Praise for Joanna Barker

"I loved this blend of intrigue, wit, and romance. Enemies to lovers doesn't get better than this!"

—**Julianne Donaldson**, best-selling, award-winning author of *Edenbrooke* and *Blackmoore*

"Historical romance readers, prepare to be riveted! Joanna Barker penned an immersive plot with an intriguing mystery and a slow-burn romance that entrances. The sparkling prose will steal your breath, while the evocative plot twists keep you turning the pages. *A Love Most Daring* is simply stunning."

—**Rachel Scott McDaniel**, award-winning author of *The Dreams We Knew*

"I'm a complete weakling for a broody hero with a tender heart, and Joanna Barker created a winner in her newest book, *A Love Most Daring*. This romantic Regency delight sprinkles suspense into the world of "exiled" Beatrice Lacey and Bow Street officer Alexander Rawlings. The story is filled with fun dialogue and mystery, but the reluctant romantic Alexander Rawlings steals the scenes and proves that not only is his stubborn heart worth winning, but this Regency romance is also worth reading."

—**Pepper Basham**, award-winning author of *Sense & Suitability*

"Unique characters and a fast-paced mystery add flavor to this sweet romance."

—***Publishers Weekly***, for *A Heart Worth Stealing*

"Beguiling. Pairs an unusual independent young woman with a compelling investigator to captivating effect."

—***Foreword Reviews***, for *A Heart Worth Stealing*

"Verity is a unique and admirable heroine, and readers will fall for Nathaniel's tender side."

—***Library Journal***, for *So True a Love*

"The sparring of Verity and Mr. Denning is crisp with underlying respect and growing attraction. . . . For those who relish Regency romances of the respectable sort, Joanna Barker delivers again."

—**Historical Novel Society**, for *So True a Love*

A Love Most Daring

Other Books by Joanna Barker

A Heart Worth Stealing

So True a Love

Otherwise Engaged

Secrets and Suitors

Miss Adeline's Match

The Truth About Miss Ashbourne

All Hearts Come Home for Christmas

A Love Most Daring

Joanna Barker

Visit us at shadowmountain.com

PROPER ROMANCE is a registered trademark.

Library of Congress Cataloging-in-Publication Data

Names: Barker, Joanna L., 1990– author

Title: A love most daring / Joanna Barker. Other titles: Proper romance

Description: Salt Lake City : Shadow Mountain Publishing, [2026] | Series: Proper romance | Summary: "When scandal-weary Beatrice Lacey witnesses an attack, she's forced into hiding with the last man she'd ever choose—a wounded and irritable Bow Street officer. She knows Alexander Rawlings wants nothing more than to return to his investigation, but close quarters and quick-witted sparks make denying their growing connection impossible. As danger closes in, love becomes their most daring risk yet"—Provided by publisher.

Identifiers: LCCN 2025039741 (print) | LCCN 2025039742 (ebook) | ISBN 9781639934713 trade paperback | ISBN 9781649335425 ebook

Subjects: LCSH: England—Fiction | LCGFT: Romance fiction | Fiction

Classification: LCC PS3602.A775526 L68 2026 (print) | LCC PS3602.A775526 (ebook)

LC record available at https://lccn.loc.gov/2025039741

LC ebook record available at https://lccn.loc.gov/2025039742

Printed in the United States of America

Versa Press, East Peoria, IL

10 9 8 7 6 5 4 3 2 1

For Nolan,
Dream big, little one.

CHAPTER 1

"Which one?" I asked. "The blue or the red?" I turned to Ginny, holding each evening gown against me in turn, first a sky-blue silk with delicate embroidery along the hem, then a bold wine red with a gathered bodice.

Ginny reclined in an armchair, eyeing me with ill-concealed amusement. "Whichever is quickest to dress in. We're late, Beatrice."

Punctuality had never been my strong suit. "Not *very* late."

"I do not think there is such a thing," she said, wrapping one hand under the swell of her belly. She did it without seeming to realize, already protecting the child who grew within her. "You are either late, or you are not."

"Then I doubt a minute or two will make any difference at this point." I shook the two dresses at her. "What do you think?"

"I think," Ginny said dryly, "that you are very concerned with what you are wearing to a simple dinner party."

"*I* think I am showing the appropriate amount of concern, considering your mother-in-law is hosting this dinner party." I dodged her insinuation.

"Which several handsome Bow Street Runners will be attending?" Her green eyes gleamed mischievously.

"You are useless," I declared, turning to my lady's maid waiting to help me dress. "Mariah, you choose."

"I think the red is very fetching on you, Miss Lacey." Her lips twitched. "I daresay Mr. Drake will think so as well."

I dropped the gowns to my sides in exasperation. "I suppose you both find this all very amusing."

"Extremely amusing, I would say." Ginny grinned widely. "I've never seen you so out of sorts."

"It is *your* fault," I pointed out. "You and your matchmaking."

"I cannot help it." She stood and came to my side. "Ever since I met Mr. Drake, I have been anxious for the two of you to become acquainted. Besides, you haven't been terribly subtle about your wish to meet Jack's friends."

She was right. I'd made no secret of how thrilling and romantic I thought my friend's courtship with her husband, Jack, had been. And since he was a former Bow Street Runner, it stood to reason that one of his brother officers might be similarly willing to sweep me off my feet. Not that Ginny and Jack's relationship could be so easily replicated. But if I could find a love half so real and passionate, I should count myself fortunate indeed.

Ginny turned me toward the mirror, then took the two dresses from my hands. We were a study in contrast, my golden hair and freckled skin against her deep-red curls and ivory complexion. "Which do you feel most confident in?"

She held them up against me in turn.

"The red," I finally decided. It was the bolder of the two options, and I liked to make an impression when at all possible.

"An excellent choice," she said, handing the gown to Mariah.

Mariah helped me dress, then touched up my hair. I was nervous but in the most delicious, anticipatory way possible. What if tonight were the night I met my future husband—the man I would fall in love with? Ginny had only wonderful things to say about Mr. Drake. And if that wasn't enough of a recommendation, her sister-in-law, Verity, also insisted that he was as good a man as they came, charming and honorable and handsome. She would certainly know, having worked alongside him at Bow Street as a sketch artist and a private investigator in her own right.

But that familiar, shadowed worry crept again into the back of my mind, the one that had lingered since I'd arrived in London. I tried to push it away. It had been two years, after all. Surely no one remembered me—or the rumors. There was certainly no reason to assume Mr. Drake knew about them. Yet I could not rid myself of the unease. I was so unused to meeting anyone who hadn't already heard my name whispered about in the darkest tones.

Mariah finished and stepped back. I took a deep breath to steady myself—I couldn't allow myself to lose this chance. I met Ginny's gaze in the mirror.

She smiled softly. "You look lovely."

There was none of her previous teasing in her expression, only kindness. I knew I could depend upon her when it mattered, and she understood how much importance I'd placed upon tonight.

She took my arm. "Come, then, let us make our very late but very grand entrance."

Jack sat waiting for us on a bench near the stairs. Well, perhaps *lounging* was the better word. My friend's husband always managed to look quite comfortable wherever he was.

"Ah, I see you've finally finished sewing your dress." Jack stood, slipping his hands into his pockets.

I raised an eyebrow. "Sewing my dress?"

"You've both been in there an age," he said with a smirk. "I couldn't imagine what else was taking so long."

"Hush, you." Ginny took his arm. "A gentleman would wait for a lady no matter how long she took to ready herself."

"A pity, then, that you did not marry a gentleman." He winked at her.

I could not help but laugh, and neither could Ginny. I followed them down the stairs as Jack leaned closer to Ginny and whispered something in her ear. She giggled—giggled!—and nudged him with her elbow. No doubt it was something only a married couple would understand.

I swallowed and looked away. I was glad for Ginny, of course. As my dearest friend for twenty years, she deserved every happiness. But there was an edge of envy as well. How badly I wanted what she had—the love of a good man, a family of her own. I'd nearly given up my dream altogether in recent years, but perhaps . . .

Perhaps this was the night that would change that.

I trailed behind Ginny and Jack as they approached the drawing room. Though the town house was a modest size, Ginny's mother-in-law had outfitted it gorgeously. Rich damask wallpaper framed the entryway decorated with polished furniture and gilded mirrors. Nothing too ostentatious but just stylish enough to display Mrs. Travers's excellent taste, befitting of London's premier actress. She'd invited Ginny and Jack to stay during their visit to Town and had generously included me as well. She'd been all that was gracious and welcoming when we'd arrived yesterday, though I could not say the same of Jack's grandmother. I admitted some relief that the prickly, elderly woman preferred solitude and would not be attending the party tonight.

Mrs. Travers waited outside the drawing room door in a gown of deep royal blue. Her ebony curls were touched by gray, which only enhanced her timeless beauty. She greeted us all warmly, fussing over Ginny and suggesting a seat near the fire, though Ginny insisted she was perfectly well.

A small crowd moved about the drawing room as we stepped inside, perhaps a dozen people. Among them, I knew only Verity Denning, Jack's sister, and her husband, Nathaniel. I'd met them when they'd visited Jack and Ginny at Wimborne, and I'd become fast friends with Verity.

Another gentleman stood with the Dennings. I studied him surreptitiously. He looked to be a few years older than my four-and-twenty, with the broadest shoulders I'd ever seen. A girl could get used to such shoulders.

Ginny glanced at me and gave a subtle nod at the gentleman. So this was Mr. Drake. For some reason, simply putting a face to the name helped calm my nerves. He *was* handsome, with an open face and a quick smile. My heart ticked faster.

What if he knows? came that traitorous voice from the shadows of my mind. I shut it away.

Ginny and Jack went to join the group, but Verity came to my side before I could follow them. "There you are. I've been waiting for you."

"Have you now?" I narrowed my eyes slightly. "Why is that?"

She quirked a knowing smile. "A little bird told Mother that you might be pleased to be seated next to a certain officer at dinner."

Oh heavens. Did everyone know about Ginny's madcap scheme to match me with Mr. Drake? I flushed. "Remind me to scold this bird very firmly later."

"Nonsense," Verity said, taking my arm. "I have little doubt you will be thanking her."

This would be the last time I ever made my interest in a man known. How positively mortifying.

Verity led me to the group. I was careful not to look at Mr. Drake as I exchanged how-do-you-dos with Verity's husband, Mr. Denning—heavens, he was attractive, the lucky girl. Gathering my courage, I then turned to the broad-shouldered man.

"I don't believe we've met," I said without preamble, smiling in a way that I hoped came across as friendly rather than forward. I seemed to succeed since he met my smile—and better yet, there was nothing in his smile that hinted he knew even a whisper of my past. The pinching in my lungs eased the slightest bit.

Ginny's lips darted up in amusement. "Beatrice is not one to stand upon ceremony, I'm afraid. Mr. Drake, allow me to present Beatrice Lacey, my dearest and most outspoken friend, as you'll soon see."

"There is nothing wrong with a woman who knows her own mind," Mr. Drake said with a bow.

I was half in love with him already.

"Unless she also insists on knowing yours," Mr. Denning said with a pointed look at his wife, and Verity slapped him lightly on the shoulder, laughing.

"Mr. Drake and Jack are old friends," Ginny said, continuing her introduction. "They served together in the army and then came to Bow Street."

I knew this, of course. I'd already pried such details from Ginny as we'd traveled to London yesterday. But I nodded with interest, as if I'd never heard it before.

Mr. Drake focused on me, clearly curious. "What brings you to Town, Miss Lacey?"

"I'm afraid I simply trailed behind Ginny and Jack," I admitted. "This case you are working seems to have gathered quite the crowd."

"We are glad for the help," Mr. Drake said. "It has gotten out of hand rather quickly."

"You may want to say that in a quieter voice," Jack said in a mock whisper, "or the general population will begin to panic that Bow Street is not the model of efficiency."

I wanted to press Mr. Drake for more information. Jack had been surprisingly tight-lipped about the whole affair since he'd been summoned to help. I already knew far more than a young lady of gentle breeding ought. I'd always had an interest in tawdry tales of crime and passion—who would not?—and this case was far from the quiet, hushed-up affair that Bow Street no doubt desired. The grisly murder of Viscount Somerton had made headlines in every newspaper, and the articles had not minced words in their descriptions. I had read every article I could find, horribly fascinated, like everyone in London, by the violence that had not spared even someone of the viscount's status.

"Where is Rawlings?" Verity asked, glancing about the room. "Is he not coming? I'm certain Mama invited him."

Mr. Drake sighed. "He was in the middle of an interview when I left the office. He said he was coming, but I have little doubt we will find him still at his desk when we arrive tomorrow morning. The man's dedication is a touch frightening."

Dinner was announced, and to my delight, Mr. Drake offered me his arm and led me into the dining room, a warm, brightly lit space, perfect for conversation. A fact I made quick use of when Mr. Drake seated himself beside me.

"You mentioned the case has gotten out of hand?" I asked, trying not to seem too curious. "What do you mean by that?"

Mr. Drake appeared not to share Jack's reluctance to discuss the case, because he leaned a bit closer. "The sheer amount of suspects, for one," he said. "The viscount was not a peace-loving man, and he had a great many enemies. As such, we have a suspect list with nearly two dozen names on it. It takes an immense effort to organize such an investigation, checking alibis, confirming possible motives, and so on. I don't envy Rawlings in the least."

A second mention of the elusive Rawlings. Another officer, no doubt, and likely the one heading the investigation.

"Do you have suspects whom you, well, suspect more than the others?" I inclined my head toward him, my voice low as a servant reached beside me to fill my wine glass.

Mr. Drake gave a half smile, as though he'd guessed my aim. "I'm afraid I cannot divulge that information, Miss Lacey, as much as I'd like to."

It was probably for the best. In my eagerness to learn more about the investigation, I'd quite forgotten I was supposed to be charming him so that he, in turn, could fall madly in love with me.

It was a plan that showed a great deal of promise, especially as the meal went on. I turned the subject toward the food and the company, asking how he knew the various guests. We had passed a pleasant quarter of an hour in conversation when the door to the dining room opened.

I looked up, along with the rest of the table, as a man appeared in the doorway. And suddenly, I gripped my fork a little tighter.

The man did not simply step into the doorway. He *filled* it, with the sort of presence that made men straighten and women forget speech altogether. His frame was long and lean—not broad but immovable as stone. His deeply brown hair, almost black, was parted and pomaded to one side, the style efficient and no-nonsense, and a light shadow crept up his jaw. He wasn't handsome in the way that normally attracted a lady's attention, but there was a fierce rigidity to his features that called to mind a painting I'd once seen of Alexander the Great.

My skin warmed, my ears buzzing. I'd never seen this man before, of that I was certain. And yet as I studied him, there was a jolt in the very middle of me. As if a part of me recognized a part of him.

His midnight eyes seemed to absorb the candlelight as they swept over the room, meeting mine for the barest of moments before moving on without so much as a twitch in his expression. Clearly, my reaction was one-sided and as ridiculous as it was impossible.

"Mr. Rawlings," Mrs. Travers said delightedly, coming to her feet at the head of the table. "How thrilled I am that you could come."

So this was the Bow Street colleague I'd heard so much about.

"I must apologize for my late arrival," he said, and his voice was just as deep and rumbling as I'd imagined. Or at least, as much as I'd imagined in the ten seconds or so since he'd appeared. What I hadn't accounted for was the lilt in his words, a slight Scottish brogue that brought to mind sweeping Highland vistas and fathomless, gleaming lochs.

Not that I'd ever been to Scotland. But if one could read, one could travel.

Mrs. Travers only beamed at him, waving him forward. "Never mind that. Come, there's a place for you just here."

I took a sip from my glass, watching over the rim as he made his way around the table. He moved with purpose, a careful confidence in his every motion as he seated himself directly across from me.

Mrs. Travers sat again, a queen presiding over her court. "Have you met everyone, Mr. Rawlings?" she asked. "Need we make any introductions?"

Though he'd given the table a cursory glance at his arrival, his shrewd gaze traveled again over the guests, stopping—at last—on me. I knew he'd seen me when he'd first arrived, but I had the impression he'd taken me in and dismissed me all in a single instant and was only now forced to acknowledge me.

Mrs. Travers followed his eyes. "Oh, yes, you haven't met Miss Lacey, Genevieve's friend from home."

He inspected me a moment longer, then nodded curtly. "A pleasure."

I was certain it wasn't. In fact, I was quite sure he'd never been pleased to meet anyone.

I returned his nod with a shallow one of my own. "Mr. Rawlings."

Pleasantries dispensed with, conversation again started up along the table. I resolved to put Mr. Rawlings from my mind and turned back to Mr. Drake, who was a perfectly amiable dinner companion. There was no need to lose any of the progress I'd made tonight simply because a brooding gentleman looked at me askance.

"What do you hope to see while in London, Miss Lacey?" Mr. Drake asked.

"Oh, everything and anything," I said enthusiastically. "I've come for the Season several times before, but I've never had the chance to explore the city."

"Never had the chance?" he repeated.

"You see, I was always scheduled rather tightly with balls and dinner parties and such," I said. "My mother saw the Season as something of an investment and did not wish to waste it on such silliness as the Royal Menagerie or Astley's Amphitheatre."

In fact, Mother and Father disliked London as a whole, making the journey only to introduce me into Society and for my subsequent—and unsuccessful—Seasons. They far preferred a quiet country life, the same as Ginny.

"Well, that simply will not do," Mr. Drake declared. "You must make the most of this trip."

"I intend to," I assured him. "I am determined to spend my time quite selfishly and do everything I've wanted to over the years."

Mr. Rawlings made a sound of disapproval across the table. I darted a glance at him, but he only intently speared a potato on his plate. Had I imagined it?

"I am glad to hear it." Mr. Drake drew my attention back to him. "A little selfishness is never amiss."

"I quite agree," I replied, picking up my wine glass to take a sip.

"Tomorrow night, we are going to Vauxhall, Mr. Drake," Ginny cut in, apparently having eavesdropped upon our conversation from down the table. "You ought to come with us so that we might have even numbers."

I shot her a look—she was being terribly obvious. But she ignored me innocently and waited for Mr. Drake's response.

He smiled, not seeming to mind her interference. "I should be delighted, assuming my schedule allows it."

"I wouldn't assume anything of the sort," came that deep Scottish brogue.

We all looked at Mr. Rawlings, who met our gazes with cool impassivity.

"We already made an exception for tonight," he said. "I can't imagine we can spare both you and Jack again tomorrow."

"Come now, Rawlings," Mr. Drake said, unperturbed. He must be used to his friend's abruptness. "We'll either find the murderer, or we won't. Leaving an hour or two early won't change that."

"It very well might," Mr. Rawlings countered. "Every minute counts in a case like this. We cannot waste our time with *frivolities*."

"Perhaps, Mr. Rawlings"—I raised my brow and offered a curled smile—"it might benefit you to join us in our frivolities. All work and no play, as they say."

I didn't know why I said it. It wasn't as if I *wanted* him to come, watching us with judgmental disdain as we dared to enjoy ourselves while he had a murder to solve. But there was something so imperious in his nature, and I couldn't resist taking a jab in his direction, if only to see what he might do.

His dark eyes met mine, unblinking and impenetrable, and slowly traveled over me—the wine glass in my hand, the string of pearls at my neck, the mischievous grin still perched on my lips. "Better all work than all play, Miss Lacey," he said slowly, pointedly, "as you seem to favor." Then he turned away, engaging Mrs. Travers with a question.

My smile dropped. I sat back in my chair, my cheeks pricking with heat. What presumption. Did he think he knew me from a glance? That he could judge me shallow and overindulgent from the barest overheard conversation at a dinner party?

The other guests shifted uncomfortably in their chairs, trying to resume their conversations, though I could feel their quick glances my way. I looked at Ginny, and she only lifted one shoulder, as baffled as I was by Mr. Rawlings's retort.

"All that to say," Mr. Drake said from beside me, trying desperately to salvage our conversation, "I should be glad to join you tomorrow night, should my presence not be needed for the investigation."

I managed a small smile, one I did not feel. "That is kind of you, Mr. Drake, though I do understand if you are unavailable."

He hesitated, casting a glance at Mr. Rawlings. "I am sorry for that," he said in a low voice. "He is not usually so . . ." He paused, apparently unable to find the right word.

"I should like to know the end of that sentence," I said dryly.

He laughed under his breath. "I hope you won't hold it against him. He is carrying the weight of the investigation, I'm afraid. There is a great deal of pressure from the magistrates."

I pointedly did not look in Mr. Rawlings's direction. I wished I could flatter myself that he was exerting the same effort, but I had little doubt he had already dismissed me from his mind once again.

"You ought to come by Bow Street tomorrow before we go to Vauxhall," Mr. Drake suggested. "I should be happy to show you around."

"I can't imagine Mr. Rawlings would be terribly happy about that."

"Rawlings can have no objection," he said, amused, "seeing as he does not own the magistrates' court."

"Then I should be glad to." I could not hide my pleasure at his invitation. "Thank you."

We turned our attention to where Verity had begun telling a diverting story about one of the cases she had worked with her husband. Mr. Denning periodically interrupted to correct her or add a detail, and they soon had us all hanging on to their every word.

Except for Mr. Rawlings, that was. The other guests around him laughed with the story, but he only traced the ceramic edge of his plate with one finger as he stared down at the table, lost in thoughts I couldn't begin to guess at. But I thought I recognized the barest emotion on his face. Worry.

He glanced up suddenly, seeming to sense my attention on him, and his expression immediately fell back into passive indifference. He looked away again, but I studied him a second longer. A man like Mr. Drake was an open book, but I imagined Mr. Rawlings was more like a wrought-iron strongbox—difficult to pry open and just as off-putting.

Thank heavens Ginny hadn't decided to match me with Mr. Rawlings. He was so far from what I was looking for in a husband, it was almost laughable.

I focused again on Verity's story, on the easy repartee she shared with her husband and the way he positioned himself to face her, as if she were his whole world.

One day, I would have that, I reaffirmed to myself. I would have what Verity and Mr. Denning had, what Ginny and Jack shared. It was the only way I could ever imagine marrying—for the truest, deepest love.

CHAPTER 2

London *bustled.*

Oh, I'd missed it. The ever-changing melee of errand boys, shopping ladies, and gentlemen out for a stroll. The carriages and carts rattling upon cobblestones, buildings towering above us with glamorous facades. There was such energy and purpose, I could not help but find it infectious as I followed Ginny along crowded Bond Street. I was fond of Little Sowerby, the village near my home, but it did not hold nearly the same thrill for me as the city. I imagined I could be perfectly happy living all my days in this fascinating blend of cultures and people.

"Here we are," Ginny said brightly, stopping before a shop window featuring a variety of hats and bonnets. "If you do not find something you like here, I can't imagine you'll find it anywhere."

I had mentioned at breakfast that I needed a new hat, and she had immediately arranged this little shopping excursion. She was perhaps trying a bit too hard to please me, determined that I enjoy every moment of our time in London.

She needn't make such an effort. I would enjoy my time with her no matter what we did. But I appreciated it all the same, the feeling of being looked after. I did not often feel that way at home. Father often seemed to forget he even *had* a daughter. And Mother, while not completely unfeeling, seemed far more concerned with trying to marry me off to anyone who would accept my tarnished reputation than in forming a real and lasting relationship with me. I knew she meant well, that she loved me in her own, absent sort of way, but it only made my friendship with Ginny all the starker a contrast.

When Jack had received a request from Bow Street asking for his help with the investigation, Ginny had decided to go along with him. Not because she loved the city, by any means, but because she knew *I* did, and she'd immediately invited me to travel with her. I'd resisted at first—my last visit to London had come to a disastrous end—but instead of accepting my response, she'd marched to my house and begun packing my belongings.

"You adore London," she had insisted as she'd tossed a pair of dancing slippers into a trunk. "I'll not let you shut yourself away for the rest of your life because of a few false rumors."

She knew very well how horrible that Season had been. How the rumors had been not just false but nasty and vicious and as widespread as the pox as well. I'd been worried that my love of London would be dampened by my experience, that the whispers would follow me still. But Ginny had convinced me eventually, and I'd decided firmly in favor of optimism. London had always lifted my spirits in the past, and perhaps it would do so again.

I'd been right, quite thankfully. The last two days in Town had left me lighter, fighting away those dreadful shadows that perched like crows in my mind. I'd needed this—a change of scene, a switch in pace.

And perhaps, with Mr. Drake, there might be other developments on the horizon.

I mustn't get ahead of myself, I thought in reprimand as Ginny and I stepped into the millinery, the little bell above the door jingling merrily. I should not worry over what might come but simply enjoy the here and now.

We browsed the shop, inspecting trinkets and ribbons and all manner of hats and bonnets. Then Ginny grinned, reaching for something behind me.

"I do believe," she said, plucking my bonnet from my head and replacing it with the item, "that this bonnet was made for you."

I turned to examine myself in a nearby mirror and burst into laughter. The bonnet was downright atrocious, with disproportionately large pink silk flowers, a thick, striped ribbon, and a billowing ostrich feather that curled over the wide brim and tickled my nose.

"You are wasted in Little Sowerby," I said, still laughing, "with such an eye for fashion as that."

"That bonnet could shade all of Little Sowerby and then some," she said with a wink. "And has enough flowers to adorn all of Hampshire."

The shopkeeper passed by and shot us a reprimanding look, her arms clutching rolls of ribbon. Ginny's mouth parted upon seeing her, and it only made me laugh again.

"Hush now," she scolded me in a whisper, taking the bonnet back even as her lips twitched. "You might've warned me she was near."

"I didn't see her!" I said, replacing my own bonnet on my head. "Though if I had, I still would not have told you."

"You are a wretch." She set the bonnet back on its stand.

"But a very lovable wretch." I grinned at her. "You ought to get into trouble more often. It keeps one young."

"Ah yes, rule-breaking," she said. "The real fountain of youth."

We wandered apart, continuing to peruse the shop on our own. I found a lovely little bonnet with a blue satin ribbon that would look well with my new walking dress. I was inspecting the quality of the trim when I heard a voice behind me.

"Miss Lacey, is that you?"

I froze, my hands tightening around the bonnet. The voice was soft, haunting. I knew whose it was before I turned around.

Clarissa Haythorne stood behind me, the very picture of sophisticated elegance in a stylish pink gown, closely cut to display her figure, and a delicate, lace-trimmed parasol in her gloved hands. She stepped toward me as her lips spread into a delighted smile.

A delight, we both knew, that she did not really feel. Nor did I. Of course I should have the terrible luck of meeting the one person I most wished to avoid.

"It *is* you," she declared, eyes gleaming. "Why, I quite doubted myself at first, but then I thought I recognized your dress from your last Season."

I forced my hands to stay at my side, though my instinct was to smooth back the skirts of my admittedly older gown. I could afford new gowns—Father provided an ample allowance, if nothing else—but I didn't see the point in refreshing my wardrobe when I socialized so rarely.

Now I wished I had invested in at least a few dresses. I looked the dowd beside Clarissa; she always wore the best clothes in the latest fashions, as if to make up for her rather plain face and slightly squashed nose. She'd never been a beauty, but that had not stopped her from ruling over her circle of Society for the last several years since her—and my—debut. She looked very much the same as when I'd last seen her. That same calculating glint in her gaze and wicked tilt to her lips. And, of course, that confident ease that came with assuming she was the cleverest person in the room.

"Miss Haythorne," I managed through my clenched jaw. Courtesy demanded I exchange polite niceties, but I could not seem to force the words from my mouth. "It is still *miss*, is it not?"

I knew very well it was. I'd kept an eye on the London papers in my absence, and it was clear from the social pages that she was still decidedly unmarried. In truth, I couldn't imagine anyone marrying such a conspiring creature, but stranger things had happened.

"It has been ever so long since you've been to Town," Clarissa said, ignoring my pointed slight as she twirled her parasol in her fingers. "A year, at least?"

"Two, actually," I said.

"Oh, how dreadful," she exclaimed. "How have you survived? I think I would go quite mad without proper Society."

Well, one makes do when one is rejected by proper Society.

That was what I wanted to say to her. That, and point out the fact that *she* was the reason Society had rejected me in the first place. But it would help nothing. In fact, it would likely harm everything I hoped to accomplish in London. I only smiled blandly and nodded.

"Beatrice?" Ginny stepped to my side, looking curiously at Clarissa.

Clarissa's razor-sharp gaze went to my friend. I fought the urge to push Ginny aside, as if to save her from a viper's bite. She'd never met Clarissa before, quite thankfully; she and Jack ran in very different circles than I had previously.

"Good afternoon." Clarissa inspected Ginny from head to foot. If she expected to find anything to criticize, she would be disappointed. Ginny was always perfectly put together, and today was no exception, her sage-green pelisse immaculate and her red hair neatly curled and pinned. "I don't believe we've been introduced."

Ginny's eyes flicked to mine, a question in her glance, then back to Clarissa. "Genevieve Travers. A pleasure to meet you."

"I'm certain it is," Clarissa said with a smile.

"Do excuse us," I said shortly. Clarissa and I were *not* friends, and there was no point in pretending. Especially if that put Ginny in her line of fire. "We've an important appointment to attend."

"Oh, of course," Clarissa said with exaggerated civility and immediately stepped aside, skirts swishing about her ankles. "Do not let me keep you."

I took Ginny's arm and pulled her with me. To her credit, she did not question me until we'd left the shop and gone down the street, out of view from the millinery's windows.

"Who was that?" she finally asked, careful concern in her voice.

"That," I said through gritted teeth, "was Clarissa Haythorne."

Ginny came to a sudden halt, and I with her. She turned to face me slowly. "Do you mean to tell me," she said, her voice hard as granite, "that that was the girl who ruined your Season? Your reputation?"

"Allegedly." I crossed my arms against my chest, trying to hold back the storm of anger and injustice that had risen inside me. "I had no proof against her."

"But you know it was her," she insisted. "She had every reason to want to destroy you."

I nodded tightly. Ginny knew everything about that fateful Season—the only person who did. Not even my parents knew the whole truth.

Ginny spun on her heel, a decidedly agile movement for one so far along with child, and started back the way we'd come.

"Ginny, stop." I grabbed her arm. "You can't."

"I certainly can," she said, trying to tug her arm free. "I have no qualms about dressing down such a horrid person in public."

"I am sure it would be both eloquent and cutting, as she would deserve," I said. "But you really mustn't. Please."

Ginny stilled. "Why?"

I sighed. "Because Clarissa Haythorne has every tool at her disposal to make my life perfectly miserable, as we've already seen. The only thing to do is to stay out of her way."

Ginny examined me, and there was a discernment in her eyes that made me squirm.

"I am sorry," she said quietly. "Only I know how difficult it was for you. I cannot bear to let her get away with such a thing."

I smiled at her, a halfhearted effort. "We've quite switched places, haven't we? Normally, I would be the one declaring war, and you would be urging caution."

"Yes, well," she said, touching one hand to her belly, "my motherly instincts are already firmly in play. Because if I see that woman again, nothing would stop me from putting her in her place."

"Let us stay far away from Miss Haythorne, then," I said with a short laugh. "I don't think Jack would thank me for getting his wife involved in a bout of fisticuffs on Bond Street."

"Jack has taught me plenty," she said tartly. "I could handle Miss Haythorne."

I linked my arm with hers. "I have no doubt."

As we started off again, heading for Ginny's carriage ahead, I had to swallow against the lump in my throat. Ginny had always been on my side, just as I had always been on hers. We'd been through so much together, and I considered myself the most fortunate of people to have so true a friend.

I forced several deep breaths into my lungs. Everything was fine, I reassured myself. It had been one chance encounter. Clarissa would forget me soon enough, if she hadn't already. Perhaps her vindictive nature had softened since I'd last seen her.

Or perhaps she would revive her war against me, the one I had lost so terribly the first time.

She'd let me run back to Little Sowerby with the scraps of my reputation two years ago. I wasn't sure I'd be so lucky should we cross swords again.

We returned to the Travers home as the sun began to set behind the rooftops. Ginny had tried doubly hard to distract me for the rest of the afternoon, and we'd purchased armfuls of new trinkets that neither of us had really needed. It hadn't helped much, but at least now I could fully anticipate our evening at the Vauxhall Pleasure Gardens. A thrill raced across my skin as I imagined dancing with the handsome Mr. Drake, strolling arm in arm with him along the lantern-lit pathways. He was a quick-witted, lighthearted fellow—the perfect cure to the melancholy that had rooted inside me since seeing Clarissa Haythorne.

I dressed carefully, selecting a pretty deep-blue gown that brought out the same color in my eyes and a cream spencer jacket. It was October, and although the pleasant weather had allowed Vauxhall to remain open later in the year than was normal, there was still a distinct chill in the air.

We'd arranged to meet Jack and Mr. Drake at No. 4 Bow Street, which was only a short carriage ride away. I was as equally fascinated by Bow Street itself as I was by their Runners, so I could not help but stare up at the rather austere brick facade as Ginny led the way down the carriage steps. I followed her through the entry and into a broad room filled with tables and desks and chairs and a great many bustling officers and patrolmen. The magistrates' court had a very distinct energy, full of purpose and determination, and I found it quite catching.

That was, until I spotted Mr. Rawlings. He was speaking with Jack, the both of them intent on the conversation. My stomach curdled. Drat. I'd hoped to avoid the man altogether. To meet both him and Clarissa Haythorne on the same day was a crime, indeed.

Ginny immediately made her way to her husband. I trailed after her, nonchalantly searching for Mr. Drake. Perhaps he was in one of the smaller offices?

"Good evening, gentlemen," Ginny said, wrapping one arm around Jack's. "Have we arrived at a bad time?"

Jack's face lit up at the sight of her. Heavens, the way Jack looked at Ginny. As if it had been a month since he'd seen her instead of a single day. It made one feel like quite the interloper.

"There is never a bad time for you to arrive." He pulled her close to his side.

I glanced away, allowing them a moment, and my gaze—quite unfortunately—landed upon Mr. Rawlings. He was looking at me as well, though his manner could not have been more different from Jack's. His coal-dark eyes held only a polite disinterest, his mouth a serious line across his face.

"Miss Lacey," Mr. Rawlings said in greeting. Well, at least he'd remembered my name.

"Mr. Rawlings," I replied coolly. "Any progress on your case?"

His expression changed not at all. "Some."

Clearly, he wouldn't give me any information on that front. I would wait to try my luck with Mr. Drake. Assuming we found him.

Ginny seemed to read my thoughts as she glanced around. "Where is Mr. Drake?"

Jack's brow lifted. "Is he not back yet? He left two hours ago for an interview in Mayfair. I imagined he would have returned by now."

"I daresay he'll be a while yet." Mr. Rawlings riffled through the stack of papers in his hands. "I asked him to confirm an alibi for the viscount's solicitor while he was out."

"And where would that take him?" I attempted a casual air.

Mr. Rawlings placed a paper on the top of his stack and peered down at it. "Whitechapel."

My heart dropped, disappointment rooting deep within me. Whitechapel was in the opposite direction of Mayfair. It could be hours before Mr. Drake returned.

Hours. My focus sharpened on Mr. Rawlings. He had to have known when he'd made the assignment that Mr. Drake could not possibly return in time to meet us. Had he done it just to spite me because of our clash last night? He seemed far too discerning to have done it by happenstance.

What a toad.

Mr. Rawlings looked up, oblivious to the daggers I was glaring at him. "Jack, do you have the notes from your interviews? Lady Somerton is arriving soon, and I must apprise her of the new developments."

Jack stepped to a nearby table to fetch his own stack of papers, much less organized. Mr. Rawlings held out a hand for them, but Jack paused, holding them out of reach. "You need a respite, Rawlings," he said. "Did you sleep at all last night?"

"Of course I slept," Mr. Rawlings said curtly.

"More than an hour or two?"

"I cannot see why that signifies."

Still irritated, I inspected Mr. Rawlings, wishing to find a flaw in him. He was impeccably dressed, his clothing well made and well cared for, if a bit too plain to be considered fashionable. His dusky-brown hair was in perfect order and his shoulders ramrod straight, but there was a weariness in the stubborn set of his face, in the shadowed crescents beneath his eyes.

"You will run yourself ragged, that's why," Jack said. "You'll be of no use to the investigation if you're dead on your feet."

A taut muscle worked in Mr. Rawlings's cheek. Ginny stepped forward, her hand still on Jack's arm. "You should come with us to Vauxhall, Mr. Rawlings," she offered. "At least for an hour or two. A distraction is just what you need."

"Or perhaps sleep would be the better idea," I cut in. "Plenty of *sleep*."

I was not being terribly subtle, but that had never been my forte.

"I thank you, Mrs. Travers," he said stiffly, ignoring my suggestion. "The dowager viscountess is due to arrive any moment, else I would be most glad to accompany you."

Thank heavens. Even if I didn't much relish the idea of shadowing Ginny and Jack without an escort of my own, it was the far superior option to having that escort be Mr. Rawlings.

"What luck, then," Jack said with a mischievous smile, holding up a folded letter, "that this note arrived from the viscountess a few minutes ago. She begs your pardon but asks to postpone your meeting until tomorrow morning."

Mr. Rawlings blinked. He did not move for a long moment, and then his eyes narrowed upon Jack. He knew he'd been had.

"Come, we'll have a grand time of it," Jack said, "and then you may return here to your endless notes and meetings."

"Yes, do come," Ginny encouraged, though she carefully did not look my way. She knew very well from last night that I did not much care for Mr. Rawlings.

"I cannot say I am in the mood for merrymaking." Mr. Rawlings did not intend to go down without a fight. "I would not be very good company for Miss Lacey."

Ginny and Jack both turned to me, as if I were the deciding factor. I opened my mouth to insist he need not come, but then I paused. There was a delicious satisfaction in knowing I could force this man to do something he very clearly did not wish to do. Since he had managed to deprive me of Mr. Drake's amiable companionship, I would keep him from what *he* wanted—to be left alone with his work. "I'm sure I've had far less pleasant company than you before, Mr. Rawlings," I said, a challenge to my words.

He regarded me closely—an unwelcome inspection. I imagined he was quickly cataloging each and every excuse he might use to free himself from this invitation. But he dropped his stack of papers on the desk behind him with a soft thump. "Very well, Miss Lacey." He stepped forward and suddenly seemed taller than he had even a moment ago, his figure rather imposing before my smaller frame. "Lead the way."

Oh bother.

Chapter 3

Vauxhall was a dream.

Thousands of glass lanterns glittered in the twilight, hung from trees and lampposts and every pavilion. I couldn't fathom how many there were—they floated and danced through the night like impish sprites, and the effect made me catch my breath. I twisted around, determined to take in everything all at once. Great trees disappeared into the night sky above us, stars sparkling through their branches. In the center of a large grove, an enormous orchestra building spilled out music for the rows of dancers, and to my left, a stately colonnade stretched beyond my sight. Supper boxes ringed the grove, outfitted with tables and chairs, and were painted with cheerful scenes. Hundreds of people milled about—eating, dancing, exploring—and I *thrilled* to be a part of it all.

I'd long wished to visit Vauxhall, but Mother had never approved, considering her views on the intermingling of classes, dining in public, and extravagant entertainment. For years, I'd read about Vauxhall's many delights, my head full of wistful imaginings. I had been afraid that the gardens could not possibly live up to my expectations.

This, however, was far beyond even what I had hoped for.

I felt myself being swept away into the magic of the night—the wafting smells of baked ham and sweets, the violins trilling, the laughter and conversation—but it took only one glance at the long-faced, reticent man beside me to leech away my enthusiasm. Mr. Rawlings's presence was like an anchor, dragging me back from that welcoming tide.

Mr. Rawlings had not offered me his arm and walked with both hands clasped firmly behind his back as if I would try to take his arm myself. He needn't fear. The last thing I wished was to be any closer to him.

I tried my best to ignore him as I took in the sights. It was my own fault, really. I should not have taunted him.

Ginny and Jack strolled ahead of us down the Grand Walk, a wide pathway that ran through the entirety of the pleasure gardens, lined with towering trees. Ginny glanced back at me, and I sent her a look of such long-suffering that she took pity on me. She spoke a word to Jack and they stopped, waiting for Mr. Rawlings and me to draw even with them.

"It looks as though the next dance is about to begin," she said meaningfully.

Did she think to force Mr. Rawlings to dance with me? He didn't seem to have heard her; he was gazing off to his right with a staid expression.

Ginny and Jack exchanged a look, and I sighed. I did not want to become a charity case wherein they were forced to look after me like a spinster sister.

"You must dance," I encouraged them. "I would enjoy watching from here. Everything is so lovely."

Ginny hesitated, not wanting to abandon me.

"I hardly think Ginny should be dancing in her condition," Jack said.

"My *condition*?" Ginny turned to him, brow raised.

"Yes," Jack said. "We really ought to find somewhere for you to sit. You don't want to grow overtired."

"I am expecting a child," Ginny said with wry exasperation, "not wasting away from consumption. I could certainly dance if I wished to."

"Undoubtedly you *could.* It is the *should* I am concerned about." Jack's eyes had a roguish gleam to them. "You might be ready to be a mother, but I am quite counting on the next two months to make myself serious enough to be a father."

Ginny bit back a smile, realizing he was teasing her, and I felt again that tinge of guilt that I was holding them back.

"Go," I insisted. Ginny dearly loved to dance, and they deserved to enjoy their evening, especially with the baby coming. "I shall be perfectly fine here with Mr. Rawlings."

Ginny still looked uncertain, so I gave her my best smile and a wink, showing her how entirely unaffected I was by the brooding gentleman beside me.

She saw right through that little farce, but thankfully, she did not protest again. "Come, husband," she said, taking Jack's hand. "While we dance, I shall instruct you on all the ways women are quite capable, even when plagued by *conditions.*"

They moved toward the grove in front of the orchestra. Several dancers stared at Ginny. Some simply looked surprised to a see a woman clearly with child preparing to dance, while others muttered in obvious disapproval. One woman even stepped to Ginny's side and said something I could not hear, but Ginny only offered a polite smile and waved the woman off. I grinned. Two years ago, Ginny would never have dreamed of flouting one of Society's rules. This was Jack's influence, no doubt.

The dance began, and Ginny and Jack disappeared into the crowd. Which left Mr. Rawlings and me standing there in perfect awkwardness. On my part, at least. He seemed entirely unperturbed, which was beginning to grate upon my nerves.

After a few minutes of silence, I couldn't bear it any longer. "Might I assume you do not dance?" I asked tartly, keeping my attention fixed on the dancers.

"Aye," he said in his even tone. "I do not dance."

"A relief, to be sure."

A long moment, then he shifted almost imperceptibly. "A relief?"

"Well, yes," I said. "It is a convenient excuse, considering I do not wish to dance with you, and you do not wish to dance with me."

I thought perhaps I'd surprised him with my bluntness, but it was difficult to tell. He reminded me of the statue in our garden at home—cold and expressionless.

"I mean no insult, Miss Lacey," he said carefully.

"Oh, I am not insulted," I said. "You would need to try much harder than that."

He said nothing in response, though he cast me a sidelong glance. Appraising me yet again, though I doubted anything could change this man's opinion once he'd formed it. I looked away, disliking his militant inspection. If only Mr. Drake could have come instead of Mr. Rawlings. Then I would not have this edgy wariness pervading my body, or the irritation that refused to dissipate.

No matter. I did not need Mr. Rawlings's good opinion. If I'd learned anything over the years, it was that I only needed the love and trust of a few good friends.

I paid no heed to Mr. Rawlings for the entirety of the dance, tapping my foot to the music and smiling as I watched Ginny and Jack move about the floor. When the dance came to an end, everyone clapped for the musicians and began to disperse. Out of the sudden lull, a bell rang, a cheerful chime in my ears. I straightened as a great rush of people swarmed past us with excited expressions.

"Beatrice!" Ginny appeared at my side again, slipping her arm through mine. "Hurry, or we shall miss the Cascade."

Oh, the Cascade! I'd read about the attraction a dozen times at least, and I would be loath to miss it.

We moved together through the crowds, all flowing down the Grand Walk, past the curve of the supper boxes, and into a more thickly forested area. Lanterns lit our way, though it was darker here than in the main grounds of the gardens. I could see now why Vauxhall had something of a reputation. How easy it would be for a lady or gentleman to slip away for a romantic assignation, hidden away by the shadows and rustling trees.

I glanced at Jack and Mr. Rawlings walking behind us. Jack spoke seriously, and Mr. Rawlings listened with an expression of irritated tolerance. Were they discussing the case?

Mr. Rawlings raised his eyes, and I snapped my head forward before he could catch me looking.

The crowd milled about a small clearing in the wilderness ahead. A wide black curtain stretched along one side of the glade. Ginny and I managed to inch our way to the front until we had a decent view, Jack and Mr. Rawlings right behind us.

A bell rang again, and the curtains parted. I could not help a gasp of delight. Before us stood a miniature scene set on a stage, a rural landscape of open hill country complete with a bridge, miller's house, and water mill. Wooden coaches and wagons crossed the scene, lifelike in their movements and accompanied by the sounds of wagon wheels. But what drew my eye was the artificial waterfall at the center, seeming to run down a sloped hill to turn the wheel of the mill before gliding away again. For a moment, it looked so perfectly real—the silver flowing movements, the clever lighting, the sound of roaring water.

"How do they do it?" Ginny asked, fascination clear in her voice.

I tried to recall what I'd read of the attraction. "The waterfall is made of tin," I said, leaning closer to inspect the scene. "Tin sheets and mechanical belts turned by a team of men. But I haven't any idea how they make the sounds."

Mr. Rawlings cleared his throat behind me, as if he wanted to answer but stopped himself.

For the best, in my opinion.

After we'd spent several minutes enjoying the spectacle, we moved to one side of the glade to allow others the chance.

"Absolutely incredible," Jack declared. "The ingenuity of man knows no bounds."

"What did you think of it, Mr. Rawlings?" Ginny tried to involve him in the conversation.

"Entertaining enough," he said. And that was it. Nothing more.

I addressed Ginny and Jack. "Shall we walk to the Hermitage and have our fortunes told?" If the stories were to be believed, Vauxhall employed a hermit to tell fortunes to any guests found wandering in the deep reaches of the gardens.

"Yes, let's," Jack agreed, holding out his arm to Ginny. She paused, glancing my way. She did not wish to abandon me to Mr. Rawlings's less-than-enviable company yet again.

But to my utter shock, Mr. Rawlings—after a moment of tense hesitation—stepped to my side, extended his elbow, and spoke in a flat, emotionless tone. "Miss Lacey?"

I stared. He hadn't so much as helped me from the boat when we'd arrived—Jack had done that—and he'd been keen to keep his distance from me earlier. I had half a mind to politely refuse him and march away by myself. But Ginny and Jack were watching, and there was no point in making a scene.

"Thank you," I said stiffly. I laid my hand on his arm with as little pressure as possible, not wishing to actually touch the man if I could help it.

He shifted his weight as if disliking my proximity. His jacket parted slightly, and something glinted from within, reflecting the bright lanterns—a brass crown fixed atop a short wooden handle, most of it hidden within his pocket. A Bow Street baton. I'd seen one before; Jack had one just like it. It was both a symbol of authority and a weapon—and a reminder that this was not a man to be trifled with.

Well, neither was I a woman to be trifled with.

We followed Ginny and Jack into the trees, the sounds of the Cascade and the gathered crowd fading behind us. I cast Mr. Rawlings a sidelong glance, examining him.

"Yes?" he questioned, looking straight ahead. The pathway around us was dark, only lit by a few lanterns, the trees stretching over us into the night sky.

"Oh, nothing," I said. "Only that earlier it seemed you were worried I might infect you with the plague."

Mr. Rawlings's mouth parted—to smile, perhaps, for the first time since I'd met him? But when he turned, there was no amusement in his iron expression. None in the least.

"Jack made it clear that I was not showing you the proper respect as his wife's especial friend," he said. "I am attempting to rectify the situation."

Ah. That was what Jack had been speaking to him about.

"You do not seem the type to allow others to command your actions." My voice was more cutting than I'd intended. But then, I did not particularly enjoy the fact that Jack had scolded Mr. Rawlings into offering me his arm.

His brow raised in challenge. "And you do not seem the type to force a man into escorting you on such a fanciful excursion."

"Yes, well, you might have avoided this entire affair if you had simply allowed Mr. Drake to keep his original appointment with us."

I hadn't meant to lay out my irritation quite so plainly, but there was no taking the words back once they'd left my mouth. In truth, I didn't wish to. It was clear that Mr. Rawlings was rarely crossed or questioned. Some caustic criticism might do him good.

He did not seem to agree, coming to a stop in the middle of the empty path and facing me directly. "Pardon me?"

I had to force myself not to release his arm and step back. He hadn't looked me full-on since we'd left Bow Street, and dash it all if he weren't something of a frightening figure, his face a harsh contrast of shadows and bare moonlight. I held my ground, however, and narrowed my gaze at him.

"I daresay it has to do with pride or some such nonsense," I said. "With you being the head of the investigation, you can't very well have your authority questioned. But you needn't have punished Mr. Drake for wanting some time away from the case."

Mr. Rawlings stared at me, the stiffness in his shoulders the only sign that he'd heard me. "You think," he said slowly, dangerously, "that I sent Drake away out of spite?"

I jutted my chin. "I cannot imagine another reason when you knew he intended to join us tonight."

His eyes hardened. "You have a very high opinion of yourself, Miss Lacey."

"I do indeed," I said. "But that is beside the point. You've yet to deny what I said."

Mr. Rawlings gave a short, humorless laugh. "Then let me do so now, unequivocally. I had no thought of you or your little outing in the least when I sent Drake out this afternoon. I was quite busy, you see, investigating a horrific murder. But I should have realized that apprehending a killer is nothing compared to the inconvenience of being deprived of your escort to a *pleasure garden*."

The truth in his words stung. When he said it so bluntly, I could not help but feel silly. Small. Foolish. But then my anger rose, resisting. "Forgive me for misunderstanding," I said tightly. "If the situation is really so dire as all that, I cannot understand why you should have agreed to come in his place."

"Because," he ground out, "I was attempting to be polite, which I now see was a lost cause. My time would have been better spent at Bow Street."

"It is not too late to leave," I said with a stretched smile. "I would hate for anyone to think you might actually be enjoying yourself. You have a reputation to uphold, after all."

"Bold words, Miss Lacey," he said, his words clipped, "for a woman in your situation."

I was not easily stunned into silence, but I found myself with my mouth parted, eyes wide. Had I misheard him? He only stared back, gaze set in a hard line, watching me as if to measure my reaction and judge me by it.

I slowly took my hand from his arm, dropping it to my side. "What precisely do you mean by that?" I said shakily, trying to remain calm but failing miserably.

"You seem quick to assume things of others when you should be more concerned about what people are saying about *you*."

And I realized then that Mr. Rawlings knew precisely what sort of rumors had circulated about me since I'd last left London.

It wasn't that I'd expected to avoid my past entirely. I'd known that would be impossible. The *ton* liked its gossip, and I had provided more than my fair share in the past. But I *had* hoped to ignore it for as long as possible, stay ahead of the rumors for at least a few days.

But it wasn't to be. They were already here, haunting me and poisoning people against me. What *had* Mr. Rawlings heard? So many scandalous falsehoods had circulated two years ago, some worse than others. I hated that I cared. Why should this man's opinion mean anything to me?

I wanted to cry, as pointless and absurd as that might be. That thought more than anything made me straighten my back and steel myself. I cried but rarely, and I would not let Mr. Rawlings be the one to push me over such an edge.

"I see," I said, my voice rough. "And here I thought Jack had better taste in friends."

My words fell into the silence between us, a stone in a pond. Mr. Rawlings said nothing, only stood with a rigid stillness, dark eyes reflecting the light of the lone lantern near us.

"Your company is no longer needed, Mr. Rawlings," I somehow managed, "nor was it ever desired. Good evening." I turned on my heel and continued along the now-deserted path. Ginny and Jack had disappeared around a bend, not realizing we'd fallen behind. No matter. I would catch them, and then I could finally begin to enjoy my night.

I heard Mr. Rawlings's footsteps behind me, a quick, loping stride. "I cannot leave you here alone," he said tightly. "I'll see you to Jack."

"That will not be necessary," I replied, quickening my pace. "They're just ahead."

"Don't be foolish," he snapped. "This is Vauxhall, not Mayfair."

I rounded on him, and he drew up short.

"I think it is quite more dangerous to be with *you*," I retorted, "than to be alone. Though you may think otherwise from my reputation."

"Miss Lacey," he began, voice hard, "I cannot—" He stopped, his eyes flicking to something behind me, then widening.

I vaguely registered the sound of pounding footsteps, panting breaths. In the shortest of moments, Mr. Rawlings's expression ran through a dozen emotions, each impossible to interpret. What was he—

He threw out his hands and pushed me to the side.

There was no chance to catch my balance. I hit the ground with an unflattering thud, my hip and shoulder taking the brunt of the impact. The hit sent a shuddering, breathless jolt through me, and I gasped, struggling to sit up, my hands sinking into the damp, muddy earth.

"Mr. Rawlings!" I yelped. "What in heaven's—" Then my breath caught again.

Mr. Rawlings grappled with a man on the path in front of me. Grasping the stranger's lapel with one hand, he drove his fist into the man's face. The man—a black mask hiding his features—stumbled back a few steps. He caught his balance, and his mouth drew into a menacing sneer.

My mind churned slowly, too slowly. I could not breathe. Who was—What was—

The man launched himself back at Mr. Rawlings.

Cold, icy fear clawed through me. I could not control myself. I screamed an awful, breathless shriek.

Mr. Rawlings spun toward me, searching for whatever threatened me. There was nothing. I was a witless idiot, distracting him from the real danger.

In that briefest of moments, the masked man yanked something from his belt. It flashed in the lantern light.

A knife.

"Mr. Rawlings!" His name tore from me, a desperate lash.

It was too late. Mr. Rawlings turned just as the man slashed him across the upper arm. Mr. Rawlings shouted and fell back, one hand clutching his injured arm.

My stomach twisted, chest tight. I opened my mouth to scream again, but the sound froze in my throat as the masked man turned his lightless eyes toward me.

Chapter 4

He started after me. Panic surged through my veins—hot and instantaneous. I scrambled to my feet, searching frantically for anything to use as a weapon. I had nothing but my reticule. Nothing but grass and earth and trees.

The man was nearly to me, just steps away. His mouth twisted cruelly below the edge of the mask. The knife was still clutched in his hand, the edge glinting with blood.

I was going to die.

I threw up my hands, clenched tightly into fists—a pitiful defense. My heartbeat was a drum in my ears.

Then he flew forward, tumbling to the ground, limbs flying wildly. I barely dodged out of the way in time. Mr. Rawlings had tackled him from behind, and the two rolled across the pathway, fists flying.

I could only watch in horror as the stranger landed a solid blow across Mr. Rawlings's jaw. He fell back on the ground, moaning and cursing, his jacket a patchwork of blood and mud. The assailant picked up his knife and stalked after Mr. Rawlings.

No. No!

Heat coursed through me. Anger. It sharpened and focused my mind. I searched my surroundings again, looking for something—anything—to stop the man.

My foot kicked something. A stout wooden stave topped with a brass crown. Mr. Rawlings's Bow Street baton, dropped in the scuffle.

I snatched it up, grasping the heavy wooden handle. Then I darted after the attacker. He was nearly to Mr. Rawlings, who was trying to sit up, dazed by the blow. He did not see the stranger coming.

The man raised his knife.

Using both hands, I whipped the baton at the back of the assailant's head with all my strength. It struck with a sickening thud. The man loosed a howl, dropping to the ground and clutching his head. He attempted to stand but fell again to his hands and knees, shaking his bloody head with a growl.

Then he looked up at me. His mask had come undone in the melee. I stared at him, and he at me. He had a face I might have passed a hundred times on the street and never noticed. Brown hair, dark eyes, thick brows, wide nose, and a stubbly chin. Unremarkable and ordinary. But there was nothing ordinary in the way he looked at me with such dark hatred that I took a step back, my hands clutching tighter around the wooden baton.

"You," he growled, his voice a broken, grasping thing. "You're mine."

He lurched to his feet, heading toward me. I fell back, gasping.

Then Mr. Rawlings was there, his uninjured arm stretched out in front of me. His balance was unsteady, movements erratic.

But it was enough. The stranger glowered at him, realizing the fight was lost, then snatched up his mask from the ground. With one last look of pure venom at both of us, he stumbled away into the dark.

Mr. Rawlings started after him. I dropped the baton to the ground and grasped his arm—the one not dripping with blood. "You mustn't."

He tried to shake me off, but it was a testament to how truly hurt he was that he was unsuccessful. "Let me go," he insisted, though his words were formless, brogue lilting. Not sharp and precise like he normally spoke.

"Stop," I ordered him. "You're injured. You'll only bleed to death, and what good will that do?"

He blinked at me, his eyes hazy. "I—" He shook his head once, and his gaze cleared a bit. "Miss Lacey. Are you hurt?"

The urgency in his voice tugged deep within me. This man hardly knew me, but what he had done tonight . . .

"No," I said, throat aching. "I'm not hurt."

He moved his arms to grasp me and hold me out for inspection. But then he winced and clutched his injured arm as if just realizing he himself was hurt.

"I'll run to find help." My voice was unfamiliar in my ears, wild and wobbly. I couldn't seem to focus my thoughts. Bright spots of light danced in my vision.

"No, you certainly will not," he snapped. "You will stay right here where I can see you."

I heard footsteps and jerked my head, terror rising again inside me. But it was Jack running back to us from up the path. Ginny followed not far behind, one hand clasped to her belly, mouth agape.

"What happened?" Jack demanded as he skidded to a halt beside us, barely winded. "We heard shouts."

"We were attacked." Mr. Rawlings was all business, even covered in blood and unsteady on his feet. "A man with a knife. Came at me first, then went after Miss Lacey. We fought him off."

We. I blinked. Yes, I'd fought as well.

Jack's face was as serious as I'd ever seen it. "Where did he go?"

"That way." I pointed in the direction the man had disappeared. Jack was gone again in an instant, jacket flapping behind him.

"Jack!" Ginny shouted after him, but he did not hear, or chose not to. She reached us in the next moment, grasping my arms. "Where are you hurt, Bea? Tell me!"

"I'm not," I managed.

"The blood!" she cried as she inspected me.

"It's not mine," I said. "Mr. Rawlings's arm is badly cut."

I met Mr. Rawlings's eyes, too dark against the pale of his face. He was not well, his breaths shallow and his shoulders bowed as he cradled his injured arm.

"We need to bandage it," I said immediately. "Stop the bleeding."

Ginny was not one to blanch at the sight of blood, thankfully, though my stomach was more riotous. We helped Mr. Rawlings ease off his jacket, then Ginny fished a handkerchief from her reticule. I folded it into a messy square, my movements hasty and imprecise, and pressed it to the wound with shaking hands. The crimson blood against the white of his shirt made everything seem garish and unreal in the hazy lantern light.

"Here," Mr. Rawlings ground out, reaching into his pocket with his other hand to retrieve his own handkerchief. "Tie the bandage on."

Ginny took it and wrapped it around his arm while I held the other handkerchief in place. We all turned as Jack appeared again down the path, anger and frustration written across his face. He hadn't caught the man. Without a word, I took the ends of the handkerchief from Ginny, and she hurried to meet him.

I tied off the ends, but I was far from a competent nurse. Mr. Rawlings needed a doctor, and soon. My breaths came too quickly. What had just happened? Had we truly almost died at the hands of an armed assailant?

"You saved my life." Mr. Rawlings was watching me, his eyes burnished by the flame of the nearby lantern. He'd spoken with a sort of detached bewilderment, as if trying to come to terms with that fact.

"And you saved mine." My voice cracked. "Now, let us say nothing more of it. We need to find a doctor, or my efforts will have been in vain."

Suddenly, voices and footsteps surrounded us—other guests at the gardens, I assumed, who had heard the shouts and come to help or to gawk. I noticed them with an odd vagueness. My vision dipped and swam, and I swayed to one side. Mr. Rawlings grabbed my elbow.

What a sight we must be, him holding me up, the both of us bloody and dirty.

"You've had a shock," he said brusquely. "You ought to sit."

"No, I'm—"

"Mrs. Travers," he ordered, not listening to me. "See to Miss Lacey."

Ginny nodded and returned to my side as Mr. Rawlings strode off to where Jack stood speaking to another man, something about closing all the entrances to the gardens.

I stood there, legs like jelly, my hands and skirts filthy. Everything felt so far away, so muted and dreamlike. Ginny was speaking beside me, holding my arm tightly, and I struggled to make out her words.

"—see you both back," she said. "We'll send for a doctor on the way." She noticed I wasn't listening. "Bea?"

"I need to wash my hands," I said distantly, holding them up before me, splotched with blood and mud. "I . . . I don't . . ."

She took my hands in hers, not caring how grimy mine were. "You're safe now, Beatrice," she said softly. "You're safe. It's over."

But it wasn't. The masked man had escaped, and the grasping, choking fear that had consumed me had yet to relinquish its hold. What if he came back?

I blinked away the strange fog that clouded my mind, the details of the night screaming back into focus. I could feel the biting chill in the autumn air. The dirt beneath my nails. My damp skirts clinging to my legs. Faint strains of the orchestra drifted on the breeze.

Then I spotted that golden gleam in the dirt again—the baton that had saved both our lives. I pulled my hands from Ginny's and bent to pick it up. There was blood on the gilded crown. Our attacker's blood.

"This is Mr. Rawlings's," I said. "I'll keep it for him." I held it gingerly as I slipped it into my reticule, shuddering at the thought of the blood staining the fabric inside. I would throw it out entirely, I already knew.

Ginny mistook my shudder for a chill. She took her shawl and wrapped it around my shoulders, then slipped one arm around me. She held me close, and I let her, her presence comforting.

But the black pit in my chest refused to dissipate. Never before had I felt truly unsafe. That I was in danger. That I might die. It was a feeling that tore one up and left one changed on the other side.

And I knew I was not the same person I had been.

Mr. Rawlings hissed as the doctor stabbed the needle yet again into his skin, stitching up the impressive gash on his upper arm. The doctor had cut away Mr. Rawlings's sleeve to reveal the wound, and though I'd known it was awful when I'd helped him at Vauxhall, seeing it now in the bright lamplight of the Traverses' parlor made me feel ill.

I looked away, stomach churning, and focused on taking deep, full breaths as I pulled the blanket tighter around my shoulders. Ginny had tried to convince me to go upstairs and change out of my soiled dress, but I'd refused. I needed people around me, needed the heat of the fire and the hum of conversation in my ears.

Not to mention that I wasn't entirely sure my unstable legs could conquer the staircase.

I had, however, washed my hands. Several times, in fact, in a manner that brought to mind a tortured Lady Macbeth. I could still see the stain of blood in my mind's eye, swirled and dried with mud.

"Tell me." Jack was seated across from me, a black book balanced on his knee, pencil poised to write. "Did the man say anything to you?"

I shook my head. "Nothing." Then I paused. "No, that's not true. He said—" I had to pause, swallow. "He said, 'You're mine.'"

Jack said nothing for a moment, brow tipped into a *V*. "You're sure?"

I nodded, and he began writing.

"And he wore a mask?" he asked.

"He did," I replied. "Though it came free in the scuffle."

Jack's pencil paused. "You saw his face?"

"It was dark," I said as Ginny brought me a cup of tea, hot and steaming. "But yes, well enough."

Jack exchanged a look with Ginny.

"Verity?" she asked.

"Yes," he said. "Send for her immediately. And Denning too."

I took the cup, brows lowered. "Why Verity?"

"She can sketch the man," Ginny explained, "if you describe him to her."

"And the sooner, the better," Jack said. "You would be surprised how quickly memory fades."

Ginny nodded and left the parlor, undoubtedly to send a message to the Dennings' nearby home.

"Rawlings, did you get a good look at his face?" Jack turned in his chair. "Recognize him at all?"

Mr. Rawlings's mouth was a tight slash, as if he were using every drop of self-restraint to keep from cursing out loud as the doctor continued his ministrations. "I did not recognize him," he grunted. "But if I saw him again, I'd know him."

Bruises were beginning to form on Mr. Rawlings's face, around his left eye and along his jaw. The assailant had gotten in a few good blows during their bout. I bit my lip, sitting there feeling stupid and useless with my soft hands and unmarred face. It had been luck. That was all. Just luck that I hadn't died tonight—that we *both* hadn't died.

My breathing was still too fast, my pulse galloping in my head. I had to get a hold of myself. I wrapped my hands around my teacup, willing my hands to *stop shaking*.

"You should sit with Verity as well," Jack told Mr. Rawlings. "We'll need both of your descriptions."

We heard a commotion outside the room, voices and footsteps. The door opened again, and Mr. Drake appeared, looking rather disheveled. I straightened, a flush whispering across my cheeks. Blast it all. I hadn't planned on him seeing me in such a state.

He quickly took in Mr. Rawlings with the doctor, Jack and me by the fire. "I just heard," he said, closing the door behind him. "I came straight here. What happened?"

Jack explained everything, though I barely heard him as I discreetly tried to sort myself out—tugging my skirts straight and brushing back my untidy hair. I hadn't yet looked in a mirror, but perhaps that was for the best.

I looked up and found Mr. Rawlings watching me from across the room, his face as unreadable as a blank book. But I could well read his thoughts. He knew I was trying to make myself presentable for Mr. Drake. I'd all but declared my intentions for the man when we'd argued at Vauxhall, after all.

I glanced away, my cheeks growing even hotter.

"And you're well?" Mr. Drake turned to face me. "Miss Lacey?"

There was a sweet concern in his voice. "I am well enough," I said. "Though the same cannot be said for Mr. Rawlings."

"I am fine," Mr. Rawlings said with a terse, manly denial.

"You are not fine," the doctor countered. I hadn't caught his name in the clamor of our arrival. "You'll need to wear a sling for at least a week or run the risk of straining your sutures. And I'm not entirely sure you didn't also crack a rib or two. You need to rest."

"Rest?" Mr. Rawlings glared at the man as if he'd offered a grave insult instead of sound medical advice. "I have work to do. We must find the culprit."

"How would we go about that?" The question escaped before I could think twice.

Mr. Rawlings moved his glare from the doctor to me. "*We* won't be doing anything, Miss Lacey. Bow Street is quite capable of handling this on its own."

"She has a point though," Mr. Drake said. "How do you propose to track this man down? We have so few clues as to his identity."

"True," Mr. Rawlings said with a scowl. "But it's quite clear why he came after us."

Clear as mud, though Jack was nodding with understanding.

"It's the case," Jack said. "You think he's trying to stop you from finding the murderer."

"Not just that," Mr. Rawlings replied grimly. "I would bet a year's salary that our attacker *was* the viscount's murderer."

I gaped at him. It was foolish, really, that I should be shocked. The masked man had attempted to kill both of us. But realizing now that our assailant had possibly been the one behind the most gruesome and sickening crime London had seen in years . . . I pulled the blanket around me, fear gathering like a knot behind my ribs.

Mr. Drake, however, was shaking his head. "That is quite the leap to make, Rawlings. We cannot know whether they're connected."

"What else could it be?" Mr. Rawlings argued as the doctor cut the thread and began bandaging the wound. "It is the only case I've been working for a week, and I'm the lead officer. I must have caught his trail somehow, and he's determined to put an end to it. Determined enough to attack not just me but an innocent woman."

Mr. Drake frowned. "What sort of leads have you been working? What might have tipped him off, if it *is* him?"

Mr. Rawlings shook his head. "It could be a number of things. I've been prying into the viscount's financial affairs, but then we've also been questioning each and every one of the household staff and close acquaintances. If we have a strong lead, I can't say *I* even know it."

Frustration burrowed into his brow, deep as a newly plowed field. This was a man who hated being ignorant, hated not understanding.

"But we'll discover it," he said as the doctor positioned a white strip of fabric under his elbow and forearm and tightened it into a sling around his neck. "If he is worried we'll learn his identity, we must be doing something right. We must get to Bow Street now, review everything we have so far."

Mr. Drake cleared his throat. "About that," he said. "Mr. Etchells sent me with a message."

Etchells. The name wasn't familiar to me.

"The chief magistrate," Jack explained to me, seeing my confusion.

"What sort of message?" Mr. Rawlings's voice was suspicious.

Mr. Drake shifted his weight. "He wants to give you time to heal. Recover."

"I don't need time," Mr. Rawlings replied immediately. "I can work."

"Yes, well," Mr. Drake edged, "there may be extenuating circumstances."

"Spit it out, Drake," Jack said mildly.

Mr. Drake sighed. "Mr. Etchells has removed Rawlings as head of the investigation. I am to take up the reins."

Silence descended, thick as a wool blanket. My eyes darted between Mr. Drake and Mr. Rawlings, tension radiating through the room.

Mr. Rawlings did not react, only sat still as the doctor finished adjusting the sling around his arm. "You cannot be serious," he finally said, more calmly than anything he'd said all night.

"There is no doubt in your abilities," Mr. Drake was quick to assure him. "Mr. Etchells is worried you have become too public a face for the investigation. Painted a target on your own back, so to speak. And now with you injured—"

"Injured or not," Mr. Rawlings broke in tightly, "I can work."

Mr. Drake shook his head. "You need time to heal."

"Not to mention," Jack said, thoughtful, "that you've seen the man's face. If he really is the killer, you've just become a key witness."

Mr. Drake nodded. "He'll be coming after you again, mark my words."

The realization came slowly—painfully so. It pricked at the corners of my mind, toyed with me, then flared to awareness in one sharp burst.

"I've also seen his face." My voice was unsteady.

The men seemed to have forgotten I was there. They all turned to me in surprise.

I tried to swallow, my throat suddenly rough as sand. "I've seen his face," I said again. "He'll be after me, too, won't he?"

They stared at me, their faces showing varying degrees of alarm as they came to the same conclusion. But it was Mr. Rawlings whom I looked at, searching in the dark angles of his face for a reassurance that I was perhaps overreacting. I did not find it. Instead, in his grim expression, I saw only a confirmation of what I feared.

I was right.

And I was in terrible danger.

CHAPTER 5

Ginny bustled back into the room in the midst of our foreboding, funereal silence. She stopped, seeming to sense the shift in mood immediately. "What's happened?" she asked, one hand going to her chest. "Jack?"

He stood, clearing his throat. "There is some . . . concern about the fact that Beatrice can identify their attacker."

Ginny inhaled sharply and came to my side. She understood immediately. Her father had been a magistrate for nearly a decade, and tonight her wits were clearly quicker than mine.

"Is she in danger?" Her face was pale against her vibrant red hair.

"We cannot know for certain." Mr. Rawlings stood with a wince. Heavens, he looked worse for the wear—white shirt caked with blood and dirt, his hair in disarray. "The attacker was after me. It is unlikely he knows who Miss Lacey is."

"But it would not be difficult for him to discover her name," Mr. Drake pointed out. "The man is clearly resourceful if he was able to follow you to Vauxhall. He knows she can identify him, the same as you."

"He spoke to her," Jack said, voice grim. "Threatened her."

The room stilled, the quiet a living, breathing thing.

"If he is indeed the murderer, as you suspect," Jack continued, "then I have little doubt he is ruthless enough to tie up any loose ends."

Loose ends. I was a loose end.

"What can we do?" Ginny's hand found my arm, as if to comfort me.

I barely registered her touch, trying desperately to keep apace of the conversation.

The doctor, finished packing up his things, appeared more than ready to leave. He quickly clasped his bag, grabbed his hat and gloves, and slipped from the room.

Jack frowned, his mouth set in a grave line. "We need to get Beatrice out of London. Immediately."

I had been clinging to the unraveling threads of my sanity, but this made me lose my grasp completely. "Leave?" I gaped at him.

"She cannot leave," Ginny insisted. "We must keep her here, keep her safe."

Jack shook his head. "London is not safe for her, Ginny," he said. "You must see that."

Ginny seemed about to protest yet again, but Mr. Drake broke in. "Where could we send her? Home?"

"No," Mr. Rawlings said shortly. "That will only put her family in danger as well. It cannot be anywhere she is known."

"Somewhere in the country," Mr. Drake suggested. "Do we have any contacts who might take her in?"

"Perhaps," Jack said. "Wily might know a place. Though we can hardly send her off by herself."

"Of course not." Ginny stepped forward. "I will go with her."

Jack turned to her in disbelief. "You?"

"Beatrice needs me," she said stubbornly.

He shook his head. "And how would you help her? What could you do if he tracked you down?"

"It would not be the first time I've faced down a murderer." She raised her chin.

"No, Ginny." I stood abruptly, heart racing. How could she think to put herself in the path of such a man? "Jack is right. You must think of the baby. I would never forgive myself if something happened to you."

Ginny stared at me. "But then . . ." She stopped a moment, her eyes glassy, then regained her composure. "Who will go with you?"

"Verity?" Jack suggested.

Mr. Drake shook his head, his face filled with regret. "We need Verity here," he said. "If we are to lose Rawlings in the investigation, then we need all the help we can get."

Ginny turned away, plainly upset. She didn't like this. Neither did I, but what were we to do?

Mr. Drake sighed. "There is an obvious solution." He turned toward Mr. Rawlings, still standing opposite the room from me, shoulders bent around his injured arm.

Realization struck me immediately, and my mouth dropped. Mr. Rawlings blinked slowly, taking longer to catch on.

"Me?" he finally said in disbelief.

"Yes, you," Mr. Drake said. "You've already been relieved of the case, and we've established that you need time to heal."

"We have *not* establi—"

"Where better to recuperate than in some sleepy village, keeping an eye on Miss Lacey?" Mr. Drake continued on, overriding Mr. Rawlings's protest.

Oh no. Heavens no. I could think of nothing worse than traveling with the reticent, high-handed Mr. Rawlings. "Is that really necessary?" I asked, trying not to reveal my absolute dread at the idea. "I could . . . I could go by myself."

It was a foolish, desperate idea, one I knew would be rejected before I'd even finished speaking it.

"I am afraid that is out of the question," Mr. Drake said, and there was no sign of the friendly, lighthearted man who'd sat beside me at dinner last night. He was all business, though there was some sympathy in his voice. "We cannot leave a lady like yourself unprotected. And besides that, you are also a witness now, important to any prosecution that should come against our culprit."

"But Mr. Rawlings is injured," I blurted out. "He isn't in any state to protect me."

Mr. Rawlings gave a dry laugh. "I managed well enough tonight, but I'm grateful for your confidence, Miss Lacey."

I glared at him. Couldn't he see that I was trying to free us both from this debacle? "As I recall, we both managed well enough," I said, jaw tight. A reminder that he hadn't acted alone. That I had saved his life as well.

His eyes narrowed on mine and held there, as if daring me to break away. I only planted my feet more firmly and stared him down.

"You needn't worry, Beatrice," Jack said. "Mr. Rawlings is more capable with one arm than most men are with two. You will be safe with him."

I did not doubt it. The man was infuriatingly competent in everything he did.

"We still need somewhere to send them," Mr. Drake said. "Or this discussion is pointless."

Another moment of silence.

"I know of a place," Mr. Rawlings said, his words clipped, expression resigned.

I stared at him. Was he giving in? He could not want this any more than I did.

"Where?" Ginny pressed.

Mr. Rawlings shook his head. "I should not say. It would be safer for everyone involved to know as little as possible." He had returned once again to his natural state, indifferent and aloof.

"Even me?" I challenged. "Are you to blindfold me in the carriage?"

He turned that penetrating gaze back to me. "If you would feel more at ease."

I made a noise of disbelief. We couldn't actually be contemplating this, could we?

"What of her reputation?" Ginny asked, crossing her arms. "They cannot travel alone together, let alone hide away for an undetermined length of time."

I nearly retorted that my reputation was the least of my worries but just stopped myself. That wouldn't help my case at all.

Mr. Rawlings broke in again. "Safety must be our first priority. But we will depart in secret, and we will take every precaution to protect Miss Lacey's reputation."

If I wasn't imagining things, he put the slightest emphasis on that last word, reminding me that he knew my reputation was already in tatters.

Ginny faced Mr. Rawlings, her face steeped in worry. "Are you sure about this place?" she asked. "Are you sure Beatrice will be safe there?"

Mr. Rawlings nodded just once, a sharp drop of his chin. "Yes."

I expected more arguments from the others, but Ginny bit her lip, the tension in her face ebbing slightly. Jack looked thoughtful, and Mr. Drake was nodding his approval. Apparently, everything was already settled.

I wasn't ready to give in just yet. "My mother is expecting me home in a week. I cannot just dash off into the country."

"I have every hope that this will all be over in a week," Mr. Drake offered. "If the murderer was so bold as to attack the lead investigator, I believe we are closer to solving this case than we realize. You and Rawlings will return soon enough."

I shook my head. They all had an answer for every protest I made. It was infuriating. "There has to be another way," I insisted. "A better way. What if—"

"Beatrice." Jack stepped forward, fixing me with a serious stare. "You must see reason. This man is a murderer. If he finds you, he *will* kill you."

His words hit me with enough force to tear the breath from my lungs. All the terror from earlier tonight swept over me again, along with the memory of the pure hate in our attacker's eyes. I tried to push the image away, but it refused to yield its hold on me.

You're mine, he'd said. He'd meant it. I knew he had. He would be looking for me, the woman who had drawn his blood and kept him from his quarry.

"There is no time for arguing," Jack said firmly. "We have to get you out of London. Now."

I said nothing, my hands curling into fists around my skirts. My pulse was like a battering ram in my ear.

"I am sorry, Miss Lacey," Mr. Drake said softly. "But I promise we shall do our best to resolve this as quickly as possible."

My mounting irritation—and the suffocating tide of utter powerlessness—dissipated at his words. This was not the fault of anyone here, I knew that. It was chance that had placed me at Mr. Rawlings's side tonight and into this precarious situation.

I took a deep breath. This was clearly going to happen whether I liked it or not. I had to adapt, make the best of things. That was always my way in life, and I would not abandon my creed so easily.

"Very well," I finally said, my voice catching in my throat. "I'll go."

I looked at Mr. Rawlings, who had said nothing more since he'd offered his unwanted port in this maelstrom. He met my gaze, and I could feel the weight of his stare like a physical thing. What was he really thinking behind that careful facade?

"We must leave tonight," he said. "The dark will help us avoid any tails."

"You'll take my carriage," Ginny said immediately. "Please."

He nodded, accepting her offer. "Can you be ready to leave within the hour?" he asked me, a challenge strung through his words, as if he expected me to need hours of preparation before we could depart.

"Yes." I kept my voice cool. "Can you?"

He ignored my jab and faced Jack and Mr. Drake. "I'll fetch a few things from home and return shortly. Have Verity begin her sketch with Miss Lacey when she arrives."

Then he left the room without so much as another glance my way. A charmer, to be sure. The next few days spent in his company would be a delight.

"We should begin packing," Ginny said determinedly, moving toward the door. She was never one to dally about once a decision had been made.

I followed, casting a glance at Mr. Drake as I passed. He offered a reassuring smile, and I returned it, though inwardly I sighed. Why couldn't I be hiding away from a murderer with him? I would almost welcome such a thing. Instead, I was to be trapped with *Mr. Rawlings*. My insides twisted yet again.

Mariah was waiting in my room, no doubt having heard from the servants belowstairs that something was afoot. Her eyes widened at the sight of me, still dressed in my ruined gown.

"What's happened?" she gasped. "Why was the doctor called? Are you hurt?"

I could not summon the energy to tell her everything. I sat heavily on the bed as Ginny recounted the rather unfortunate turn our evening had taken. I needed to change, to pack, but exhaustion crashed into me. Gone was my excitement and anticipation for a visit to London with my best friend. Instead, I was left with an emptying dread and a hollow chest.

"They leave within the hour," Ginny finished as she opened the wardrobe. "We need to ready Beatrice as quickly as possible."

Mariah was speechless, her mouth gaping as she glanced between the two of us. "But surely I will come with you," she said. "To help."

"No," Ginny said, sorting through my dresses. "Questions will be asked about Beatrice's sudden absence. Perhaps we can say she is ill? You must remain to make it look as though she is here. It would be simple enough to bring food, clean clothes, whatever we need to keep up the ruse."

Clearly, she'd thought everything through while I was still struggling to come to terms with my new reality.

"And, Mariah, you must promise you will not tell anyone what you've heard tonight," Ginny said sternly. "This is of the utmost importance."

She nodded seriously, face pale. "Yes, miss."

Mariah helped me out of my soiled gown, and I washed myself as best I could at the basin since there was no time for a proper bath. Once I was relatively clean, Mariah dressed me in a traveling gown and fixed my hair into a simple coiffure. I looked through the many things I had brought to London, though they all seemed quite useless. Silver combs and pearl necklaces and painted fans. None of that would do me any good now.

We packed my trunk, filled it with stockings, chemises, and the plainer of my dresses. Ginny, however, folded the one ball gown I'd brought to London, a beautiful pink affair in embroidered silk.

"I hardly think I shall need such a gown," I said dryly.

"One never knows," she said.

I'd never thought of Ginny as obtuse, so she must be quite mad if she thought I'd be attending any balls while on the run from a murderer and in the company of the dour Mr. Rawlings.

But I let her pack it because it seemed to give her some comfort. I added a few things to the top of my trunk—pieces of small jewelry, various perfumes and cosmetics, my hairbrush and pins.

"How will you manage without me?" Mariah fretted, hands at her waist as she gazed at the full trunk.

"I shall bravely soldier on." I closed the lid with a thump. "Perhaps Mr. Rawlings is an expert on French hairstyles."

Mariah did not appreciate my attempt at levity, swiping a sudden tear from her cheek. I took her hand. "Please do not fear," I said more softly. "You'll be perfectly safe here with the Traverses."

"I am not worried for myself, Miss Lacey," she said. "Who will keep you out of trouble?"

"Out of trouble?" A wry smile found my lips. "I believe I am quite in the thick of it already."

A knock came at the door, and Verity peeked inside. "Might I come in?"

"Certainly," I said. "It is something of a party already."

Verity smiled sympathetically. "Your London visit took an unexpected turn, I understand."

"*Unexpected* is one word for it." Ginny laid my thick winter cloak atop the trunk. She turned to Verity. "You are ready to sketch?"

Verity held up her sketch pad and pencil, and Ginny nodded. "Come, Mariah, let's leave them to it. We can sort out some food for the journey."

They left, and then it was just Verity and me, the crackling of the fire, and the beginnings of a headache in my right temple.

Verity sat at the writing desk in the corner and gestured for me to sit in the nearby armchair. "I am going to ask you a few questions about the man you saw," she explained. "I will do my best to recreate his face as you remember it, but it is an imperfect science. We can only hope for a decent enough likeness to be useful to the investigation."

She spent the next twenty minutes questioning me, asking for specifics about the man's eyes, the shape of his nose, the color of his hair. His features were something of a blur in my memory, but she managed to pry small details from me. The outline of a face began to appear on the paper before her.

At last, she held it up for my inspection. "What do you think?" she asked. "Am I close?"

I blinked. It was very close. She'd captured his dark brows and thick jaw, and while it wasn't perfect, when I looked at the shadowed eyes—menacing, haunting—it twisted me back into that moment of terror. When he'd come after me. When I'd been helpless. A shiver traced over my spine. "How did you do that?" I asked quietly. "I can admit to some skill in drawing, but nothing like this."

She gave a slight shrug. "Nathaniel calls it a gift," she said without any sense of self-importance. "Until recently, I simply considered it a diversion. But whatever the word, I intend to do as much good with it as I can." She collected her pencils and stood. "Rawlings should be back by now. I will interview him and see what other details he might add."

I made a sound of irritation at his name—an inadvertent reaction.

Verity paused, eyeing me. "Might I assume you and Mr. Rawlings are still on the wrong foot since the dinner party?"

I grimaced. "Let us simply say that nothing but the threat of a murderer would induce me to spend another minute of my time in his company."

Verity tilted her head as she clasped her sketch pad to her chest, amused. "He is not so bad as that."

Curiosity sparked inside me. Ginny barely knew Mr. Rawlings, having only met him a time or two. But Verity had been acquainted with him for years and worked with him at Bow Street, besides. "What do you know of Mr. Rawlings, then?" I asked. "Because he seems quite determined to uphold my opinion of a straitlaced, long-faced, impossible-to-please officer of the law."

"He is that," she conceded with a short laugh. "But you mustn't let him intimidate you, Beatrice. He is kinder than he lets on. You can trust him."

Trust. I snorted. I very much doubted that.

She only smiled and patted my arm. "You will both have to trust each other, I'm afraid."

"I'm quite afraid of that too," I said. "Please, do everything you can to find this man"—I gestured at her drawing—"so that I may return as soon as possible."

"Indeed I will," she said with a wink. "Then perhaps you might regain your footing with a different officer of the law."

I did not bother to hide my grin. "Perhaps."

She moved to the door. "Good luck, Beatrice. I do hope we meet again soon under less dire circumstances."

"As do I," I replied soberly. "Thank you, Verity."

Quiet descended after she left. It was the first time I'd been alone since this whole ordeal had begun. I went to stand before the trunk at the foot of my bed. I took another deep breath—how many had I consciously taken tonight, trying to center myself?—and laid an unsteady hand atop the trunk.

This was an adventure, I told myself. The type of experience I'd so often wished for amid my ordinary, uninteresting life. And while I was afraid, I could not let that emotion rule me. I was stronger than my fear, my uncertainty, my apprehension. I would face this obstacle head-on, with all the dogged optimism I could muster. This was my chance to prove my mettle.

I spotted my reticule on the floor near the door. I must have dropped it there when I'd entered earlier. I bent to pick it up. Mr. Rawlings's Bow Street stave was still inside. I moved to my washbasin and tipped the open reticule so the stave slipped out into the water, splashing in the silence. The crown was smeared with dried, rust-red blood. Before I could grow too nauseated, I took a rag and scrubbed the stave clean, trying very hard not to think about the man I'd injured with this weapon. When I finished, I dried it and placed it into the new reticule I'd be taking on tonight's journey.

A manservant came to fetch my trunk. I donned my cloak and followed him downstairs, feeling an ache in my side from where Mr. Rawlings had pushed me out of harm's way. How had that been only a few hours ago? It seemed my entire world had upended since then.

Everyone was waiting in the small entryway, conversing in quiet voices—Ginny and Jack, Verity and Mr. Denning, Mr. Drake.

And Mr. Rawlings.

He stood by the front door, apparently having finished meeting with Verity. He spoke with Mr. Drake, their faces serious. I had no doubt they were speaking of the case. Mr. Rawlings obviously did not enjoy having his authority stripped away, but he had every reason—just as I did—to want this case solved as quickly as possible. His white sling stood out in bright contrast against his clean clothing, nondescript and dark. His hair was fixed again, back into that rigid style he wore. The bruises around his eye and jaw had continued to darken, which only made him look that much more dangerous. Intimidating.

Ginny met me at the bottom of the stairs, hair coming loose from its pins, posture weary. She took my hands. "Please, be careful, Beatrice. No unnecessary risks. Bide your time, stay out of sight, and everything will be right in the end."

I kissed her cheek. "I will. You must take care as well."

She nodded, and there was so much more we could have said to each other, but we left it at that. With a quick embrace, she stepped back.

I turned to face the rest of the party—all watching me—but I fixed my attention on Mr. Rawlings. He waited beside the door, hat in hand, expression staid.

"Are you ready, Miss Lacey?" There was no warmth in that Highland lilt, no matter how it softened the edges of his words.

Every doubt returned with a vengeance, like glowing embers stoked back to life. Was I truly going to travel to an unknown location with a man I barely knew? Did I really trust that he would protect me?

I dragged a deep, cold breath into my lungs, then released it. I had to have faith. Pushing away the battering thoughts, I nodded. "I am ready."

With one last glance back at Ginny, standing with her arm through Jack's, I followed Mr. Rawlings out the door and down the front steps.

He stopped beside the coach and held out his good hand to me. I hesitated, then took it. Through our gloves, the steady press of his fingers sent a bolt of awareness through me—the touch of this man I barely knew. He helped me inside with no sign of aggravation from his injury.

I seated myself on the forward-facing bench, while he sat across from me. Wonderful. We'd have to stare at each other for hours on end. But then I imagined him sitting beside me, bumping into me with every turn in the road, and decided his choice was the preferable option.

I met his eyes, and I could read nothing in those dark depths, no hint of emotion in his features.

He set his mouth in a serious line, then knocked on the roof. "Drive on," he commanded.

Chapter 6

We rode in silence, winding through the midnight streets of London. Mr. Rawlings said nothing, only stared out the window, one hand splayed against his jaw. For nearly thirty minutes, he did not look at me or acknowledge me in any way, as if he'd forgotten I was there altogether. It would not surprise me if he had, really.

Eventually, the buildings around us faded into the blackness of the countryside. Our coach had lanterns, but I could not see beyond the sphere of light that enveloped us. We could be surrounded by anything—farms, quiet towns, sleepy meadows.

Or perhaps menacing figures on horseback, keeping pace with our coach and waiting for the right moment.

I shivered and pulled my cloak tighter around me. I needed a distraction. Silence had never been my natural state.

"I suppose the driver knows our destination?" I asked.

Mr. Rawlings did not glance my way. "The general direction."

"What of me?" I pressed. "May I know to where I am being absconded by a near stranger?"

He dropped his hand and straightened in his seat. "Somerset."

"And what is in Somerset?"

"A house," he said.

"A house," I repeated dryly. "Well, thank goodness for that. Will it have walls and a roof, do you suppose?"

His eyes finally turned my way, briskly inspecting every inch of my face. "You are rather mouthy for someone who nearly died tonight." He spoke matter-of-factly, with no hint of insult to it.

"I'm always rather mouthy," I said almost cheerfully. "I imagine that even dying would do little to change that."

A shift in his expression, the slightest recalculation. This conversation was doing me good. It was challenging me, forcing me to think of his words and reactions instead of the threatening shadows outside my window.

"The house was my grandfather's." He abruptly turned the subject back. "Left to me on his death a few years ago. I visit but rarely. We will be safe there."

"I see." I leaned back. "But if no one knows where we've gone, how are they to contact us when the murderer is caught?"

"I told Drake," he said. "He will send us updates on the case and pass along any letters."

My brows lowered. "If you told Drake, why could we not tell Ginny and Jack?"

He shook his head. "Even those with the best of intentions can slip up. What if they spoke of it in private, but a servant overheard through a closed door? Or they sent us a letter, but the post office worker had been bribed to collect such information? If our murderer is determined, any tiny mistake could lead him to us."

I felt somewhat insulted on my friends' behalf, that Mr. Rawlings would think them so careless. "But Drake will not make such mistakes?"

Mr. Rawlings frowned. "I did not say that. Only that it is better for everyone if knowledge of our location is restricted as much as possible."

"Better for everyone or better for you?"

I must be irritating him. The muscle ticking in his cheek was clue enough of that.

"I am trying to keep you safe." His voice deepened as if he intended to intimidate me with pure masculinity. "It would be helpful if you allowed me to."

"I wasn't aware I had a choice in the matter."

He closed his eyes briefly, no doubt to gather his remaining stores of patience.

Guilt pricked inside me. Yes, he was overbearing and abrupt and callous, but he *had* saved my life not two hours ago. He had put himself between me and danger.

He could have died.

A swallow caught in my throat as I observed him now—the darkening bruises on his face, how he held his injured arm close to his body. I dropped my gaze to my gloved hands, clenched in my lap. I relaxed my grip.

"I am sorry," I said softly, seriously. "I do not mean to sound ungrateful for what you did tonight. I—I've never—" My voice cut out. Inhaling deeply, I retrieved Mr. Rawlings's stave from my reticule and leaned forward to set it on the seat beside him. "Thank you, truly."

He said nothing, staring down at the stave. Then he picked it up and slipped it inside his jacket.

"Get some sleep, Miss Lacey," he said. "We've a long road ahead of us."

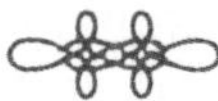

I awoke to a violet sunrise, the barest brush of light. I jolted upright, having lain across the bench sometime during the night. My back ached, and my head pounded as the coach rattled down some country road. How had I managed to fall asleep? I'd thought for certain that the residual energy from Vauxhall would keep me wide awake, but I'd dropped off quickly, my body giving in to my deep weariness.

I blinked across at Mr. Rawlings, my mind still fuzzy with sleep. He watched me, fully awake and not looking at all like he'd spent the better part of the night bouncing around inside a coach.

"Where are we?" My throat was dry and scratchy.

"We just passed into Berkshire," he replied.

"When do we arrive?" It was too much to hope that it would be soon.

"Tomorrow morning, if we face no delays."

Tomorrow? I barely stopped a groan. I had to spend another full day alone in this coach with Mr. Rawlings.

His gaze drifted over me, from my head to my boots, and a sudden awareness flooded me. I gave myself a cursory inspection. My skirts had twisted themselves around my knees, revealing a shocking amount of stockinged legs. The fabric of my dress was wrinkled beyond anything, and my hair—oh, I could not even begin to imagine what my hair looked like.

Blushing fiercely, I quickly straightened my skirts to cover my legs and asked the first thing that came to mind. "Did you sleep?"

He glanced back out the window. "No."

Revelatory indeed.

"You ought to have slept," I said. "No matter how ardently you protest, you *do* need rest to recover."

"Yes, I am quite aware of what the doctor said," he replied sagely.

My stomach growled, and though the rattling of the coach was loud, my stomach was louder. The corner of Mr. Rawlings's mouth pulled back.

I refused to be embarrassed. "Shall we eat something?"

"Please," he said. "I would have eaten earlier but you were using the basket as a pillow."

"Oh." I looked down at the bench beside me, and sure enough, there was the basket Ginny had sent with us, packed with food. My blush grew hotter. Perhaps it was good I was here with Mr. Rawlings and not Mr. Drake, considering how I continued to embarrass myself.

I sorted through the food and came up with a meal of thick bread and butter, cold sausages, and fresh apples. It was filling enough, but I would have given almost anything for a scalding cup of tea to warm my hands. The country air felt colder outside of London, autumn tightening its hold.

The sun had risen fully by now, and I found myself rather entranced by the passing countryside, soft and ethereal in the golden morning light. It was difficult to feel the same fear as last night, when all had been hidden by menacing shadows. This dreamy daytime made it seem impossible for us to be in any real danger.

After eating, Mr. Rawlings pulled out a copy of *The Times* and began reading without so much as another word in my direction. I settled back into my seat and resigned myself to the dullest day I'd ever known. I hadn't thought to bring along so much as a book, and clearly, Mr. Rawlings would not be a willing source of entertainment.

When he finished with his newspaper, he folded it precisely and set it on the bench beside him.

"May I?" I gestured to the paper.

He tilted his head by the barest degree. "The gossip columns are not terribly interesting today." *Or ever*, his tone seemed to say.

"I shall be the judge of that," I said lightly.

He handed me the newspaper. "If you like."

He was being so terribly polite that one could almost pretend he hadn't said such stinging things to me last night about my reputation. But I could not quite forget it, nor the way he'd looked at me with that infuriating surety, as if he already knew everything about me.

It would do no good to resuscitate that argument now, though, not when we had to endure each other's company for the foreseeable future.

I happily spent the next hour perusing the newspaper. Taking my time, I pored over the advertisements, the political news, Society gossip, and announcements of births, deaths, and marriages. I smiled when I spotted a notice touting Mrs. Travers's upcoming appearance in *Henry VIII*, though that smile quickly faded. I would not be there to attend—Ginny and I had planned to go only yesterday.

"What is it?"

I started. I hadn't realized Mr. Rawlings was watching me.

"Oh," I said. "Nothing, really. Only, I'd so looked forward to seeing Mrs. Travers play Queen Katherine. I have heard she is unrivaled in the part." He scrutinized me with an angled brow. Judging me, likely, for caring about missing a theatrical performance when our lives were quite literally at stake. "But it's not important," I added quickly, dropping my gaze back to the paper. "Of course it isn't important any longer."

I could feel his eyes on me still, but I forced myself to continue reading.

I always enjoyed each section of the newspaper, though it might seem odd to some to see a lady reading the ship news from the London docks. But every article, advertisement, and snippet was a glimpse into the lives of others—lives that were far more interesting and compelling than my own. I craved even the smallest bits of information, desperate for connection with a world that seemed impossibly out of my reach.

My world was so small, so confined, in Little Sowerby. Each day was the same—daily instruction from Mother, seeing to the household management, hosting callers and returning visits, attending church, embroidering handkerchiefs, avoiding Father, and trying very hard not to scream into my pillow at the end of every day.

Ginny was a bright spot among the gray, and our friendship was often the only thing to keep me afloat. But reading the papers and books and magazines and gossip sheets . . . It gave me something to focus on, to dream of, to find fascination with. It helped, however little, to imagine that my life would not always be summed up by a handful of repetitive tasks.

I turned the page and began to read the section on reported crimes and court appearances. It was a subject I found more interesting than the rest, letting me imagine what might drive a person to commit a crime. I was reading almost lazily, gaze drifting across the page, when a sentence caught my attention.

> *A housebreaking occurred on the twentieth of October at Peak House, the London residence of Lord Osterson. A rare diamond brooch was taken. Further inquiries to be made.*

"Odd," I murmured. Hadn't I just read something about Peak House? I flipped back through the paper, skimming over the tiny black print until I found it—a bit of gossip tucked in among the news of the royal family.

> *A certain young miss of lately questionable morals was seen emerging from the gardens during the ball at Peak House on Thursday last. Whether she met with a Mr. Falmouth, who exited soon after, remains to be determined.*

"Very odd," I said again, my voice low.

"What is?" Mr. Rawlings sounded frightfully uninterested.

I flicked a glance at him, debating whether I should keep my insights to myself. But the coincidence was too strange. "This here," I said, pointing to the newsprint, "says that a robbery occurred at Peak House on the twentieth."

"And?"

"And," I said, pushing on despite his clear indifference, "does it not seem odd that Peak House should have hosted a ball just the evening before?"

He considered it. "Perhaps," he said, "but not terribly unusual. I imagine that guests often wander off with valuables that don't belong to them."

I shot him an exasperated look. "I may not currently enjoy the good graces of the *ton*, but even I know there aren't a great many hot-handed thieves among them."

"Just one would be enough, I imagine," he said.

"Hmm." I tugged on a curl as I gazed out the window.

"You have another theory?"

I shrugged. "No, not really. I was simply stating something I found curious in order to pass the time. And it worked splendidly. Why, we enjoyed an entire two minutes of stimulating discussion." I flashed a saucy grin at him, expecting nothing beyond a look of long-suffering at my mouthiness.

Instead, he raised one eyebrow as he held my gaze, his posture as poised and proper as one could be in a coach. "Stimulating indeed."

His voice was serious, but I could not shake the feeling that he was toying with me, laughing at me somehow. Well then, he did not deserve my delightful company. I looked back down at my paper, determined not to speak again unless necessary.

We passed the rest of the day with little to no conversation, stopping every few hours to switch horses and stretch our legs. I read the newspaper through twice, composed a terribly rhymed poem in my head about endless rutted roads, and tried not to think about all I was missing back in London. The excitement over the case, the hustle and bustle, the sense of purpose.

This was still an adventure, I tried to convince myself. I'd never been to this part of the country before. Surely Mr. Rawlings and I could avoid each other well enough once we arrived. I could go on long walks and explore the nearby countryside or write letters to Ginny and Mother. I wished I could look forward to escaping into a book, but I doubted Mr. Rawlings's house would have much of a library, if any. Likely, it was a tiny, derelict cottage with little in the way of luxury. But it would be safe, if Mr. Rawlings was to be believed, and that was certainly the most important quality a house could have at the moment.

As the day wore on, the clouds overhead grew thicker and darker. I watched with no small amount of apprehension, and I knew Mr. Rawlings did as well. His posture was tight as he looked out the window, foot tapping restlessly against the floor. No doubt he wished to be done with this miserable journey as much as I did, and rain would do nothing but delay us.

Sure enough, the rain began to fall late in the afternoon, and the road grew muddy and slick. Twice, the coach's wheels stuck fast, and it was only by the coachman's expertise that we managed to continue on.

But finally, the coach came to a stop, and the door opened. The coachman looked half drowned, hat soaked through and limp.

"Very sorry I am, sir and miss," he said. "But I don't think we can be continuing much longer. We'll need to find somewhere to stop for the night."

I couldn't help my relief. As anxious as I was to reach our destination, the ride had grown increasingly bumpy, and a chill crept through even my thick cloak. Mr. Rawlings exhaled deeply, though his expression remained unchanged. I couldn't tell what he felt at the news.

"Very well," he said. "I believe there is a town another mile or two up the road. We can seek shelter there and hope the storm passes quickly."

The coachman nodded eagerly, and for the first time, I realized that he had to be utterly exhausted. He'd slept not a wink last night, all because we needed a quick escape from London.

"Thank you," I said sincerely. "Mr. . . . ?"

He flushed, touching his hat. "Barton, miss."

"You've been very helpful today, Mr. Barton." I offered a grateful smile. "Truly, thank you."

He grinned and bowed. "You're too kind, miss. Thank you, miss."

He closed the door behind him. I looked over at Mr. Rawlings, and he was regarding me strangely.

"What is it?" I asked, already defensive.

But he only shook his head and glanced away.

We arrived in a small village shortly after, the rain a steady thrum on the roof of the coach. I peered through the window as we came to a stop outside a rather rickety-looking inn, its walls in peril of toppling over in the wind. But light glowed in the windows, and the thought of a warm fire made my heart lift.

Mr. Rawlings did not bother to wait for the coachman. He opened the door and splashed down into the mud, his boots sinking a good three inches. My sudden enthusiasm for a fire was doused. I had only my half boots, which would surely be sucked into the mud as though it were quicksand.

Mr. Rawlings held out his good hand to me, but I hesitated at the door of the coach. I didn't have any other boots for tomorrow. Even if I cleaned these tonight, would they dry by the time we set out in the morning? How would I—

"Shall I carry you?" His voice was dry even as rain dripped from his hat.

I raised my eyes to meet his, which held a daring gleam, as if he thought his challenge would drive me into the mud to prove a point—that I did not need his help.

But it was abundantly clear that I would never win Mr. Rawlings's good opinion. So why would I ruin a perfectly good pair of boots over it?

I spread my lips into a wide, catlike smile. "Oh, would you, Mr. Rawlings?" I said with gushing relief. "Such a gentleman. So kind."

He stared at me, completely caught off guard. He'd expected me to refuse and stubbornly wade through the mud.

Mr. Barton appeared around the corner of the coach. "Yes, yes," he said. "You assist the lady, sir, and I shall see to your things."

I grinned and batted my eyelashes, holding out my hand. "If you please, Mr. Rawlings. I do think my hem is getting damp."

He made no move, the rain soaking through his jacket and his boots sinking deeper with every passing second. Then his eyes narrowed. My heart skipped one significant beat.

In a single, fluid motion, he stepped forward, grasped me behind the knees with his uninjured arm, and threw me over his shoulder.

I gave a small, unladylike yelp as my stomach hit his sturdy shoulder. He turned back toward the inn, swinging me haphazardly, with no thought to my comfort.

I pushed myself up on my elbows against his back. "Mr. Rawlings!" I gasped. "What on earth are you doing?"

"Carrying you, as requested." His ridiculously deep voice rumbled in his chest. He tromped through the mud, kicking up great clods that no doubt speckled my dress with brown. "If you prefer to walk . . ."

He would delight in that, dumping me here in the mud because I protested his so-called chivalry. I grasped the fabric of his jacket with both hands in case he tried to follow through.

"You should not cling so, Miss Lacey," he said shortly. "Someone might have the wrong idea."

"Oh?" I asked in a clipped tone. "Concerned about mixing your sterling reputation with mine? I shouldn't be surprised, considering how well informed you are about my past."

"It is my job to be informed."

Even using one arm, the other still in a sling, he carried me with ease. I wished I'd eaten a few more sweets lately to make it more difficult on him. I could just see the corner of the inn as we approached. He jostled me to the side as he reached his slinged hand for the door.

"A pity," I said hotly. "I was under the impression you were good at your job."

He stiffened—whether from some pain in his arm or the insult in my words, I could not say. But in the next second, he swung open the door and dropped me unceremoniously to the floor. I just managed to get my feet under me, throwing a hand against his chest to catch my balance.

"Here we are," he said abruptly, as if I'd been a load of firewood.

He looked down at me, and I realized then how very close our faces were.

His eyes were deeply brown, almost black in the storm. The rain had softened the precise lines of his hair, now curled into a slight wave about his ears. The width of his jaw was shadowed with dark stubble, and I thought—vaguely and wildly and all in the space of a single second—how it might feel were I to touch my fingers to the sharp angle of his cheekbone. My hand still balanced against his chest. My fingers twitched.

He stepped away, and my hand dropped. Without another word, he turned and strode toward the long counter at the back of the taproom.

I tugged my dampened pelisse straight with a jerk as I followed him, heat simmering just beneath the surface. I was frustrated with him—and myself. I should not be thinking such ridiculous things about him, not when he clearly cared not one whit about me.

Mr. Rawlings waved over a stout woman, who was serving a nearby table. She delivered the food and then came behind the counter. I refused to look at Mr. Rawlings, my temper still boiling.

"Needing a room?" she asked pleasantly, pulling a ledger toward her.

"Yes." I spoke before Mr. Rawlings simply because I knew it would irritate him. "Two rooms, please."

"Certainly," she said. "I have several still available, and—"

"We need only one room."

The woman and I both turned to gawk at Mr. Rawlings. He looked back with an unruffled countenance, leaning on the counter with his good hand.

The innkeeper darted a glance back to me before returning her gaze to Mr. Rawlings. "Are you quite certain? I assure you we have plenty of space." I wasn't sure if she was concerned for my sake or if she simply wanted the profit of letting two rooms.

"One room." Mr. Rawlings left no room for argument. "The key, please. We've had a trying day."

He'd had a trying day?

"Very well." She turned to the row of keys hanging on the wall behind her. "Up the stairs, third door on the right."

Mr. Rawlings paid without another word, then took the key—and my elbow—and guided me toward the stairs.

I tried to shake him off, but his grip was like steel. "One room?" I asked in a low hiss.

"How am I to keep an eye on you if we are in separate rooms?"

"I think the idea of separate rooms is to keep your eye *off* me," I retorted.

"And if the murderer tracks us here?" He leaned closer to me, and I hated how my skin flushed at his proximity.

"I can scream very loudly, I assure you."

"Yes, I recall."

I pressed my lips together, remembering all too well the uncontrolled shriek that had escaped me at Vauxhall.

"Hearing you scream is not the problem," he said grimly. "It is getting to you in time *after* you scream."

Cold flooded my veins, sweeping away the heat of my anger. He urged me up the stairs, and I did not protest, my chest suddenly cinched tight.

"You do not think he has followed us all the way here?" I asked in a small voice when we reached the top of the stairs.

Mr. Rawlings moved toward the third door on the right. "We would be fools to rule it out."

He slipped the key into the lock and opened the door. After a quick inspection, he hurried me inside. There was a weary-looking bed next to a dirty window, a wooden chair before a small fireplace, and a threadbare rug that did nothing to hide the splintering floorboards.

"Charming," I said.

Mr. Rawlings ignored me and went to the window. He checked that the latch was fastened and rattled the frame besides. Then he turned and surveyed the rest of the room. "Secure enough," he said, all business.

Mr. Barton arrived at the open door with my trunk, coming inside to set it down beside the bed. "Anything else, miss?"

I forced a smile, though it felt as false as a mask at the theater. "No, thank you."

He bowed, then departed, leaving the door ajar.

I turned back to face the room, clasping my hands rather fiercely in front of me. I refused to look at Mr. Rawlings, the reality of the situation finally settling around me, stifling and smothering. We'd spent the entire day alone in a carriage together, yet this felt dramatically different. Perhaps because there was a bed positioned so obviously in front of us.

"I'll help with the rest of our things and see the driver settled," Mr. Rawlings said, not seeming to notice the shift of emotions in the room. "Then I will take a look around to ensure everything is as it should be. I'll return in a quarter of an hour. That should allow you sufficient time to prepare for bed."

"Very well," I rasped, my throat unaccountably dry.

He glanced my way, as if wondering why I acted so strangely, but decided not to comment. He moved to the door.

"I will lock it behind me," he said. "Do not open it for anyone else."

"I am not a complete half-wit," I retorted, some of my fire returning in the face of his heavy-handedness.

Mr. Rawlings paused, his hand on the doorframe. "I do not think anyone could accuse you of that, Miss Lacey." He left, closing the door firmly behind him.

I stood there a moment, taken aback. That had almost sounded like a compliment. The thought nearly made me laugh. *You are not a complete half-wit* was precisely the sort of compliment Mr. Rawlings would extend.

The key turned in the lock, then Mr. Rawlings's footsteps drew away. I gulped a deep breath, trying to regain control of my racing heart. But nothing I did made any difference. This sudden panic could not be contained.

I would be spending the night in this room with Mr. Rawlings.

Chapter 7

My precious seconds were already ticking away, so I hurried to my trunk. The last thing I wanted was to hear Mr. Rawlings's key in the lock while I was tangled in my stays.

Everything was a bit more difficult without Mariah, but I managed to remove my wet, mud-speckled dress and change into a clean chemise. Obviously, I could not sleep in only that, so I also took my thick dressing gown and wrapped it around me, knotting it firmly at my waist and ensuring the edges crossed snugly under my chin.

Then I removed a mountain of pins to let down my coiffure and wrangled my hair into a passable braid. I did not bother with curling papers. I had only Mr. Rawlings to impress, after all, and I hardly wanted him thinking I'd made such an effort for him.

As prepared as I could be, I next faced the dilemma of where to *be* within the room when he returned. Sitting by the fire? Standing at the window? In bed under the covers? I rejected the last idea immediately. If Mr. Rawlings could be nonchalant and cool as a winter's breeze about our shared accommodations, then I certainly could as well.

I paced the small room until I again heard footsteps outside the door. A knock came, sharp and precise.

"Yes?" I called, my voice remarkably steady.

"It's me," came Mr. Rawlings's dulcet Scottish brogue.

"Who?" I asked sweetly. I didn't know what possessed me, only that I felt absolutely alarmed at sharing a room with him and was still rather annoyed at him for carrying me through the mud like a sack of flour. I was desperate to reclaim even a tiny bit of control.

There was a pause, then, "Are you toying with me?"

He did not sound either amused or annoyed but rather in disbelief.

"I can hardly say," I said, "since I do not know who *you* are."

"Open the door, Miss Lacey," he ordered. "Or I shall."

Smothering a grin, I went to the door and unlocked it, opening it just a crack as I peered out. "Oh, it is you, Mr. Rawlings. You might have said."

He frowned and pushed past me into the room. I thought I heard the word *impossible* muttered under his breath. I liked that. Impossible, I could be.

Mr. Rawlings went to stand before the fire, pulling off his gloves. He'd changed already, his clothing dry and clean, and had fixed his hair from the rain, as if unable to bear any sign of dishevelment. "I walked around the inn," he said, not looking at me. "All was quiet outside, and the taproom is beginning to empty."

"And you saw nothing to stoke your suspicions?" I asked.

"No." He set his gloves and hat on the rickety table. "But that is hardly reason to drop our guard."

He turned, opening his mouth to say something more, but then stopped. His eyes swept over the length of me—my unruly braid and my dressing gown and my stockinged feet. Then he cleared his throat and pointedly looked away. "Are you hungry?" he asked briskly. "I can have something sent up."

"No, thank you," I said. "I cannot say I have much of an appetite."

He frowned again. Was his mouth permanently set in a downward slant? I thought he might argue with me, but he only grabbed the back of the wooden chair and turned it to face the fire. "I'll keep watch," he said. "You get what sleep you can."

"You won't be terribly comfortable in that chair," I said.

"Are you offering me the bed?"

"Oh, no," I said. "I was simply pointing it out so that you would be more fully aware of your discomfort."

"Your kindness is too much, Miss Lacey," he said dryly. "You mustn't make such a fuss."

I almost laughed. His staid humor was just so unexpected. But I refused to give him the satisfaction of making me laugh.

He sat facing away from me and leaned back in the chair, making the wood creak. I retreated to the far side of the bed, putting as much distance between us as I could manage. Feeling supremely awkward, even though he wasn't watching, I pulled back the covers—roughspun and certainly not clean—and forced myself to lie down. The pillow was lumpy, the mattress smelled of damp straw, and the heat of the fire did little to help my chilly feet.

But I exhaled, shook my head once, and refused to fall prey to the negative. "Good night, Mr. Rawlings," I offered, my gesture filling the quiet room.

He straightened but did not turn. "Good night," he finally responded.

I closed my eyes, breathing through my mouth so as not to inhale the less-than-lovely scent of the blankets.

It was going to be a very long night.

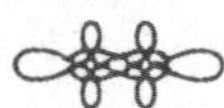

The darkness was all-consuming.

I ran down the path, winding and endless, the trees towering above me, pressing in, smothering. I looked over my shoulder, saw the shadow pursuing me. I wanted to scream, but it was trapped in my throat. I was voiceless. Helpless.

Sudden lights ahead. Lanterns, bright against the night. I ran faster, desperate. I could make it. I could—

My foot caught on a root, and I went down. My legs failed; I couldn't stand. I crawled, one inch at a time, tears streaming down my cheeks.

Then I heard his breathing. I spun to face him. He stepped from the shadows, knife dripping with blood.

"You're mine," he seethed.

He lunged.

I awoke with a jolt, scream stillborn in my mouth. I lay there in my bed, panting, blinking, pulse a constant drum in my head. Then I realized that was the thrum of rain against the roof and window. It was pitch-black outside, the stars and moon engulfed by clouds as the storm lashed against the glass. The inn. I was at the inn.

My heart refused to slow, trying to warn me of danger I knew was only a dream. A nightmare.

Then I heard it. A muttered curse, barely audible above the sound of the storm. I pushed myself up onto one trembling elbow, my vision bleary as I squinted across the room. I did not know what I'd expected to see, but it was *not* this.

Mr. Rawlings still sat on his chair, but whereas a few hours ago he'd been fully clothed, he now wore only breeches and half a shirt. Half a shirt because his injured arm had been freed from both the sling and its sleeve, and he was attempting to wrap a fresh bandage around his arm.

I stared. I could not help it. The fire still flickered behind him, and the shadows lining Mr. Rawlings's chest and shoulders did little to hide the lean muscles there, his skin painted in dancing golden light.

I nearly jumped when he released a muted groan. One of pain but perhaps also of frustration. He could not tie off the bandage by himself.

"I can help," I said without thinking.

He turned on his chair, startled, and saw me watching. I could not guess what thoughts crossed his mind at that moment. I'd caught him in a rather vulnerable position. Clearly, he'd meant to take care of this while I slept, with me being none the wiser.

For a moment, it looked as if he might refuse me, in some sort of claim to masculine pride. But then he nodded—one short drop of his chin—and I realized he might be in more pain than I'd thought.

I slid to the edge of the bed, ensuring my dressing gown was still covering me as I stood. Then I tread softly to his side, my feet whispering against the floorboards. My body was still recovering from my dream, weak and weary, but I tried not to show it.

His eyes did not leave me as I approached, taking in my every movement with wariness. But why should he have any reason to be wary of me? He held out the fresh bandage to me, and I took it.

I focused on his injured arm and blinked in surprise. "You're bleeding again."

Indeed, his cut looked nearly as awful as the night the doctor had tended him. Though the sutures held, there was new blood among the dried around his wound.

"Why are you bleeding?" My brow furrowed. "You haven't done anything to stress the wound, have you?"

"Besides carrying you through the mud?" He spoke gruffly, and I could not tell if he was angry.

My stomach dropped. "That was your choice, if you'll recall."

Mr. Rawlings let out a short, humorless laugh. "I don't recall you giving me much of a choice at all."

"Silly, prideful man," I muttered under my breath. Still, guilt pricked inside me. Had it truly hurt him to carry me? I hadn't meant for that to happen.

He regarded me with tense awareness as I moved closer, then held out his arm, pressing his lips together fiercely from the pain.

I would do this quickly, for his sake. That was my plan, at least, though it was more difficult to execute than I'd thought—mainly because of the absolute distraction that Mr. Rawlings was without a shirt. His skin was fire-warmed beneath my fingertips as I wrapped the bandage around his arm. The angles and shadows of his muscled chest made it nearly impossible to focus, and a prickling blush climbed my neck and cheeks, refusing to leave.

He sat stiffly, his body tense. Was it the pain, or did I cause his unease? Finally, after winding the bandage several times around his upper arm, I knotted the ends as firmly as I could.

My eyes—which I'd kept fixedly on the bandage—finally darted to Mr. Rawlings's. He did not watch my ministrations, as inept as they were. He watched *me*, looking up at me with an intensity and focus that set my pulse tripping.

I tore my gaze away and moved to the washbasin in the corner. Wetting a small cloth, I returned to his side and cleaned his arm around the bandage. It was not strictly necessary—he could have done it—but that guilt would not leave me be. After I finished, I washed my hands in the basin while he slipped his arm back into his sleeve and quickly buttoned up his collar.

Then I took the sling and did my best to copy what I'd seen the doctor do, wrapping it tightly under his elbow and forearm and knotting it behind his neck. My fingers brushed the skin there, and he froze, not moving or even breathing.

"There." I stepped back, my own skin far too heated for how small the fire beside us was. "You're like a new man."

He adjusted the sling around his neck. "I did not mind the old one."

His tone was lighter than I'd ever heard from him before. Was he teasing me? Wonders never ceased.

He leaned back in his chair and grimaced as he shifted his injured arm. I eyed him. "Did the doctor not give you anything to help with the pain?"

"He did," Mr. Rawlings said. "But it seems rather contrary to dull my senses while keeping watch for danger."

"Then let me keep watch," I offered. "I've had a few hours of sleep. I can rouse you if I see or hear anything."

His eyes seemed to draw the shadows into them, making it more difficult than normal to guess his thoughts. Did he think me impertinent? Foolish? Useless?

"Thank you, Miss Lacey," he said quietly in the end. "But I should feel better doing it myself. I can sleep in the coach tomorrow. We should arrive in the early evening if the storm passes quickly."

I nodded, knowing it was pointless to argue with him. I'd learned that much in the last three days. Once he made up his mind, there was no changing it.

Except . . . I could not help but think I might have changed his opinion of me, however slightly, since we'd been thrown together in this misadventure. But perhaps that was wishful thinking.

"Can I—" I cleared my throat. "Can I do anything else?"

He shook his head. "No, thank you. I am sorry to have woken you."

"You didn't," I said honestly. "But you needn't fear to ask for my help, even if you find it difficult to do so."

"I shall remember that in the future," he said, and I almost believed him.

It seemed silly to wish him good night when it was early morning, so I simply returned to the bed and slid beneath the blankets gone cold. I could feel him watching me, which ought to have made me uncomfortable.

It was really quite peculiar—unaccountable, really—that instead I felt *safe*.

Mr. Rawlings was gone when I awoke, though the fire was stoked, and the sun shone weakly through the window. I'd slept well—surprisingly well, considering the nightmare that had woken me and the intimacy of our encounter. It would be easy to believe that I'd imagined our middle-of-the-night conversation, if not for my visceral memories—the scandalous heat of his nearness, the gravity of his gaze anchoring mine.

I threw off my blankets, welcoming the chill of the room outside the sphere of the fire's warmth. I needed to rid myself of such thoughts. Things that happened in the hush of night had no place in daylight.

I did my hair in such a way that would surely make Mariah groan, then struggled with my stays until they were adequately snug. But when I began buttoning my dress, I realized, with no small amount of horror, that I could not reach the uppermost buttons on the back.

It was then, of course, when Mr. Rawlings knocked.

At least, I assumed it was he since it was identical to his knock last night, sharp and direct. A bolt of panic darted through me. I did not want him to see me in any sort of undress, even just a few missed buttons, and I could hardly ask him for help.

"One moment," I called, my voice squeaking slightly, and I hurried to slip on my pelisse. That would have to do. Once we arrived at his cottage, I could retreat to my room—assuming we did not have to share one again, perish the thought—and change into another dress that I could more easily fasten.

I crossed the room and opened the door to find Mr. Rawlings standing there. He looked weary but not alarmingly so. Had he found a chance to sleep last night?

He held a small tray, balancing a mug of tea and a bowl of what I assumed was porridge but could very well be pig slop. One could not be certain in an inn like this.

"Good morning." I forced a ridiculous amount of cheer into my greeting. No need to let him know how off-balance I still was by our interaction last night.

"Good enough, I suppose." He moved past me and set the tray on the small table.

I closed the door, glancing at the food. "Is that for me?"

"I've already eaten," he said briskly.

For a moment, a softness filled the space between us. He'd brought me breakfast?

"Eat quickly," he ordered, ruining the moment as only he could.

I sighed as I dropped onto the chair beside the table. "Did you think I intended to linger over such a meal?"

"I never quite know what you intend, Miss Lacey." He crossed the room to the window and peered outside. "The coach is being prepared as we speak. I've ordered Mr. Barton back to London and procured a hired coach and driver."

I straightened. "What? Why?"

"To limit the number of those who know our location," he said as if that were perfectly obvious.

It was logical, of course, but then, *everything* Mr. Rawlings did was logical.

"You might have let me say goodbye," I said, somewhat indignant.

"Why?" He appeared baffled.

A good question. I had no real attachment to the kind Mr. Barton. But it was a stark reminder of my new reality, and I could not help but feel slightly abandoned. He'd been my last link to London, to Ginny. I was now entirely at the mercy of Mr. Rawlings.

"No reason," I managed.

Mr. Rawlings did not seem to sense my sudden unease. "I'll have the driver fetch your things." He exited without another word.

"A delightful conversation, to be sure," I murmured to the empty room. I regarded the porridge suspiciously, decided not to risk it, and picked up the mug of tea. It was weak but warm, and I sipped it gratefully. I needed fortification against whatever this day would bring.

Which was more boredom, apparently. After loading our coach and setting off, Mr. Rawlings and I returned to our status quo of the day before—quiet. But it felt more strained today. Likely because I'd seen him without his shirt not six hours ago, which had the tendency to make any subsequent interactions a touch on the awkward side.

I eyed him across the coach, and he stared steadfastly out the window. His free arm braced his injured one across his stomach, and his face seemed tenser than normal, even for him.

"Are you still in pain?" I asked.

"I can manage," he said.

"That is not what I asked."

"I can manage," he said again, more shortly.

"You could not manage last night."

"A singular experience, I assure you."

I clasped my hands in my lap. "You still have not answered my question. Is your wound hurting you?"

He exhaled a long breath, still refusing to meet my gaze. "Of course it is. But as there is no solution for the pain besides medicine I will refuse, I see no point in discussing it again."

"Do not be so quick to write off alternative treatments," I said smartly. "I find complaining about one's grievances to a sympathetic audience to be quite effective."

"And are you volunteering for such a task?"

"You are injured because of me." An unexpected ache claimed my throat. "The least I can do is lend you my ear."

He finally looked at me, his expression perplexed. "You think this was your fault?" He raised his slinged arm just an inch, wincing as he did so.

"I do." I swallowed to clear my throat. "If I had not been such an imbecile as to scream and distract you, I imagine you would have caught the man there in Vauxhall. Instead, you are injured, and we are both exiled to the country."

Mr. Rawlings's gaze narrowed but not in anger or frustration. Rather, it was how I imagined I looked whenever I read a particularly fascinating article in *The Times*: curious or perhaps intrigued.

"I do not blame you in the least," he said. "I blame myself for letting my guard down and for putting you in such a dangerous position."

"Then I suppose we will both continue to blame ourselves," I said. "It is better than blaming each other, at least. In fact, I think we are as close to a truce now as we've ever been."

"A truce?" He shifted forward with the slightest lowering of his brow. "I did not realize we were at war, Miss Lacey."

I laughed. "That is because you are a man. All straightforward attacks and unforgiving sieges. Subtle strategy is a woman's specialty."

"Of that I have little doubt," he murmured.

I ignored that. "Now, we've still a long day of traveling ahead. I suggest we stop every so often to allow you a reprieve. I imagine the jostling is not helping the pain. And"—I raised my chin, forcing myself not to blush—"if your bandage should need changing, then I should be glad to help you again."

Mr. Rawlings sat back in his seat, looking amused—if that was possible without actually smiling. "Are you always so eager to entrench yourself in the affairs of others?"

"Oh, yes," I replied. "I find it passes the time quite nicely."

He shook his head and looked out the window again, but if I was not mistaken, a bit of stiffness left his shoulders.

The day went on without too much hardship. Mr. Rawlings did not fuss when I ordered him out of the carriage every few hours to give him a rest from the constant bumping and swaying, which was a relief. I'd assumed he was prideful even to his own detriment, but I was glad to see he had at least some sense. He also slept a few hours, which eased my guilt. We even spoke here and there, keeping to banal topics such as the road and the holding weather.

As the sun began to set toward the tree line, Mr. Rawlings sat forward and peered out the window.

"Are we nearly there?" I asked. I'd restrained myself from asking as long as I could.

He nodded. "We're close. Another half hour, I'd imagine."

We traveled in silence, the shadows growing long around us as we passed through a small village. I wished I could have seen more of it. I wasn't sure whether Mr. Rawlings would give me any freedom to explore once we were settled, if last night's unexpected protectiveness was an indication of how our time in the country would progress.

"We ought to think of a new name for you," Mr. Rawlings said suddenly. "To use while we are here."

"A new name?" I repeated.

"Yes," he said. "It would be pointless for me, since I'm already known, but giving you another name would offer an added layer of security."

"A new name," I mused. "What an opportunity. I've never much liked Beatrice, you know, though I would never tell my mother that." I sat forward, warming to the subject. "Perhaps another Shakespearean woman? I've always been partial to Ophelia, though I should not like such a tragic ending. But we needn't limit ourselves to Shakespeare. Perhaps Lysandra or Seraphina? Something exotic and exciting. One doesn't get to choose a new name every day."

Mr. Rawlings stared at me, mouth parted.

"What?" I asked, a bit miffed. "Have you never considered changing your name?"

"No, I have not," he said slowly.

"You've no imagination at all," I said. "Or perhaps it is a womanly pastime. We do, after all, spend our lives preparing to change our names when we marry. One cannot help but wonder."

Mr. Rawlings looked nonplussed, as if I were a strange creature from a fairy tale come to life. "I had thought," he said, trying to regain control of the conversation, "that we would only change your last name."

I frowned. "That is practical, I suppose. It would be easier to remember if it was Beatrice So-and-So."

"Smith?" he suggested.

"Beatrice Smith? Oh, heavens no," I replied distastefully. "That is dull to the extreme. No one would think I was interesting at all."

"Might I remind you," he said, "that being dull is much to our advantage in this situation? We must do everything we can to keep from attracting undue attention."

"Then you really should have been banished with someone less like me." I flashed him a grin.

He exhaled a long, tortured breath. "Miss Lacey, please."

"Oh, very well." I considered for a moment. "What about Albright? The name of my mother's abigail when I was a girl."

"Miss Albright," he repeated, as if testing the name. It seemed to meet his approval since his eyes lifted to mine and held there a moment. "It suits you."

I blinked. Again, this strange sort of compliment, coming at the oddest of times.

The coach bumped as we turned onto a long lane that disappeared into the twilight.

"Here we are," Mr. Rawlings murmured, sitting forward on his seat.

My nerves grew exponentially. I swallowed hard, peering out my window, trying to catch a glimpse of my new home for the foreseeable future.

"Shall there be food, do you think?" I asked suddenly.

Mr. Rawlings raised an eyebrow. "Food?"

"At your cottage," I said. "You said you do not visit often, so I only wondered if there were any goods stocked there or if we might return to a local tavern for dinner. Although even if there *is* any food, I cannot say I will be of any use in preparing it in an edible way. Mother did not insist on cooking lessons as part of my education, and I see the lack very clearly now."

But my words only seemed to baffle him further. "I never said it was a cottage," he said, chin pulled back. "I said it was a house."

Had he? Somehow, I'd fixed it in my mind as a cottage, run-down and overcome with brambles and climbing ivy.

He cleared his throat. "You ought to know," he began, "that there are some parts of my life I've kept private, even from my closest friends."

That was a very strange road to take our conversation down. "Oh?" I tried to hide my confusion.

"I did it for a few very particular reasons," he went on, "of which I have little desire to explain at the moment." His words lost some of that precise edge I was used to hearing, his Scottish lilt taking over.

"I see," I said cautiously, though he was making positively no sense.

"All that to say, you might be somewhat surprised when you do see my . . . house."

"What on earth are you talking about, Mr. Rawlings?" I finally asked straight-out. "You are running me about in circles, which is no easy task, I assure you."

He said nothing more, only set his mouth in a grim line and waved a hand to the windows on my right. I moved to the edge of my seat and peered out the window.

Then I *stared*.

CHAPTER 8

Out of the looming shadows came a massive, overwhelming shape, the size of which I could only truly grasp by the number of illuminated windows lining the dark stone walls. A columned portico towered above the front door and steps, and the walls extended so far on either side that they disappeared beyond my view. It was four stories tall, made of solid gray stone, and seemed to await our arrival with domineering superiority.

"*That* is your house?" I squeaked.

"Aye," he said, the word clipped.

I whipped my head around to stare at Mr. Rawlings, who looked defensive, as if prepared to actually start that war we'd discussed earlier.

I was tempted to fire the first shot. Why had he kept this from me?

"That," I said as we approached the front steps, "is not a house."

"And what should I have called it?" he challenged.

"Oh, a great many words come to mind." My voice snapped more than I'd intended. "An estate? A manor? A *palace*?"

"It might not be a cottage," he said, eyes flashing, "but it is certainly *not* a palace."

"That remains to be seen," I replied shortly. "Was your grandfather a duke, by any chance? Am I addressing a lord?"

"Don't be ridiculous," he said. "My grandfather made his money in trade. We've no illustrious family line or esteemed connections, I assure you."

"We?" I repeated.

He grimaced, but before I could press him further, the coach came to a stop at the front door. Neither of us moved for a long moment, then he reached up behind his neck and pulled the sling over his head.

"What are you doing?" I asked, irritated. "The doctor said—"

"The doctor is not here." He gathered the sling and tucked it in his pocket. "And I'll thank you not to tell anyone of my injury."

Without another word, he opened the door and stepped down, turning to offer me his hand.

I looked at him, then up at the imposing house. I was not at all prepared for this. But I had little choice. I clenched my teeth and took his hand. He helped me down, dropping my hand as soon as my feet touched the gravel. How flattering.

He started up the wide stone steps, and I followed, smothering the flare of panic inside me. Why couldn't it have been a cottage? I'd prepared myself for rustic and isolated, not grand and formidable, and I found I far preferred my imagined version of Mr. Rawlings's country home. It stayed neatly within the structure of what I knew about him, what I'd assumed about him.

This, however . . . This changed everything.

The front door opened as we reached the top step, and a man appeared in the doorway—the butler, I presumed. He was tall and thin, with a balding head. He frowned as if he might scold us for interrupting his evening. Then he pulled back, staring at Mr. Rawlings.

"Sir!" he said in surprise.

Mr. Rawlings strode directly past the man, sweeping off his hat. "See that the horses and carriage are cared for, Stroud," he ordered.

Any doubts as to his claim over this house vanished. No man would enter a home not his own in such a presumptuous manner.

I skirted around the butler, nodding a greeting. He only blinked at me as if I were some sort of curious mirage following in his master's wake.

The entryway was just as regal as the outside. An enormous staircase wrapped around one side of the lofty space, ascending to the next story in effortless grace. The floor was white marble with gold flecks sparkling in the candlelight, and an endless array of artwork, gilded mirrors, and tapestries covered the walls. I gaped upward at the opulent chandelier floating directly overhead. It wasn't even lit, and it still drew my awe.

Stroud followed us inside, signaling a footman, who immediately went out the front door to see to the carriage.

"Sir." Stroud addressed Mr. Rawlings again, regaining his composure as he clasped his hands behind his back. "We did not expect you."

"I should hope not." Mr. Rawlings tossed his hat and gloves onto the polished table beside the door. "That would have defeated our purpose entirely."

"Yes, sir," Stroud said, shooting a glance my way.

Mr. Rawlings did not notice his butler's unspoken curiosity. "Where is my mother?"

"In the drawing room, I believe," Stroud replied.

It took my mind a few seconds to connect their words. But then . . .

Fear spiked inside me, just as hot and bold as when the murderer had fixed his aim on me at Vauxhall.

His *mother*.

A wide, heavy door opened across the entryway, and a small woman stepped out onto the marble floor. She wore a deep-blue gown, well-tailored and expensive, and her russet-brown hair—tinged with gray—was pulled into a severe chignon.

She paused, her sharp, dark eyes sweeping across the entry in an instant. They stopped on Mr. Rawlings. "Alexander?"

Alexander?

Mr. Rawlings stepped toward her, and his face softened by the slightest measure. "Mother."

I almost laughed from the sheer madness of it all. I had traveled halfway across the country with this man—had shared a room with him, had bound his wounds—and I was *just* realizing I hadn't known his given name. *Alexander.*

And now I was to meet his mother.

"What are you doing here?" she asked, her words precisely enunciated. "We've had no notice from you."

How odd. She did not seem to have the same Scottish accent as her son. Where would he have gotten it?

"Our departure was rather unexpected, unfortunately." Mr. Rawlings bent to kiss his mother's cheek, and she grasped his elbows, staring wide-eyed up at him in shocked pleasure.

Heavens, and I thought he towered over *me*. Mrs. Rawlings was diminutive beside him.

"What has happened to your face?" She touched the dark bruises around his left eye, her words somehow both concerned and scolding.

"A scuffle is all, nothing to worry about." He sent me a knowing glance, a reminder not to speak of his injury.

Only then did Mrs. Rawlings seem to realize I was there. Her mouth tightened as she took me in. "What is this?" she asked.

What? Not *who*? It was clear from whom Mr. Rawlings had inherited his charming personality.

"There was a complication in the case I was working," Mr. Rawlings said. "I will tell you everything, but some food and tea would do us both some good, I think."

Mrs. Rawlings pursed her lips, no doubt biting back a protest. "Go into the drawing room," she ordered. "I shall speak with Cook and join you shortly."

Stroud led us into the drawing room, then turned to face me. "May I take your things, Miss . . . ?"

"Oh," I said. "Yes, thank you." I did not offer my false name; I did not think I was capable of that lie just yet.

I tugged off my gloves, then allowed Stroud to help me out of my pelisse. When I faced him again, he was blinking rapidly, his mouth parted.

What on earth? I glanced at Mr. Rawlings, but he was moving to stand beside the massive stone fireplace, oblivious to this strange reaction from his butler.

"Stroud, will you see that the blue room is prepared for Miss Albright?" Mr. Rawlings directed as he warmed his hands over the fire.

Stroud stepped back from me and offered a curt bow. He hurried from the room, shutting the door behind him with an ominous thud.

"That was odd." I frowned at the door. Why had he stared at me so?

"Stroud?" Mr. Rawlings said. "Yes, he can be a bit off-putting."

"No, not that," I said. "He looked at me like . . ." Then it hit me. I gasped. "My buttons!"

I reached over my shoulder and felt the undone buttons at the nape of my neck. My stomach lurched, and I felt the blood leeching from my face.

Mr. Rawlings looked positively baffled. "Your buttons?"

I swallowed hard, dropping my hand. "I—I could not reach all the buttons on my dress this morning. I put on my pelisse thinking I could simply change when we arrived, but . . ."

"But you did not anticipate a butler helping with your wraps," he finished for me. And then—miracle of miracles—he gave a short laugh, his lips sporting a ghost of a smile.

"It is not amusing," I insisted. "What must he think of me, a strange woman arriving unannounced with his master after a long carriage ride, and her dress *unbuttoned*?"

"Who cares what the man thinks?" He leaned his good forearm on the mantel.

"I do!" I paced across the room, wringing my hands. "What if he tells your mother? Drat it all, what if *she* sees? I will have ruined my reputation yet again and all within the space of five minutes."

"Stop blathering and come here," he ordered. "I'll set you to rights."

I turned to face him. "You?"

"Yes, fortunately I understand the complicated workings of a button," he said dryly.

I did not move. There were only a few buttons left undone, and I doubted he would get a glimpse of anything scandalous. But still. A woman liked her privacy.

"My mother will return any moment," he pointed out.

"Oh, very well." I hurried to join him beside the fire and turned my back to him. "Do hurry."

In my anxiety over Stroud and Mrs. Rawlings, I had not anticipated the proximity of such a task as buttoning a dress. But when Mr. Rawlings's fingers brushed over the skin of my upper back, I realized quite belatedly how suddenly *intimate* this felt. I fought a shiver, my skin heating, my mind going utterly blank.

I tried to think of something—*anything*—to say to distract myself.

"Why did you not tell me about this place?" My words came out softer than I'd intended. I was still rather put out with him for keeping such a secret, after all. But it was difficult to summon much anger when he stood so close to me, the warmth of his body mixing with that of the fire.

He did not respond immediately. "That is a difficult question to answer," he finally said. "And best done at another time."

I frowned. I wasn't satisfied by that in the least. "What is it called?"

"Briarstone," he said. "Briarstone *House*, naturally."

I exhaled a laugh, though it was brief. "And your mother? You should have told me she would be here."

"And endured your worries and complaints for the last two days? I think not." A slight tug at the very top of my dress, and then he stepped back. "Done."

I turned to face him, crossing my arms over my stomach. "Thank you," I managed.

He nodded, his expression unreadable as his eyes traced over me.

It was then that Mrs. Rawlings opened the door and found the two of us standing a bit too close in front of the fire. I cleared my throat and moved away.

"Food is being prepared," she said, closing the door behind her and narrowing her gaze at us. "Now, let us sit. Tell me everything."

She arranged herself on the sofa, and Mr. Rawlings sat beside her. I claimed an armchair across from them.

Mr. Rawlings gestured to me. "Mother, this is Miss Beatrice Lacey. Miss Lacey, meet my mother, Mrs. Ruth Rawlings."

Well, apparently we would not be keeping anything from his mother if he was beginning with my real name.

"A pleasure, Mrs. Rawlings." I attempted as much civility as possible. "I do apologize for arriving so unexpectedly. I promise it was a matter of great urgency that prompted our flight from London."

Mrs. Rawlings inspected me, her expression hard. "What sort of matter?" She did not greet me in return.

Mr. Rawlings succinctly explained all that had happened in the last few days—the case, the incident at Vauxhall, our theory about the murderer coming after us. He spoke in a low tone to keep from being overheard by anyone passing the drawing room.

"We left London two nights ago," he finished, "and traveled straight here. We mean to keep a low profile, hide away until Bow Street can find the man who attacked us."

Funny he did not mention our night at the inn together. I imagined his mother would not take too kindly to that.

"And why should you be safe here?" she asked. "Wouldn't this man know to look for you here?"

An excellent question, which I rather foolishly hadn't previously considered. Besides that, I couldn't help but be irritated that Mr. Rawlings had had no reservations about telling his mother everything when he'd refused to even inform Ginny and Jack of where we were going. Why should we trust his mother not to let anything slip?

Mr. Rawlings's mouth tightened. "Perhaps if anyone knew about Briarstone, that would be an issue."

Mrs. Rawlings made a sound of irritation. "Why do you insist on hiding your inheritance? What difference does it make? For that matter, why do you persist with this absurd profession when you have everything you need right—"

"We do not need to have this discussion again." Mr. Rawlings's voice was hard, commanding. "Not in front of Miss Lacey."

"Bah!" Mrs. Rawlings threw up one hand, rising to her feet and stalking toward the window.

Mr. Rawlings took a deep breath, his shoulders stiff. He glanced at me, and there was something very . . . exposed in his expression. Since I'd met him, I'd seen nothing that indicated a weakness or vulnerability in him. But this house, his mother—there was so much I did not know.

"And what is your plan?" Mrs. Rawlings questioned sharply, turning back to us. "How are we to explain this woman's presence at Briarstone? We cannot keep her a secret. The servants will talk; you must know that."

"Miss *Lacey*," he said, and I was gratified to hear a bit of rumbling in his voice as he corrected her, "will have a perfectly rational reason for being here."

"Will I?" I raised my brows at him.

Mr. Rawlings nodded firmly. "We will tell anyone who inquires that you have come to be my mother's companion."

Silence gripped the room for all of two seconds.

"Her *what*?" I asked in astonishment, grasping the arms of my chair as I leaned forward.

"Absolutely not," Mrs. Rawlings snapped.

Mr. Rawlings set his jaw, motioning for us to be quiet. "It is the only explanation that makes sense," he said, his voice low but firm. "We shall say that I brought her here with me from London to be at my mother's side, to keep her from growing lonely."

"Lonely? I haven't been lonely a day in my life," Mrs. Rawlings declared in a harsh whisper. "This is ridiculous, and everyone will see right through such a farce."

"Then you will have to convince them," Mr. Rawlings growled. "It is a ruse, yes, but one designed to keep a dangerous criminal from finding us."

I sat back in my chair, my insides a riot of indignation—me, a lady's companion? And to the standoffish Mrs. Rawlings?

"It is only for a week or so." He braced his forearms on his knees as he looked between his mother and me. "You needn't like it, but it is what must happen."

I wanted to reject everything he'd said, but as I cast about my mind for any other solution, none came to mind. It appeared Mrs. Rawlings had a similar struggle, if her irritated expression was anything to judge by. Undoubtedly, this was why he had decided to tell his mother the true reason for my coming here, knowing how she would react if he had actually tried to pass me off as her companion.

"Can I count on you, Mother?" he asked. "We cannot do this without you."

Mrs. Rawlings said nothing for a long minute. Then she gave one tight nod. "Very well."

"Thank you." He allowed a long exhale. "I know it is an imposition, but I am grateful for your help."

Mrs. Rawlings looked slightly mollified, settling back in her seat.

"Miss Lacey is to go by Miss Albright while she is here," Mr. Rawlings said. "We shall keep her away from Society as much as possible and hopefully return to London soon, putting this whole mess behind us." He turned to me. "While you are here, Miss Lacey, it is imperative that you remain within the house."

I blinked. "What?"

"You are safe here," he said. "Outside of these walls, I cannot guarantee that."

I let out a disbelieving breath. "What of Briarstone's grounds? Surely they are secure."

"I'm afraid this is not something we will be negotiating." His voice allowed no room for argument. "Unless I accompany you, you shall not leave this house."

Who did this man think he was, to imagine he had such full and unequivocal authority over me? I'd thought that I'd been coming to know him, at least in some small way, but it was clear now that everything I believed about him was only what he had wished to show me. I forced back the retort that rose in my throat. I needed time to make sense of these new developments. I would play by his rules . . . for now.

"Very well," I said but in a tone that made it clear how much I disliked acquiescing.

Mr. Rawlings nodded, a flash of relief in his eyes. "Shall we put our plan into motion?" He stood and strode to the door, pulling it open. "Stroud?"

The butler appeared in the doorway a moment later. Had he been listening just outside? Thank heavens Mr. Rawlings had insisted on keeping our discussion quiet.

"Yes, sir?" the butler said, standing straight.

Mr. Rawlings gestured at me. "Miss Albright will be staying with us as my mother's companion for the time being."

The lie fell rather easily from his lips. Was it because his manner was *always* brusque and commanding and one learned not to challenge him?

Except for me, of course. I delighted in challenging him.

Stroud stiffened slightly. "I see," he said slowly.

"Take her to her room and ensure she has dinner and anything else she might need," Mr. Rawlings said, returning to stand by the fireplace. "I need a word with my mother. Alone."

Stroud nodded, turning halfway back toward the door. "Miss Albright, if you please."

I had no choice but to stand, dismissed as if I, too, were a servant. My temper still roiled just beneath the surface, though I knew it would help nothing if I were to argue again.

I met Mr. Rawlings's eyes with cool defiance. I might now be trapped here at his *palace* with his shrewlike mother, but I was not beaten. I bent my knees in the barest curtsy. "Mr. Rawlings," I managed. Then I did the same to his mother. "Mrs. Rawlings."

At least they could not say I was uncivilized.

CHAPTER 9

Stroud showed me to my room, a spacious chamber that boasted a wide, canopied bed, a delicate set of rosewood furniture, blue floral wallpaper, and two windows overlooking the front drive. Compared to our room at the inn last night, the difference was almost amusing.

A footman delivered my trunk, and a maid left a tray with sandwiches and a steaming teacup. I stood in the center of the room, feeling out of sorts as I took it all in.

"Will you be needing anything else?" Stroud asked from beside the door.

In truth, I would have liked a bath, but I did not want to appear overly demanding, even to a butler. Or perhaps just *this* butler, who had seen my scandalously unbuttoned dress.

"No," I said. "No, thank you."

He nodded and left, frowning the entire time. Wonderful. How I enjoyed being mistrusted by everyone.

When the door clicked shut, I exhaled a shuddering sigh. I was finally alone.

I ate and drank to my heart's content, then unpacked my trunk. I changed into my night rail and let down my hair. The bed called to me, soft and inviting. I slipped under the covers—terribly comfortable and smelling of lavender soap—and laid my head on the feather pillow. *Bliss.*

I was certain I would fall instantly asleep, as exhausted as I was. But instead, I lay there in the dark, my body tense and my mind awhirl.

I still could not comprehend what had happened tonight, that Mr. Rawlings owned this estate, that he'd brought me here. Heavens, it was only just occurring to me just how very wealthy the man must be. I could not help but echo his mother's questions. Why on earth did he persist in a career at Bow Street when he had *this*?

My thoughts turned to Mrs. Rawlings, and I could not help a frown. Her chilly reception had been disheartening, to say the least, especially considering I had to spent the next week or more playacting as her companion. But we *had* sprung this on her rather unexpectedly. I imagined that I would not have reacted much differently had I been in her place. Perhaps tomorrow, after a night of sleep, we could both start again.

I heard footsteps in the corridor outside my room, brisk and purposeful. Mr. Rawlings. I sat up, listening. His steps slowed outside my door, then continued past. There was a creak and the soft thud of a door closing.

His room was near. It had to be intentional. In this great of a house, I could easily have been placed in a separate wing entirely. He likely wished to keep a close eye on me.

I tried not to think what Mr. Rawlings could be doing in his room, which was surely much larger and grander than even the room I'd been given. Master of the house. It was very odd to think of him that way. I'd only known him as the gruff and straitlaced Bow Street officer, but somehow, he had an entirely separate life, hidden from everyone he knew in London. Despite my irritation with him, curiosity flared within me. What made him keep such a secret?

I burrowed my face deeper into the pillow, refusing to entertain my thoughts any more. How desperately I needed a full night's rest. Hopefully I could sleep clear to morning without Mr. Rawlings and his middle-of-the-night awakenings to keep me—

Oh.

I'd helped Mr. Rawlings dress his wound last night at the inn. Did he have no one to help him tonight?

"Surely he does," I whispered to myself. He had a dozen servants who could assist him. A footman or a valet or perhaps Stroud himself. Except Mr. Rawlings had asked me not to tell anyone about his injury. Did he mean to keep this from the entire household?

I deliberated a long minute, until I realized that the longer I waited, the more likely it was that Mr. Rawlings would attempt to do it himself. I threw off my blankets and jerked on my dressing gown, muttering under my breath. I did not *want* to help him after what he'd put me through tonight. But I knew it would niggle away at me all night unless I tried.

I opened my door an inch and peered out into the corridor. Empty, with just a single candle burning in a sconce. I shut the door silently behind me and crept along, passing two doors until I spotted firelight underneath one. A shadow passed, blocking the light.

I raised my hand to knock, then hesitated. This was foolish. Someone could come along at any minute, a servant or even Mrs. Rawlings, and there would be no explaining why I was outside this door. But then I pictured his expression from last night, the twist of pain on his face, the horrible wound bleeding. I had to ensure he was cared for.

I knocked.

A pause, then footsteps. My pulse hammered.

The door opened, filling the corridor with sudden light, and I blinked up at Mr. Rawlings. He'd removed his jacket and waistcoat and tugged his cravat so it hung loosely around his neck. His sleeves were pushed up, revealing lean, muscled forearms. I gulped, forcing myself to breathe . . . and trying very hard not to stare. I'd seen the man nearly shirtless, for heaven's sake. Why should his forearms send me into a swoon?

Mr. Rawlings froze, then his eyes darted up and down the corridor. "Miss Albright," he said. "You should be in bed."

It was less an expression of concern and more a pointed observation. What was I doing *here*, outside his door?

"So should you," I managed, clasping my hands behind my back. "The doctor prescribed rest, if you'll recall."

"Yes, well," he said dryly, "a rather impertinent young lady knocked at my door. Makes it difficult to sleep."

I arched a brow. "Do forgive me. Only I recalled how you wished to keep your injury a secret from the household—or, more specifically, from your mother—and thought that perhaps you might again require help with your bandages."

"Oh." Mr. Rawlings cleared his throat as if he'd expected me to say something entirely different. "Thank you, but I found help."

"I am glad," I said with a brisk nod.

"Are you?" He lifted a brow.

My lips parted. Was he implying I'd *wanted* to help him with his bandage and that he was depriving me of such an opportunity?

"I was under the impression that you are quite angry with me," he said, "and would be glad to see me inconvenienced or, better yet, in some pain."

I coughed, heat pricking in my cheeks. "I do not wish to see you in pain." I tried for an air of superiority. "But you mustn't mistake my common decency for forgiveness. Indeed, I am still thoroughly irritated with you. I only offered my aid because of my misplaced sense of responsibility for your injury, which you have already insisted I should not feel toward you. I admit it is rather a jumble, but then, that appears to be my life as of late."

Mr. Rawlings almost—*almost*—looked amused. "I know the feeling, I assure you."

The corridor was chilly, and I pulled the edges of my dressing gown tighter about me. I should have returned to bed, what with our rather precarious situation here in the corridor, but there was a question begging to be asked. "If I may," I asked quietly, "why is it you do not wish your mother to know about your wound?"

He did not answer right away, and I thought he might refuse altogether. But then he leaned against the doorway with his uninjured arm in a way that made me far too aware of his casual attire. "My mother," he said, "does not approve of my working at Bow Street."

"I gathered."

He exhaled a quiet, humorless laugh. "Yes, she is not one to keep her opinions to herself."

"She thinks it beneath you?" I ventured a guess.

"In a way," he replied. "She believes I have a responsibility to this estate and that I should devote myself to its running." He rubbed his thumb against his jaw. "If she learned I've been wounded, she would only use it as ammunition in our ongoing battle."

"It is a compelling argument on her part," I said. "Why keep a dangerous job in London when you have such a life here?"

Mr. Rawlings scrutinized me, no doubt guessing my game. His expression grew guarded once again, any sign of our earlier camaraderie vanished. "You look dead on your feet, Miss Albright. You should go to bed."

I tipped my head to one side. "That was very neatly dodged."

"One picks up a thing or two after a few years at Bow Street."

"If I were not positively exhausted, I would press you now," I said. "But do not think you've escaped my curiosity."

"Is that so?" He sounded less than worried.

"Certainly." I allowed a sly grin to take my lips. "I dislike being in the dark. If I am to serve as your mother's companion, I shall use my position to shamelessly root out all your secrets."

Mr. Rawlings shook his head. "I do not know that I've ever been so threatened by a young lady."

"You must have very dull acquaintances indeed."

"I am beginning to think so."

The clock on the mantel behind him struck midnight, chiming into the quiet of the corridor.

"Heavens, midnight already," I said. "You must stop keeping me up so late, Mr. Rawlings."

The corner of his mouth twitched. "'Tis a habit I shall attempt to break." He stepped back into his room. "I trust you'll sleep well."

"And I trust you'll know where to find me should I scream?"

"Hence the proximity of our rooms." He paused, his hand on the door. "Good night, Miss Albright."

"Good night, Alexander," I said saucily.

I was rewarded by the startled look in his eyes before I turned on my heel and headed for my room. It felt good to catch him off guard. The man was impossibly set in his ways, so very sure of his every move. I enjoyed tilting him off-balance.

I reached my room and glanced back over my shoulder just in time to see his door close. Had he been watching me the whole way back?

Perplexed, I turned back to my door, more than ready to tumble to my bed in an exhausted heap.

Then I heard something to my left. A scuff. A breath.

I stared down the other end of the corridor, toward the stairs. The candlelight glowed weakly against the shadows, and I could see only a few feet ahead of me. I watched a few moments but heard nothing else, saw nothing else. Yet there was something about the silence that filled my chest with dread. My heartbeat ticked faster.

I slipped inside my room and shut the door firmly behind me. I pressed my ear to the wood, listening. Again, I heard nothing. No footsteps, no breathing. I was being silly. Likely it had been a servant going about their work.

Still, I hurried to my bed, dropped my dressing gown on the chair, and slid under the covers. I clutched the edges, pulling them under my chin, and tried very hard not to listen to the noise of the settling house, the wind scraping the window.

And foolishly—hopelessly—I wished that Mr. Rawlings could sit in the chair beside me, watching as I slept.

Chapter 10

A quiet knock woke me the next morning.

I jerked upright, my blankets tangled about me. "Yes?" I called, my mouth dry as cotton.

A young maid slipped into the room, red-haired and freckled. She bobbed a curtsy. "Beggin' your pardon, miss," she said. "Mr. Rawlings sent me to wake you."

"Wake me?" I rubbed my bleary eyes and peered at the clock. "It's not eight o'clock."

"Apologies, miss." She strode to the windows and tugged back the curtains, flooding the room with sunlight. "He insisted."

"I am certain he did," I muttered under my breath as I threw my feet over the side of the bed. "I do not think he knows how to speak without *insisting*."

I caught a flash of a grin on her face before she wiped it away in a look of politeness. "He asked me to give you this."

She retrieved a note from her apron pocket and handed it to me, then went to stoke the banked fire. I opened it and read.

Miss Albright,

I apologize I cannot meet you for breakfast; I'm afraid I've much work to catch up on.

My mother is an early riser and would expect her companion to be the same. Perhaps you might get better acquainted today.

A. Rawlings

I grimaced at the note. Mr. Rawlings had to maintain our ruse in case anyone saw the note, but his meaning was clear all the same. I was to spend today with his mother in order to convince the household of our story. And now I would not even have Mr. Rawlings there.

"What should you like to wear?" the maid asked, moving to my wardrobe.

"Pardon?" I asked.

"Mr. Rawlings insis—that is, he *asked*—that I help you dress." She paused with one hand on the wardrobe door. "If you like."

My annoyance with him faded. This was a thoughtfulness I hadn't expected, considering I was now practically a servant in his house. Why had he done it? Did he simply not wish to repeat my button mishap of the evening before? Or was this some attempt to help me feel more comfortable here?

"Yes, thank you." I cleared my throat. "The green will do."

After the maid—Agatha, as she introduced herself—helped me into my spring-green morning dress, she also quickly arranged my hair into a neat chignon, much better than my sad attempts during my journey here. I felt a little pang in my chest, missing Mariah. I hoped she wasn't too terribly worried.

Gathering all my courage, I descended the main staircase a few minutes later and found the breakfast room quiet and empty. Filling a plate with eggs and pastries from the many covered dishes on the sideboard, I ate as slowly as I could. I continued putting off the inevitable with a second and then third cup of tea, but eventually, there was nothing for it. I sighed deeply, stood, and went in search of Mrs. Rawlings.

Clasping my hands behind my back, I inspected Briarstone House in the light of day. It was even more impressive than it had been at night, if that was possible. Clearly, whoever had decorated the house had expensive taste. Silk wall coverings, gold candlesticks, and delicate furniture with richly colored cushions adorned every room

I peeked into. It was something of a maze, and I hadn't the slightest clue where Mrs. Rawlings might be.

I heard footsteps. I turned, catching the profile of a man crossing the corridor. For the wildest, panic-filled moment, my heart leaped into my throat. He had mahogany hair, thick brows, wide shoulders. *It is him!* my body screamed at me. *He found me!*

Then the man looked in my direction, and I saw him full-on. While there were certainly similarities, I knew at once this was not our attacker from Vauxhall. He was too tall, eyes light instead of dark, and much younger. Not to mention he wore the livery of a footman.

"Miss?" He'd stopped in the middle of the corridor, staring at me. "May I help you?"

I tried to catch my breath. My pulse still raced, convinced I was in danger.

"Yes," I managed. "Can you direct me to Mrs. Rawlings?"

"Yes, miss." He eyed me with no little curiosity. "She is in the morning room. Around the corner, at the back of the house."

"Thank you." I attempted to sound how I imagined a lady's companion would: mature, cultured, responsible. None of my actual attributes, unfortunately.

I continued on, my chest tightening with every step. I had to get a hold of myself. I could not be flinching at every shadow or thinking that every man who appeared suddenly was a murderer. I had a role to play, and I needed to avoid suspicion.

I focused on the unpleasant task ahead. My impression of the severe Mrs. Rawlings last night had not been overly flattering. To say I was dreading this meeting would be a massive understatement. I fleetingly imagined crying off and exploring the estate instead, but I knew that would be a mistake. Not only would the staff wonder why I'd neglected my duties as a companion to Mrs. Rawlings, but she would also find reason to dislike me even more.

Then again, perhaps my hope from last night would prove true, that with a fresh day and some introspection, Mrs. Rawlings might also wish to start anew with me.

I arrived at the open door of the morning room. Sunlight streamed across a thick, luxurious rug and several comfortable-looking armchairs. The room was decorated in golds and taupes, light and bright and welcoming. It was a direct and striking contrast to the woman dressed in deep blue sitting before the fire, needlework in hand, her posture so erect as to almost look painful.

Mrs. Rawlings looked up when I stepped inside. She sniffed in clear disapproval. "It is nearly nine o'clock."

It appeared we would *not* be starting anew.

"Is it?" I moved into the room. "I am early."

Her gaze narrowed. "I am dressed and breakfasted by eight o'clock every morning."

I sat across from her, folding my hands neatly in my lap. "An accomplishment, to be sure."

She pressed her lips into a thin line, made a sound of disapproval, and looked back down at her needlework.

We spent nearly ten minutes in silence, she determinedly stitching while I gazed about the room, the clock ticking loudly. I wasn't precisely sure of her aim. Was she attempting to frighten me off with her iciness? It might have worked if I had anywhere else to go.

Finally, I squared my shoulders and faced the storm head-on. "How precisely shall we go about this?" I asked. "I must admit that I've never pretended to be a lady's companion before."

"I haven't any idea," she said with a steely expression, still looking down. "I do not think we need to bother with the pretense overmuch. You'll not be here long."

That was my desire as well, but her saying it made me want to dig in my heels. "Oh, one never knows in a case like this," I said. "It could be weeks. Months even."

Her hands paused in her work, the only indication that she felt the same horror at the prospect that I did.

"Let us hope Bow Street is more competent than that," she said sourly. "Even without my son."

"Bow Street employs a great many dedicated officers," I replied, attempting to keep the edge from my voice but not entirely succeeding. "But cases can be unpredictable, as evidenced by my very presence here. I would not have chosen this, I assure you."

"Oh?" Her eyes shot to mine, dark and sharp. "Would you not?"

I pulled back my chin. "Pardon?"

But Stroud interrupted us, entering with the day's mail on a silver tray.

"Thank you, Stroud," Mrs. Rawlings said, taking the small stack of letters.

The butler's mouth tightened in distaste when he saw me, but he only bowed and left the room.

Without a word, Mrs. Rawlings stood and retreated to the writing desk in the corner. After reading her letters, she pulled out a blank paper, took up a pen, and began to write.

So ignoring me was her chosen tactic. That was perfectly fine with me. I had little desire to converse with someone so unpleasant.

We sat there, Mrs. Rawlings working industriously on her correspondence as I slumped back on the sofa and stared gloomily out the window. The gardens outside looked lovely in the sunlight, and I longed to explore them. How long did we have to play at this charade? An hour? Two? The entire day?

This was not what I had expected when I'd left London with Mr. Rawlings. I'd assumed we would be shut up in a tiny house somewhere, left largely to our own devices. Not this ornate prison with a cold and aloof warden. I wished I had a book, a newspaper, letters of my own—anything to detract from this debilitating boredom.

I wondered what Ginny was doing in London. I could only hope she was resting and not worrying overmuch, though I doubted she was keeping to the busy schedule she and I had drawn up for our visit to Town now that I was gone. I pictured her and Mariah going about the business of pretending I was ill, a farce that could only fool people for so long.

My thoughts darted to Clarissa Haythorne. Did she know about my supposed illness? Would it keep her from renewing her vengeful rumors against me? Or was she even now whispering in every estimable ear she could find? What sort of reception was waiting for me when and if I returned to London?

Twice, a servant passed in the corridor, glancing inside as they did so. I could only imagine what they thought at seeing Mrs. Rawlings and me together. I doubted our playacting was fooling anyone.

When footsteps again approached, I glanced up, expecting to see another servant. But Mr. Rawlings stood in the doorway, brow furrowed as his gaze went between his mother and myself. I straightened, impossibly relieved to see him.

Heavens, what a thought.

"Good morning." He stepped into the room and closed the door behind him.

I stood. "Good morning," I said with false brightness. I did not want Mrs. Rawlings to know how very much she'd affected my mood.

Mrs. Rawlings stood as well, not looking at me as she regarded her son. "Where have you been?"

"Attending to some business," he said, utterly vague and unhelpful. "I thought to see how you were getting on."

"About as well as one might expect," Mrs. Rawlings said, "having a stranger thrust into the innermost parts of one's life."

"We are fast friends," I said. "As you can see."

Mr. Rawlings raised one eyebrow but did not comment. He held himself stiffly, his arm without the sling, and I was quite certain he was in pain. But I could not inquire after him with his mother in the room, so I kept my concern to myself.

"Do we really think this will work?" Mrs. Rawlings folded her arms. "The servants are already suspicious."

"We have little choice but to persist," Mr. Rawlings said. "At least until we have word from London that Miss Lacey is safe to return."

Mrs. Rawlings obviously found that answer dissatisfying, but she said nothing more, only sat and returned to her correspondence with a scowl on her face.

Mr. Rawlings warily stepped toward me, as if afraid I might snap at him for abandoning me this morning.

"I heard no screaming last night," he said quietly so his mother could not hear. "You slept well?"

I bit my lip. In the light of day, I'd almost forgotten the strange sound I'd heard last night in the corridor, and the distinct feeling of being watched. But it seemed silly to mention it now. Clearly, it had been nothing, and telling Mr. Rawlings would only make me seem nervous and oversensitive.

"I did," I said. "And I must thank you for sending Agatha to help me this morning. That was very gracious of you."

He clasped his hands behind his back. "I thought you might prefer her help to mine."

The memory of his fingertips brushing the sensitive skin on my back flashed through my mind again. Yes, it was certainly for the best that he *not* help me in future.

Mr. Rawlings nodded to his mother seated across the room at her desk, her posture more rigid than ever. "I am sorry if this morning was . . ." He paused. "Uncomfortable."

"I have certainly dealt with worse," I said. "But I daresay your mother and I will not become bosom friends anytime soon."

He turned back to me. "Let us simply hope the case progresses quickly. I am eager to return as soon as possible."

"Are you so keen to escape your life of luxury here?" I asked. "Or perhaps you are escaping something else?" I shot a meaningful glance at his mother.

Mr. Rawlings did not take my bait. "I am only keen to return to work," he said firmly.

I did not believe him. Not entirely anyway. He was certainly attached to his work—though *obsessed* might be the better word—but there was more to it than that. This was his home, yet he did not look any more comfortable here than he did at Vauxhall or at the Travers home. In fact, he seemed even less so, if that was possible.

"How is your wound?" I nodded at his arm, still speaking quietly.

"Better," he said. "I imagine I'll be returned to normal within a week or two."

I did not expect the small surge of relief that came at his words. No matter our small disagreements and irritations with one another, I was truly glad he was on the mend. I was about to make a quip about all the unwanted rest he would be getting here in the country when a quick pattering of footsteps echoed from the corridor outside the room.

The door opened, and a child stood on the threshold, a young boy with dark curly hair and devastatingly blue eyes. He could barely be three years old, his small frame still clinging to babyhood in the roundness of his cheeks and limbs.

He spotted Mr. Rawlings, and his face lit like the sun, a toothy grin spreading over his face. "Uncle Alex!" he shouted and barreled toward us, nearly knocking over a small table in his haste.

Mr. Rawlings bent and scooped him into his arms, the boy giggling madly. "Who is this strapping young man? Not Elijah, surely."

"I am Elijah!" he protested. "Me, me!"

A tall woman swept through the open doorway, dark-haired and lovely, dressed in a neat, green walking dress. She had the same blue eyes and pert nose as the boy, and she smiled brightly. "I am sorry," she said. "He quite got away from me at the front door."

Then she spotted me standing beside Mr. Rawlings, and her expression turned to surprise, brows raising. "Oh, I am sorry. I did not realize you had company."

Mrs. Rawlings made a sound, half scoff, half laugh, as she stood. "Company indeed," she muttered, coming to greet the newcomer.

The woman seemed utterly perplexed as she kissed Mrs. Rawlings on the cheek. "How are you, Aunt?"

Aunt. She must be a cousin. I could certainly see the resemblance between her and Mr. Rawlings in their height and coloring, though I could never imagine a smile like hers gracing his lips.

"Do not ask a question you do not want an honest answer to, Helen," Mrs. Rawlings replied.

Elijah squirmed, and Mr. Rawlings bent to set him down. The boy darted off immediately, running toward the window and bumping a small table on which perched a ceramic statuette.

"Do be careful," the woman—Helen—cautioned him.

"Bah," Mrs. Rawlings said, looking rather fondly at the boy. "Let him be. I can buy new things."

"You say that now," Helen replied. "You may feel differently after he shatters your Meissen figurines." Her gaze returned to me, and she moved closer, offering a curtsy and a smile. "I do apologize for our abrupt arrival. I heard Alexander had returned, but I wasn't expecting a guest."

The way she said it made it sound as though this were the very first time Briarstone had ever had guests. Although, considering Mrs. Rawlings's prickly nature, it very well could be.

Mr. Rawlings stepped forward to introduce us. "Helen, this is Miss Beatrice Albright. Miss Albright, this is my cousin, Mrs. Helen Millard."

How odd it felt to be addressed so wrongly. I managed a curtsy. "A pleasure, Mrs. Millard."

"Most exceedingly," she said, clasping her hands before her, still smiling. "A true delight to meet you. What brings you to Briarstone?"

"Oh." I cleared my throat. "A new position."

"Position?" Helen tipped her head. "What position is that?"

A moment of purely awkward silence passed. Mr. Rawlings exhaled. "I brought her here to be Mother's companion."

Helen blinked. "Truly?"

"Yes," Mrs. Rawlings said dryly. "Alexander has got it into his head that I am *lonely*."

Helen recovered from her surprise admirably. "Well, how wonderful," she said in a firm voice. "No doubt you will cheer the place up immensely, Miss Albright."

I could feel the touch of her smile like a sunlit breeze. With Mr. Rawlings's reticence and his mother's active dislike and Stroud's suspicion, I had not had a very warm welcome at Briarstone. But the simple kindness Helen showed now made my spirits lift. How different the room felt with just the smallest bit of graciousness.

Elijah went to a small bureau against the far wall and opened the bottom drawer. He immediately began pulling out armfuls of tin soldiers and lining them up on the floor.

Mr. Rawlings nodded at the boy. "I hardly recognize him. He's grown so much."

"Yes, well, if you visited more often, you might know your own godson," Helen said matter-of-factly. "When were you last here? Spring?"

"It is not an easy journey," he said evenly. "And you know very well I am kept busy at Bow Street."

"Oh yes," she said. "Far too many criminals to catch to spare a few days for your family." She regarded me again, and the curiosity there made my stomach tumble. "Where do you hail from, Miss Albright?"

I swallowed. "London, most recently."

"I might have guessed." She glanced at Mr. Rawlings. Did she wonder about us traveling together? I hoped she would not question me on that. I did not like to lie, and I particularly did not want to lie to this woman.

"How old is your son?" I turned the conversation back toward her.

"A very rascally three," she said. "He will tell you he is almost four, but his birthday is not for nine months."

I smiled, watching him play with his soldiers. "He looks the very picture of you."

"That is very kind." Helen watched Elijah as well, pride in her voice. "But he takes after his father in spirit. He has already decided to join the Royal Navy to accompany Captain Millard as soon as he possibly can."

"Your husband is in the navy?" I brightened. "Oh, that must be fascinating indeed."

"It certainly was more so before Elijah came along," she said with a laugh. "I often joined my husband on his ship, but we've since decided I'm to be landlocked until Elijah is older."

I really could not imagine it. To live on a ship and go where the wind took you, to see the world and experience *life*. My existence suddenly felt very small.

A clatter. I looked down to see one of the toy soldiers tumbling across the floor toward me. It came to a halt right at my feet, and Elijah scuttled after it on his hands and knees. Then he pulled back, looking up at me in surprise. I did not think he'd noticed I was in the room until that instant, and he was suddenly very aware of the stranger in his midst.

His eyes went to his mother and back to me, wariness filling his expression.

"Good morning," I said with a smile, reaching down to pick up the soldier. I held it out to him. "Here you are."

Elijah made no move to take it from me, though he seemed to be debating, head tilted.

I'd always hated it when people towered over me, and I assumed children felt no different, so I crouched there on the ground, skirts pooled around me, and held the soldier a little closer to Elijah.

He finally grew brave enough, scooting the last couple of feet and taking it from my hand. I expected him to return to his line of soldiers, but he grinned up at me, apparently overcoming his fear. "Play with me," he said, then reached out and tugged on my hand.

"Oh." I was taken aback. "I don't . . ." Then I realized this was the perfect excuse to escape more conversation with Helen. Not that she wasn't perfectly kind and agreeable, but I was quite certain I would be caught up in our charade sooner or later. "Yes, very well." I followed him back to his play area. "Which shall I play with?"

"These." He shoved a pile of five or six soldiers at me. "You're the Fwench."

"Ah," I said. "I speak French very poorly, but I shall give it my best effort."

He laughed, though I did not think he really comprehended my words, and began forming his own soldiers into a circle surrounding mine. I sat on the ground, legs to one side, skirts spread modestly over my feet, and lined up my soldiers to face his. As he pretended to shoot my troops, I gave them all very dramatic deaths befitting the battlefield, and he giggled in pure delight.

"Again!" he demanded when all my soldiers were defeated.

"If you insist," I said. "But I think I've earned a cannon, at the least."

He shoved a cannon on wheels in my direction, then bent his face to the floor, ensuring his soldiers were lined up perfectly straight. I glanced up and blinked.

All three—Mrs. Rawlings, Helen, and Mr. Rawlings—stared at me. Mrs. Rawlings had a perplexed furrow in her brow while Helen looked on with a smile. Mr. Rawlings, however, watched with his mouth parted slightly and a softness to his expression that I'd never seen before. When our gazes clashed, a strange, fervent heat lit up my spine, and a thread of energy strung between us.

My heart thumped wildly in my chest. "I'm sorry," I said quickly, words tumbling over themselves. I made to stand. "I should have asked."

"No, no," Helen protested. "Please, don't stop on our account."

I settled back down with no small amount of trepidation. Had I overstepped? I'd simply wanted to be friendly, but Mrs. Rawlings was glaring at me like I'd killed the family pet. And Mr. Rawlings . . .

Well, the way he was looking at me was very different indeed.

"Play with us, Uncle Alex," Elijah insisted. It appeared as though he had much of his uncle in him, with that domineering tone.

I expected Mr. Rawlings to make an excuse. Instead, he came and sat beside me, one elbow propped on his upright knee. He ought to have looked a little ridiculous, a man as tall as he sitting upon the floor, but he could not quite manage it. Instead, he looked almost at ease, and when his eyes flitted over to mine again, there was something in them that settled my racing pulse.

"You be the Scots." Elijah pointed to a group of soldiers painted with red-and-green plaids and kilts.

"Terribly apt," I said.

Mr. Rawlings gathered his soldiers, arranging them into a tight formation. "I'm not Scottish, you know," he said quietly, so only I could hear.

My brows lowered. "I find that hard to believe, what with your accent."

He shook his head. "I lived near Inverness for many of my formative years, but I was born here."

I chanced a glance at Mrs. Rawlings, who was speaking with Helen on the sofa, pretending not to cast furtive looks at us every few seconds. "I did wonder why your mother does not speak the same."

"Yes, she did not adopt the language as I did," he said, "eager as I was to blend in."

I wanted to pry more, to ask why he had lived in Scotland for so many years. It did not fit in my mind with the picture I'd been forming of him, that of a rich and privileged child. But he said nothing more, so I followed his lead.

We played with Elijah, waging silly wars against one another. Mr. Rawlings won my cannon in an epic battle, and I retaliated by pretending a rockslide had pummeled half his army. Elijah delighted in it all, laughing and charging the both of us with his cavalry.

A few times, I caught Mr. Rawlings watching me over the boy's head. And whenever that inscrutable, fascinating gaze of his met mine, it never failed to send a curl of heat through my stomach. Which was curious and baffling and *entirely* unexpected.

I resolved to ignore it.

A resolution I already knew I would be hard-pressed to keep.

Chapter 11

Helen and Elijah stayed another hour, and it seemed to be a weekly ritual, the two of them coming to visit Mrs. Rawlings from their home nearby. I gathered from their conversation that Mrs. Rawlings and Helen's mother had been sisters, though the latter had died a few years ago.

I watched them all with scientific interest as I sipped my tea—mother, son, and cousin. They seemed to get along well enough, and there was an easy rapport between them. But there was a distance, too, a shadow I could not quite put my finger on. As if they danced about certain subjects that I, a stranger to their family, could not begin to comprehend.

I tried to avoid Mr. Rawlings's eyes, not at all willing to risk re-awakening that strange heat in my stomach.

"He likes you, you know," Helen whispered, sitting beside me.

I nearly spat out my tea and resorted to choking instead. "Pardon?" I managed.

"Elijah." She nodded to where Mrs. Rawlings sat beside the boy, reading him a story. "Though you should not be too flattered, I suppose, since he likes nearly everyone. But at least you are not in the select few he dislikes."

I gave a nervous chuckle and set down my teacup. "He is a darling child."

Helen observed me. "You were very good with him. Have you a great many younger brothers and sisters?"

"None at all," I admitted. "I am an only child, and all my cousins are much older than I. But I've always wished—" I stopped myself, swallowing tightly. "That is, I've always liked children. Thank you for letting me play with him today."

"Of course." Helen touched my hand as if she knew there was more I was not saying. She looked over at Mrs. Rawlings, then back to me. She sat up straight. "Miss Albright, you must come to the assembly on Friday night."

"Assembly?" I repeated as if I'd never heard the word before.

"Yes, absolutely," she said. "Everyone of importance in Camberwell will attend, and it will be the perfect opportunity to introduce you to local society."

"Why should she need to go if *I* am not attending?" Mrs. Rawlings asked shortly. "She is my companion, you'll recall."

"Oh, do not be so dour, Aunt," Helen said playfully, and she might have been the only one who could call Mrs. Rawlings *dour* and not be boxed about the ears. "Miss Albright will need some friends if she is to stay here. She is young. You cannot think to lock her away in Briarstone."

I almost laughed. She did not know how close she was to the truth.

"Alexander, you must come with us," Helen went on, turning to Mr. Rawlings. "The matchmaking mamas have been bereft in your absence. Do make an exception and let them parade their pretty daughters in front of you."

"I doubt they've noticed my absence at all," he said distractedly as he looked out the window. "Surely there are other eligible gentlemen they can focus their attentions on."

"None so eligible as you, as I think you are quite aware." Helen set her teacup down.

Mr. Rawlings exhaled heavily. "I have far better things to do with my time than dance with lasses I have no intention of courting."

"Well, if you will not come, Miss Albright and I shall go together." Helen determinedly linked our arms.

Mr. Rawlings's eyes flashed to mine, and I could read his thoughts in a thrice. He would, under no account, be allowing me out of the house without him.

"Miss Albright has other responsibilities," he replied shortly.

"Come now," Helen protested. "She should not be deprived of a ball simply because neither of you has any desire to attend. And perhaps we might find some of these other eligible gentlemen for Miss Albright to dance with."

Mr. Rawlings's features tightened, and for a split second, I wondered if it was the thought of me dancing with another man. But that was ridiculous. Clearly, it was because of the case, of the danger in allowing me into such a public setting. And he was right, though I hated to admit it. As much as I wanted to attend the assembly, it would draw too much attention to myself.

"Perhaps it is too soon," I said to Helen, disappointment settling into my boots. "I've only just arrived. There will be other opportunities, I am sure."

Helen was too perceptive. She had not missed my unspoken exchange with Mr. Rawlings, and her lips pressed into a slanted line.

"Thank you for the invitation though," I hurried to say. "That was very kind of you."

She nodded. "Perhaps next time."

Little did she know there would be no next time if everything went according to plan. I had no intention of remaining at Briarstone even a second longer than necessary.

Helen and Elijah took their leave a few minutes later, and I sighed as his small body skipped out of sight. Their visit had been a welcome distraction, and the quiet that immediately descended was tense and thick.

Mr. Rawlings stood. "I've correspondence to catch up on," he said, not looking at me. "I'll leave you ladies to it." He strode to the door and out into the corridor.

My stomach dropped. Oh, not him too.

Mrs. Rawlings sat silently across from me. She met my gaze steadily, posture perfectly straight.

Heavens, I couldn't do this for another minute, let alone several more hours. I jumped to my feet. "Pardon me." I did not allow her the chance to protest, not that I thought she would. No doubt she needed a reprieve as much as I did.

I left the room and spotted Mr. Rawlings just ahead, striding purposefully away. I hurried after him as he reached the entryway.

"Mr. Rawlings," I hissed in a low voice.

He turned, looking not at all surprised to see me bearing down on him.

"You can't truly mean to leave me alone with your mother again," I demanded.

"You *are* her companion," he replied with a hint of acerbic humor. "I daresay it is part of the job."

"Amusing, to be sure." I crossed my arms. "She likes mold growing on her bread more than she likes me."

His lips did not so much as twitch at my joke. Did this man ever laugh—or even smile?

"What do you suggest I do?" he asked. "We have to keep up the pretense, else the servants will suspect."

I considered as I glanced around the entry hall. "Offer me a tour," I said. "Of the estate. I need to know my way around, do I not?"

"A tour?" he repeated flatly.

"Yes." I raised my chin. "You've brought me here. The least you can do is show me around."

"I was not lying when I said I have correspondence I need to see to," he said. "I still have work."

"Very well, then." I leaned closer so only he could hear. "I shall show myself around. If I should happen to wander off and am found by the murderer on our trail, then that is something you shall have to live with." I turned on my heel and started off toward the back of the house.

He groaned deeply as his footsteps came after me. "You enjoy irking me, don't you?"

"I have little else to amuse me." I turned to walk backward a few steps, facing him. "You've taken me from my entertainments in London, so I have to make do here."

Mr. Rawlings only shook his head, clasping his hands behind his back.

"It is a pleasant day," I said. "Should we begin with the grounds?"

He sighed heavily. "By all means."

He led me through the house until we reached the back door, with steps leading down to a wide lawn. The house was perched on a low, meandering hill that slanted down toward a lake just distant. The trees and surrounding thickets were slowly changing colors, reds and oranges and yellows peeping through the browns and green. It was beautiful and made me miss home just a little. Mother always did love autumn.

"A lovely prospect, to be sure," I said.

"Aye," he agreed.

Just beyond the lawn grew dozens of aspen trees, planted in an orderly procession among the wilder trees and brushes. I shaded my eyes. "What is over there?"

"The water garden." He spoke shortly, as if the quicker he answered all my questions, the sooner he could return to work. Unfortunately for him, I had little intention of letting him abandon me anytime soon.

"Perfect," I said. "We'll start there." I started forward, and he matched my pace.

Even though it was October, the sun shone brightly, warming my back. Escaping the awkwardness of the morning room felt so very refreshing, and I exhaled, lifting my face to the breeze.

"I like Helen very much," I said. "I suppose I should call her Mrs. Millard though."

"She would not mind such a breach in propriety, I assure you." Mr. Rawlings walked beside me, his deep voice a strange contrast to the gentle brush of the wind in the trees.

I shot him a sidelong glance. "Do you have other family here besides?"

"No," he said. "Helen is my only cousin, and her parents died years ago."

"I see." I touched the leaves of a rosebush as we passed. "You seem close."

"We were." His voice grew a bit gruff. "As children, we were more like brother and sister."

"But no longer?" I asked curiously.

"Circumstances drew us apart."

Were these the same circumstances that had sent him to Scotland? I imagined if I posed that question, he would close himself off again. Better to stick to more innocent topics. "Elijah is a handful," I offered.

His expression softened by the smallest degree. Ah. Elijah was his weakness, though I should have realized earlier. "He is quite like I was growing up," he said, a barely discernible pride in his voice.

"You?" I laughed. "No, I cannot imagine it. You were born with a scowl and a command on your lips."

"I do not scowl," he said with a scowl.

"Oh, to have a mirror." I grinned up at him.

He crossed his arms. "Is it so terrible to have a serious disposition?"

"Of course not," I said. "Who would I tease if we were *both* cheerful and idealistic?"

He seemed not to have a response for that, staring at me in an odd sort of way. I quickened my pace to reach the first water feature, a quatrefoil pool with a bronze mermaid spouting water in the center. Beyond the fountain, a stone-edged canal made its way gradually toward the lake, the water running over narrow rills and down miniature cascades and under a beautiful balustraded bridge. The autumnal colors of the foliage provided a truly stunning backdrop.

"Oh, it is beautiful," I said, a bit breathlessly.

Mr. Rawlings stopped at my side. "My grandfather had it constructed when I was a child." His voice lacked any sort of emotion or inflection. "He was determined to impress the local gentry."

"It does its job nicely," I said. "You may consider me quite impressed."

He gestured toward the stairs that flanked the canal. I chose the left side, descending to the next level where a rectangular pool boasted dozens of water lilies. He followed, though he kept several steps between us.

"Helen seemed rather put out with you for not visiting more often," I said carefully.

"She misses her life at sea, that is all," he replied. "She wishes to entrap me here with her."

"I could think of worse places to be trapped," I observed. "And I am sure Elijah would wish to see more of you."

"You are incredibly obvious, Miss Lacey." He spoke mildly, seeming unconcerned about my shameless prying. "Simply ask your question."

"Very well," I said. "Do you not visit because you are trying so very hard to keep all this"—I waved a hand back toward the manor house—"a secret from your London circle?"

"Aye."

"And why is it so important to keep it a secret?"

His eyes slid to mine, narrowed slightly as if gauging how much he could tell me. "My friends know nothing about Briarstone," he said finally, "because I do not want my past unduly influencing my future. I am accepted as I am, which is how I prefer it. I would hate for anyone to look at me differently because of something so arbitrary as money."

"Surely they would not reject you now, even if you *are* ridiculously wealthy." My lips twitched. "It is an unfortunate shortcoming, to be sure, but they seem an accepting lot."

He ignored my little joke. "There is also the matter of keeping my mother, Helen, and Elijah safe. I have no shortage of enemies because of my work at Bow Street. If my connection to them was known, it could put them in the line of fire from any number of criminals seeking revenge."

"Oh." His words took me aback. Perhaps I should not have been surprised, considering I'd refused Ginny's company for the very same reason. I simply hadn't realized until today that Mr. Rawlings also had people he wanted to protect.

He said nothing more, and I gave up on my prying. I continued down the side of the canal, taking in the details of the water garden.

"If I had such a garden," I mused, sensing that we desperately needed a change in topic, "perhaps I would pine less for London. I'm afraid my home is rather dull in comparison to this."

"Why is it you pine for London?" he asked.

It was carefully worded, revealing none of his motive in posing it. But I could hear the unspoken question. This was not precisely the change in topic I'd been wanting.

"I've always loved the city," I said. "Even if it no longer loves me."

We strolled in the quiet, my words lingering between us, the trickling of the water filling my ears.

"The rumors about you," he said finally. "They're not true, are they? Any of them."

It wasn't a question but an observation. He stated it as fact, as if he had no doubt in its veracity.

And I hadn't realized how much I'd needed to hear those words from him.

"No." My voice was scratchy. "No, none of them are true."

His footsteps slowed, and I turned to face him as we both came to a stop. He regarded me with furrowed brows. "Where did they come from?" he asked. "And why?"

"Ah," I said lightly. "You are determined to dive right into the thick of it, are you?"

"You have no qualms about prying into my affairs," he pointed out.

"Your affairs are not so black as mine."

"That is debatable."

I eyed him, wrestling within myself.

His expression shifted slightly. "You needn't tell me if you don't wish to. You hardly know me."

"I do not think *that* is true," I said. "You brought me to your family home, after all, and introduced me to your mother and cousin. We've spent nearly every second of the last few days together. Heavens, I've even seen you without your shirt." As soon as the words left my mouth, I froze, heat rushing to my cheeks. *Why* had I said that?

But then, of all the unlikely things, Mr. Rawlings's lips twitched. "Yes, you have." Was that a touch of amusement in his eyes? "In fact, your blush that night was the first thing to make me doubt the rumors. You seemed far too . . ." His voice trailed off.

"Naive?" I prompted, even now fighting the same blush. "Green?"

"No." He shook his head. "Sincere."

"I see." I had to pause a moment, clearing my throat. I remembered trying to imagine what he'd been thinking as I'd bandaged his arm. It had *not* been this. I pressed on. "But all that to say, we are not precisely strangers anymore, Mr. Rawlings, and I find myself wanting you to think well of me."

His eyes fixed on mine and held me there. "Go on, then."

This would be easier if I did not have to look him in the eyes. I clasped my hands before me, turning to walk again beside the canal. He followed just a step behind.

"Two years ago," I began, "I attended a ball in London, hosted by the Earl of Granville. I was not normally included in such functions, but my mother managed to procure an invitation. It was my chance, you see, to make a good impression on the very best of Society. My two previous Seasons had been unsuccessful, and all my mother's hopes were pinned on this ball."

Mr. Rawlings remained quiet, listening intently.

"I was introduced to a great many people," I said, "and several promising gentlemen asked me to dance. I left the ballroom halfway through, needing a few minutes to collect myself." I paused, uncertain my voice would support the words I wished to say. "I saw something I should not have."

"What do you mean?" His gaze was a focused steel.

The memory came flooding back to me, my senses overwhelmed just by the thought of it. I'd left the ball, glad for the break in noise and chatter. As I'd wandered the corridors, I'd recalled reading in the paper that Lord Granville collected valuable books and that he'd recently procured a copy of Shakespeare's first folio, a rare version with faintly purple-tinted pages. I'd decided to find the library to see if I could discover my namesake within the pages of the first folio, since *Much Ado About Nothing* was one of the plays included.

I'd peeked in several rooms, searching as I went, and finally found the library door ajar, dancing with firelight. I'd stepped inside and inspected the room, a welcoming space with every wall lined in bookshelves, a tall-backed sofa facing the fire, and a large folio stand in the corner. I went to the folio stand immediately, sensing that Lord Granville would have put his new acquisition on display. I was right—the folio was there, all dark calfskin and gold lettering—but it was closed rather than opened to a favorite passage. And besides that, the large volume was off-balance, looking as if it might topple off the stand at any moment.

I frowned, reaching out to adjust the book on the stand to a safer position. How odd.

Then I heard it. The rustle of clothing. The hushed whisper.

I spun just as two heads appeared over the sofa in the middle of the room. A man, whose face was a blur to my mind, then and now. Because my eyes immediately snapped to the woman's face.

Clarissa Haythorne.

We'd known each other since our debut Season, passing in and out of each other's spheres. I'd never been important or interesting enough to catch her attention, for good or for ill.

Until now.

I stared at her, at the sleeve of her dress slanted off her shoulder, her mussed hair and flushed cheeks, the smudged rouge on her lips.

I gasped. *That* I remembered with perfect clarity. It was the sound that had broken the crystal glass of the situation, had brought it shattering down around me.

"I stumbled upon a romantic meeting," I whispered now to Mr. Rawlings. "The woman was an acquaintance of mine." I lifted my eyes to meet his, to make my meaning clear. "An *unmarried* acquaintance. She was with a man. They were—" I shook my head. "Well, I am sure you can imagine what they were doing."

"Well enough," Mr. Rawlings said tightly. "What happened then?"

"I fled," I admitted. "I didn't know what else to do. I ran back to the ballroom, acted as if nothing had happened. But she found me a few minutes later. She threatened me."

I could see her cold expression in my mind, the iron glint in her eyes as she'd gripped my elbow tightly enough to leave a bruise. Her high, nauseating voice had whispered directly into my ear. *If you tell anyone what you saw tonight*, she'd hissed, *I will destroy you. Do not doubt I have the power.*

Then she'd patted my arm with a catlike smile and disappeared into the crowd.

I shook my head at Mr. Rawlings. "I wouldn't have said anything, of course. She is far higher in Society than I am, and what business was it of mine?"

His head tilted as if attempting to piece together what I was saying. "But if you didn't say anything . . ."

"I can only assume she panicked," I said quietly. "She was afraid her threat would not be enough to keep me silent, so she decided to ruin me before I could ruin her. By the next morning, there were already stories circulating about me. Each worse than the last. Each as false as the last."

"So she ruined your reputation," he said, "*your* life, because of her own foolish indiscretions?"

"Yes." There was nothing more to say, really.

He turned away as if to shield me from the brittle flash of anger in his eyes. But I saw.

"Did you not fight back?" he said, his voice tight. "Tell everyone the truth?"

"No," I said. "I wish I had. But I was out of my depth and terrified that my future was gone. I did not have the weapons she did, the connections and status. The war was over before it had truly begun." I sighed, brushing back a curl. "I retreated home to lick my wounds, though the rumors chased me there as well. I cannot go anywhere without whispers and censure following in my wake."

Mr. Rawlings finally looked back at me. "I am sorry," he managed roughly, "that this happened to you. She must be a hoyden indeed to spread such slanderous lies. The things I heard—" He stopped abruptly, realizing where he was leading the conversation.

"Oh, I've heard them all." I pretended an indifference that I certainly did not feel. "That I'm secretly wed to a gardener and carrying his child. That I am dying of a mysterious illness and my parents are desperate to marry me off before anyone discovers it. That I have a problem with drink and spend my days in a sodden stupor . . ."

He said nothing, though his shoulders tightened.

"How *did* you hear such things?" I asked, suddenly curious. "I'd only been in London for a day or two before we went to Vauxhall, but you knew even then. I assumed it would take longer for the rumors to catch up to me."

A muscle in his jaw ticked almost imperceptibly. "That is my fault, I'm afraid. At the dinner party, I realized you had an interest in Drake, so I asked around, wanting to know more of you." Mr. Rawlings cleared his throat before continuing. "I did not expect to find what I found."

"Oh." That was certainly not the answer I'd anticipated, and it took me a moment to consider all the ramifications. Then I jolted to a stop. "So you knew of the rumors before we coerced you into coming to Vauxhall with us?"

"Yes," he admitted.

"Ha!" I jabbed a finger into his chest. "So you *did* send Mr. Drake off on that ridiculous errand on purpose! To miss our meeting!"

"Would you have not done the same for your friend?" he asked, brow raised, not looking at all remorseful. "If you believed what I did back then?"

"That hardly matters," I declared. "I am heartily offended. You were so high and mighty about how important the case was and how you would never deign to muddy your boots with such silly antics. But I was right all along!"

I made to prod him with my finger again, wound up in my righteous indignation, but his hand caught mine, grasping it just beneath the wrist. Neither of us wore gloves, and the feel of his warm skin against mine sent a bolt of pure energy shooting up my arm.

My breath faltered, tangled in surprise, and I stared up at him, into those ink-dark eyes that seemed to hold an endless array of secrets. The wind whisked through my skirts, blowing them against his boots, tossing my curls into disarray around my face.

"I think," he said, his gaze roaming my face with a slow, deliberate intent that left my lungs aching for air, "that we can both admit we judged each other wrongly at first."

The trees rustled above us, a soft stirring that did nothing to mask the inescapable drumming of my heart.

"I do not think I judged you wrongly," I managed, breathless. "You *are* abrupt, arrogant, and aloof, just as I surmised within five minutes of making your acquaintance."

"You flatter me," he said dryly.

We stood so close together. I could have stepped away, tugged my arm from his grasp, but I did not.

"*But*," I amended, "you are certainly more than that." I dared to lean an inch closer. "I have much to discover about you yet, Alexander Rawlings."

He did not move for another long moment, staring down at me, his large hand wrapped firmly around my wrist. Then he released me and stepped back. I took a short breath, trying to hide how very much he'd unnerved me.

"You mustn't call me Alexander in public," he said.

"Only in private, then?"

He let out a sigh of exasperation, but there was a slight upward turn of his mouth, if I was not mistaken.

I turned away, focusing on a nearby stone figure atop a column—some Roman god, I assumed. I attempted to calm my racing pulse but did *not* succeed.

"Why did you return to London?" He moved past me to inspect the statue as well. "If your previous visit ended so poorly?"

"Ginny convinced me," I replied. "She was the only one who did not abandon me after the rumors spread and the only one who knew the truth of what happened. She insisted I had to reclaim my life. And so I went, determined to conquer my demons. It did not work quite as I intended."

"No," he said. "It seems you have only added new ones." He paused. "I am sorry for it. I wish you had not been caught up in this case."

"I can hardly blame you," I said. "You did not choose this."

His eyes found mine again. "No, I did not."

There seemed to be some hidden meaning in his words that only he knew.

He cleared his throat and turned away. "We ought to go back to the house."

"Yes," I said. "Your mother will have missed me, I am sure."

I thought that maybe he smiled again, but I could not be certain.

CHAPTER 12

When I returned from the gardens, Mrs. Rawlings was prepared. She had a neat pile of linen baby clothes—for the poor, she said—and instructed me to hem the edges as she performed her duties as mistress of the house.

I wanted to refuse and would have done so rather colorfully if the housekeeper hadn't been in the room at that moment. Instead, I bit back my retort and took the sewing with a smile. In the end, it was better that my hands were occupied. It saved both of us the trouble of filling the room with empty conversation or, worse, pointed slights and ill-concealed irritation.

I inspected Mrs. Rawlings as I hemmed the sleeve of a baby gown. She sat stiffly at the nearby table, reviewing the week's food orders and menus with the housekeeper.

She glanced at me as if feeling my gaze, then frowned and turned away. Why, precisely, did she dislike me so much? I was perhaps a little outspoken and sometimes flippant, but I wasn't a *terrible* person.

And yes, I'd appeared unexpectedly to disrupt her life and invade her privacy, but shouldn't she instead be annoyed at Mr. Rawlings for bringing me? I doubted that would ever happen. I had the feeling she was the type of mother who thought their child could do no wrong.

Save for her obvious annoyance with him for working at Bow Street.

The afternoon dragged like a wagon with a broken wheel, but I managed to finish a somewhat decent baby gown, which Mrs. Rawlings only sniffed at. We parted—gratefully, on both our parts—to dress for dinner.

When I came back down after changing into my evening gown, a simple dark-blue silk, I made my way toward the drawing room. I heard voices through the partially open door and paused just outside, recognizing Mr. Rawlings's deep voice.

"—don't wish to discuss it now," he said in low, sharp tones, attempting to be hushed but not quite managing it.

"You never wish to discuss it," Mrs. Rawlings retorted. "And you've been avoiding me all day. Don't think I haven't noticed."

"I've been busy, Mother."

"So have I," she snapped. "Running *your* estate while you gallivant about London, chasing criminals."

"I do not gallivant." Mr. Rawlings's words were clipped. "My work is important."

"And Briarstone is not?" I heard footsteps and imagined her moving closer to Mr. Rawlings. "This is your legacy, whether you want it or not. I fought tooth and nail for it, and I'll not have you throw everything away because your position at Bow Street gives you an inflated sense of heroism."

Silence. I held my breath, listening intently. What did Mrs. Rawlings mean, that she'd had to fight for Briarstone? Hadn't Mr. Rawlings inherited it from his grandfather? Perhaps I should have had qualms about eavesdropping, but I would deal with the moral implications of my actions another time.

"You have made your choices," Mr. Rawlings said, and I was surprised to hear his voice even and unaffected, not hard, as I might have expected, considering what she'd said to him. "And I will make mine. Is that not what you really fought for? The power to choose for myself what I want?"

Mrs. Rawlings made a noise of irritation, and her footsteps paced away from him again.

"I am grateful for everything you have done," he said, his tone softening. "Please know that. But my life will be my own."

Mrs. Rawlings did not respond again, and it seemed as good a time as any to make my appearance. I allowed a bit of noise as I approached the open door, scuffing my feet. When I stepped inside the drawing room, they both regarded me expectantly.

"Punctuality is not a strength of yours, is it, Miss Albright?" Mrs. Rawlings pursed her lips.

I looked at the clock. It was two minutes past six o'clock. Her criticism was entirely unfair, but I could hardly admit that I would have been perfectly on time if I hadn't been listening to her conversation from the corridor.

"I do beg your pardon," I said with a bright smile. "Only I found myself with a few minutes after dressing and decided to continue working on those baby clothes for the poor. I'm terribly sorry I lost track of the time."

She looked at me, rather astounded, as I swept into the room and seated myself directly across from her, smiling all the while. Perhaps this was the best tactic to take with her, pretending I did not notice her derision and acting in simple innocence.

Mr. Rawlings turned his head, and I had the sneaking suspicion it was to hide a grin of his own. Whatever the reason, it gave me the opportunity to inspect him from beneath lowered lashes. I hadn't seen him in such formal clothing since the dinner party at the Traverses', and I hadn't properly appreciated it then. The man certainly filled out a dinner jacket.

He caught me looking and raised one brow. I refused to be embarrassed and simply broadened my smile.

"Thank you for showing me the water garden today, Mr. Rawlings," I said, perhaps louder than I needed to, but I wanted to ensure Mrs. Rawlings took notice. "Briarstone has some very pretty land about."

Mr. Rawlings narrowed his eyes slightly, as if knowing precisely what I was doing. Which would have been interesting since I wasn't even fully sure. I simply wanted to remind Mrs. Rawlings that she was not the only one with a claim on her son's time.

"Of course," he said. "I would hate to have you wander off and get lost."

Stroud entered the drawing room, regretfully cutting off my pert response. "Dinner is served."

Mrs. Rawlings made to stand, but Stroud stepped forward. "If I may have a moment of your time, ma'am?"

Mrs. Rawlings paused. "Yes, what is it, Stroud?"

He turned to Mr. Rawlings as well. "I should like to address you both, actually. I just had word that my sister in Bath is ill. She begs that I come and see her back to full health."

Heavens, what a prospect. Disapproving, contrary Stroud acting as a nursemaid? I could think of nothing worse for someone suffering with a serious illness.

"I wondered if you might allow me to go to her," he said, bowing his head deferentially. "No more than a week. The under butler should be able to manage in my place, though I realize this is quite the imposition."

"No, no." Mrs. Rawlings waved him off. "You must go to her. Family comes before all, does it not?"

She cast Mr. Rawlings a meaningful glance, which he pretended not to notice.

"Sir?" Stroud turned to Mr. Rawlings.

He nodded. "By all means. Just be sure your duties will be attended to in your absence."

We stood to go into the dining room, and as I passed Stroud, I cast him a sidelong glance. He was already watching me, his expression cool and unreadable. A chill ran over my skin, a strange premonition. As if Stroud's leaving had something to do with *me*.

I hurried after Mrs. Rawlings. That was preposterous, I told myself. Stroud disliked me, but that did not mean everything he did related to me in some way.

We seated ourselves at the table, and dinner proceeded in a most awkward manner. As we ate, Mrs. Rawlings refused to acknowledge my presence and spoke only to her son, who seemed less than inclined to carry a conversation.

Though he barely spoke, Mr. Rawlings watched me a great deal during the meal. What he was looking for, I couldn't say. But when our gazes caught across the table, awareness flared within me, heating me from the inside out.

I hated to admit it, but I knew precisely what it was. *Attraction.* The very idea of it was absurd. I did not even *like* Mr. Rawlings. Well, not much, anyway. How could I be attracted to a man who ordered me about like I was one of his servants, who had dug into my past and involved himself in my private affairs and irritated me to no end?

Except our conversation at the water garden had caught me off guard. I hadn't expected him to be so accepting of my story about Clarissa Haythorne—or so frighteningly angry on my behalf.

And when he'd captured my hand, when we'd stood so close, I'd felt . . .

Mr. Rawlings broke our gaze, his mother claiming his attention with some complaint from a tenant. I forced air into my lungs, ducking my head. I remembered very well how I hadn't thought him handsome at our first meeting. He'd been too fierce, his features harsh and unyielding. Now, though, I was beginning to see him differently. As if knowing the more hidden parts of him changed what my eyes were telling me.

And I realized that even if Mr. Rawlings was not handsome in the usual way, he was incredibly—and quite unfortunately—attractive.

It did not matter. It *could* not matter. I couldn't guess how long I would have to stay here at Briarstone House, and allowing myself to dwell on such things—even within my own head—set a dangerous precedent. Mr. Rawlings was charged with my protection. Our relationship could only ever be purely professional.

Besides, he gave no sign that *he* felt any of this baffling attraction I sensed between us. Perhaps it was only me reading more into our interactions than I should. He was far too in control of himself; whereas, I acted before I thought in almost every situation.

It would be best for both of us if I simply ignored this untimely attachment. It had no permanent bearing on my future—it was only the unfortunate side effect of spending too much time with a man.

I simply wished that this specific man did not intrigue me so very much.

Chapter 13

The next morning plodded along much like the first. Mrs. Rawlings continued to assign me various mind-numbing tasks—mending, arranging flowers, and declining social invitations. But while these chores occupied my hands, they left far too much time for my mind to wander. What was happening back in London? Had Mr. Drake and Jack made any progress in the case? Was Ginny worried for me? How was she feeling this late in her pregnancy?

I missed her desperately. Besides my Seasons in London years ago, I had rarely spent much time apart from my best friend. She balanced me, kept me grounded and realistic, and I could feel myself more and more on edge without her steadying influence.

After luncheon, I escaped to my room for a few hours. I first wrote to Mother, a false, ridiculous letter describing all the delightful diversions she would assume Ginny and I were spoiling ourselves with in London. I read my letter over several times before signing and sealing it. Mother would not have the slightest indication that things were not as they seemed. There was no point in worrying her.

I did not bother to write to Father. He would not have read my letter anyway.

Next, I scribbled page after page to Ginny, informing her of everything that had happened since we'd parted and begging for any information she could share with me. I was withering away in my ignorance, trapped so far from the center of it all.

I could only imagine how Mr. Rawlings was managing, with it being his investigation. Did he feel as helpless and useless as I did? He'd kept himself shut away with work since we'd arrived, but what precisely did that work entail? Was he still investigating the murder from afar? Was he receiving updates from London?

I gathered my letters and went in search of him. A servant directed me toward his study, and as I approached the door, my heart ticked a little faster. Silly, I told myself. I had no reason to anticipate seeing him.

Still, when I knocked and heard his deep, commanding voice call out "Come," a thrill ran through me.

Stupid, foolish attraction.

I stepped inside. Mr. Rawlings sat at a desk in the corner, a great hulking affair no doubt meant to intimidate whoever stood before it. The study itself was rather sparse, functional but with little ornamentation.

He looked up at my entrance, and his pen stilled. "Miss Albright." He stood. It seemed odd that he should use my false name even here when it was just the two of us. But I supposed one never knew when there were servants about.

"Good afternoon." I left the door ajar and stepped forward. "I have a letter for Ginny I'd hoped you might post for me." I'd enfolded Mother's letter in Ginny's and asked her to forward it from London so Mother would not wonder why it came from Somerset.

He eyed the letter. "I assume you haven't given away relevant details of our location or the case."

"No, I decided against sending the map I drew of our exact route from London," I quipped.

I thought I might see that muscle in his cheek twitch, like it did when he held back a smile, but he sadly gave me no reaction at all.

"A wise choice," he said, holding out a hand.

I moved toward him. "The letter, however, is full of rather colorful descriptions, if you are intent on peeking." I flashed a grin as I handed it across the desk.

He took the letter, our hands not so much as brushing. "I would not dream of invading your privacy so, Miss Albright."

The man really should just smile and get it over with before his face cracked right down the middle from the stress of holding it back.

"How was your morning?" He sounded rather distracted, asking only to be polite. He glanced back down at his papers on the desk. Had I interrupted some important doing?

I almost made a joke about his mother acting as my taskmaster, but something in the air felt strange. The connection we'd forged yesterday in the water garden had faded, leaving a weak remembrance in its wake.

"Well enough." I took a step back. "Thank you for posting that."

Mr. Rawlings looked me in the eye for the first time and opened his mouth as if to say something. Then he pressed his lips together and nodded. "Of course."

I hurried from the room, my stomach in a twist. Had I imagined everything yesterday? I thought back on our conversation, recalling how he'd deftly pulled my story from me, my deepest secret. How he'd listened and questioned and reacted just right.

I stopped there in the corridor. Had it all been a front? Not a deception, per se, but had he simply treated me like he would have treated someone he interviewed at Bow Street? Seeking details, trying to understand and solve a problem.

That was how it felt anyway. Especially now, after he'd barely acknowledged me in his study.

I gave a huff of a laugh. Well, there it was. He certainly did not feel anything toward me, and I need not waste any more time wondering. I was just a case to him, a duty to fulfill.

I would do well to remember that.

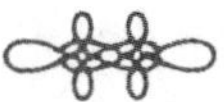

The days passed, each as numbingly slow as the last. I spent my mornings with Mrs. Rawlings, both of us avoiding speaking as much as possible, though she still cast calculating looks my way. In the afternoons, I escaped to my room or the small library on the main floor, where I was quickly making my way through the limited selection available there. Clearly, the Rawlings family were not great readers.

I tried to keep hold of my dogged optimism, but it seemed as if my defenses wore away with every passing hour. It did not help that I barely saw Mr. Rawlings. He kept to his study, working on heavens only knew what. When I saw him at dinners, it was in the presence of his mother, which certainly discouraged me from asking him any reaching questions. He barely glanced at me, resorting to impersonal inquiries and polite observations.

He seemed to be healing well enough, at least. His bruises had begun to fade, and he held his arm less stiffly. I wondered if his mother suspected anything or if it was simply that I watched him so closely that I could see his small improvements.

Four days after I'd asked Mr. Rawlings to mail my letters, I stood at the morning room window, staring out at the gray clouds that hovered forebodingly over Briarstone. I begged them to rain, to match the blackness of my mood. Loneliness perched on my doorstep like an unwelcome houseguest, and for the first time since I'd left London, I felt no desire to push it away.

I knew my life was in danger in London, that a murderer was even now searching for me, but at the moment, I could not think of anything so terrible as being right here—alone, abandoned, and utterly defeated.

"Miss *Albright*."

Mrs. Rawlings's voice came from behind as she entered the room. She always said my false name like that, like it was a personal offense to her.

"Yes?" I asked politely. That was the only way I'd survived the last few days, doing what I'd determined to do: pretend her unkindness did not bother me.

"Alexander received a bundle of letters from London." She held up a thick, folded note. "He asked me to pass this on to you."

My heart leaped. I hurried across the room and took it from her, not caring if she disapproved of my eagerness. My name—my real name—crossed the front in Ginny's familiar hand. Drake must have sent it to Mr. Rawlings for her.

"Thank heavens," I breathed. I returned to the window and sat on the seat nearby, then wasted no time in breaking the seal and unfolding the papers. A smaller note dropped to my lap. I glanced at it but set it aside to read Ginny's letter.

Dearest Bea,

It has been only two days since you departed, but I have nearly gone mad for worry. Jack assures me that Mr. Rawlings would never allow anything to happen to you, but you know how I always fear the worst. I can only hope that you are safe wherever you are.

I wish I could write with good news, but I have none. The case has continued as it did before, sprawling and complex and seemingly impossible to pinpoint a clear suspect. Jack, Mr. Drake, and Mr. Denning have worked all hours of the day and night along with so many other officers, but there have been no truly promising developments.

Mr. Drake has written to Mr. Rawlings with the same news, though undoubtedly with more detail than I can supply you here. We can only continue to hope that a break in the case comes swiftly so you may return.

I can almost hear you demanding to know how I am, even though I am not in any danger whatsoever, but I shall satisfy your imagined questions. Despite a severe lack of sleep—my reasons are obvious, I think—I am well. Jack was worried that the shock of Vauxhall might have stressed the baby and insisted on calling a doctor to see to me the day after. But everything is perfectly fine. I rest when I am able and worry about you in between.

Please write to me soon, Bea. Reassure me that you are well and cared for, and perhaps I might sleep a little easier. Be careful.

All my love,

Ginny

I lowered the letter, fighting tears. To know that someone was thinking of me, missing me, cracked the careful veneer I'd built around myself the last few days. Heavens, how desperately I wished I could embrace her right now! I needed that physical reassurance more than I ever had before.

I looked back at the letter and noticed a postscript through my blurry vision.

PS You have likely seen the note accompanying my letter by now. I received it yesterday morning and debated whether to even send it to you. I haven't read it, of course, but the servant who delivered it came from the Haythorne household, so I have little doubt who it is from. If you read it, know that whatever she says to you, she has no power over you anymore. Or better yet, simply throw it in the fire as I was tempted to.

I straightened, my skin going cold. I dropped Ginny's letter on the table beside me, then slowly picked up the smaller note that had fallen to my lap.

I did not recognize the handwriting, but *Miss Lacey* was dashed across the front in a decidedly feminine hand. It had to be from Clarissa Haythorne, but why on earth would she be writing to me?

I knew myself too well. There was no possible way I would burn the letter before reading it.

I broke the seal and opened the letter, dread filling every empty space in my chest.

My dearest Miss Lacey,

What a fortuitous coincidence it was to come across you while shopping yesterday! If I hadn't, I would not have had a single clue you had returned to London. You are ever so private these days, though I can hardly blame you after the business with those awful rumors. I never believed a word, my dear!

I tightened my grip on the page, bending and twisting it.

I did wish to remind you of our conversation when last you were in London. I hope time has not dulled your memory! I would hate for there to be any misunderstanding between us. The past should stay firmly in the past, do you not agree?

Perhaps we might take tea together soon. I imagine we would have much to talk about.

Clarissa Haythorne

Her name was signed with a ridiculous flourish, overbearing and presumptuous.

I stared at the note, throat tight as if it might close over entirely. My eyes pricked for a very different reason now—anger. Anger at the unfairness of life, at the futility in attempting to reclaim my reputation, at the absolute injustice that Clarissa Haythorne ruled her London world while I cowered in the country. That she could pretend such innocence about ruining my reputation when she was the mastermind behind the entire affair.

"Are you well, Miss Albright?"

Mrs. Rawlings's words were cool, yet there was a strange tone to her voice that I hadn't heard before. Concern? Curiosity?

I stiffened. I did not want her to see me like this. "Perfectly well." I choked on the words. "If you'll excuse me." Grasping my letters in one hand, I stumbled to my feet and hurried from the room. I started for the stairs, then came to a wobbly halt. I did not want to go to my room. Agatha might find me there.

Instead, I turned on my heel and darted for the library. In all the time I'd spent there, no one else had ever entered, and I craved that quiet, that privacy.

Closing the door behind me, I retreated to the spot I'd claimed as my own—a particularly comfortable chair settled behind a thick bookcase, which shielded me from the door. I curled into the chair, bringing the letters to lay against my knees. I stared at them.

Ginny's kind words—her sweetness, her worry—blazed at me from the page. I attempted to focus on them, reminding myself that it did not matter what Clarissa said or thought or did. It was the same thing I'd tried again and again to believe in the last two years, but I'd never completely succeeded. When one had so little control of one's life, it was easy to feel helpless and hopeless.

Normally, whenever I crumbled under this grasping, deepening powerlessness, I knew how to counteract it. I went for a brisk walk or visited Ginny or made myself useful to Mother. But here, so far from all that was familiar to me, I had no defenses.

I turned on my side, the pages tumbling from my lap to the ground.

And I cried.

"Miss Albright?"

The voice came from far away, distant and muffled, as if in a dream. I lifted my head and tried to open my eyes, but they resisted, swollen and tender. Why should I bother?

I dropped my head again and drifted off to sleep once more.

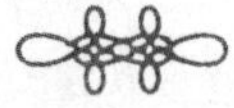

"Miss Albright!"

I jolted upright. The room was growing dark around me, and I squinted to make out my surroundings as my eyes adjusted to the setting sun. The library. I was in the library. But who was shouting?

The door to the library was thrown open, banging against the wall. The sudden sound was like fireworks in my brain, and I winced, holding my head. What on earth—

"Beatrice, so help me, if you don't answer me in the next—"

"I'm here," I called, my voice scratchy. "Just here."

Mr. Rawlings rounded the edge of the bookcase in the next moment. The light from the corridor outside the library shone on him dimly, and I stared. His eyes were fierce, angry, and there was a tension in his body I'd never seen before, not even after our incident in Vauxhall. Those dark, wavy locks, normally so rigidly arranged, had fallen into a disheveled mess, and his clothing was wet, his shoulders drenched.

"Where the *devil* have you been?" he asked, voice edged like a blade.

My mouth parted. "I—I've been right here," I stammered. "I fell asleep, and—"

"You fell asleep?" He stepped closer, that alarming glint in his eyes only sharpening.

I realized then that I might be a little disheveled myself. My hands straightened my skirts and hair even as my brain attempted to unravel the meaning behind his words.

"Yes," I said defensively. "I came in here to read and fell asleep. Is that such a crime?"

He ignored me, throwing a wild hand toward the door. "And you did not hear the dozens of calls for you? Blast it, the entire house has been looking for you for two hours!"

Two hours.

I gaped at him. "What do you mean?"

"I *mean*," he said, "that you disappeared and no one knew where you went. You weren't in your room, and you did not answer our calls. We searched the house, every outbuilding, and the entirety of the gardens, and I thought—" He stopped, breathing hard. "I thought something happened to you," he finished.

His words hung there in the silence, twisting and breaking the tension between us.

"I'm sorry," I whispered. "I didn't know. I was crying, and then I was asleep. I didn't—" I pressed a hand to my forehead, taking a shuddering breath. "I'm sorry."

He said nothing, only stood there, the rough scrape of his inhales and exhales filling the entire room. Then he turned and stalked out the door. "She's here, Mother," I heard him say. "Call off the search."

Mrs. Rawlings said something in return, though I could not make out the words. I crossed my arms on my knees and dropped my head on top of them, so many emotions rushing through me it was impossible to identify them all. Embarrassment, though, was quite prevalent. Had the entire household really been searching the four corners of the estate for *me*? How had I not heard them?

The library door closed again. Well, at least Mr. Rawlings had left me to wallow in peace.

But his footsteps came again, slower, until he stood before me. I blinked, staring at his muddy boots on the rug beside the letters I'd abandoned there.

"Why were you crying?"

His question was so unexpected, so quiet that I thought I'd heard him wrong at first. I looked up at him, my hands trembling in my lap. The fading daylight caught the distinct lines of his face, the habitual furrow between his brows. But there was also something new in his expression. Concern. It stood out in stark contrast—Alexander Rawlings was not a man accustomed to softness.

"I . . ." I gulped. "It was a moment of weakness. I was simply overwhelmed."

He inspected my face, perhaps searching for signs of my tears. He fished about in his pocket and pulled out his handkerchief, offering it to me.

"I'm not crying now," I pointed out, though something about his gesture reached inside and touched the coldest part of me, warming it slightly.

"Well, it is the only thing I know to do in such instances," he said gruffly, "so take the blasted thing, will you?"

I took it, settling it between my hands in my lap.

Mr. Rawlings noticed the letters at my feet and bent to pick them up, placing them on the table beside him. He paused, fingertips balanced on the top page, not looking at me.

"I've neglected you," he said. "Haven't I?"

"You are busy." My words came out uneven.

He gave a short, humorless laugh. "You needn't be polite. You can be honest."

"Very well, then, I shall be honest." I raised my chin. "I know hardly a soul in this house, in this *town*, and in the last four days, I've exchanged perhaps twenty words with you, the only person I do know. I'm quite certain you do not even like me, which would make sense, considering your mother despises me for reasons I cannot ascertain, no matter how I try. Not to mention that Ginny says there have been no developments in finding our attacker, which means I shall be trapped here for time indefinite, which led to me crying and falling asleep and you shouting at me. So yes, you've neglected me, though *abandoned* might be the better word, and I am just very, very tired."

I took a deep breath and locked my lips together. It had all spilled out of me in a rush. I could not take it back, and neither did I wish to.

Mr. Rawlings stared down at me, his face as confounded as I'd ever seen it. He gave one shake of his head, dragging a hand through his damp hair, his waistcoat and jacket pulled taut against his chest. Watching him sent a tingling swoop through my stomach, and I firmly scolded my body. There was to be none of that while I was angry with him.

"I am sorry," he finally said, dropping his hand again. "Truly. I thought it for the best if we did not act too familiar, considering what the household believes about your presence here. I distanced myself, believing it the professional, responsible thing to do. But I did not stop to think how it might make you feel."

He paused. "And I am sorry for shouting at you." His voice grew lower, rougher. "I was not myself."

I toyed with his handkerchief, the memory of him storming into the library searing through my thoughts. He certainly hadn't been himself. He'd been desperate, untethered, his eyes blazing with something wild and unspoken. Had it been fear . . . for me?

I gave a tight nod, accepting his apology. "Thank you."

He stood there, his tall frame silhouetted against the setting sun, and seemed not to know what to say next. I took pity on him.

"You truly had the entire household looking for me?" I asked.

Mr. Rawlings shifted his weight. "Yes."

"You thought . . ." I paused. "That *he'd* found me?"

His gaze flashed to mine. "Aye. For a time."

This sent another jolt through me. That Mr. Rawlings thought our attacker could find us here . . . It was easy to pretend I wasn't in constant danger here in the quiet, dull isolation of Briarstone. But it would take only one wrong move to bring devastation down upon us both.

I pressed my lips together. "I did not mean to worry you."

"Yes, well, suffice it to say," he said, "I shall be keeping a much closer eye on you."

Perhaps I ought to have felt irritation at that, that he felt the need to watch my every move. Instead, a strange pleasure bloomed inside me. "Likely for the best," I managed.

"To be safe."

We looked at each other in the hush of sunset, the room awash in gold and amber, and it felt as if we stood on the edge of a cliff.

Teetering. Uncertain.

But tempted.

He cleared his throat and glanced out the window at the darkening sky. "Come," he said. "It's nearly time for dinner."

"I'll be along soon." The edges of my mind were still frayed and unraveling. I needed a few minutes to compose myself.

Mr. Rawlings nodded, his eyes returning to rake over me, as if reassuring himself that I was there, that I was safe. Then he turned and strode from the room without a backward glance.

I fell back against my chair, breaths shallow. Something had shifted, that much was clear. In myself. In him.

Never had a man reacted to me, to my safety, in such a way. As if the thought of me in danger might be his undoing. I brought my knees to my chest, curled my arms around them, and sat in the quiet chill of the library. But for once, I did not feel the cold.

Chapter 14

Dinner that night was a remarkably different experience than the first week of my stay.

Mr. Rawlings made a point to involve me in the conversation, to ask after my opinions and to listen with care. I knew he only did it because he felt guilty, yet it still helped. My flagging spirits found a bit of hope.

Mrs. Rawlings looked on with clear disapproval. No doubt she wondered what had changed between Mr. Rawlings and me, and she certainly did not like it. I did my best to ignore her, focusing on the lifeline Mr. Rawlings was throwing to me.

I slept better that night than I had since I'd left London, and I woke feeling refreshed and more like myself. Though the actual circumstances of my situation hadn't changed—I was still trapped here at Briarstone—just knowing that Mr. Rawlings was on my side now made a world of difference. I could even face a morning with Mrs. Rawlings with a cheerful smile and an indomitable will.

I went down to the breakfast room, half expecting to see Mr. Rawlings there waiting for me. But the room was empty, as usual, and I tried to stifle my disappointment with a hot cup of tea.

After finishing, I stood and went out into the corridor. I had just started toward the morning room when his resonant voice spoke behind me.

"Miss Albright."

I spun, taken off guard. Mr. Rawlings stood in the doorway of his study, one hand resting against the frame. Morning light poured in behind him, casting his figure in sharp relief. Was it possible that he was taller than last I'd seen him?

"Yes?" I managed.

"I hoped to catch you before you went in," he said. "Do you have a moment?"

I hesitated, for reasons I wasn't quite sure of.

"Unless you are eager for another morning with my mother?" he suggested with a slight narrowing of his eyes that I was beginning to recognize as humor.

"Oh, always," I said. "But I shall delay that pleasure as a special favor to you."

I followed him inside his study. He went behind his desk and riffled through a stack of papers.

"Do you recall during our journey here," he said, "when you noted that odd coincidence in the paper?"

I squinted. "The robbery?"

"Aye," he said. "The one that took place after the ball hosted at Peak House."

"I recall," I said slowly.

"Well, I thought it odd as well." He straightened, a paper in his hands. "That morning at the inn, I posted a letter to Bow Street, asking for more information on the case."

I blinked. "You did?"

He waved me closer. I approached, hands clasped behind my back.

"I also asked one of the clerks to search amongst our case files and other newspapers for any similar occurrences," he said. "I just received his preliminary notes this morning."

He handed me the note, which was a list of six dates and locations. I examined it, not entirely certain what I was looking at. "What does it mean?"

"It means," he said, "that you were right to find the robbery at Peak House suspicious. It is far from being the only case of its kind in the last year. All these"—he pointed at the paper in my hand—"are robberies with remarkable similarities to the Peak House case. In each one, there was a large social gathering the night something was stolen, and generally, the items taken were small and easily hidden on a person. In fact, I am beginning to wonder if there are many *more* cases like this, but we are simply overlooking them because the robberies were reported much later, the owners not noticing their missing items right away."

"So you think they are all connected?" I asked. "That there is a thief among the *ton*?"

"I'm hesitant to draw any conclusions without more information," he said, "which is difficult to come by so far from London. I am waiting on more from my clerk, who is continuing to look back even further in our files. In the meantime, I've been attempting to track down any newspaper I can get my hands on, old and new, and look for the coincidences you noticed. I've found another two robberies that I think could be connected to these six."

Mr. Rawlings was sorting through his papers again, brow furrowed in concentration, and heaven help me if I did not find his competence and intelligence *wildly* attractive. Not to mention that he was speaking to me as if I were an equal to be consulted or that he had acted when he'd felt my suspicion had merit.

"So this is what you've been up to the last few days?" I tried to distract myself from being mesmerized by the capable way he sorted through papers.

"I am of no help in the murder case," he said. "I had to occupy myself or else go mad."

"I can relate," I said. "I'm half mad already."

He met my eyes, and for a moment, I felt that pull again, that unraveling thread between us.

I forced myself to look down at the paper in my hands, my cheeks heating. "I admit, I am quite fascinated by the idea of a thief moving amongst the ranks of London high Society. Heavens, I wonder if *I've* even met him at one point."

"Not terribly likely," he said. "These robberies were all within the last year."

And I had been in the country, hiding. He did not voice that, thankfully.

I held the list back out to him. "You'll tell me if you discover anything new?"

He took it. "Yes, I will."

My hands felt awkward now with nothing to hold. I dropped them to my sides. "What news from Mr. Drake? Did he have anything to report on the case?"

Mr. Rawlings frowned. "No. But then, I can hardly expect him to send anything of a sensitive nature in a letter. But he said nothing to make me assume they were close at all to catching the culprit."

I sighed. "I daresay it will be a while yet before we can return to London."

He paused in the midst of straightening his papers. "I am sorry. It is far more of an inconvenience to you. This has no doubt thrown off your . . . your plans for your time in London."

I stilled. Was he referencing the clear interest I'd shown in Mr. Drake? "Yes," I said hesitantly. "Ginny and I had a great many hopes."

He nodded, not looking at me. "Certainly, you can still pursue those when we return."

I swallowed hard. "Perhaps."

He finished tidying his desk and turned to me, his face clear of emotion. "I hope you'll not think me presumptuous," he said, "but I wished to ask you something."

I sent him a wary look, instantly on guard. "Yes?"

"My mother said that after you read your letter yesterday," he began, "you fled the room. And I have been wondering—" He paused and looked down to where he'd placed one hand on the desk, as if trying to find the right words. "In the library yesterday, I noticed that you received two letters, and I feared you'd received more bad news than just Mrs. Travers's update on the case."

I blinked. He was a man of great detail, so I wasn't surprised he'd notice my letters. But I *was* surprised that he seemed to care.

"You are irritatingly perceptive, Mr. Rawlings," I said. "How is a woman meant to keep any secrets around you? I shall lose my appeal without some sense of mystery."

"You are nothing *but* mystery, Miss Lacey." He said it mildly, though the corner of his mouth inched upward.

"Am I?" I managed, his words sparking a low flame beneath my ribs. "I shall take that as a compliment. I daresay it shall go straight to my head."

"You're avoiding the question." His tone had gone serious again.

I pursed my lips and went to the window, that familiar dread rising inside me yet again. "You're right, of course." I parted the curtain with one hand but didn't truly see anything beyond. "I received another letter, from a Miss Clarissa Haythorne."

"And she is?" His voice was close. He'd followed me to the window, coming to stand beside me.

I sighed. "The same woman who took my reputation from me."

He said nothing for a long moment. "What did she want?"

"To remind me to keep what I know about her to myself." I dropped the curtain. "Also to have *tea*, as one does with blackmailers."

Mr. Rawlings crossed his arms. "Avoiding that appointment is one benefit of no longer being in London."

I laughed, a quiet burst of unexpected mirth. "Very true, though I daresay I will have to deal with her eventually."

"Or your friends can," he said. "You are far from unprotected."

"A blessing I am well aware of." I cleared the lump forming in my throat. "That is something I did not have the last time."

Indeed, I'd had only Mother and Father, and I'd been far too frightened to tell either of them what had happened with Clarissa. Mother knew the rumors were false, of course, though I hadn't told her the truth about their source. If she'd known, she likely would have tried to denounce Clarissa without proof, making a mess of her own reputation and ruining any chance I might have had of reclaiming my place in Town. Father, on the other hand, had been indifference personified. It was baffling how little he'd been affected by my fall from grace.

But Mr. Rawlings's words—his insistence that I was not alone in this trial—gave me a new strength. He was right. I had friends now, and I was far from the naive, uncertain girl I'd been two years ago. If it came down to it, if it were me against Clarissa when I returned to London, this time I would not retreat. I would rally. I would fight.

Mr. Rawlings fixed his eyes on me. "Miss Lacey—"

Footsteps sounded outside the study, and I realized very quickly how precarious our situation was. Notwithstanding the open door, we were alone. What would a servant think, stumbling upon the master of the house with his mother's companion?

Mrs. Rawlings appeared in the doorway. She took in the two of us, standing beside the window, and she darkened immediately. "I have been waiting for you, Miss *Albright*."

"It is my fault, Mother," Mr. Rawlings said. "I waylaid her."

Mrs. Rawlings's mouth only tightened more. "Come along. We've work to do." She half turned, waiting at the door. I sighed and started toward her, but Mr. Rawlings caught my elbow.

"You needn't if you do not wish to," he said in a low voice. "We can find some reason."

I could not look away from where his hand held my arm—firmly, confidently, as he did everything. "It is fine," I managed. "I can survive a few hours."

He nodded and let me go. I strode across the room and past the watching Mrs. Rawlings, and even though I knew she would likely make my day even more miserable because of how she'd found us, I could not bring myself to care.

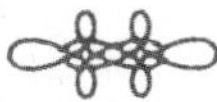

Later that afternoon, Mrs. Rawlings and I had just finished a very stilted, tense tea when a knock came at the parlor door, and a footman stepped inside. "Mrs. Millard to see you, ma'am."

Mrs. Rawlings looked up in surprise, and I saw immediately the gladness in her eyes. I felt a sudden jolt of . . . Was it *jealousy*? She certainly never looked at me like that. In fact, I'd never seen anything close to approval from her.

"Send her in," Mrs. Rawlings said.

Helen swept into the room, smiling brightly. "Good day, Aunt. Good day, Miss Albright."

I stood and curtsied, impossibly pleased to see her. "Mrs. Millard."

She went to kiss Mrs. Rawlings on the cheek, then sat beside her, directly across from me.

"Where is Elijah this afternoon?" Mrs. Rawlings asked.

"Playing with the vicar's sons," Helen replied, straightening her skirts. "We passed them on our walk here, and he begged so very much."

Mrs. Rawlings gave a slight frown, clearly missing the boy. "Will you take any tea?"

"No, thank you," Helen said. "I only mean to stay a minute."

"Oh?" Mrs. Rawlings stirred her tea. "Why is that?"

The parlor door opened again, and Mr. Rawlings stepped inside. He must have heard Helen's arrival. My stomach dipped as his eyes met mine, and he closed the door behind him.

"Helen," he said. "To what do we owe this pleasure?"

"I come begging for a fight, I'm afraid," she said quite cheerfully.

"What sort of fight?" Mr. Rawlings crossed his arms.

Helen turned to me, mischief in her smile. "I came to convince Miss Albright to attend the assembly with me tonight."

I perked up. "You did?"

"Oh yes," she said. "The more I thought on it, the sillier it seemed that you should not attend. It will be such a jolly time, and there are a great many people anxious to make your acquaintance."

"People?" Mr. Rawlings asked, perhaps a touch sharply. "What people?"

"Everyone in town knows Miss Albright is here," she said. "She is the object of much speculation."

Mr. Rawlings stiffened, and I knew why immediately. My presence was not supposed to be noticed.

"Why should that be?" Mrs. Rawlings demanded. "What business is it of anyone's?"

Helen laughed. "People make it their business, Aunt. You know that. And we can hardly blame them for talking. A beautiful and mysterious woman come to Briarstone House?"

I laughed. "Beautiful and mysterious? I'm afraid I shall quite disappoint."

"Nonsense." She waved me off. "You're a stunning creature, and far too lively to be cooped up in this house. No, you are coming with me, and that is that."

Mr. Rawlings's arms were still crossed, his expression stern. What was he thinking?

"You know they will only talk more if she does not come," Helen pointed out. "You might as well face it full-on. People will grow tired of the topic soon enough."

Mr. Rawlings considered that, his brow furrowed. Then he met my gaze, his dark eyes intent. "Do you wish to go, Miss Albright?" he asked.

My chin pulled back. "I . . . well . . . yes. I suppose I should like to." In truth, I would do nearly anything to escape this prison of a house for a few hours.

"Very well." He dropped his arms. "Helen, we will come fetch you at a quarter to eight o'clock."

"We will?" I stood, unable to stop the surge of excitement in my veins.

"You will?" Mrs. Rawlings's reaction was less than pleased.

Mr. Rawlings set his shoulders. "Yes, I daresay an hour or two won't do any harm."

"You are coming as well?" Helen sat straight. "What has brought this on, Alexander?"

He gazed at her, narrow-eyed. "Did you not wish me to come?"

"Of course I do," she said. "I simply thought I'd have to drag you behind the carriage."

"I'm only attempting to be neighborly," he said.

Helen arched a brow but turned to Mrs. Rawlings. "And what of you, Aunt? Will you join us as well?"

Mrs. Rawlings snorted in derision. "No, I am quite content without any neighborliness in my life. I shall remain at home and enjoy my hard-earned solitude."

Solitude indeed. I'd been here almost a week, yet I hadn't realized until now that Mrs. Rawlings hadn't had any visits aside from Helen. No friends, no neighbors, no acquaintances. It was little wonder Mr. Rawlings might have assumed no one but the household would notice my presence at Briarstone. But I was quite certain it was the household itself who had spread the news to the town.

I couldn't help but wonder what they'd said about me.

Helen stood, grinning widely. "Do dress your best, Miss Albright. I shall have a mountain of introductions."

With a curtsy and a farewell, she left the room.

The second the door closed behind Helen, Mrs. Rawlings turned to face her son. "Are you sure this is wise?" Her voice was harsh, critical. "Miss Lacey will not be staying here much longer. Why should we ingratiate her with the local society? Why would *you* wish to?"

He waved her off. "It is one night. They will see her and gossip and move on, just as Helen said. It is better for them to see there is nothing strange about Miss Lacey being here."

He spoke logically, as if he'd planned the entire affair himself. Yet I knew that logic was not why he'd agreed to take me. I was fairly certain he would be perfectly happy never leaving this house for our entire stay.

No, he'd agreed because *I'd* wanted to go.

Perhaps he still felt guilty for abandoning me. But I found I did not care. My excitement was already building. An assembly! With dancing and food and laughter and people. What a treat it would be after the last week of bitter boredom.

Still, I hesitated. "Will it be safe, do you think?"

He exhaled. "As safe as anywhere at the moment. If the murderer *has* tracked us down somehow, I doubt he will choose a ball as his moment to strike." He straightened the lapels of his jacket. "Besides, I will be keeping watch."

I nodded, a small smile blooming on my lips. "Thank you."

His eyes roamed across my face. "You're welcome."

Mrs. Rawlings stood abruptly. Her expression could have frozen over a lake in summer. "Well, I do not like it," she said. "But it appears I have no say about anything in my own house anymore."

She shot me one last icy glare before stalking from the room, her skirts rustling in her wake.

I sighed, folding my arms over my stomach. "I do not think she will ever like me."

"Possibly," Mr. Rawlings said without an ounce of sympathy.

I sent him a mock scowl. "You are not supposed to say that. You are supposed to assure me that she will soon realize what a delightful person I am, and then we shall be thick as thieves."

"That would be a lie," he said. "Should you like me to lie to you?"

"Every now and again," I replied. "For morale."

He chuckled, a low rumble in his chest that caught me off guard. When he smiled, it changed the structure of his face so drastically that he almost seemed a different man entirely. It lightened his darkness and smoothed his sharp edges.

And sent a soft flutter through me, as if I'd swallowed sunlight.

Had I truly thought he wasn't handsome? Because that seemed like foolish denial now.

"My mother will come around in her own time, and *only* her own time," he said. "There is little point in rushing it."

"Quite easy for you to say," I replied tartly. "You can hide away in your study."

"*Work* in my study," he amended.

I waved a hand. "One and the same."

He started for the door. "I'll have the maid sent up to assist you in dressing. The townsfolk would have far too much to talk about if you missed your buttons again."

"You are not so amusing as you think," I called after him, and I swore I saw him smile again as he disappeared down the corridor.

CHAPTER 15

Agatha came to help me dress a few hours later, and I could not keep a smile from my face. Not even Mrs. Rawlings's continued disapproval could dampen my spirits. I was venturing beyond Briarstone, even if just for a few hours, and I would spend the night *dancing*.

I was grateful now that Ginny had insisted I pack a ball gown. I would have had nothing appropriate otherwise, and even though I would likely never see these people again, I still wished to make a good impression. They hadn't heard the rumors about me, did not even know my real name. This was my chance to reinvent myself, just for an evening, and I planned to take full advantage of that.

Agatha spent extra time on my hair, braiding my golden curls into an elegant coiffure atop my head. When I stepped in front of the mirror to inspect myself, I smiled. I looked rather lovely, all things considered. My silk gown was the lightest of pinks and had the most beautiful embroidery at the hem and sleeves. My neckline skimmed a bit lower than my normal day dresses, and I thought the gown showed my figure rather well.

Leaving Agatha in my room, I made my way down the grand staircase. I was early, and Mr. Rawlings had yet to descend. I paced the entryway as I waited for him, practically bouncing on my toes, anticipation humming inside me.

Finally, I heard footsteps and turned to see Mr. Rawlings descending. He buttoned his jacket as he made his way down, focused intently on his task, so I had the chance to fully appreciate the effect of Mr. Alexander Rawlings dressed to impress.

And I was *very* impressed.

He wore a black jacket with a fawn waistcoat, both of which did remarkable favors for his towering physique. The raven waves of his hair were tamed ruthlessly by pomade, as though he had made a marked effort to appear as resolute and unaffected as ever. The stubble that often crept over his face this late in the day shadowed his neck and jaw, and he had a pair of gloves tucked under one arm. The bruises from our altercation in Vauxhall had faded over the last few days, though I could still see the slight discoloration around his right eye.

He looked so terribly dark and dashing that I suddenly wished to hide, certain I would not make it through the night with such a man at my side. My skin radiated a tingling energy, my stomach a hive of nerves.

He glanced up, then back down at his buttons. "There you are, Miss—"

He looked back to me, eyes intense and focused as they swept over me from head to foot. He slowed as he reached the bottom of the stairs, his hands seeming to forget altogether what they'd been doing.

A surge of pleasure rushed over me. How long had it been since I'd felt this way—since a man had looked at me with admiration rather than judgment?

"Good evening, Mr. Rawlings," I said, surprisingly calm. "You look very nice."

I smoothed the fabric at my stomach, drawing his attention to my narrow waist. Sometimes, a girl simply could not help herself, and I'd had so few moments of power in the short time I'd known Mr. Rawlings. I would enjoy this.

He cleared his throat, tearing his eyes from me and finishing the last button on his jacket. "Are you ready?"

"Do you not wish to return the compliment, sir?" I asked with an innocent expression. "How do I look?" I gave a small turn, bringing my shoulder to my chin and flashing him a mischievous smile.

"I think you know how you look," he said, his voice even and unbothered.

How well he masked himself. But I'd seen how he'd stared at me.

"Oh, I do," I said coyly. "I simply wish to hear it from you."

"That is very reaching." He made his way toward the front door, tugging on his gloves as he went. "Should not a compliment be offered freely and sincerely?"

I followed him. "I quite agree. I am simply providing you with such an opportunity."

"So generous."

"I do try."

His carriage waited at the foot of the steps as we went outside, the chill October air sweeping over us. Mr. Rawlings stopped next to the carriage and offered me his hand. I paused beside him but did not take it.

"You mustn't keep a lady waiting for reassurances about her appearance," I told him, attempting to keep my expression stern. "I shall begin to doubt myself entirely and wish to stay home."

"Do not tempt me," he replied. "You are far too sure of yourself as it is, and I have little desire to attend the assembly."

I simply waited, eyebrows raised in expectation.

He exhaled a long, frustrated breath. "Very well. You are as lovely as you are vexatious. How is that?"

I considered a moment, then smiled. "That will do."

I took his hand, and the moment his strong fingers closed about mine, my heartbeat sped into a rapid staccato, a shiver running through me. Heavens, we wore *gloves*, yet my body seemed to react as if I'd touched a pan too hot from the stove.

I dared not look at him as I stepped up into the carriage and took my seat. He followed me inside, closing the door behind him and sitting across from me. He seemed to fill the space that remained, making me all too aware of how alone we were—and how quickly my heart was beating.

"I wanted to discuss how you will comport yourself tonight," he said without preamble. He knocked on the roof, and the carriage started off.

"Oh? Do enlighten me."

"It would be best if you made very little impact on the gathering," he said. "Do not speak or laugh overmuch. Be polite but not memorable. Do whatever you can to keep from drawing undue attention to yourself."

"What a pleasure this will be," I said dryly. "Shall I fetch my copy of Fordyce's *Sermons* to read in the corner and reject anyone who asks me to dance?"

"Ideally, yes."

"I would not put too much hope in that." I settled my hands on either side of me and leaned forward, looking him in the eye with a daring grin. "I intend on fully enjoying myself tonight."

His lids lowered. "It is not too late to turn around."

"A bluff," I countered.

He raised his hand to the roof as if to signal the driver, his brows arched in a challenge.

"Oh, very well," I said with a wave. "I shall behave. You must know I have no desire to compromise our story."

He lowered his hand. "Good. Because it could happen in an instant, a slip of the tongue that reveals too much. If anyone asks you questions, use as much of your real life as you can. It will be easier to remember than anything fabricated."

I stored away his advice. No matter that I teased, I very much did not want to give away my true identity tonight, and not just because a murderer was after me. "I will take care. I promise."

He nodded. "I will remain close should anything happen. Simply look for me, and I will extricate you from any conversation you wish to avoid."

Why did my stomach flutter at his words? They weren't romantic in the least.

"And will you dance?" I couldn't resist asking. It was difficult to picture him on the dance floor, hopping through the steps of a spirited country reel.

Mr. Rawlings cast me a look of such disgusted disbelief that I laughed.

"I shall take that as a no," I said, still grinning. "You will disappoint so many young ladies."

"That is not my concern tonight," he replied. "Or any night."

Perhaps it was a very good thing he did not dance. For purely selfish reasons, I had no desire whatsoever to see another woman on his arm.

The ride to town took only a few minutes, and I spent most of it peering out the window, glad for any view that wasn't Briarstone. When we came to a stop in front of an unassuming townhome on the edge of the village, I straightened in surprise. "This is Helen's home?"

"Yes," he said, opening the door and stepping out.

I examined the house from inside the carriage, curiosity rising inside me. The flower boxes were neat and tidy, and the door had seen a fresh coat of paint, but all in all, it was much smaller and more modest than I would have imagined for the cousin of someone of Mr. Rawlings's status. Not that I cared one whit about Helen's wealth or position in Society, but I found that I had to constantly reevaluate everything I learned about Mr. Rawlings and his family.

Helen appeared at the front door, wearing a cream ball gown with a lace overlay. "A beautiful night, cousin," she greeted Mr. Rawlings. "Isn't it refreshing to step outside of Briarstone every now and again?"

"I am already regretting it," he said stoically.

She took his hand as he helped her inside. "Oh, Miss Albright, don't you look a picture," she exclaimed as she sat beside me. "Absolutely lovely. Isn't she lovely, Alexander?"

He followed Helen back inside. "I have already pronounced her precisely so, under much duress."

"I cannot guess at what you mean," I said with false sweetness.

Helen's eyes flicked between the two of us, too perceptive for my taste. No good would come of her thinking there was anything between Mr. Rawlings and me.

I turned to her, wanting to distract her. "Your dress is beautiful," I said. "I've never seen such exquisite lace."

She smiled, touching the lace. "My husband brought it home after his last voyage to India. He spoils me so."

"Where is he now?" I asked.

"Patrolling the Channel," she replied. "Thankfully, nowhere near as far as India."

We chatted easily as the carriage wound its way through town, discussing Elijah's latest antics and comparing which dances we hoped would be called tonight. Mr. Rawlings watched me with Helen, one hand propped against his chin, the lantern outside lighting his face. I tried very hard not to guess what he was thinking.

We arrived at the assembly rooms, which looked very cheery indeed, though much smaller than those I'd visited in London. The windows glowed from within, cozy and welcoming, and I could already hear the sounds of the orchestra tuning their instruments.

After Mr. Rawlings handed us down, Helen took my arm and pulled me ahead. "Come," she said, inclining her head. "Let us *really* talk now that Alexander cannot hear."

I laughed, even if my insides squirmed at her attention. "A kindness, I am sure. My endless talking is driving him quite mad."

"Mad indeed," she said under her breath.

"Pardon?"

"Nothing." She gave a bright smile. "How are you getting on with Aunt Ruth? She does like to make life difficult, does she not?"

I hardly knew what to say to that. I was supposed to be Mrs. Rawlings's companion; if I spoke ill of her, it would not reflect very well on my character. "She is coming around," I said carefully. "I think."

She laughed. "You are too kind, Miss Albright. I know precisely what my aunt is like, though I love her dearly."

"Please," I said, "call me Beatrice." It would make me feel just a little less deceitful if she called me by my real name.

"And you must call me Helen," she insisted.

I glanced behind me as we entered the front doors. Mr. Rawlings followed us, looking as if he were about to enter a boxing ring instead of a ballroom.

The large room bustled with ladies and gentlemen all in their finest—silks and white gloves and pearls and feathers aplenty. The energy of the space swept me away, reminding me in a small way of London. How I missed it. But this would have to do in the meantime.

"Should you like to make the rounds with us?" Helen asked Mr. Rawlings.

"Not in the least," he said and disappeared into the crowd.

I blinked after him. That had been rather abrupt.

"Come along, my dear Beatrice," Helen said, tugging on my arm. "You are about to become very popular."

She took me around the room, introducing me to all her friends and all her friends' friends, it seemed. If anyone was popular, it was most certainly Helen. But that was hardly surprising. She was as friendly and charming as anyone I'd ever met. I curtsied and smiled and made polite conversation, and though it was a bit overwhelming, I was heartily enjoying myself. No one here sent me dark, sidelong glances or whispered behind their fans as I passed. What a relief it was to hide behind my false name.

A tremor of unease passed through me. I hadn't moved so easily in Society since before I'd crossed Clarissa Haythorne. What would it be like when I finally returned to London? If her note was anything to judge by, she was not sitting idly by during my "illness." I had little doubt she was fanning the flames of those rumors anew, discrediting me and ruining me all over again.

I caught a glimpse or two of Mr. Rawlings as we made our way around the room, but he did not approach, only prowled about the edge of the dance floor like a brooding wolf. Had he noticed Helen's look of curiosity in the carriage and decided to again distance the two of us? If so, it was probably for the best. But it did nothing to help the jolt in my stomach every time our eyes met through the crowd.

"Mrs. Goodall, how are you, my dear?" Helen exclaimed, greeting a middle-aged woman.

"Oh, very well indeed." Mrs. Goodall smiled pleasantly at me. "And who is this?"

Helen laid one hand on my arm. "Mrs. Goodall, may I present Miss Beatrice Albright, lately of London."

"So pleased to meet you, Mrs. Goodall." I offered a curtsy. Heavens, my knees would give out if we kept this up much longer.

"Likewise!" Mrs. Goodall exchanged a knowing glance with Helen. "What good fortune. My son is just nearby." She waved to a young gentleman a few feet away. "Francis!"

The man came to join us, friendly looking, with bright-red hair and a broad smile—a smile that only broadened upon spotting me. I had a feeling he had already been watching us before his mother had called him over.

"Miss Albright, might I introduce my son, Francis Goodall?" Mrs. Goodall said with obvious pride.

"A pleasure." Mr. Goodall bowed.

I curtsied again, and at that moment, the orchestra began playing, and the first dance was called.

"Might I have the honor of this set, Miss Albright?" Mr. Goodall asked, holding out one hand.

"You may." I was certain my cheeks were pink from pleasure. I truly could not remember the last time someone had asked me to dance.

Mr. Goodall led me to the line of dancers, and I did not think I was mistaken that there were several—or possibly dozens—of eyes on me. I took a deep breath, trying to calm my nerves. It was just a dance.

"How are you finding Camberwell, Miss Albright?" Mr. Goodall asked as the dance began, and we moved toward one another.

"I haven't seen much of the town, I'm afraid." I took his hand, and he led me around our partners in a circle. "I'm kept quite busy at Briarstone."

I was trying to do just as Mr. Rawlings had instructed: keep to the truth as much as possible.

"You are Mrs. Rawlings's companion, is that right?" He sent me a curious glance.

"Yes," I said brightly. Wishing to avoid any further questions in that direction, I asked him, "Tell me about yourself, Mr. Goodall. Your mother seems lovely indeed. Do you have any other family?"

We continued our conversation through the entirety of a Scotch reel and then a quadrille. I was careful to always direct the topic back to him, smiling and giving him all my attention. That was my aim tonight: I would be pleasant and lively, but I would try my hardest not to be interesting.

When he led me back to Helen, she had another gentleman at her side, a Mr. Rogers, who seemed rather eager for an introduction and a dance. Again, I dodged questions and directed plenty at him in turn. But in between our exchanges, I allowed myself to get lost in the music, in the rhythm of the steps, and in the smiles of my partner. How wonderful this was, to clap and bounce and simply *enjoy* myself.

The next two hours were a delightful blur. Helen provided no shortage of partners, and at one point, there were at least three gentlemen waiting to meet me when I returned after a dance. I knew it was an anomaly—I was something bright and new in a small-town society—but dash it all if I didn't take an immense amount of pleasure from the apparent demand for my hand.

"I do love being right," Helen said with a grin after my sixth partner—or was it my seventh?—returned me to her side. "You have made quite the impression, my dear."

I waved her off. "It shall fade soon enough. But I cannot deny that I am having a wonderful time. The last few days have been so very—" I stopped myself just in time. I was about to say *trying*.

"So very what?" She took my arm and stepped closer so we would not be overheard.

"So very different from what I am accustomed to," I managed. "It has been an adjustment, that is all."

Helen nodded sympathetically. "I am sure."

She looked as if she might press me, so I cleared my throat. "I haven't seen Mr. Rawlings lately. He hasn't abandoned us, has he?"

"I would not be surprised if he has," she said, allowing me my retreat. "But no, he is still here somewhere, lurking about and doing his best to avoid the legions of women intent on becoming the new Mrs. Rawlings."

I could hardly blame them. He was ridiculously rich, broodingly handsome, and mysterious besides. Women were not born to withstand such a confluence of attractive attributes.

"Well, I think he's being rather silly," I said. "What harm could it do to dance a few sets? It's only polite."

"Oh, he is convinced it could do a great deal of harm," Helen replied. "He has no desire to form any more ties to this place than necessary."

I tipped my head. "Why is that? One would think he'd be eager to find a wife and secure an heir for Briarstone."

Helen shook her head. "One might think that," she said, "if one did not know Alexander. But Briarstone holds no happy memories for him. I am surprised he has stayed as long as he has."

"No happy memories?" A thought connected in my mind. "Is that why he and Mrs. Rawlings removed to Scotland?"

Helen suddenly straightened. "I am sorry," she said. "I think I've said too much."

"Oh," I said, taken aback. "I apologize. I did not mean to pry."

Her face softened. "I know. It is simply not my story to tell." She looked away, carefully shifting her expression back to neutral territory. "Look, here comes another hopeful for you," she said, nodding toward an approaching gentleman.

I'd barely caught my breath from the last dance. "Waylay him a moment for me?" I begged. "I only need a drink."

"I am sure he would be happy to fetch you one," she called after me as I started for the table of lemonade.

I slipped through the crowd, my steps quick, and was just nearing the table when a hand gripped my elbow.

"A word, Miss Albright." Mr. Rawlings's deep brogue sounded in my ear.

Chapter 16

I looked up at Mr. Rawlings, startled. How had he approached without my seeing him?

"Now?" I asked. "I was only fetching a drink, and then I'd hoped to dance a few more—"

"That is precisely what we must speak about." The muscles in his neck corded. "Come." He pulled me alongside him without another word.

My stomach twisted. Had he seen something? Were we in danger? Thankfully, everyone was in the midst of finding their partners and spots on the dance floor, and our sudden exit went relatively unnoticed. His grip on my elbow remained firm, commanding, and I dared not pull away.

He led me to a set of french doors that opened to a small garden, ill-tended but with a stone fountain gurgling in the center. A brisk breeze whisked over me, rustling my skirts and chilling the fevered heat of my skin, warm from my hours of dancing.

Nodding tightly at a pair of older gentlemen strolling near the fountain, Mr. Rawlings directed me toward a corner of the garden steeped in shadow—still public but allowing us as much privacy as could be expected at an event like this.

When he finally released my arm and turned to face me with a stony expression, I stared up at him with bated breath. What had made him hurry me out of the assembly?

"I thought," he said, his voice knife sharp, "that we'd decided you would *not* draw attention to yourself."

I stared, then blinked. "Pardon?"

"You are a witness to a crime, Miss Albright." A spark ignited in his eyes. "Must I remind you again what is at stake, what sort of danger you are in?"

I drew my shoulders back. "No, you do not," I said hotly. "I remember quite clearly."

He seemed not to hear me. "I am trying to keep you safe, a rather thankless task, I might add. It helps nothing when you flirt your way through the ballroom."

"I wasn't flirting!" I protested. "I was dancing."

"Whatever it was, you drew the eye of every gentleman in that room." His words were quick, clipped, angry. "That was precisely the sort of display I'd hoped to avoid."

"It wasn't a display," I snapped. "I was *enjoying* myself, though perhaps you simply do not recognize the feeling, having never experienced it yourself."

He ignored me yet again. "We mustn't depart too abruptly, or it will only raise suspicions. Go back inside and plead exhaustion to the next man who asks you to dance. Then, in a few minutes, I—"

"I will *not*." I stepped closer, my stubbornness snapping taut inside me. "For the first time in nearly a week, I haven't felt alone or frightened or looked down upon. Unless you have seen anything to indicate we are in any real danger, I refuse to believe it necessary to—"

"*I* will be the one to decide what is necessary." He leaned toward me, eyes glittering in the lantern light.

We stood toe-to-toe, locked in a glare that heated the air between us. I inspected every inch of his face, stern and unyielding. There was something else he wasn't telling me, something he did not want me to know. What else had he seen tonight as I'd danced with man after man? Could it be . . . ?

"You are jealous," I said in sudden realization.

His expression shifted infinitesimally, his head drawing back an inch.

"You do not truly believe I've risked our cover. You simply cannot stand to see me dancing with other men." My words ran away from me, and I could not rein them in.

"You are badly mistaken," he ground out.

His denial was so harsh it only served to confirm my suspicion. But Mr. Rawlings, jealous? I'd never before experienced such a thing, never imagined a man might have such feelings toward me. It was . . . rather thrilling.

I tried to ignore the surge of sparks in my veins. "If you wished to dance with me, perhaps you should have asked rather than watched from the corner and glowered at all those who *did*."

"I do not wish to dance with you," he said, the edges of his voice rough. "I detest dancing."

"Oh?" I moved even closer, our faces only inches away. "Shall we make a bargain?"

"You are in no position to negotiate, Miss Lacey."

"I rather think the opposite," I countered. "You can hardly drag me away kicking and screaming."

"You wouldn't—"

"I might."

He exhaled a rattled breath, and I thought, for the first time, that perhaps I really *was* driving this man mad.

"Unless . . ." I dangled the word in front of him, a tempting carrot.

"Unless what?" he asked.

"I will leave the assembly without a word of complaint," I said, "*if* you dance with me."

Oh, how I enjoyed the look of utter stupefaction that crossed his face.

"Why on earth would you—" he began.

"Because it would entertain me to no end," I said. "And because you should feel, for once, what it is like to have someone else holding the puppet strings of your life."

He stiffened. "I am not one to bow to pressure."

"Then it seems we are at an impasse. I shall let you know when I am ready to leave." I turned to go, but he grabbed my arm, pulling me back to face him. My breath left my body. My arm was trapped against his chest, his fingers wrapped tightly around my forearm.

"We are not finished," he growled.

We were nearly pressed together entirely. I could feel the heat of his body, the brush of his breath. I raised my chin, and my knees weakened. His dark eyes burned, fierce and fiery. He glared back at me, then—

His eyes dropped to my lips.

I froze.

An eternity passed in those two seconds. Eons and ages. The world was a blur around me, the night sky fading upward into oblivion.

Then he swallowed and tore his gaze away. He released me, stepping back.

My skin hummed where he'd touched me, blood pounding in my ears. I took a shuddering breath to fill my lungs with much-needed air.

He stood still, the silence between us thick and unwieldy. Then he brushed past me, striding toward the open doors.

I spun, staring at him. What had happened? What had *nearly* happened? I came to myself and hurried after him. "Where are you—"

"The next dance is starting soon," he said brusquely. "I do not wish to stay here a moment longer than necessary."

Was he serious? Was he truly going to dance with me just to force me to leave the assembly early? I'd extended that challenge without any real thought that he might agree.

He stopped at the open doors and held out his arm to me, not even looking back to see if I was coming. Oh, this man! The pure presumptuousness of him!

Biting my tongue, I took his arm, hating how firm it felt under my hand.

He led me inside just as the orchestra began to play again. We joined the line of dancers, those around us sneaking curious glances at Mr. Rawlings. He stood there without an ounce of expression, seemingly indifferent to the stares. Had he *never* danced at a local assembly before?

The dance began. I curtsied, and Mr. Rawlings bowed, his mouth set in a hard line. Then we stepped together, and he took my hand.

I'd already danced for hours tonight, with half a dozen other men, but the moment our hands met, it was clear that this would be *very* different.

He led me through the dance as he did everything in life, with a commanding assurance that he knew precisely what he was doing. Even if I hadn't already known the steps, I imagined he could have steered me through without incident. The crackle of energy that I'd felt out in the garden had followed us inside and now worked its way through every limb in my body. My heart was tapping out a stilted rhythm, my lungs hard-pressed to keep pace.

We parted, the movements of the dance taking us to different partners. The man now holding my hand smiled at me, and I managed a weak one in return. I was far too occupied in trying to control the chaotic pace of my breathing.

He returned me to my place in the line, and I forced myself to look up. Mr. Rawlings watched me with his lips set in a thin line, and there it was again. The burning in his eyes.

The ladies moved to circle their partners, and I followed, turning with the rhythm of the music, feeling his gaze scorching me at every angle. Then my hand was in his again, and despite the turmoil spinning inside me, it felt . . . steadying.

We were close enough to speak, but we did not, the music a faded strum. He turned me under one arm, his other hand skimming my waist, leaving tendrils of heat in its wake.

And I wondered if perhaps the reason Mr. Rawlings did not dance was because it made all his partners fall irrevocably in love with him.

We took each other's hands, our arms crossed behind our backs, and turned in time to the music. His eyes fixed on mine as if challenging me to look away. But why would I when I had never in my life—*never*—had a man look at me the way he was now? I forgot that we were in a public ballroom. I forgot that I was trying to convince everyone here that I was someone else entirely. No, I was single-minded, my senses fully and completely immersed in this moment. The melody of the violins carried through my mind, and a heady warmth filled my chest.

It ended too soon. Much too soon. I might've danced with him until the sun blazed over the horizon, but the music came to a stop after a long, legato note. The dissonant sounds of applause and voices rang out around me.

Mr. Rawlings had yet to look away from me, my hand still in his. We stood there a moment longer as the dancers moved around us. He opened his mouth as if to say something. Then he stepped back. Dropped his eyes and my hand.

He bowed, short and sharp. I was too stunned to manage more than a wobbly half curtsy. A girl simply did not recover quickly from a dance like that. It had tugged me every which way, intoxicating and exhilarating, and had left me *aching* for more.

He escorted me to where Helen stood on the edge of the dance floor, holding a glass of lemonade and watching us with her mouth parted.

"Gather your things," he said to her. "We're leaving."

He turned on the spot and strode away. He certainly wasn't dallying about.

Helen faced me, expression concerned. "Are you well, Miss Albright?"

"Yes," I said briskly. "Perfectly well."

She did not seem to believe me. "You are sure? I was watching the two of you dance, and it looked rather . . . tense."

That was certainly one word for it.

It was then I noticed the whispers, the curious glances sent toward me—and toward Mr. Rawlings as he started for the front doors. How many people had been watching us like Helen had? My plan to go relatively unnoticed was certainly dashed away.

But it was hardly my fault that Alexander had danced the way he had.

I took Helen's arm and moved her with me away from the dance floor, trying my best to hide from those searching gazes.

"We simply had a disagreement," I said. "It is nothing, really."

Helen nodded, still appearing doubtful.

"I had a wonderful time," I assured her. "Truly, I did. You've been so kind. I never thought to expect it."

She patted me on the hand. "It is not difficult to be kind, Beatrice."

I gave a short laugh under my breath. "You might be surprised."

She said nothing to that, though a shadow crossed her face.

We fetched our shawls and reticules, then made our way out to where Mr. Rawlings stood waiting beside the carriage. He did not meet my eyes as he helped me inside, and so I returned the favor by ignoring him entirely after he seated himself across from us.

Helen and I exchanged a few remarks about the evening on the ride to her home, but the tension was so thick I think we were all quite relieved when we arrived. Mr. Rawlings again alighted to help her down.

Helen paused before exiting, looking over at me. "I shall call on you soon, Beatrice," she said meaningfully. "To see how you are getting on." She spoke louder than necessary, as if wanting Mr. Rawlings to know she would be checking in on my well-being.

I smiled, touched that she would be so thoughtful. "Thank you, Helen. I should like that very much."

Mr. Rawlings helped her down, and she leaned close to him and whispered something. He stood frozen a long moment, then seemed to come to himself. He said a few words in return, all too low for me to hear. Helen looked back at me, her lips curving up on one side.

"I think you might," she said to him, then patted him on the shoulder and went inside her house.

Mr. Rawlings stared after her. Then his shoulders tightened, and he climbed back inside the carriage, which seemed to have suddenly grown much smaller without Helen's presence.

He seemed preoccupied with his gloves as we started off again.

I cleared my throat. "What did she say?" I asked carefully.

He did not meet my gaze. "Nothing of import."

He clearly did not wish to speak. Very well, I could keep quiet for once. Especially because I was afraid of what might escape me if we *did* tumble into a conversation after such a night. My tongue had never been particularly obedient, and I was already loose-willed and at odds with myself.

The rest of our journey was silent. I kept my knees carefully turned away from him so they would not brush his. The last thing I needed was more physical reactions proving my ridiculous attraction.

The carriage had not even come to a complete stop outside Briarstone when Mr. Rawlings had the door open. He stepped down on the pebbled drive and turned to offer his hand to me.

"You needn't be polite," I said, though I took it and stepped down. "I know you are angry with me."

"Angry?" he repeated as though he'd never heard the word before.

"For making you dance." I pulled my shawl closer about my shoulders, the breeze twisting my skirts.

He finally looked at me for the first time since we'd left the assembly. "I'm not angry."

"Oh." I'd truly expected something of a lecture upon arriving. Perhaps he felt bad for how he'd treated me in the garden.

"I am, however, thoroughly irritated at your muleheaded inability to ever listen to me."

Or perhaps not.

"I'd rather be a mule than a sheep," I said.

"Unfortunately." He started for the front door. "A sheep would be much easier to protect."

I cast my eyes to the cloudy night sky as I went after him.

Inside, only a few candles were burning, draping the front hall in shadows and silence. We made our way up the staircase, quiet again falling between us. It was just the two of us now, alone in an upper corridor of his house, and that fact made me wary, on edge.

He did not seem to feel the same. He strode directly past my door and stopped before his own, his gloves and hat clutched in one hand.

"Good night, Miss Albright," he said, then went inside. The door closed behind him with a loud click.

"Good night," I said pointlessly to the empty space.

I stood there in the silence, wrestling with my riotous emotions. Why should I feel disappointed? Why should I feel as if there was something left unsaid? Undone?

"Preposterous," I muttered under my breath as I opened my door.

I'd already told Agatha she need not wait up for me. I could manage myself well enough for one night—and undressing was certainly less arduous than dressing. I strode to my dressing table in the corner and dropped my reticule there, draping my shawl over the back of the chair. I sat and began removing my hairpins, my tightly coiled locks falling against my neck and shoulders.

I had just removed the last pin when I noticed it. My hairbrush. Hadn't Agatha set it on the left side of the dressing table earlier? I remembered because I'd remarked on the fact that she was left-handed. But now my brush was nearer the middle of the table.

I was being silly. Agatha had obviously just moved it again, tidying up.

I sighed, turning in my chair to regard my room. How much longer would I be trapped here? Tonight's escape into town had only made Briarstone feel more like a prison, especially not knowing when I might be released.

My thoughts began to creep back to that shadow-swept garden outside the assembly rooms, back to the moment when Mr. Rawlings had slid his gaze down to my lips. He had, hadn't he? Or had I only seen what I wanted to see?

That was a sobering thought. Because it meant that I had *wanted* Mr. Rawlings to kiss me.

But that couldn't happen. I was nothing more to him than a duty, a responsibility. Kissing him would help nothing, no matter how easily my body remembered the touch of his hands.

Drat it all. I needed a distraction, or my thoughts would never let me be.

Perhaps rereading Ginny's letter yet again would calm my nerves. I opened the drawer of my dressing table. Then I paused.

My stomach turned cold.

When Agatha had come to help me dress earlier, I'd placed Ginny's letter here in the drawer, with Clarissa Haythorne's note folded and pushed to the back so I did not have to see it.

Both letters were still in the drawer. Now, however, Clarissa's was perched on top, unfolded, her snide words peeking out at me.

And I knew immediately.

Someone had been in my room.

CHAPTER 17

Within ten seconds, I was out of my room and rushing down the corridor. I caught myself against Mr. Rawlings's doorframe and raised a hand to knock. Just in time, I remembered that his mother's room was right beside his, so instead of pounding frantically on the door, I managed a short series of quick knocks.

He answered immediately, perhaps having heard my approaching footsteps. He was still dressed, thankfully, though his cravat had been loosened. His brow furrowed. "Miss Lacey?"

My breaths were coming too quickly. "Someone has been inside my room."

He paused to take that in, apparently baffled about why that should cause me concern. "I do employ several maids."

"No," I said. "Someone was reading my letters."

His expression changed in an instant, hard and serious. "Show me."

I led him to my dressing table, quickly explaining how I'd left everything before we'd departed for the ball earlier.

"But the letter is unfolded now," I said. "Someone was reading it."

He stared down at the open drawer, hand grasping the back of the chair. He was silent for several seconds. "Are you certain?"

He did not say it as if he doubted me. Instead, he asked with complete sincerity, simply wanting my absolute assurance that what I'd said was correct.

"Yes," I replied. "I am certain."

The line of his mouth was set like iron. "It could be nothing," he managed. "It could be that a maid was simply cleaning too enthusiastically."

"Do you really believe that?" I folded my arms over my stomach, trying to ward off the sudden chill that had sunk into my bones.

"No," he admitted. "No, I think it is very possible that someone in this house wanted information about you."

My hands went numb, and I balled them into fists. "Why?"

He shook his head. "Perhaps our cover is not as convincing as we thought."

I straightened, a thought occurring to me. "Or perhaps someone is eager to be rid of me."

Mr. Rawlings looked at me doubtfully. "You mean my mother?"

"She has made no secret of her dislike for me."

"But she already knows who you are," he countered. "Why would she have any need to poke about your room? She would never stoop to that."

He had a point about her already knowing who I was. But unlike him, I had no difficulty picturing her snooping about my room. Still, if it *wasn't* her . . .

"My real name is on these letters," I said.

"I know," he replied grimly.

"So whoever read these knows it now."

"Yes."

I suddenly felt dizzy. All of tonight's events came together in a whirlwind, and I sat heavily in the chair, bracing one hand on the dressing table.

"Miss Lacey?" He crouched beside me, gasping my elbow as if to steady me.

"I thought—" I gulped. "I thought I was safe here."

"You *are* safe here." His voice was firm, fierce. "I will question the staff tomorrow and discover who was in here."

"No one will be likely to confess to that." I took a deep breath and looked at him. "You don't think he's found us, do you? That perhaps he employed someone to search my room?"

"No," he said firmly. "That wouldn't make any sense. If he already knew where you were, why would he need to? No, he would—" But he stopped, perhaps realizing that voicing what a murderer would do to me might be a terrible idea.

"He would kill me without a second thought." A tremor laced my words.

It was too real. It was too *possible*, that the man had somehow tracked us here. I hadn't felt this fear since we'd left London, and it twisted and churned inside me, climbing my throat to choke me.

He said nothing, only gazed at me with some unknown emotion. Our faces were near, me sitting while he crouched beside me. His hand still grasped my elbow, and it felt like the only thing that kept me from flying apart.

"I would *never* let that happen," he said in a low voice, his Highland brogue fierce. "You are under my protection, Beatrice Lacey, and I would die before I let that man touch you."

I looked him in the eyes, so firm and unyielding, and felt the truth of his words. I knew he meant them. My galloping heart began to calm, and I swallowed hard. "I've never . . . I've never had this," I said softly.

His head inclined, brow dropping. "Had what?"

"A man to protect me," I whispered.

A pause. "What of your father?"

I shook my head. "He cannot be bothered by me enough to care." It was so terribly sad as to be true. Ever since I'd been so disappointedly born a girl, Father had rarely concerned himself with me, instead turning my raising entirely over to my mother and governess. And two years ago, when he'd heard of Clarissa's rumors, he'd written it off as "women's business" and refused to involve himself. Defending me from such an attack against my character had never even occurred to him. Though

I'd learned long ago to guard my heart from him, sometimes the hurt still broke through, especially when I compared him to Ginny's late father, a man who had treated his daughter as his greatest treasure.

I'd dreamed over the years of how it might feel for a man to see me as the center of everything. Of *his* everything. It had been hard to imagine before.

It was not so difficult now.

Mr. Rawlings's hand tightened on my elbow. "Then he is a common fool."

I could not help a smile at the vehemence in his words. But then we stayed there, gazing at each other, and my smile faded. An unfamiliar current hummed between us, quiet but unmistakable. This was not the fiery tension of our standoff in the assembly room gardens, nor the playful teasing before the ball. No, this was so much more.

My hand moved of its own accord, reaching up to graze the line of his jaw with my thumb. His skin was rough, needing a shave, but it did nothing to quell the molten gold simmering in my chest. His dark eyes held to mine, and he stayed perfectly still, barely breathing, as if I were a wild animal that he might frighten off. But I wasn't frightened by him. Not in the least.

A creak came from somewhere in the house, the sound of the roof settling. But it was enough to jar us both from our trance. My hand dropped. Mr. Rawlings stood abruptly and backed away a few steps.

"I'll stand guard outside your door tonight," he said.

"Oh." I came to my feet, my face flushed. "You needn't do that."

"I wasn't asking." His tone left no room for argument.

Some part of me thought to protest, insist that I would be fine and that he should get some sleep. But I knew he would never listen, and I knew that I would sleep not a wink if he weren't just outside my door.

"Thank you." My voice was the barest brush of a whisper.

He nodded, took one hesitant step forward. Then he seemed to come to himself. He strode to the wooden chair placed before the hearth and carried it out of my room.

I followed him to the door as he set the chair across the corridor. No doubt he would look strange to any servants who happened to pass, but I could not bring myself to care very much.

"I'll stay until dawn," he promised, one hand braced on the back of the chair.

I bit my lip, wishing I could tell him exactly what it meant to me that he would do this. But too much had already passed between us tonight. I only nodded, my throat thick.

"Good night, Miss Lacey," he said quietly.

"Good night, Alexander," I said.

I closed the door as he moved to sit on the chair. He would *not* be comfortable. I smiled softly as I remembered this same situation that first night at the inn, when he'd stayed awake to keep watch over me. I'd wished him discomfort then, strangers as we were.

But I already knew I would feel the same as I had that night. Safe. Sheltered. Protected.

I changed and climbed into bed. I blew out my candle and waited for the darkness to settle, for the fear to come. But it never arrived, not with Alexander keeping watch. I soon fell deeply asleep.

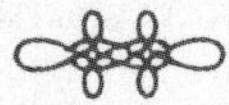

Morning came too quickly, weak daylight bleeding through the sides of my curtains. Slipping into my dressing gown, I knotted the ties and crept to my door, peeking out into the corridor. Empty. Alexander was gone, the chair as well. But I knew he'd stayed the whole night. He was a man of his word, and I trusted his word beyond anything.

I rang for Agatha to help me dress, and after she arrived, I watched her in the mirror, humming a folk song while she worked on my hair. There was nothing suspicious in her bearing. Was it at all possible that she had been the one to read my letters?

"Did you enjoy the assembly last night, miss?" she asked, brushing out my hair.

Her question startled me from my thoughts, and I coughed slightly. "Yes, I did. I love to dance."

At least, I *had*. Now that I knew what dancing with Alexander was like, I did not think I could ever fully enjoy dancing with anyone else. There was simply no comparison.

"Were all the gentlemen so very taken with you?" She smiled knowingly.

I forced a smile in return. "I was pleased with the attentions of a few." Or one, at least.

She returned to her work, and I studied her again. "Agatha," I asked carefully, "did you tidy my dressing table last night? My drawers, perhaps?"

She did not even look up, focused on her task. "No, miss. I am sorry. Did you wish me to?"

"No," I said. "No, thank you."

She finished a few minutes later and left. It was after eight o'clock now, and I had no reason to linger in my room. But I fussed with the covers on my bed, dabbed on some perfume and a touch of rouge, and straightened the dresses hanging in my wardrobe.

I knew what I was doing, of course. But I couldn't avoid Alexander forever.

Emotions warred within me, tugging every which way, fears and doubts and desperately dreamed dreams. Things had drastically shifted between us last night. I'd accused him of being jealous, for heaven's sake. And even if I were right, and he had been jealous . . . where did that leave us? I knew I had feelings for him—feelings that seemed to grow by the hour—but how did he regard me?

His words came back to me, from the moment I'd been trapped in my terror. *You are under my protection, Beatrice Lacey*, he'd said. There'd been a delicious possessiveness to his words that I hadn't fully appreciated last night but that now sent a shiver across my skin.

I stood on a precipice, of that I was quite certain. It would take only one more small push, the tiniest of breaths, to tip me over. And

I knew that if I fell in love with Alexander Rawlings, I would never recover. My life would never be the same.

I would never be the same.

Even if somehow we did both feel the same way, there was so much to hold us back. His mother. His career at Bow Street. My reputation, even if he seemed to accept me in spite of it. No, it was better not to even think of it at this point. There was still a murderer on our trail, and I could be here at Briarstone for some time yet. I needed to be careful not to complicate things any further, put away my feelings.

I nodded, resolute, and started for my door.

That resolution went sailing out the window as I started descending the stairs and spotted Alexander pacing the entryway. He was a sight to behold, his serious, dark features a sharp contrast with the bright sunlight surrounding him. He had shaven and dressed in fresh clothes, and though he must have been exhausted from lack of sleep, he looked none the worse for wear. Indeed, one might argue—myself, to be precise—that he had never looked better.

He glanced up the moment he heard my footsteps, his eyes piercing, penetrating.

Blast and bother. This was going to be impossible.

"Miss Albright," he said, his deep voice carrying up the stairs. "I need to speak with you."

"Always to the point," I said, one hand gliding along the rail as I made my way down. "Not so much as a 'good morning' or a 'how did you sleep?'"

Alexander remained unruffled. "How *did* you sleep?"

Everything in me softened. "I slept well," I said quietly. "Thank you."

He nodded. "Good."

"What did you need to speak to me about?"

He shot a look around, and even though we were alone in the entryway, he lowered his voice. "Let us speak in my study."

I followed him down the corridor. He opened the study door and ushered me inside, his fingers grazing the small of my back. Fire leaped through me, and I scolded myself very firmly.

He closed the door again, which I noted distinctly. Last time we'd spoken in here, he'd left it wide open.

Alexander turned to face me, his expression entirely serious. "We need to leave Briarstone."

I stared at him. "Leave?" I repeated. "Why?"

"I was planning to question the staff today," he said. "About your letter. But I had a great deal of time to think last night, and I realized that that course of action would not help us. In fact, it would likely only draw attention to our charade and make it more obvious we were hiding something."

"But why leave?" I wasn't sure why I was questioning him—I'd wanted to leave almost from the moment I'd arrived. But this was so sudden.

"If the person who read your letter—and now consequently knows your name—has any nefarious intent, we cannot risk staying here. We need to get ahead of whatever danger might be coming our way."

I swallowed hard. "You're right. But where would we go?"

He pressed his lips together grimly. "I do not know yet. But we need to leave as soon as possible."

I nodded. "I agree."

Alexander inspected me skeptically. "Why are you being so amenable? You generally fight me much more."

"Only when I disagree," I replied. "Besides, I find I am in your debt this morning." He was the only reason I hadn't spent the entire night clutching my pillow in fear.

He shook his head. "You owe me nothing."

I ignored that. "Your mother will not like us leaving," I warned. "Especially together."

"That hardly signifies," he said. "Her feelings are irrelevant in this decision."

"You should certainly word it precisely like that when you tell her," I said in an attempt at humor.

His mouth twitched up into a half smile—a rather attractive half smile—but it faded quickly. "Are you sure you are in agreement with this?" he asked quietly. "I cannot say where we will go. Your reputation would be in much more danger than here, where we have my mother as a chaperone."

I bit my lip. "Better to have my reputation in danger than my life."

He nodded. "Let us tell my mother, then."

I followed him to the morning room, where Mrs. Rawlings sat at her writing desk. She barely glanced up as we entered, distracted, but when she saw the two of us, she straightened and set down her pen.

"What is this?" she asked bluntly. Like mother, like son.

Alexander once again closed the door behind us. He shot me a wary glance as he faced his mother. "We are leaving," he said. "As soon as possible."

Mrs. Rawlings blanched. "Leaving? Why?"

Alexander stepped closer, hands clasped behind his back, his face set in determination. "We discovered that someone searched Miss Lacey's room last night, though we haven't any idea who they are or what their motive may be. We think it best to leave now before anything can come of it."

We.

"You cannot leave," Mrs. Rawlings exclaimed.

Alexander shook his head. "We do not have much choice in the matter. This is the best decision for everyone, to keep Miss Lacey and everyone in this household safe."

Mrs. Rawlings sent me an icy look, and it nearly froze my bones. Did she blame me for taking her son away from her so soon?

"What if," she said haughtily, "I can provide you with a very good reason why you should not leave?"

My eyes narrowed on her. "What do you mean?"

"Miss *Lacey*," she said tartly, "is not in any danger." She stood, chin held high. "It was I who searched her room."

"You?" Alexander was stunned into stillness.

Even though I'd mentioned my doubts about Mrs. Rawlings last night, I was still caught off guard. I gaped at her.

"Yes," she said. "Though I admit I am not so practiced in subterfuge. You arrived home much sooner than I expected and nearly caught me."

"Why?" I managed, perplexed. "What on earth were you looking for?"

"Evidence," she said. "To prove my suspicions."

"Suspicions of what?" Alexander moved a step closer, his voice dangerous.

Mrs. Rawlings did not answer him but instead went to the door that led to the parlor. She opened it a few inches. "Stroud? Come in here, please."

Stroud?

"When did Stroud return?" Alexander's shoulders were tense, his expression rigid. This was precisely the type of situation he hated—a situation quickly spinning out of his control.

I was not enjoying it very much either. My stomach was a mass of nerves, shooting through every inch of my body. What was Mrs. Rawlings about?

"He arrived last night," Mrs. Rawlings said coolly as Stroud appeared in the doorway, his expression rather stormy. "After you left for the assembly."

"What has this to do with anything?" Alexander asked. "This is a confidential matter, Mother. We should not discuss this in front of—"

"Stroud knows everything," she interrupted.

I blinked. "Everything?" I asked in disbelief.

Her eyes turned to me again, dark and calculating. "Yes, Miss Lacey, everything. Including the real reason you are here."

Chapter 18

"What do you mean, the 'real reason'?" I took a step forward, completely baffled and truly a bit irritated. "You *know* the real reason, Mrs. Rawlings."

"I know the reason you gave me," she said, voice harsh. "But I am not one to believe what I am told without doing my own research."

"What on earth are you talking about?" Alexander demanded, bracing his hands on the back of an armchair. "We told you the truth, Mother."

"Perhaps *you* did." Mrs. Rawlings sounded rather smug now. "But *she* did *not*."

"You are going to have to explain better than that." Alexander was practically growling, frustration biting in his tone.

"Very well," she said. "My suspicions began when Stroud told me what he saw during your arrival here."

I stiffened, dread pooling in my chest. "My buttons."

"Quite," she said. "Just the first warning sign. Then that first night, I saw you going to my son's bedroom door. He turned you away, as was proper, but you cannot deny that it happened."

It was all so ridiculous I could hardly draw a breath, let alone mount a defense.

"The next day, you forced him to take you out to the water garden, a secluded, sheltered place, where you might have attempted any number of tawdry things." She was warming to her speech, no doubt long planned and long practiced. "You have sought every chance possible to be alone with him, in the library the day you conveniently 'disappeared' and yesterday in his study and last night at the assembly." She pointed a finger at me. "You have only been ungrateful and insolent to me and to him. You are a scheming, fortune-hunting trollop, and you have done everything in your power to entrap my son into marriage."

The silence that fell upon the room was stifling. My heart beat too quickly, and I feared it would give out entirely. Entrap him into *marriage*?

"Mother, you have never been more wrong in your life." Alexander could barely speak for how tight his jaw was. "Miss Lacey has been nothing but proper in all her interactions with me. Why would you slander her so?"

"Ask her, why don't you?" Mrs. Rawlings replied. "Ask her what she is hiding from you, why she would stoop so low to capture a husband."

A thread of shadowed unease began to uncurl inside me. What did she mean, 'hiding'? She couldn't possibly know about . . .

"You can ask me anything," I managed, trying to keep my voice even. "I will answer."

"Very well." Mrs. Rawlings's eyes glinted. "Stroud, if you will."

The butler stepped forward, all cool composure amid this room of hot tempers. "After Mrs. Rawlings and I discussed our suspicions that first night," he said, addressing Alexander, not me, "I immediately set out for London."

"You lied," Alexander said, anger simmering under the even tone of his voice. "You said you were visiting your sister in Bath."

"Yes, I lied," Stroud said without remorse. "But for a very good reason. When I arrived in London, I set out investigating. Mrs. Rawlings had informed me of Miss Lacey's real name, and I was determined to know the truth of her."

Oh no. Heavens, no.

"The things I was told about this woman," Stroud said, voice thin, "the things I learned, would curdle your blood, sir. And you have a right to know them. She is every inch the sort of woman Mrs. Rawlings accuses her of being."

I could not breathe. How had it happened? How was it possible that the rumors had followed me *here*, where I was no one? Where I was hurting no one? Mrs. Rawlings glared at me, self-assured and self-righteous. Stroud kept his nose in the air, disdainful as he looked down on me.

"You know *nothing*," Alexander spat out.

My head jolted to my right. Alexander took two steps forward, placing himself in the middle of the room, directly between his mother and me.

"You know nothing about Miss Lacey or what she has suffered," he declared. "You know nothing about the sort of woman she is."

Mrs. Rawlings's expression only grew harder. "Ask her then, Alexander. Ask her about the rumors that still circulate about her, even years after her disgrace."

"I do not need to," he said tightly. "I've already heard them, before we ever left London."

Mrs. Rawlings stilled. "What?"

"Everything you seek to shock me with, I heard myself," he said. "And I asked Miss Lacey about them our first day at Briarstone." He turned to me, face lined with determination.

I steadied myself. He was giving me this chance to defend myself. I would not go to pieces.

"Everything you've heard about me is a lie," I said, my voice surprisingly steady. But then, hadn't I been practicing this very defense in my head for the last two years, wishing so desperately that I could shout it out to all of England? "The rumors were a creation of a woman with a vile mind and a vicious character. She wished to ruin my reputation because I knew a secret of hers, one that could have ruined her in return."

Mrs. Rawlings only shook her head, and I was quite certain she wasn't even listening. "Why should I believe you? Everything I've learned about you only confirms my first suspicion."

"Let me address your concerns, then," I said. "Starting with my buttons: My buttons were undone simply because I lacked a lady's maid, and I could not reach them. I forgot until Stroud helped me out of my pelisse upon our arrival, and I even expressed my embarrassment at forgetting to your son, which Mr. Rawlings can confirm. But nothing untoward happened."

I spoke briskly, matter-of-factly. I had to keep my simmering anger at bay, else risk losing my head altogether. Mrs. Rawlings watched me, her mouth pressed into a slit.

"That night, I did knock at Mr. Rawlings's door," I said. "But not to proposition him, as you so blatantly suggested. You see, your son was injured in the attack at Vauxhall, cut by a knife on his arm. I helped him bandage and care for the wound on our journey here, and that night, I was only checking that he did not need further assistance."

Mrs. Rawlings's eyes darted to Alexander. "Is that true?"

"Of course it is," he said, his posture rigid.

"Why would you not tell me?" she snapped.

"Because you would once again demand that I leave Bow Street," he said without an ounce of expression to his face. "But the fact is that Miss Lacey saved my life that night. You should be thanking her, not condemning her."

Mrs. Rawlings's hands formed into fists. She said nothing. I did not imagine a thank-you was immediately forthcoming.

"Your third complaint," I continued on, "has more to do with you than Mr. Rawlings. Yes, I coerced him into taking me to the water garden, but only to avoid spending any more time in *your* company."

Mrs. Rawlings turned away, as if that might shield her from the repercussions of her attacks.

"Both of the other instances you mentioned," I said, "the library and the study, were entirely innocent and unplanned. I never had aims upon marrying your son and certainly had no such aspirations in coming here. My situation is exactly as we told you when we arrived."

Silence fell again, broken only by the crackling of the fire. My words had spilled from me faster and faster until I had only the barest control over the tremors in my voice. It was more than anger. It was hurt, frustration, hopelessness. Would I never be free of these rumors? Would they always haunt me like a vengeful spirit?

"Stroud, please leave," Alexander said suddenly. "I will have words with you later."

Stroud said nothing as he slipped out the door, but I thought, perhaps, I saw some guilt in his demeanor. It did not make me feel any better.

"Are you satisfied?" Alexander asked in a low, dangerous voice. "Have you any other qualms about Miss Lacey?"

Mrs. Rawlings squared her shoulders as she faced us again. "You needn't sound so high-handed, Alexander," she hissed. "Can you really blame me for my suspicions with circumstances as they were?"

"Yes," he said. "If you had but deigned to ask Miss Lacey or me, we might have avoided this altogether. She did not deserve any of your accusations, nor did she deserve to again face the pain of her past." He exhaled. "An apology is in order."

"An apology?" Her eyes flashed. "You must be joking. I have opened my home to a stranger and consented to provide her with a lie to keep her safe. Just because I had my doubts as to her intentions—"

"Doubts?" I repeated in disbelief. "Do not paint this so prettily, Mrs. Rawlings. You have assaulted my character and insulted my integrity." I dropped my hands to my sides and took a deep breath. "I neither want nor need an apology from you. Good day." I spun on my heel and left the room.

As I went, I heard Alexander's raised voice and Mrs. Rawlings's defensive tones, and I could not stand it. I ran, heading straight for the back door overlooking the lake. It was drizzling outside, the clouds dark and heavy, but I did not stop. My slippers were soaked through in seconds as I darted through the grass, my damp hem clinging to my legs.

At last, I arrived at the water garden, where the towering trees overhead provided some shelter from the light rain. I found a marble bench tucked away alongside the trickling canal. It was wet, dark with rain, but I sat anyway, bracing my hands on either side of me, curling my fingers around the frigid marble.

I stared down the length of the canal toward the lake in the distance, where a rowboat was tied to a small wooden dock. For half a moment, I imagined taking it out onto the water to get as far from the house—from Mrs. Rawlings—as I possibly could. How often had I taken our own tiny boat at home out on the nearby pond? But the thought flitted from my mind. All the energy seemed to have left my body, and I sat there, the rain a chorus all around me.

The scene played again and again in my head—Mrs. Rawlings's haughtiness, her superiority, her downright hatred of me. It all made sense now, why she'd treated me so. She'd assumed I was a woman of loose morals intent on entrapping her son.

But to bring back the rumors to torment me yet again . . . Had Clarissa's falsehoods not ruined my life enough? Now they had to poison Mrs. Rawlings against me as well. Because no matter what I or Alexander said, I would not be surprised in the least if she still doubted we were telling the truth. I was a seductress, after all. Perhaps I'd tricked her son into lying for me. I could certainly see her convincing herself to believe that.

I wrestled with the darkness that grasped and clawed at my mind. I'd hoped for so long that one day I might escape my past, that I could create a future free from that bitterness. Now though . . . Now it seemed impossible, when women like Mrs. Rawlings wielded my ruined reputation like a broadsword.

It was cold, my feet wet, and my shoulders soaked through, but I refused to go inside. I would not go where I was not wanted.

Eventually, I heard Alexander's footsteps. He came down the stairs alongside the canal and found me there on my bench, as if he'd known all along that I'd be here. He did not come sit beside me. Instead, he stood there, hands at his sides, looking at me with the strangest restlessness in his eyes.

"I shouted at my mother," he said.

I said nothing, only gripped the marble under my fingers harder.

"I've never raised my voice to her in all my life." He shook his head. "Though she's certainly deserved rebukes in the past. But she went too far today."

"She is very protective of you," I said stiffly. "Such a trait in a mother is to be commended."

"Not when she attacks someone entirely innocent."

A few raindrops fell on me from the tree above, and I shivered, a chill climbing my spine. Alexander moved to me, shrugging out of his jacket and settling it around my shoulders. It was warm, far too big, and smelled of him.

He sat beside me and eased my left hand free of the bench, my fingers bent into rigid claws. "We should go inside. You're near to frozen."

I shook my head. "I cannot."

His hand curved around mine. "Then give me your other hand."

I allowed him to take it, having no argument left in me. He took my hands between his larger ones and rubbed them until heat built under my skin, warming me.

I watched him as he coaxed life back to my fingers. "Thank you," I said simply, my mouth suddenly dry. "For defending me."

His lips flattened into a slash, his eyes shadowed pools. "I should not have needed to."

"Still," I said.

We sat there in the quiet, dripping stillness, the water running under the balustraded bridge just a few steps away. After a minute, his hands stopped moving over mine.

"I do not wish to try to excuse her actions," he said, his brogue soft, "but I do feel that you are owed some truths about my family and me. If you'll allow me."

I gazed at him, feeling the gentle tenderness of his hands around mine. I nodded.

He swallowed. "You know that I lived here as a child but that I also spent many years in Scotland. But I've never told you why."

"No," I said. "You never have."

His thumb ran over the line of my knuckles, his touch raising bumps along my skin. "My grandfather," he began, "made his money in trade. He built this house, determined to propel our family to new heights and join the ranks of England's most elite. He depended on my father to make a good match, to force our family to be accepted.

"But my father had other plans. He fell in love with my mother, though she was but the daughter of an apothecary, and married her against my grandfather's will." Alexander paused. "I have only the barest memories of my father. He died when I was four years old."

My fingers tightened around his. "I am sorry."

Alexander went on as if he hadn't heard me. "My grandfather hated my mother. He made his opinion quite clear. After my father died, Grandfather took over the entirety of my upbringing, employing stern and harsh governesses, refusing to let me see my mother but rarely."

Sympathy tore at my heart—how hard that must have been, for the both of them—but I resisted it. I was still too angry at Mrs. Rawlings to feel sorry for her.

"My mother endured this for years," he said. "Suffered the cruelty and mistreatment of my grandfather so as not to abandon me. It hardened her, I think. Formed her. When she began to see how he was changing me, teaching me to be like him instead of like my father, she knew she had to take me away from here before it was too late. But escaping my grandfather was no easy task."

"Why?" I asked softly.

He exhaled. "Grandfather knew very well that Mother hated him, that she wanted me away from his influence. But he gave her no money, refused to allow her guests, even her own family. When still she defied him, he threatened to have her committed to an asylum if she did not obey."

I stared, mouth parted. I could not imagine such cruelty. My father was indifferent but never needlessly mean.

He glanced at me. "I learned this later, of course. I was only seven years old at the time. But I knew very well what sort of man my grandfather was. When my mother told me we were running away, I listened. We left in the middle of the night, with only one bag each. She'd hidden away a small amount of money, enough to take us across the border to Scotland, where she'd visited once as a young woman. Grandfather would search everywhere for us, and she wanted to be as far away from him as possible. We eventually settled in Inverness."

"Where you lived until you were grown," I said.

"Yes," he said. "We kept in contact with my aunt, Helen's mother, but beyond that, we were cut off from all we had known."

Alexander looked at me then. "In those long years between, Mother and I lived a life far from luxury. She worked endless hours to support us, in a multitude of positions—seamstress, laundress, maid—but never complained. She educated me, made me who I am."

My jaw tensed, again fighting any small surge of sympathy inside me. I could not deny that I was surprised, however. I could never have imagined the aloof and proper Mrs. Rawlings bent over a washboard for endless hours, all to keep her only son from the clutches of her horrible father-in-law.

"She always talked of returning here, to my and my father's inheritance, and taking back what belonged to us," he went on. "It was what drove her and gave her strength. But my desires were different." He paused, his leg bouncing slightly as if agitated—or nervous.

"What did you want?" I asked quietly.

His throat bobbed. "My life in Scotland was not an unhappy one," he said, "but I needed more than our small world there."

His words took me aback. They described so perfectly my own feelings of home, of my parents.

"Against my mother's wishes," he went on, "I left Inverness at seventeen. I went to London, found a few odd jobs. I was aimless, really. Wandering. Eventually, I did some work for Bow Street, helped an officer with a case. He took me under his wing and mentored me." He shook his head slightly, as if in amusement. "It was luck, really. The most fortunate twist of fate. Because it was at Bow Street that I found my calling. I found friends. I could help right wrongs and catch criminals and be *useful*."

"But your mother wishes you to give that up."

"Yes," he replied. "A few years after I arrived in London, my grandfather died. Briarstone was left to me."

He said it with such distaste that I knew immediately. I remembered the conversation I'd overhead between him and his mother when we'd first arrived here. *My life will be my own*, he'd said. "But you did not want it," I suggested.

"No," he said. "My happy memories of my early childhood had been tainted by my grandfather's cruelty. I wanted nothing more than to sell the place and move on."

That was why he seemed so ill-at-ease here. It was his house, but it was not his home.

"But Mother refused to let me sell," he said with an exhale. "'Briarstone is ours,' she insists. 'We earned it.' And so I let her take over the running of it while I returned to Bow Street. She still does not understand why I remain in London, though I've told her a dozen or more times. I've built a life there, one I'm loath to give up."

"Nor should you." I shifted to face him. "She might enjoy isolation, but not everyone does."

"It is more than that." He exhaled. "My mother does not trust easily. Though she had many friends here in Camberwell, during those few years after my father died, all those so-called friends abandoned her, intimidated by my grandfather's power. When she decided to run with me, she had no one to help her, save my aunt. Mother has never forgotten their abandonment. And then, in Scotland, she was always so afraid that my grandfather would find us that she never allowed us to grow close to anyone, to have anything more than passing acquaintances. That is why she holds herself apart from Society here, why we both do. And that is also why she was immediately suspicious of the woman I brought home with me."

I swallowed. I could see it—understand it, even. But my emotions from when she'd confronted me still refused to abate. It would take time. "Thank you for telling me," I said.

"No one knows this about me." He sounded almost baffled, leaning forward to brace his elbows on his knees. "I never thought I would tell anyone. I always intended to keep my two lives completely separate. But because of you . . ."

"Because of me, your two worlds came crashing together," I said lightly. "I ruined everything."

"No," he said. "That is not what I meant."

My lungs were tight. "What did you mean?"

He said nothing, only stared at his hands clasped in front of him. Then he stood and offered me his hand. "We should go inside."

I wanted to ask him again. What was he not saying?

But I took his hand, so warm even in this chill, and he helped me to my feet. He did not offer me his arm as we started back up the stairs of the water garden.

I pulled his jacket tighter, wishing—pointlessly—that it was his arms wrapped around me instead.

"We still need to take care," he said, walking beside me.

"Take care?"

"Stroud's questions in London may have stirred something up," he replied. "And we know now that my mother was the one in your room, but that does not mean you are not still in very real danger."

I gazed down at the damp grass, drops of rain hovering on their tips. He was right. Mrs. Rawlings's meddling was a stark reminder of our reality, of how quickly one small slip could ruin our cover. I swallowed back a sudden bitterness on my tongue, the familiar bite of fear.

"You are in danger as well, you know," I managed.

"My safety is secondary," he said. "You are my priority."

He said it so briskly, businesslike, as if to pass over the true significance of his words. But I heard them. I felt them. For a moment, my stomach warmed with the knowledge that Alexander would do anything to keep me safe. Then that warmth withered and seeped away. If our attacker should find us, I knew Alexander would put himself, willingly, between me and death. The idea of him in any sort of danger made my blood turn to ice.

When we reached the house, I was shivering terribly, even under the jacket. Alexander noticed, of course, and immediately sent for Agatha.

"A hot bath," he instructed her when she arrived, "and then some rest. I'll see that a tray is sent up immediately. She hasn't eaten breakfast."

"I'm not an invalid," I protested even as my teeth chattered.

"And bring her some books from the library," he went on, ignoring me. "Whichever she wants."

It was all too much. I didn't need such a fuss. And yet with every command he gave—each one for my well-being—my heart beat a little faster.

Agatha began to lead me away, Alexander's jacket still draped around my shoulders. I looked back at him standing there in the corridor, his shirt and waistcoat nearly wet through, his hair damp and curling. All because he'd sat in the rain with me.

My eyes rose to his. He watched me go, and though he wore, as always, an expression of careful neutrality, I could read him better now. I saw the worry in the set of his mouth and the slight furrow in his brow.

Verity had been right. *He is kinder than he lets on*, she'd said. *You can trust him.*

It was a very good thing, because I was fairly certain I'd just given him my heart.

Chapter 19

Agatha was quick and efficient. Within an hour, I was bathed, dressed, and wrapped in a thick blanket, seated on the window bench overlooking the lawn. It was remarkable what a scalding bath, a hot cup of tea, and a good book could do for one's mood.

Not that I had forgotten the morning's events or the revelations that had turned my world upside down.

Now that I had the time and distance to attempt to view Mrs. Rawlings's treatment of me with any sort of objectivity, I tried. I thought back to our first meeting, when I'd appeared so unexpectedly with her son in her home. Then she'd learned that I would be staying there, acting as her companion, invading the privacy she held so fiercely.

And somewhere in the midst of all that, she'd heard from Stroud that I'd been in a most inappropriate state of undress when we'd arrived.

I shook my head, hating that I was beginning to understand her point of view. How might I have reacted if *my* son had shown up with a suspicious woman and a rather far-fetched story about a murderer on their trail?

Still, I did not think I would ever have been half so awful as she had been to me. Disapproval in every glance and making me sew until my fingers went numb. Instead of trying to learn more about me and form her own judgments, she simply saw what she wanted to see and set herself against me at every turn. I knew from experience how impossible it was to please people like that.

My eyes wandered across the landscape, back toward the water garden. The bench where I'd sat with Alexander was hidden from view, but just the thought of it made every emotion I'd felt during our conversation rush back into my chest.

Everything he'd told me about his childhood simply made so much sense. It fit into the puzzle I'd been constructing about him, filled in the gaps and made the picture more complete. It explained why he'd been so standoffish and reticent when we'd first met, why he disliked Briarstone with a passion, why he kept everything a secret from his friends in London.

Why he tolerated his mother's nosiness and irritability. Because of all she'd sacrificed for him.

I did not want to think of Mrs. Rawlings any longer—my emotions clashed too much. Instead, I recalled the way Alexander's hands had warmed my own, the feel of his heavy jacket around my body, the way his damp hair had swooped across his forehead.

How had it come to this? How had I lost myself to him so quickly?

I certainly hadn't expected it or even hoped for it. I'd spent the last week longing to return to London. But now, all I longed for was to be with him. I wanted to make those lips dart up in surprise and feel his hands on my waist. I wanted to sit beside him before a crackling fire, reading as he worked on this case or that. I wanted those dark, enigmatic eyes to follow me—and only me—for the rest of our days.

I wanted a great many things from Alexander, but I did not know if he wanted them as well. He kept his emotions so tightly inside him. I knew he felt *something* for me—a woman could sense these things—but was it simply a passing physical attraction? An inevitable result of our forced proximity since we'd left London?

Or did he also feel that invisible thread between us, pulling us closer with every moment we spent together?

I sighed and took a sip of tea. It was all so very tangled—Alexander, my feelings, the case, Mrs. Rawlings, Briarstone. Perhaps once this was all over, once we could return to London and our normal lives, we might have a chance to see if this connection between us was anything *more.*

A sudden, sharp knock at the door nearly made me drop my teacup. I hadn't heard any footsteps, and the knock did not sound like Alexander's. "Yes?"

There was a pause, then—"May I come in?"

I sat up straight. It was Mrs. Rawlings. Her voice was stiff and stilted, but it was her.

I dearly wanted to refuse her. I had every right, considering what she had accused me of not three hours ago. But my curiosity—my Achilles heel—had to know what she wished to say. "Very well," I said.

The door opened, and Mrs. Rawlings stepped inside. She found me immediately, still seated on the window bench.

I stood slowly, gaze narrowed, and I kept my blanket wrapped around my shoulders. I did not curtsy. "Mrs. Rawlings," I said, my voice flat.

Her lips pressed into a thin line, and she closed the door behind her. So this would be a conversation she did not wish anyone to overhear.

"If you are here to demand I leave—" I began.

"No," she interrupted. "No, I am not."

But she did not say what she was here for, only clasped her hands behind her back and paced to the other window. I let the silence stew between us. She could speak when she wished to.

"Alexander said you saved his life," she finally said.

That was not what I'd been expecting in the least. "Pardon?"

"At Vauxhall." She turned to face me, though she inspected the rug instead of looking at me directly. "When you both were attacked—he said you saved his life."

I swallowed hard, gripping my blankets around me. "He saved mine as well."

She seemed not to hear me. "He told me you hit the man over the head. That he would be dead now if not for you."

I said nothing, staring at her. Where precisely was this conversation headed?

"I feel it my duty as his mother," she went on, "to thank you."

My brows shot up. "Thank me?" I repeated skeptically.

She looked me in the eye for the first time since entering. "Yes," she said. "If you had not done that, I would have lost my only son. And so I must thank you"—she took a deep breath—"and ask your forgiveness."

The silence that grew between us was as thick as the blanket around my shoulders and filled with an echoing disbelief.

"Do you mean that?" I said quietly.

"Yes." Her chin held a stubborn tilt, as if she were determined to pretend this was not strange in the slightest. "I made assumptions about you that were entirely incorrect, and I—I am sorry for it. Please accept my sincerest apology."

I inspected her face. *Was* it sincere? Or had Alexander forced it?

But I saw something there that I'd never seen before. Regret. Whether it was for her actions or the consequences she now faced, I did not know. But I decided to offer her the benefit of the doubt. My anger faded away. "You were protecting your son," I said. "As any mother would have."

"Perhaps next time, I will do so a little more judiciously."

Her unexpected levity caught me by surprise, and I exhaled a short laugh. "Heavens, was that a joke, Mrs. Rawlings? You mustn't shock me too much, or I shall expire on the spot."

She did not laugh or even smile, but a tiny muscle in her cheek gave the slightest twitch. "We cannot have that. Alexander would be even more put out with me." She eyed me. "He was very defensive of you."

I lifted one shoulder. "I imagine he would defend anyone who needed it."

"Perhaps not quite so ardently."

I coughed a little. "I'm not—that is, we aren't—"

"Aren't what?"

I paused, seeing that spark of interest in her eyes. She wanted information from me. She wanted to know what was happening between Alexander and me, which meant he hadn't told her anything. Neither would I. It was none of her business, though she would no doubt attempt to make it so.

I smiled at her, which I knew would only aggravate her further. "Nothing, Mrs. Rawlings. Nothing whatsoever."

I would accept her apology, but I did not owe her anything beyond that.

She sniffed, knowing very well that I'd thwarted her. "Alexander told me I am to beg that you come to dinner tonight. I've never begged in my life, and I do not intend to start now." She paused. "But I should appreciate it if you did come. He is rather angry with me, I think."

I almost denied her. It would have been a lovely, sweet sort of justice. But continuing this feud between us would help nothing, especially . . .

Especially not knowing what the future held. For me. For Alexander.

"I will come," I said.

Mrs. Rawlings nodded, paused as if she meant to say something more, then seemed to decide against it. She turned and left, closing the door behind her.

I gave a shake of my head, still rather shocked at what had unfolded. Mrs. Rawlings—stubborn, arrogant, aloof Mrs. Rawlings—had *apologized.* To *me*. What was the world coming to?

Perhaps I should still be angry with her, but I found I could not summon the emotion. She'd asked for my forgiveness, which was more than many in my life had ever done. I did not have it in me to hold a grudge. It was far too exhausting.

I curled up again on the window bench, the tightness in my lungs easing ever so slightly. I stared out at the rain-drenched landscape, not truly seeing, my mind preoccupied.

Then I blinked. I sat up, pulling the curtain farther back. My breathing quickened. I focused on a spot in the distance, just beyond the stables, where a crowd of silver birch trees grew. For a moment, I thought I'd seen a figure in the dreary gloom of the storm.

Shadows gathered around the trees, the wind rustling the leaves. I watched for a minute longer, but there was nothing else. No sudden movement. No figure. And yet my body braced—muscles tight, veins racing, thoughts tangled—as if it knew something my mind did not.

"You're being silly," I whispered to myself. This business with Mrs. Rawlings had simply set me on edge, and I was conjuring up phantoms.

I stood and drew the curtains closed. It would do no good to indulge my imagination. There was no nefarious villain searching my room and no vengeful murderer hiding in the shadows.

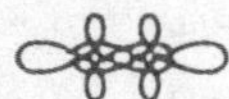

I'd never enjoyed extended periods of idleness, so in the early afternoon, I dressed and went searching for Alexander. I found him, as always, in his study. I stepped inside, and he stood immediately.

"Miss Lacey," he said, and the way his voice formed my name sent a pleasant tingle up my spine.

"Mr. Rawlings," I said overly formal, teasing him.

His eyes swept over me. "How are you feeling?"

I wandered into the room, inspecting the row of bookshelves along the southern wall. "Much better now. Your mother came and apologized, so I expect the end of the world is likely nigh."

"She did?" There was no hiding the surprise in his voice.

"Yes, this morning." I turned to face him. "You did not know?"

"No," he said. "She is prideful to a fault. I thought she would never admit to being wrong."

"Well, she did." I bit my lip. "In truth, I think she felt worse about it than she showed to either of us. Though I cannot be sure. She is as difficult to read as you are."

Alexander's brows lifted. "You find me difficult to read?"

"Oh, immeasurably," I said. "You've a face like the statues in your water garden."

"Is that an insult or a compliment?"

"Must it be one or the other?" I seated myself at the chair before his desk. "What are you working on? I'm terribly bored since I've been relieved of my companion duties for the day."

He sat as well and gestured to the pages of scrawled notes and newspaper clippings that littered his desk. "The London robberies again. I've found another two instances that might line up with what we've learned, but it's difficult to be sure without more information. I'm hoping to receive more from Bow Street in the next day or two, but until then, I can only muddle through newspaper after newspaper."

I straightened. "I could help, you know."

Alexander lowered his brow. "You would wish to?"

I would do nearly anything if it meant I was able to sit across from him, share the same air, feel the press of his gaze. But I reined myself in and managed to answer quite nonchalantly. "If you'd like."

"It is not interesting work," he warned.

I smiled. "I don't mind. I'd like to be useful."

He watched me a moment longer, as if expecting me to rescind my offer. When I did not, he stood and went to a stack of newspapers on a nearby table. "I had these delivered yesterday," he said, picking up the stack and moving them to the desk in front of me. "London papers all, dating within the last two months. Look for anything out of the ordinary."

I saluted him crisply. "Yes, sir."

He seemed not to know what to do with that, which only made me grin more. Heavens, how I liked discomfiting this man.

He returned to his seat, and I took a paper and began reading. We fell into a comfortable quiet, broken only by the rustle of paper and scratch of his pen.

After a few minutes, I sneaked a glance at him over the edge of my paper. He was reading, an elbow propped on the desk, his head leaning against splayed fingers. He had to be tired. Last night seemed an age ago, with all that had happened this morning.

"You *could* go sleep," I said, turning the page of my newspaper. "I can do this."

"I'm fine," he said unconcernedly.

"Predictable." I raised my brows at him.

"One night without sleep will not be the end of me." He did not even look at me. "Besides, now that we've established there is no immediate threat—"

"Debatable with your mother."

"—I am certain I will sleep perfectly fine tonight," he finished.

"Oh, very well, I shall stop fussing," I said.

We settled in to our research again, and this time, I lost myself in the words, the printed stories, the lives and people intertwined on the pages before me. When at last I looked up, having read upward of half a dozen newspapers front to back, the sun had begun lowering toward the distant horizon, casting long shadows across the study.

I folded my newspaper and set it on the desk, then sat forward and pressed my hands to my lower back, stretching. "Heavens, reading is terrible for one's posture, is it not?"

I glanced at Alexander. He had been watching me, the pen in his hand poised over a paper, though he did not write. He swallowed, quickly dropping his gaze. "Yes. Quite."

What had that been about?

"I'm sorry not to have found anything helpful," I said.

"*I'm* sorry," he said briskly as he jotted down a note. "I wasted your afternoon."

"It wasn't a waste," I said. "It was a step forward, no matter how small."

"Your positivity is almost catching," he said, setting down his pen and straightening his papers.

"It would not be the worst thing to take a more hopeful view of the world, Alexander."

His hands paused a moment, then continued forming his pages into a neat stack. "We ought to dress for dinner." He looked over at me. "If you are coming, that is."

"I promised your mother I would." I exhaled. "But now I find myself quite undecided." He said nothing, a slight frown on his face. I watched him, a smile toying with my lips. I knew very well he'd instructed his mother to ask me. "If *you* wanted me to come," I said pointedly, "then perhaps I might make the effort."

"Why would I not wish you to come?" He stood and began tidying the rest of his desk.

"I didn't say that," I replied.

"What did you say?"

"I said that my decision depended on who was asking."

"My mother asked you."

I narrowed my eyes at him. "You are being purposefully obtuse."

Alexander released a long breath. "And *you* are running me in circles, Miss Lacey. Simply tell me what you want me to say."

"Very well. Repeat after me." I stood and leaned one hand on his desk, holding the other against my chest. "'I, Alexander Rawlings, desperately wish for you, Miss Beatrice Lacey, to attend dinner tonight, or I shall be most bereft and likely left sobbing at the table.'"

"I will most certainly *not* be saying that."

I sighed. "A shame. I suppose I shall dine in my room."

He moved around the desk and headed for the door. "A shame indeed. I believe we are having roast beef."

"Oh, fine, then," I said, following after him. "Do stop begging; I shall come. You oughtn't debase yourself so, Alexander."

"I've never done so in my life."

"Most assuredly," I replied pertly.

He made a noise that was either amusement, frustration, or—most likely—both, and I grinned widely as I trailed him up the stairs. If he *did* like me, heaven help this man. He would need all the patience he could muster.

Chapter 20

The roast beef was delicious, and I did not regret my decision to join the dinner table. Mrs. Rawlings was decidedly quiet, no doubt reevaluating everything she knew about me. I leaned on all the skills Mother's careful tutelage had driven into me and managed the conversation gracefully, avoiding anything sensitive. I was not desperate for Mrs. Rawlings's good opinion, but neither did I want to give her any additional reasons to find me wanting.

After dinner, we retired to the drawing room, where Mrs. Rawlings seemed to regain some of her spirit. She berated Alexander for his "drab" wardrobe unfitting of someone of his station, and he fought her off with every reason why a Bow Street officer would wish to avoid frippery and showiness. It seemed a well-worn, comfortable argument, one they took out and dusted off every now and again, and seemed to help reestablish their normal repartee.

I stayed quiet, amused by their antics. When Mrs. Rawlings declared his jacket for the gutter, Alexander sent me such a look of amused long-suffering that I laughed. This was a new side of him, and one I liked very much. But then, I was discovering I liked every side of him, for different reasons.

Heavens, how much I wanted to see Ginny and tell her everything that had happened. Keeping my feelings for Alexander to myself was almost painful. They would surely burst from my chest if I did not talk to her—or *someone*—soon.

Thankfully, I slept well that night, and the dove-gray dawn woke me gently. I lay there dozing, wishing I had the motivation many seemed to possess to rise and be immediately productive, when I heard a noise.

The sound of a horse's hooves on the pebbled drive below my window.

I blinked, staring blearily at the clock across my room. It was only six o'clock in the morning. My ears must be deceiving me. Who would be here at this hour of the day? Falling back against my pillow, I turned on my side and gathered my blankets up to my chin, trying to keep the chill air at bay. I closed my eyes, intending to find sleep again for another hour or two.

But then a horse whinnied outside. I sat up. I had not imagined that.

I slipped from my bed and padded to the window, parting the curtains with one hand. A groom led a horse up the lane from the stables, saddled and prepared to ride. Alexander's horse. I recognized it from the time I'd seen him ride out to visit a tenant a few days ago.

What on earth? Was Alexander going somewhere?

I dropped the curtain, straightening suddenly. Was it possible he'd had word from London?

I scrambled to my wardrobe and dressed as quickly as I could, picking a simple dress I could fasten by myself. I did not bother with my hair, leaving it in a wild braid tumbling down my back. I opened my door and peeked out into the corridor. Even with Mrs. Rawlings now realizing the error of her ways—at least in regard to me not being a light-skirt fortune hunter—I hardly wanted her to come across me knocking at her son's door at an ungodly hour yet again.

I crept down the corridor and knocked quietly at Alexander's door. I shifted my weight as I lingered, but he did not answer. I hurried back the way I'd come and started down the main staircase, my stockinged feet hardly making a sound on the steps, my hand gliding like a whisper on the rail. Likely, there were servants awake somewhere belowstairs, but the main part of the house remained silent and echoing.

As I approached Alexander's study, I heard rustling from within. The door was slightly ajar, and his dark figure moved about inside, barely lit by the coming sunrise.

My heart thumped loudly. Something was happening, clearly. And I had a feeling that whatever I heard in the next few minutes might again change the trajectory of my life.

I pushed the door open.

Alexander's head snapped up, his body still bent over his desk. When he saw it was me, he did not relax, as I might have expected him to. Instead, he straightened, regarding me with . . . wariness.

"Miss Lacey," he said, his voice brisk. "What are you doing awake?"

"I saw your horse outside." I stepped inside and closed the door behind me. "You weren't in your room."

"No." He tapped one finger on the papers on his desk, as if anxious to return to them.

"I couldn't help but wonder if you'd had word," I said, moving closer, "from London."

His expression shifted. "Yes," he said. "Early this morning, I received a letter from Drake. It's there, if you want to read it." He nodded at a folded letter on the edge of his desk.

I shot him a sidelong glance as I moved to pick up the letter. He only returned to his task, which appeared to be sorting through his papers.

I stepped to the window and unfolded the page.

Rawlings,

I must be brief. This morning, we apprehended the man we believe is responsible for the attack on you at Vauxhall and the viscount's murder. I cannot say more, but I urge you and Miss

Lacey to return to London with all possible haste so you might identify the man.

Drake

"They caught him?" I gasped, my stomach performing a series of mad flips. Had I read it correctly? I skimmed the letter again, and the words became a joyful blur. Finally—finally—we could leave! I would not have to playact any longer, would not have to bear Mrs. Rawlings's oppressive company. We could return to London, and I could reunite with Ginny, tell her everything, feel her comforting arms around me. "Oh, thank heavens." I spun on my heel to face him, beaming. "We can start for London today! I will go and pack immediately."

I was prepared to dash upstairs and throw every one of my belongings into my trunk. I could almost feel the blessed bustle and energy of the streets of London. Even the thought of going home to Little Sowerby did not fill me with dread. I wanted my room, my things, even my parents, such as they were. Normality had never seemed so wonderful.

Then I saw Alexander's face, the steel of a decision already made in his eyes.

"What is it?" I asked, taken aback.

"You are not coming to London," he said. "I am going alone."

I blinked, staring at him, his words incomprehensible. Then I remembered the lone horse waiting outside, saddled and ready.

"You are leaving me *here*?" My voice was suddenly dry, scraping up my throat.

"Yes," he answered, picking up a stack of papers and tucking it inside a leather folio.

"Why?"

"I explained everything in my note." He held up a folded paper without looking at me.

I exhaled a disbelieving laugh. "You were going to abandon me for London and leave me a *note*?"

"It seemed the simplest solution," he said sharply, "so as to avoid this exact scene."

"Oh, I am terribly sorry to have ruined your easy escape," I snapped. "Pray tell, *why* am I to be left behind?"

"A very simple reason." He dropped the note onto his desk. "They might have the wrong man."

"What do you mean?"

"Just what I said," he replied. "We cannot be sure the man they arrested is the same man who attacked us at Vauxhall. Until I can identify him, I have no intention of waltzing you back into London with the murderer potentially still on the streets."

Mr. Drake's letter in my hands was bent and twisted, my grip too tight. "How is that your decision to make? Do I have no say in my own life?"

"I am the one charged with your safety." He picked up the folio containing his papers. "I will not put you into any unnecessary danger. You will stay here at Briarstone until I return to fetch you."

"Fetch me?" I gave a wild laugh. "Flattering. Yes, I shall await your return like an obedient puppy."

"Good." There was no emotion in his voice as he tucked his folio into a large traveling bag, the same one he'd brought when we'd journeyed here. That detail brought everything into full focus. He was really leaving me here. How long would I have to be trapped here still, wondering what was happening in London? Wondering if he was safe?

A memory reared in my mind of Alexander bleeding on the path at Vauxhall, wounded, disoriented. I'd been there that time. I'd helped him. But what if it happened again? How could I keep him safe if I was trapped here at Briarstone?

He picked up the bag and rounded the edge of the desk. "Stay in the house. You must keep up every precaution as before."

I blocked his path to the door. "You are *not* leaving me here," I said, my voice like ice.

His eyes narrowed. "It is too dangerous to take you. That is my final decision."

He began to move around me, but I blocked him again. "That is *your* decision, not mine. Who will watch your back if I am here?"

"I've watched my own back for a dozen years."

He tried to go around me, so I backed up until my shoulder blades hit the carved wood of the study door. I took the door handle in one hand, gripping it tightly and glaring defiantly up at him, daring him to physically move me out of his way.

"Step aside," he growled.

"No," I insisted. "I am coming with you."

"You are *not*."

"I am safer with you, and you are safer with me."

"Blast it all, Beatrice." He stepped closer, no doubt trying to intimidate me. There was a look in his eyes I'd never seen before, desperate and uncontrolled.

I raised my chin. "Give me one good reason why we are not better off together, and I'll—"

He dropped his bag, took my face in his hands, and kissed me.

His lips were hard, fierce, unrelenting. The rough skin of his hands encircled my cheeks, fingertips weaving into my hair at the base of my skull. A crackle of heat burst through me, dry wood on a raging fire. It was a furious kiss. An angry kiss. But there was more—so much more—behind the powerful press of his mouth.

The door behind me was solid, steadying. He was so much taller than I, his shoulders curved into a stoop so he could reach my lips. I rose onto my toes and kissed him back, clutching his waistcoat in great fistfuls of fabric. His hands dropped to my shoulders, pulling me closer until our knees knocked together. The warmth of his touch sank deep into my bones, stirring up a great whirlwind of embers and sparks.

We tore apart to breathe, both of us desperate for air.

"If you think," I rasped, clutching his lapels, "that kissing me will make me forget about London, then you can—"

He kissed me again. Arrogant, infuriating, impossible man.

He did not slow nor rein in his passion. His lips grazed along my jaw, brushed the vulnerable, sensitive skin below my ear, and then returned to my mouth. I raked my hands through his hair, an irrational desire surging through me to throw his carefully arranged locks into disarray.

Poems would never be written about this kiss. It was too real, too imperfect, so ragged and raw.

But it was *mine*. Just like I was forever—and inarguably—*his*.

Our kiss unraveled, softened, and deepened all at once. I trembled against him, unable to believe I was in his arms, that he wanted me as much as I wanted him. He finally pulled back, lips parted and eyes heavy. We inhaled in tandem—deep, scraping breaths entering our lungs. He held my face in his hands, thumbs sweeping across the rise of my cheekbones.

"I am still angry with you," I whispered.

"I do not care," he said. "You are not coming."

How could he be so unmoved? Had our kiss not affected him as it had me? I hit his chest once, my hands curled into fists. He did not so much as flinch. I raised my fists to pound him again, needing some reaction from him, *anything*. He caught my wrists.

"You are a danger to me, Beatrice Lacey," he said, a dark huskiness shadowing the curves of his voice, that Scottish brogue claiming his tongue more fully. "Since the first night we met, you have invaded my every thought. There is a madness—a wildness—that consumes me when you are near. I cannot—" He broke off, jerking his head to one side, eyes closed as his chest rose and fell.

I stared up at him, my wrists still in his firm grasp. His words flooded through me. I could barely focus, my thoughts flitting about. He was speaking about *me*.

"I *cannot*," he said through gritted teeth, "allow myself to be distracted by you." He forced himself away, dropping my hands and taking several steps back. But there was no easing of the tension between us. It was tangible, smothering. "Having you with me would be dangerous for us both," he said. "I cannot do what needs to be done if you are there."

All I wanted to do was kiss him again, feel the burn of his fingertips pressing into my back. But I was also angry. I was overwhelmed. I was as likely to shout as I was to cry.

I was in love.

"Do you understand?" He spoke in a brusque, businesslike tone, as if that kiss hadn't just happened.

I forced myself to nod, the barest flick of my chin. That was, I was just beginning to understand.

"You will stay inside the house," he commanded. "You won't come after me or take any unnecessary risks."

"Yes." My voice was low, throaty.

There was no point in arguing. He would not relent, and I could not find it in me to continue a doomed campaign.

And I had yet to fully comprehend his words or navigate the emotions that pounded through me like a torrent in a drought-ridden riverbed. His kiss still burned inside me, my frustration and exhilaration and desire melding together until they were hardly distinguishable.

He picked up his bag from where he'd so unceremoniously dropped it. "I wrote my mother a note as well," he said. "If you would give it to her."

"Very well." I could not seem to move. If I moved, I would shatter to pieces.

"I will make all haste to London," he said, and his words felt softer, even if they didn't sound it. "I *will* return as soon as possible."

I nodded again, not trusting my voice.

He looked at me then, his jaw set into a rigid line against his face. But his eyes . . . His eyes told me he wanted nothing more than to claim my lips once more.

And then he turned and left.

CHAPTER 21

I stood there for several long seconds, his footsteps echoing back to me. I half expected him to return, to kiss me again, or to relent and allow me to come with him. But he did not.

The front door opened and closed. I couldn't help myself and moved to the window overlooking the front drive.

Alexander stood beside his horse. His raven hair, normally so neat, was disheveled from our kiss. He spoke to the groom holding the reins, but I could not make out his words. As I watched, Alexander took the reins and mounted smoothly. Turning toward the road, he kicked his horse into a canter. Heavens, the man looked fine on horseback.

He did not look back as he rode away.

I watched him until he disappeared into the distance, the trees swallowing him up. Despite my anger and the betrayal of being left behind, I touched the window, the glass cool against my trembling fingertips. "Please be safe," I whispered. "Please."

My knees shook. The events of the last few minutes were catching up to me. I stumbled to the great leather chair behind his desk and sank into it.

He'd kissed me. Alexander had kissed me.

I could still feel the shape of his lips on mine. His words echoed in my ears—he'd called me a danger, a distraction. I knew I was. I wasn't Ginny or Verity. I wasn't born into the world of solving crimes. I wasn't *useful.*

But still, he'd kissed me.

My anger was fading. Yes, I'd proved myself capable that night at Vauxhall. But that did not mean I would not crumple entirely the next time I faced some unexpected danger.

He'd been right to go without me. Even if I did not like it.

I looked around the empty study, cold and quiet. The letter on his desk called to me, the one he'd written when he'd assumed he could leave without informing me. I huffed. The audacity, truly.

My irritation somewhat rekindled, I snatched up the letter.

Miss Lacey,

I have received a letter from Drake summoning me back to London to identify a suspect they have apprehended, whom they have charged with the viscount's murder. I made the decision to return alone, leaving you within the safety of Briarstone's walls until we can be sure you are out of danger.

There is little point in begging you not to be angry with me, so I shall only ask that you do not do anything foolish while angry. Such decisions are never well made.

There was a line of words next that had been so thoroughly crossed out I could only make out a letter or two. I bit my lip. What had he written? And would he have left it legible if he'd known we were about to kiss?

If you find yourself bored beyond reason, you are welcome to continue our research into the robberies. A new batch of notes from my clerk arrived with Drake's letter, and I've left the bulk of my own records as well, which you may peruse at your leisure.

I shall return as soon as possible. Please be safe.

A. Rawlings

I tossed the paper to the desk, relishing the messiness of it against the strict and tidy lines of his ink stand, pens, and papers. The smallest of rebellions against him, but it made me feel a bit better. Perhaps

I would begin a vast renovation of his study while he was gone, painting the walls or tearing down the curtains. Then he would regret leaving me here.

"He's gone, hasn't he?"

I sat up abruptly. Mrs. Rawlings stood in the doorway, hands folded against her stomach. She was fully dressed, with her hair done in its usual austere knot. She took in my state of undress with little expression.

"I saw him ride away," she went on, stepping into the room. "Has he returned to London?"

"Yes," I managed. "There was a development in the case."

"But you did not go."

It was not a question.

"No," I said. "Apparently, I would be a danger to him." I tried to speak without any emotion, as she seemed so easily capable of, but some of my hurt came through, my voice cracking.

She said nothing, only gazed at me with those perceptive eyes.

I swallowed. "He left you a letter." I searched the desk until I found it, *Mother* scrawled across the front in Alexander's confident, masculine hand.

She took it from me and read quickly, then folded it again.

"Well, Miss Lacey," she said, "it appears we have been left to our own devices. You, of course, may choose to do whatever you wish. But I think it best to continue our charade as long as possible to keep you safe."

This was certainly a turn of events. Not once in the last week had she ever given any sign that she wished to keep me *safe*.

"What on earth did he say in that note?" I asked, baffled.

She barked a laugh. "You think I would not do something like this of my own free will? That I must be ordered to by my son? No, this is my own attempt at recompense. I cannot change how I treated you in the past, but I can do my part going forward." She turned back for the door. "Go and dress. I expect you in the morning room in an hour."

"And if I do not come?" I challenged. I was not feeling particularly amenable this morning.

She stopped, one hand on the door, and for a brief moment, I was lost to my memories. Alexander had kissed me against that door not ten minutes ago, his lips greedy and possessive. My face flushed, and I tore my eyes from it to look defiantly at his mother.

"It is your choice," she said. "But you are not so unintelligent as to make the wrong one."

A delightful woman, truly. And somehow, still a marked improvement from two days ago.

She left, and I sat alone in the study once again.

It would be a long few days indeed.

I did join Mrs. Rawlings in the morning room, and she said nothing to gloat. Instead, she politely asked my opinion on the dinner menus for the week and whether I thought the gardener should plant white or yellow tulips along the front of the house. I'd never had an opinion on tulips in my life, but I decided firmly on the side of white, if only to seem more informed than I was.

Mrs. Rawlings did not assign me any tasks, and I quickly grew restless. I could have read a book, but I did not think even a novel would prove an adequate distraction. Instead, shocking even myself, I fetched the basket of clothes from near the fireplace. I found the little-boy-sized muslin shirt I'd been working on and threaded my needle.

Mrs. Rawlings furrowed her brow. "You do not need to do that."

"Why?" I asked. "Are these not really for the poor?" I would not put it past her to have simply thrown all my work into the fire, not wanting my taint on even such humble garments as these.

"Of course they are," she said sharply. "But I only forced you to because . . ." She stopped, apparently not wishing to remind me of how little she'd thought of me before.

"I have time," I said, "and nothing else to do with it. I see no reason why I should not spend it so."

She said nothing as I began to sew. I did not mind the actual task of sewing, but as in the past, it left far too much time for my thoughts to wander. And inevitably, they wandered right back to the study, to Alexander's lips on mine and his hands on my face.

I cleared my throat, glancing at Mrs. Rawlings. Thank goodness she could not read my mind. I should not dwell on those memories, or she would eventually ask why my skin was flushed and my eyes hazy.

We had only a few minutes of quiet before we heard footsteps in the corridor—quick, hurried footsteps. For a moment, my pulse tripped, fear spiking like an arrow through my heart. Then the door opened, and Elijah stood there in the doorway, beaming, with Helen right behind.

I had to catch my breath, trying to rein in the sharpness of my reaction. I'd grown so used to having Alexander in the house, to seeing him throughout the day and knowing he was keeping watch. Having him gone was sure to set my nerves on edge. I would simply have to manage them.

"My, what long faces," Helen exclaimed. "Are we in mourning?" Her ready smile was as welcome as the spring sun after a bitter winter.

I smiled at her in return, though it was perhaps a touch forced.

"In a way," Mrs. Rawlings said crisply, standing to greet her niece. I stood as well. "Alexander has gone back to London."

"Already?" Helen looked taken aback. "I thought he planned to stay a while longer."

"His work could not be delayed." Mrs. Rawlings held out her arms, encouraging Elijah.

Elijah ran and threw his little arms around Mrs. Rawlings. Mrs. Rawlings smiled down at him, wrapping him tight in an embrace. For a moment, I could see her as a young mother, holding her son, desperate to protect him. A lump formed in my throat, and I glanced away.

"Will he return?" Helen came to sit beside me on the sofa. "Elijah was so hoping to see him again."

"When his business is concluded," Mrs. Rawlings replied. "He still has matters to attend to here."

"I see." Helen glanced my way, and I did not think I imagined the curiosity in her gaze.

I smiled brightly. "It is good to see you again. It seems so long since the assembly."

"It's not been two days," she said with a laugh. "Aunt, are you still torturing your poor companion?"

"I take great offense at that," Mrs. Rawlings huffed as she let Elijah play with her gold pendant.

"No," I said with a small smile. "Mrs. Rawlings and I have come to a sort of truce."

"I am glad to hear it," Helen said. "I greatly like the both of you, and I see no reason why you should not like each other."

"Let us not be too hasty in that regard," Mrs. Rawlings said.

A laugh bubbled out of me. "No, we would not want that."

Helen shook her head and, thankfully, decided to change the subject. "I hope you enjoyed the assembly, Miss Albright, though we left early."

I winced slightly, both at her use of my false name and the reminder of how abruptly Alexander had forced her to leave that night, because of me. "Yes, I did, though . . ."

"Though what?" She tipped her head to one side.

Quite suddenly, I did not wish to lie to her anymore. She was the only person who had been genuinely kind to me since I'd left London, and she did not deserve this deception.

"Though I must admit I have not been honest with you since our first meeting," I said quietly.

Helen pulled her chin back. "Pardon?"

"Miss Lacey," Mrs. Rawlings hissed at me.

Helen turned to stare at her aunt. "What did you call her?"

Mrs. Rawlings looked stunned, mouth agape as she stared back. Oh, what irony, that Mrs. Rawlings should be the one to spoil our great charade.

"My name," I said. "My *real* name: Beatrice Lacey."

Helen shook her head, entirely baffled. "I am terribly confused."

"I would be surprised if you were not." I clasped my hands in my lap, unaccountably nervous. "I am sorry for it and for lying. But the ruse was necessary."

"It is still necessary," Mrs. Rawlings said shortly.

"I think not," I said. "The perpetrator will soon be identified, and I think there is little danger in telling the one person we both trust entirely."

"Telling me what?" Helen looked exasperated, glancing between the two of us. "What on earth is going on?"

I took a deep breath. "I am not truly Mrs. Rawlings's companion. It was simply a cover we invented to explain my presence here at Briarstone."

Helen blinked but said nothing.

"In London, before we came here, Mr. Rawlings and I were attacked by a brutal criminal, a murderer," I said. "During the brawl, I saw the man's face, though he escaped. It quickly became clear that I was in danger and could not remain in the city. Mr. Rawlings brought me here to keep me safe. We created this story so as to keep my true identity hidden."

"Oh!" Understanding began to dawn in Helen's eyes. "Oh, my dear, I am so sorry." She took my hand, pressing it into both of hers. "What a horrible thing! How afraid you must be."

"At times," I admitted. "When I allow myself to think too long."

"Is that why Alexander returned to London?" she pressed. "Something to do with this man?"

I nodded. "We received word this morning that Bow Street has arrested the man they believe attacked us. Mr. Rawlings has gone to identify him, and then he will come back for me."

"Thank heavens for that," Helen breathed.

"Yes indeed." I squeezed her hand. "I hope you will forgive me for deceiving you. It was only ever intended to protect all of us."

Helen shook her head fiercely. "No, I understand. And I would be foolish to hold it against you. In truth, it makes a great deal of sense." She raised her brows as if just realizing something. "That is why Alexander did not want you to go to the assembly at first."

"Yes, and why he forced us to leave early," I said apologetically. "He claimed I was drawing too much attention to myself."

"I daresay he was not entirely wrong," she said. "You did make something of an impression. But not nearly so much as *he* did when you danced together."

Mrs. Rawlings huffed. "Alexander never dances."

"Oh, he most certainly did this time," Helen confirmed. "The town has been positively ablaze with gossip about the two of you."

"About us?" I blinked.

"Yes," she said. "All the young ladies are terribly heartbroken."

"Why should they be?" Mrs. Rawlings's face was pinched.

Helen finally seemed to notice that Mrs. Rawlings was not particularly thrilled that gossip had linked Alexander to me, especially in regard to a dance. "I'm sorry," she said, glancing warily between us. "I did not mean—"

"Why should the ladies be heartbroken, Helen?" Mrs. Rawlings repeated.

"Because . . ." Helen coughed slightly. "Because Alexander seemed to show Beatrice a very special . . . favor."

I had to bite my lip, though I wasn't quite certain if I was withholding a grimace or a grin. Mrs. Rawlings was only just coming to tolerate me. She would not like hearing this, that Alexander had singled me out so publicly.

I braved a glance at her. She sat quite still, lips pressed together.

"I see," she said finally.

"It was just a dance," I hurried to say. "One that I forced upon him. He was angry, that is all. I'm certain his emotions were interpreted in quite the wrong way."

Although I knew very well they hadn't been. Not if this morning's kiss was any indication.

"I see," Mrs. Rawlings said again, more tightly. Then she stood and walked over to where Elijah was setting out his toy soldiers, clearly needing a moment away from us.

Helen cleared her throat. "I am sorry. I did not intend to cause any trouble."

"Yes, thank you for that." I sighed. "I was just starting to make the smallest progress with her."

"I do not know why she is shocked." Helen kept her voice low. "The way Alexander looks at you is far from subtle."

My pulse sped up. "I do not know what you mean."

"Yes, you do," she said with narrowed eyes.

A smile fought to claim my lips. I turned away so Mrs. Rawlings could not see. "Very well," I said. "Perhaps I do know."

"Good," she said. "I was beginning to think you were either extremely oblivious or deeply in denial." She leaned forward, suddenly eager. "Are the two of you engaged?"

I nearly choked. "Engaged?"

"I think it a fair question."

"No, indeed we are not," I managed, shooting another glance at Mrs. Rawlings. She seemed not to have heard my response. "It is nothing like that. It is . . ."

Except *I* did not even know what was between Alexander and me. We had no arrangement, no understanding. All we had was ten days' worth of stolen moments and conversations and that beautiful, scorching kiss in the study.

"I'm quite certain we both feel something for each other," I said softly. "But the future is so unsettled at present. He's never spoken to me about it."

"Of course he would not," she said. "He is a man and, thus, terribly vexing in every way."

I laughed, surprised that I could feel such lightness amid this conversation. "In that, you are correct."

Her smile faded, and she regarded me more seriously. "I know that Alexander's walls can be difficult to breach," she said. "Even as a child, he kept to himself. But he is different with you."

I could hardly breathe. Did she really mean that?

"Do you know what I said to him the night of the assembly?" she asked. "When you returned me home?"

I remembered now that they'd exchanged a few low words, impossible to hear, as he'd helped her from the carriage.

"No," I said, my stomach suddenly in knots.

"I told him, 'That woman is in love with you.'" She smiled softly. "And he said, 'I do not think I will ever be so fortunate.'"

Heavens.

Heat rushed to my cheeks. I touched them unconsciously, staring at her. "He said that?"

"No, I invented it because I am a scheming matchmaker," she said wryly. "Yes, he said it."

I could find no response, my tongue unable to form words. Helen simply patted my hand.

"I'll leave it there for the moment," she said. "I can see I've interfered enough already. But know I would be more than happy to see this entire adventure end with the both of you at the altar." She touched my shoulder as she stood, going to join Elijah and Mrs. Rawlings.

I watched in a strange sort of stupor, my heart aching. I hadn't dared imagine before now what might come of this . . . this . . . *situation* between Alexander and me. But now.

Now hope bloomed inside me—beautiful, fragile, terrifying hope. And I wanted nothing more than to see what might come of it.

CHAPTER 22

Sleep was impossible that night.

I stared up at my ceiling, rain lashing against my windows, wind whistling through the chimney. It was after midnight, and I'd been trying to fall asleep for close to two hours now. It wasn't the storm that kept me awake or that I felt unsafe. I knew the house was locked, that Mrs. Rawlings was in the room beside me, that there were servants who would come at the ring of a bell.

It was simply that I felt the lack of *him*. It was the first night without having Alexander within the reach of my voice, and I was left unsettled and restless. I hated the feeling and wickedly hoped that at whatever drafty inn he was spending the night, he, too, was unable to sleep for thinking of *me*.

When the clock finally struck twelve thirty, I gave up. I threw on my dressing gown and paced my room, hoping some exercise would calm my mind. The floor was cold against my feet, the chill of the storm outside leeching through the house. I spotted the writing desk in the corner and stopped. If I could not sleep, perhaps I could work.

I slipped quietly from my room, not wanting to wake Mrs. Rawlings, and started down the stairs. The third step from the bottom creaked loudly as I stepped on it, and I winced, pausing. But I heard nothing else and continued on.

Reaching the study, I went to Alexander's desk and sorted through the papers. Here were his notes, several pages in his own handwriting. A different bundle held the unfamiliar script of another man, which must be the new notes the Bow Street clerk had sent. They looked to be cases dating further back, two years or so.

Beneath the notes, I also found the sketch Verity had done of our attacker. A copy, I imagined, that must have arrived with Drake's letter. I wondered if Alexander had requested it, thinking it might jog his memory. I glanced it over, stomach twisting at the man's shadowed eyes, and then I quickly placed the sketch at the bottom of my stack. Closing the study door behind me, I hurried back up the stairs, skipping over the third step to avoid the creak.

Reaching my room, I lit a candle, then organized the papers neatly on the writing desk. I prepared a pen and ink to take notes and began to read.

First, I skimmed over Alexander's records—thorough, detailed, and clear. He'd written down each of the robberies he suspected could have been connected through Society events along with what was stolen, the dates, and any mentions of guests who had attended. Thus far, there seemed to be no obvious suspect—none of the names appeared more than once, at least.

Next, I picked up the information sent by the Bow Street clerk who'd been tasked with searching through the records at the magistrates' court for any similar cases. The first page started with occurrences dating just over a year ago. I read through them carefully. Some did not seem to line up quite right—either the robberies occurred much later than whatever event was hosted, or the missing item was eventually found and recovered.

It took me close to thirty minutes to read through the notes, and by then, my eyes were growing heavy and dry. I rubbed them with my fingertips as I turned to the last page of the clerk's notes, determined to finish before once more attempting to sleep.

I squinted at the words in the flickering candlelight, reading quickly. Then I frowned and read it again, slowly.

July 7, 1801

A robbery was reported at the household of Lord and Lady Granville. They hosted a grand ball the evening before with close to a hundred guests. The item stolen was a rare copy of Shakespeare's first folio. The book was never recovered.

A bell rang in my head, vague at first, then stronger, more alarming. I stared at the passage, disbelief hot in my veins. *I'd* attended a ball hosted by Lord and Lady Granville in July two years ago. In fact, it had been the last ball I'd ever attended in London because it was the same unhappy evening that I'd seen Clarissa Haythorne in the midst of her romantic tryst.

It was also the same evening I'd seen Lord Granville's copy of the first folio in his library. I remembered it so clearly—the calfskin cover, the thick pages, the volume slightly askew on its stand.

The robbery had to have been the same night as the ball. Lord Granville would not have hosted more than one ball that Season. But why hadn't I ever heard of the theft? I imagined it would have made some waves in Society. Then again, I hadn't been particularly aware of other goings-on in London in the days following that particular ball. I had been far too concerned about my absolute ruination at Clarissa's hands.

I sat back in my chair, staring at the notes in front of me, my vision glazed over. What were the chances that I would have seen the folio the same night it had been stolen? Indeed, I'd likely been the last to see it. I was lucky I hadn't happened upon the thief in the midst of the robbery.

I straightened as that thought struck itself into my mind.

Or perhaps I *had*.

Breathing hard, I drew back my memory of that night, one I usually did everything in my power to avoid. In my mind's eye, I moved down the corridor, the music from the ball following after me. I found the library, crossed the room to the folio stand. Then I'd heard the rustle and seen Clarissa's head rise above the sofa. The man she'd been with appeared beside her, scowling.

And I froze—not the memory of me, but the real me, sitting in the cold of my bedroom. The man's face seemed to take up every inch of my memory. Brown hair. Shadowed eyes. A lowered brow, faintly menacing.

I sat unseeing, my heartbeat slowly quickening as if my body understood before my mind. That man. I knew that man.

I riffled through the papers in front of me, my hands shaking, throat tight, until I found the sketch Verity had drawn. I held it up to the candlelight. The attacker's face stared back at me, eyes dark and intent, lips grim.

And my breath left my body entirely.

Because I was nearly certain that this man—the stranger who had attacked us in Vauxhall—was the same man I'd seen with Clarissa in the library that night.

I couldn't be sure. I knew that. I'd been so focused on Clarissa's face, on the shock of seeing her in such a state. But the other details filled in around my realization. *Someone* high in Society had been involved in these robberies, that much was clear. What if that someone had been Clarissa? What if she'd been helping this man the night of the ball, and I'd caught them about to steal from Lord Granville? That would explain why the folio had been askew. And perhaps their romantic tryst had all been a cover as well. After all, an impassioned embrace was much easier to explain than an interrupted robbery.

Doubt immediately flared. It couldn't be. It made no reasonable sense. Why would this man have attacked Alexander at Vauxhall? Was he somehow involved in the viscount's murder?

Unless . . .

My chest froze, breath and heartbeat suspended.

Unless he hadn't been there for Alexander.

Unless he'd been there for *me*.

I remembered how he'd glared at me with such hatred. I'd thought it had been because I'd fought back against him. But what if he was angry because I was a threat to him?

Because I'd caught him in the midst of a robbery?

You're mine, he'd snarled.

My lungs were working too hard, breaths coming rapidly. I did not have a memory for faces like Verity did, but everything in me was screaming the truth of this. If I was right—and I was feeling more and more sure with every passing second—then I was not a witness to the identity of a murderer. I was a witness to a *robbery*, and only one of many over the past few years, if the notes spread before me were any indication. How many cases might I implicate this man in? And Clarissa?

I sat back in my chair. I had no proof. No real evidence of anything, save for a memory that was two years old. The conclusions I was leaping to seemed impossible. How could I explain this to anyone? It *felt* right, but feelings meant nothing in a court of law. How I wished Alexander were here. I would not have hesitated to tell him everything I'd discovered. He would have listened and then decided whether my theory had merit.

Just then, I heard footsteps from the room beside mine. Mrs. Rawlings. What was she doing awake at this hour?

I went to my door and peeked out into the corridor. Candlelight shone from beneath her door. I hesitated. Did I really think Mrs. Rawlings cared one whit about what I'd learned tonight?

Then again, this involved her son and possibly the safety of her home. Perhaps she deserved to know.

Or perhaps I simply knew I wouldn't be able to sleep if I did not tell someone.

Either way, she was awake, and it would not hurt to try. She'd rejected me enough in the past that I was quite used to the feeling.

I fetched the clerk's notes about the Granvilles' ball, then went out into the corridor. I closed my door behind me, then crept toward Mrs. Rawlings's. I knocked lightly.

The door opened a few seconds later, spilling candlelight into the dark corridor. She was wrapped in her dressing gown, her hair in two precise braids. She looked so very different—so informal—that I simply blinked at her.

"Miss Lacey," she said, raising one eyebrow. "Strange time for a social visit."

"I heard you moving about," I blurted out. "And I saw your candlelight. I thought—that is, I hoped—that we might talk. I think I've discovered something, and I'm rather reeling from it. Mr. Rawlings isn't here, so I've no one to speak of it to. Could I—may I—"

"Oh, come in," she said a bit grumpily, opening the door wider. It was not the warmest of receptions, but neither was it a no.

I slipped inside, leaving the door partway open behind me.

Mrs. Rawlings crossed her arms. "What is this you are blathering on about?"

"I found something," I said. "I've been helping Mr. Rawlings research a case separate from the murder. And tonight, I made a connection I'd never made before."

I explained everything as plainly as I could. I told her what I'd seen that night at the ball, about my realization tonight that Clarissa's beau and the attacker from Vauxhall were the same man, and my theory that it was *me* the man was after, not Alexander.

She listened with narrowed eyes. Not narrowed in irritation or disbelief but rather in focus. When I finished, she stood there, considering everything I'd said.

"I know it sounds far-fetched," I said, my throat tight. "I *know* it does. But there is also some logic to it, is there not?"

Mrs. Rawlings frowned. "There are holes to the story though. Why did the man attack you at Vauxhall? How did he even know you'd returned to London?"

A spark lit up my spine, sharp and hot. "Clarissa," I breathed. "I saw her that same morning. She knew I was in Town."

Mrs. Rawlings tipped her head. "So you believe she saw you, and then she told her lover, who decided to eliminate you as a witness before you made a move against them."

Mrs. Rawlings might be ornery and difficult, but she was also as intelligent a woman as I'd ever met. She was making connections I hadn't yet considered.

"Yes," I said. "Yes, I think you are right. He could easily have followed us from Bow Street to Vauxhall. It was the perfect place to mount an ambush, strike when I was most vulnerable."

"But he did not account for my son," she said, pride clear in her voice.

"No, he didn't." My thoughts were racing. "He must have assumed that catching us by surprise would be enough to overpower the both of us." I swallowed. "It nearly was."

Mrs. Rawlings began pacing slowly, crossing the shadowy length of her room. "But even if it is true—of which I am far from convinced—what does this all matter at this point? Bow Street has caught the man. All Alexander needs to do is identify him as the attacker, and this is over. The man's motive is secondary."

Something niggled like a worm in my brain. Alexander's words came back to me from that morning—or yesterday morning, rather.

They might have the wrong man, he'd said.

"But . . ." I began, my thought half formed.

"But what?" Mrs. Rawlings sounded impatient—I *was* keeping her from her bed.

"They arrested the viscount's murderer," I said slowly. "But if I am right about this, and the murderer is *not* the same man who came after us in Vauxhall, then our attacker remains free."

She stood unmoving, hands at her sides, staring at me. Then she shook her head. "Ridiculous," she declared. "It is far too late at night for us to be spinning such tales. Alexander will return in a few days, and you can sort it all out with him. This has changed nothing."

"Except," I said, "I have every reason to believe that *I* am the target, not Alexander. And now that he is gone . . ."

She waved me off. "You are creating fantasies in your head, Miss Lacey. It will do nothing but rob you of sleep and inflate your sense of self-importance."

I did not agree. But again, I had no proof. And the more I tried to sort through everything I *did* know, the more tangled my thoughts and theories grew.

Still. There was a dread inside me, a fearful knowing that made my stomach feel like the inside of an anthill.

Then I heard it.

A creak. But not any creak. It was the long, sharp groan that I'd heard earlier tonight when I'd trod on the third step on the stairs.

My blood ran cold. The air fled from my lungs.

Mrs. Rawlings noticed my reaction. "What is it?" she asked sharply.

I couldn't breathe. "Put out the candle," I hissed.

"Why—"

"Put it out!"

Such was the fear in my voice that she moved without further protest, stepping quickly to the candle on her bedside table and blowing it out, leaving us in the blinding blackness.

"What did you hear?" she whispered, the smallest unease in her voice.

I only shook my head and crept to the door, which I'd left partly open. I peered out, only able to see a sliver of the corridor.

We waited, the quiet and the dark playing tricks on my mind. Mrs. Rawlings made as if to speak, but I held a finger to my lips.

A minute passed, then two, then three. I saw nothing through the gap in the door, no movement or figures. I bit my lip. I could have sworn I'd heard that creak. But Mrs. Rawlings was right. My fear had gotten the better of me, had gone straight to my head and made me invent dangers.

My shoulders relaxed. I exhaled in relief.

Then a shadow in the corridor moved.

Chapter 23

I clasped a hand to my mouth to keep from screaming.

A figure unfolded from the darkness—a man, large and thick shouldered. He was perhaps twenty feet away, but I already knew he was too tall to be Stroud or any of the footmen. He wore all black, his boots wrapped in cloth to muffle his steps, and in his hand—

The faintest gleam of metal in the bare light. A knife.

I pulled away from the gap in the door, my pulse thundering in my ears. Could he hear it? Could he hear me breathing? I kept my hand pressed tightly over my mouth to hide any sounds I might make, not just a scream.

A hand grabbed my arm, and I nearly screamed anyway. It was Mrs. Rawlings, her face pale. She could not see what I saw, but she'd seen how I'd reacted. I pointed one trembling finger at the door, and she leaned forward.

Then she went rigid. Her eyes flew back to mine, and her hand clutched me tighter.

We watched as the man made his way closer, step by step, making not a sound. I could feel Mrs. Rawlings's cold hands around my arm, hear the ragged draw of her breathing.

The man stopped outside my bedroom door, just down the corridor. He paused, leaning one ear toward the door. When he was apparently satisfied, he slowly—slowly—opened the door. The flickering light from the candle I'd left burning in my room danced across his face, and I knew in an instant.

It was *him*. The man from Vauxhall. The man I'd seen with Clarissa. His features registered in my mind like lightning strikes—dark eyes, brown hair heavy with rain, thin lips curled into a snarl. His knife flashed once more as he stepped inside and vanished from sight.

"What do we do?" Mrs. Rawlings's words were barely audible, breathed into my ear.

"I—I don't know." Panic was setting in, bright lights painted across my vision, heat surging in my chest. "He'll see I'm not inside. He'll come looking for me."

How had he tracked me here from London? How had he known which room was mine? Had someone in the house betrayed us, or had he been watching? A memory from the day before darted through my mind—the figure I'd imagined out the window. Or the one I'd thought I'd imagined. He was all too real now.

"We can hide." Mrs. Rawlings was trembling, but her words were quick, determined. "Under my bed."

Something told me that would not be enough. This man had come with a *knife*. He had come to kill. If he wanted me, he would find me.

"Or I'll ring for a servant," she said next.

I shook my head fiercely. "Then they will be in danger."

There was really only one thing to do, and we both knew it. There was only one way to safety.

"We go past him," I whispered. "Now. Sneak belowstairs while he's distracted." We could raise the alarm down there, find some way to defend ourselves.

Mrs. Rawlings hesitated for only a second, then nodded.

I opened the door a few inches more, the hinges thankfully silent. We slipped into the corridor. Mrs. Rawlings held my arm like a vise, and we nearly tripped over each other. This was pure foolishness, plain *idiocy*. How could we think to escape this man, outrun him? He would hear us in a second.

We approached my bedroom door, open only a few inches. My candle on the desk still burned but left most of the room in shadow. When would he discover that I was not in bed?

A low curse came from inside the room.

"Hurry," I mouthed at Mrs. Rawlings. We quickened our steps, moving past my room and farther down the corridor.

Then Mrs. Rawlings's foot caught on the rug. She stumbled and caught herself on the wall with a dull thud. We both froze, staring at each other.

Footsteps pounded inside my room.

"Go!" I hissed at Mrs. Rawlings and shoved her ahead of me. We made it to the end of the corridor before the man burst out of my room behind us.

We clattered down the stairs. I could hear him behind us, those heavy, fast footfalls that matched the frantic pace of my heart. What could we do? Where could we run to escape him?

A bolt of an idea shot through me.

"Go to the servants," I gasped at Mrs. Rawlings as we neared the bottom of the stairs. "They'll help you."

"But you—"

"I'll draw him away." Our feet hit the marble floor of the entry. I flung a haphazard glance over my shoulder. The man was starting down the stairs, taking them three at a time. "Go!"

I pushed her away again, then ran for the front door. *Follow me*, I begged. *Follow me.* I had to keep him from Mrs. Rawlings and the servants. It was me he was after. I couldn't put anyone else in danger.

The door was unlocked. Had he picked the lock? I threw open the door just as the man reached the ground level, the impact shuddering through me. He did not hesitate. He charged after me.

Rain pelted my skin like lashes of ice as I fled. I wore no shoes, and the gravel bit into the soft flesh of my feet. My stockings were shredded in seconds.

I barely registered it. All I felt was the heat in my veins, the fear that climbed my throat like thorns. I did not have a plan; I did not know where to go. My only thought was to *run*.

I rounded the corner of the house, and *there*! The towering trees surrounding the water garden, with its many grottoes and recesses. I could hide. Hide until help came.

The ground turned to grass beneath my feet, muddy and slippery. I dared not look behind me. I knew the man was there, though the rain masked the sounds of his footsteps. My only chance was to lose him in the shadows.

Suddenly, I felt grasping fingers at my back, yanking at the fabric of my dressing gown. My body jolted, gown straining against me. I screamed.

The man swore, his footsteps stumbling behind me. Then the pressure was gone, and I dashed away. I chanced a glance back to see him sprawled on the grass. He'd tried to catch me, but I'd slipped through his fingers. He rolled and came to his feet, his eyes like lightning in the blackness of the storm.

I faced forward, heart exploding from my chest, and I ran. I had a head start now. I could do this, hide from him in the gardens. I knew them better than he did.

The few seconds it took for me to reach the first trees felt like hours. I was exposed to the wind and the rain and his *eyes*. Finally, I crashed into the brush and shadow, flung myself into their safety. The darkness enveloped me. As soon as I was hidden from his view, I sharply changed direction, going toward the lake. I slowed my pace, trying to stay quiet.

My breaths came too quickly. I was just the barest step from collapsing into a panic. Every one of my senses was alight.

I picked my way through the garden, moving as quickly as I dared. Indecision racked my brain. Should I hide, find a shadowed nook and keep my head down? Or would that spell certain death? If I kept moving, he would be more likely to hear me, see me. But so could anyone who came to help me. Assuming Mrs. Rawlings sent anyone after me. And did I want Stroud or any of the poor footmen to face this monster with his knife?

A sob hitched in my throat, and I forced it back, releasing only a crying gasp. Why wasn't Alexander here when I needed him the most? He'd sworn to protect me, but he'd left. He'd gone, and I was alone yet again, desperate and vulnerable.

There was a boat.

I remembered in a flash. There was a small rowboat on the shore of the lake. I'd seen it that day Alexander had told me of his past. I could manage rowing, I was certain. I'd done it often enough at home. And if I could find it, I could get away. I could keep everyone from danger.

Decision made, I crept through the deepest shadows. My entire body trembled, awareness raising the hair on my neck and arms. I looked every which way, alert for any sign of the man. But he'd lost me, just as I'd lost him.

A break in the brush revealed the house, a hulking blackness against the roiling rainclouds. No lights glowed in any of the windows. Had Mrs. Rawlings reached the servants? My stomach wrenched. What if this man had an accomplice who had followed her? What if help *wasn't* coming?

I forced air into my lungs. I needed to keep breathing—now was *not* the time to faint.

I moved swiftly, quietly, making my way through the gardens. I had a sole purpose now. Find the boat. Escape.

The darkness ahead peeled away. I'd reached the main section of the water garden—the canal that ran perpendicular to the shore of the lake. There was no shelter ahead, nothing to hide me. I crouched in the protection of a large tree trunk and peered around me but saw no sign of my pursuer. I had to cross. There was no way around it.

I started forward, my bare feet slipping on the stones of the walkway. A balustraded bridge crossed the canal a few feet away. I made for it.

A shadow rushed me from the side, and a shriek escaped my lips before he slammed into me, knocking the breath from my lungs. His hand clamped over my mouth, an iron arm grasping around my waist.

"There you are," he rasped. "Slippery one."

I struggled, throwing an elbow into his side. He grunted. One arm released me. But a moment later, the knife flashed, the edge stopping against the skin of my throat. I froze.

"You've been a great deal of trouble." His words were tight in my ear, angry and harsh. "Taking up with the Runners, fighting me in London, fleeing to the country. But I like a challenge."

My hands, trembling and useless, clutched at his arm.

"Clarissa insisted you wouldn't report us." His hot breath curled against my neck. "But I have less faith in you, Miss Lacey. I think you told your *noble* Bow Street man everything."

I couldn't breathe. I couldn't escape. He would cut my throat and fade into the night.

All hope fled.

"I'll take care of him soon enough," he said. "For now, I'll enjoy ending this game between us. Finally."

One blazing thought flashed through the terror, in the fragment of a second after he finished speaking.

Alexander.

This man would be after him next. He would kill him. I could not let him.

He moved his knife, angling to one side of my throat. I had one chance.

I dropped.

I gave up all my weight, my legs collapsing under me. The hot edge of the knife sliced against my neck, but I slipped through his grasp. My knees hit the walkway with a painful crash, and I scrambled away, my fingers scraping the stones, desperate to find purchase. I rolled as he came after me, and I kicked out.

He grunted as my foot connected with his knee. "You little devil."

I tried to rise, but I stumbled, tripped, fell again. I turned. He was there, looming over me, knife held high.

I threw up my hand in a pitiful defense.

A blast cracked through the night—a flash of light and smoke.

The man staggered back. Dropped his knife. Clutched his chest. Blood between his fingers.

His eyes met mine. The hatred there drained away, replaced by cold realization. Then his face slackened, and he fell, splashing back into the stone pool of the canal. He did not move.

I stared, still splayed on the ground, half sitting. What had—How had—

Alexander.

He appeared out of the dark like an avenging angel, features fierce and bold. He held a pistol in both hands as he ran to me from the direction of the house, eyes focused, chest heaving.

He fell to his knees beside me, dropping his pistol with a clatter. "Beatrice!" His hands flew over me—my arms, my face, my shoulders—searching for injuries. "Did he hurt you?"

"Alexander." I grasped his arm, trying to convince myself he was real. His greatcoat was soaked through, his hair dripping. But how? He was miles away, on his way to London.

"Did he hurt you?" he repeated desperately.

I shook my head wildly. "No. No, I'm well."

"Stay here," he ordered, and then he darted toward the pool, where the man had fallen.

I watched Alexander, tears pricking even as I tried to catch my breath. I could not convince my body that the danger was gone, panic still surging through my veins. Only minutes had passed since I'd been with Mrs. Rawlings in her room.

He bent over the pool for a few seconds, then returned, a grim set to his jaw.

"Is he . . . ?" I whispered.

He nodded tersely as he knelt beside me again.

Dead. My hands shook. The man had tried to kill me, and now he was dead. My shock, brittle and dizzying, swept through my body.

Alexander took my shoulders, inspecting me again. His fingers tightened. "Your neck."

I felt it then, the sting at my throat. I reached up to touch my neck, and my fingers came away slick with blood.

Alexander's expression turned murderous, and if he hadn't already spent his bullet, I imagined he would have shot the man again. Alexander jerked a handkerchief from his jacket pocket and pressed it against the cut, a low curse escaping his lips.

I barely heard his words or felt the rain that fell on us. I stared up at him, still trapped in absolute disbelief. His eyes rose to meet mine. They held there, raindrops sliding down the planes of his cheekbones.

He'd come. He'd protected me. Just as he'd promised he would.

I threw my arms around him, and I wept.

He pulled me against him, holding me so tightly I could scarcely breathe. "It's over," he said again and again, the words a balm. "It's over."

After a few moments, I heard shouts and footsteps coming from the house.

"Here!" Alexander shouted. "We're here!"

I did not pull away from him as the household approached. I kept my face buried in his chest, clutching him tightly around the waist. He did not release me either, one hand keeping the handkerchief pressed to my neck, the other wrapped firmly around my shoulders.

"What's happened?" Mrs. Rawlings asked, voice sharp and brisk.

"I shot him," Alexander said grimly. "He's dead."

A stunned silence followed.

"You are sure?" That was Stroud, shocked.

"I am sure." Alexander's deep voice reverberated in his chest.

"Is Miss Lacey . . . ?"

Was Mrs. Rawlings expressing *concern*? I peeked up through Alexander's arms and could just see her face reflecting the light from the lantern she held. She stood there in the rain, her brow set in a deep furrow, her mouth parted as she gazed at me in her son's arms.

"She's hurt." Alexander took my hand and helped me press it against the makeshift bandage at my neck. Then he shifted me more solidly against his chest and rose to his feet. "I'm taking her up to the house."

"I can walk," I whispered, and I knew Alexander heard me, but his arms only tightened around me. He wasn't going to put me down, and I found I did not mind.

"Williams," Mrs. Rawlings barked at a footman. "Send for the doctor, now."

Alexander said something else to Stroud about fetching the constable, but my mind was growing hazy. I did not want to listen. I just wanted to feel Alexander's warmth and strength around me, hear the beating of his heart through his damp shirt.

Then he was carrying me away, through the rain and dark and cold. Mrs. Rawlings trailed behind, and then there was Agatha at the door of the house, her eyes wide with fear. Alexander brought me into the parlor, Mrs. Rawlings calling orders for the servants to build up the fire and fetch a blanket, hot tea, and food.

I watched it all from a strange distance. Everything had happened so quickly. It felt surreal. Impossible. I'd almost died *again*. I'd come so close. My body shook, the events of the last few minutes taking their toll.

Alexander set me on the sofa and knelt beside me. My eyes flicked to him. And there they stayed.

His chest rose and fell, no doubt from the exertion of carrying me to the house. His expression, always so indifferent, was carved with emotion, the shadows of worry and regret. Gently, so gently, he leaned forward and moved the handkerchief away from the cut on my throat, which stung in the open air. There was blood on my clothing, I noted distantly.

"The bleeding has slowed," he said quietly, and his soft brogue wrapped around his words, comforting and gentle. "I think we might avoid sutures, but the doctor will wish to see it."

He took my head in his hands and tilted my face toward the fire, searching for other injuries. Though his skin was rough, he held me so tenderly that it made me wish to weep again.

"Are you hurt anywhere else?" His thumbs brushed over my cheekbones, featherlight.

I attempted to shake my head with his hands still cradling me. "No," I managed. "No, I don't think so."

With a healthy dose of skepticism in his eyes, he looked me over, carefully, thoroughly, taking my arms in turn and inspecting them for injury. After seeing the state of my muddy feet, I thought he might order me upstairs to take a bath and change, but he only had Agatha bring a cloth and basin to quickly wash my feet. Perhaps he knew I would have refused to leave him. Perhaps he was as reluctant as I was to be parted, even briefly.

Another servant brought a blanket, which Alexander wrapped around my shoulders. After a few minutes, the servants left, and the room quieted.

Only Mrs. Rawlings remained, standing at the door. "I'll see to the tea," she said quietly, then closed the door behind her.

Alexander moved to sit beside me on the sofa, adjusting the blanket around my shoulders as if needing something to occupy his hands.

"How are you here?" I asked, my voice finally beginning to steady. The warmth of the fire and the blanket and Alexander's attentions were doing a world of good. "You should be halfway to London."

"I was," he said. "I stopped at an inn for the night, and who should I come across but a messenger from Bow Street, on his way to Briarstone with an urgent letter."

I straightened. "What?"

He nodded grimly. "Apparently, the man Bow Street arrested for the viscount's murder had an alibi for the time of the attack at Vauxhall, which meant he could not have been our assailant. They only discovered it after Drake sent us that letter, so they dispatched a messenger to urge us to remain in the country."

He faced me. "And I realized," he said, "that this might have been the opportunity our attacker was waiting for. If he had somehow tracked us to Briarstone, then I'd abandoned you at the worst possible moment."

I took his hand, laced his fingers between mine.

He seemed strangely distracted by that, staring down at our intertwined fingers before continuing on. "I turned back. I rode hard and fast. I—" His voice broke off.

I searched his face. His expression was haunted, tortured.

"I was almost too late," he whispered. "When I saw him standing over you, I thought I was."

"You weren't," I said fiercely. "You saved me."

"I shouldn't have left you here unprotected." He tore his hand from mine and stood, going to stand before the fire, one hand bracing the mantel. He took deep breaths, his shoulders bowed. "You nearly died." His words were rough. "And it was my fault."

My heart ached. I rose and went to his side, my bare feet still cold, even on the fire-warmed floor. I slipped my hand into the crook of his elbow, leaning my forehead against his upper arm. He tensed at my touch.

"I am alive because of you." My voice held no frailty now. It was certain, true. "I know that without any doubt. You acted with the information we had. You made the choice you believed was right."

"But if I'd listened to you"—he protested quietly, still facing the fire, his left hand gripping the mantel—"if I'd brought you with me, then—"

"We cannot say what might have happened," I said. "If I had gone with you, he might have followed and murdered us both on the road. If you had stayed, he might have broken in and killed me anyway."

He did not move, did not seem to hear my words. I stepped closer, reaching up with one hand to gently sweep his face toward me. His eyes met mine, darkly reflecting the light of the fire below us. The heat reached to me, lit the space between us.

"None of that matters." I traced the shape of his jaw with my fingertips, stopping with my thumb on his bottom lip. He watched me, not seeming to breathe. "You saved me, Alexander Rawlings," I whispered. "And I shall never forget it." I rose onto my toes and pressed the lightest of kisses to his lips. He let me, his hand going to my waist, pulling me close for one beautiful second. The cut on my neck twinged, but the pain was distant—unimportant—when his lips were against mine.

Then he stepped back, breath ragged. "Please, Beatrice," he said. "I can't. We can't."

I blinked. "Why is that?"

"I should not have kissed you yesterday." He ran a hand through his hair, damp and curling at the ends. "I am your protector, and you are a guest in my home. I will not take advantage of you in that way."

"Yes, because clearly I find your kisses abhorrent," I said dryly.

"It is no laughing matter," he said. "I am trying to be a gentleman. What I did yesterday, how I acted—"

"Heavens above." I threw up my hands. "We both nearly died tonight, and you are worried about propriety?"

"With you?" His eyes flickered. "Always."

My head lightened suddenly, my stomach flipping. I took a deep breath and one step forward. He did not back away again.

"If you hadn't kissed me, I would have kissed you," I said. "Does that make you feel any better?"

His mouth parted, and he swallowed, and I thought that perhaps I'd gotten through to him and that he would finally take me in his arms and kiss me. After tonight, there was nothing more I wanted in all the world than his arms around me.

The door opened, and Mrs. Rawlings stepped inside with a tea tray, and I could not think of anything so frustrating as being interrupted by the mother of the man one wished to thoroughly kiss.

She saw us standing close together, and there was not one jot of surprise in her expression. She only came to set the tray down on the table in front of the sofa.

"Take some tea, Miss Lacey," she said briskly. "It will do you good."

She poured me a cup, added liberal amounts of cream and sugar, and held it out to me. I took it with a sigh and sat again on the sofa.

"The doctor and constable have been sent for," Mrs. Rawlings said to Alexander. "They should arrive within the hour."

He nodded absently. How I wished I knew what thoughts were trailing through his head at that very instant.

"They took the body to the coach house," she said in a quieter tone. "You said you wanted to search it."

Alexander exhaled. "Yes. I'll do that now."

Yet he hesitated, not wanting to leave me, I was sure. I gave him a slight nod. I was well enough here without him, even if it was certainly not what I preferred. His expression loosened slightly, and he strode from the room.

Mrs. Rawlings sat on the sofa beside me and served herself a cup of tea. For a long minute, there was nothing but silence between us, the clink of spoons against teacups almost deafening.

"I feel I must thank you yet again, Miss Lacey," she said suddenly, setting down her teacup.

"Thank me?"

"For what you did tonight."

"For luring a dangerous criminal into your home?" I asked, incredulous.

"No," she said, and there was a tone in her voice I'd never heard before. Softness. "For risking your life to save mine."

"I didn't—"

"You did," she said firmly. "I would never have been able to outrun him. You drew him away."

I shook my head. "He was there for *me*. How could I let him hurt you or any of the household?"

She gave a short laugh—not in humor but in disbelief. "What sort of woman are you, Miss Lacey? I cannot, for the life of me, understand you."

"Perhaps because your foundational beliefs about me were so very misguided," I said, my tone only slightly sardonic.

"There is truth to that," she admitted. "I am finding it difficult to reconcile what I assumed about you with what I now know. But what I know, little as it might be, is . . ." She swallowed. "Good. In fact, I think you might be a very good person indeed."

Tears pricked my eyes, and I dropped my gaze, a lump in my throat.

"And perhaps," she went on, her voice gruff, "*perhaps* you might even be good enough for my Alexander."

I exhaled a little laugh, raw and raspy. "Do not say things you do not mean, Mrs. Rawlings."

"I never do."

I met her eyes again. She held her head high, hands clasped primly in her lap.

"Thank you," I said softly.

She nodded, picked up her tea, and began sipping as if she hadn't just bared her soul to me.

Alexander returned a half hour later, shaking the rain from his coat. He looked immediately to me, as though reassuring himself that I was safe. Stroud followed him inside, looking rather pale as he closed the door.

I sat up straight, holding my teacup tightly. "Did you find anything?" I wasn't sure I really wished to know. I was only glad I did not ever have to see that man again, dead or alive.

Alexander's jaw tightened, and he gestured to Stroud, who suddenly looked as if he'd rather swallow glass than be in this room. "We've had another development."

"What has Stroud to do with this?" Mrs. Rawlings asked.

The butler stepped forward, gulping. "I helped carry the body to the coach house," he said, his voice weak, though I imagined carrying a body would do that to a person. "And I recognized him."

I stared. "You knew him?"

"I did not *know* him," he clarified. "That is, I spoke to him in London, when I went to—" He stopped, but we all knew. When he'd gone to investigate me.

"He found me in a pub," Stroud went on, addressing the ground. "Said he'd heard that I'd been asking about you. He told me a few things, which I know now to be false"—his gaze finally flicked to me—"and asked me some questions in return. I thought it was simply conversation, but looking back . . ."

"It is clear that he was searching for Miss Lacey," Alexander finished tightly, the muscles in his neck drawn tight as a bowstring. "In fact, I am quite sure he followed Stroud to Briarstone. If so, he was likely here for days."

I blinked. "Days? But then . . ." My voice cut out.

"What is it?" Alexander asked, brow furrowed.

I tried again. "Two days ago, before you left for London, I thought I saw someone watching the house."

Alexander's gaze sharpened on mine. "And you did not tell me?"

"I should have," I said. "I'm sorry, truly. But I convinced myself I imagined it. Now I can only assume that was how he knew where my room was."

Stroud hung his head. "I must beg your forgiveness, Miss Lacey," he said, remorse clear in his voice. "And I shall resign my post immediately."

The room was quiet, the crackling of the fire the only sound. Mrs. Rawlings gaped at Stroud.

I was past feeling, exhaustion catching me in its hold. I could not summon any amount of anger. "You'll do no such thing," I said tiredly. "You acted out of loyalty to Mrs. Rawlings and to Mr. Rawlings. I see no reason why such a thing should be punished."

Alexander raised his brow. "Near death is not reason enough?"

I shot him a look. "That is hardly what Stroud intended."

"I think I can manage my own household," Alexander replied.

I sat back, waving him forward as if to say *by all means*.

He narrowed his eyes at me but turned to face Stroud. He paused a few seconds. "I do not trust you, Stroud," he said finally. "Not now, at any rate. You must earn that back."

Stroud nodded, his expression sober. "Yes, sir. I will do everything I can."

Alexander sighed. "Very well. We'll speak more of this later. You may go."

Stroud left, sending me a look of gratitude as he exited. But Alexander gripped my attention once again as he turned to face me.

"I found something else," he said, "when I searched the body."

"What?" I asked, feeling as if I could not quite handle any more revelations tonight.

"A note," he said, "addressed to a Jasper Rowde. I assume that was his name, though we will make further inquiries in London."

Jasper Rowde. My mouth twisted to one side. I did not like that the man had a name. It made him human, and I did not want to think of him that way.

"The note was also signed," Alexander said, "with the initials C. H."

My eyes flew to his. "Clarissa Haythorne."

It took a moment for the name to settle in his mind, then he stared at me. "The woman who threatened you? Why would she be writing to this man?"

I held a hand to my forehead. I was just realizing, in the jumble and rush of the night's events, that I had forgotten entirely what I'd discovered earlier.

"They are working together," Mrs. Rawlings cut in. "Those robberies you have been investigating were undertaken by Miss Haythorne and this man. Miss Lacey made the connection not an hour ago."

I nodded, grateful as she explained everything I'd told her tonight. Alexander listened with a furrowed brow, shooting me an occasional glance until she finished.

"I admit I was skeptical when she came to me," Mrs. Rawlings said finally. "It sounds rather fantastical. But I think now we have little reason to doubt. The man proved it himself."

I remembered suddenly, sitting forward. "He mentioned Clarissa tonight." The memory was foggy at best, blurred and warped by the terror I'd felt in the moment. "I can't quite remember what, but they are certainly in league together."

Alexander pressed his lips together, crossing his arms. "It actually makes a great deal of sense," he said finally. "I kept wondering why the man attacked us at Vauxhall when he might have followed me to any dark and quiet corner of London in the midst of my investigation. But if he was after Beatrice, then Vauxhall was the perfect place to ambush her. Anywhere else, she was too well protected."

Alexander clasped his hands behind his back and paced the room. I followed him with my eyes, drawn by his steady stride and fierce brow.

"But we have no proof," he murmured. "Nothing tangible to tie Rowde to the thefts."

I bit my lip. "There is someone else who could provide that proof, though she won't do so willingly."

He turned my way. "Miss Haythorne."

I nodded. "I would not be surprised if she was indeed the true mastermind." She'd always been cunning. I could only imagine how she'd been swept up in this affair.

"Then we need to go to London," he said. "Right away, before she has word of what's happened."

My stomach leaped. *We.* He saw my reaction, and his stern mouth softened.

"We'll leave at dawn," he said, confirming my hopes.

"We can leave now." I sat up straight.

"No, you cannot," Mrs. Rawlings protested. "The doctor is on his way at this very moment to tend to you, and the constable will need words with you both, I am sure. And you *must* sleep. I will hear no arguments. There will be no starting off in the middle of the night."

I was taken aback by the motherly protectiveness in her voice. It appeared that once Mrs. Rawlings decided one was worthy of her approval, she gave it wholeheartedly.

"Very well," I conceded.

"And," she said, "I will be coming with you, as Miss Lacey's chaperone. One must do things *properly*."

I opened my mouth to argue but realized quite quickly that it would be pointless. Mrs. Rawlings did not easily give up a position. Besides, in this case, she was right. We should do it properly, considering how vastly everything had changed between Alexander and me.

I nodded, meeting Alexander's eyes. "At dawn."

Chapter 24

As Briarstone House disappeared behind our coach the next morning, I wasn't sure what I felt. My time there had not been without sadness or difficulty. I'd longed for London every day. I'd been lonely, terrified, and overwhelmed at various points throughout my stay.

And yet the other memories I'd made—the good memories, the *beautiful* memories—made all the rest fade into twilight. Alexander. Our walk in the gardens when I'd told him about my past. The night he'd slept outside my door. Our kiss in his study. And the deep, bone-shattering relief I'd felt when he'd plunged out of the rain-drenched night to save me.

Perhaps . . . perhaps I might return to Briarstone someday. I could not help but think I would, though I wasn't entirely certain what Alexander's intentions were. Besides, I hadn't had the chance to say goodbye to Helen and Elijah. I wasn't ready to give them up just yet, no matter what happened.

I faced forward, and a sharp pain lanced through my neck. I winced and touched my bandaged cut. Last night—or rather, early this morning—the doctor had seen to my wound, thankfully agreeing with Alexander that I did not need sutures.

"Are you in pain?" Alexander asked from across the carriage, nothing escaping his perceptive eyes. Mrs. Rawlings sat beside me.

"Only a little," I said. "It's perfectly manageable."

He frowned. "I wish you'd take the medicine."

I gave a laugh. "This conversation feels very familiar, does it not? Do you enjoy being on the other side of it?"

"Do *you*?"

"Oh, certainly," I said. "I quite like being fussed over."

Mrs. Rawlings made a sound that had the makings of a laugh, though she stifled it immediately.

The day went quickly. We spoke of the case, and Alexander made detailed notes of everything that had happened since we'd left London. He also wrote down everything I remembered of that night at the Granville ball and anything I could remember of Clarissa. We threw around ideas of how we might approach the situation. Clarissa was too smart, too wily to allow herself to be easily caught.

We stayed that night at an inn, all in our own separate rooms, of course. But that did not stop me from sending Alexander a knowing glance as I stepped inside my room, causing the corners of his lips to curl upward. How long ago that night seemed now, at the inn when he'd guarded me as I'd slept. When I'd bandaged his arm and seen the first glimpse of the man behind his stoic facade.

With Alexander in the room beside mine, I slept well that night, and we resumed our journey the next day. If all went according to plan, we would arrive in London late that night. I was desperate to see Ginny. I needed to tell her everything that had happened. Until I did, it almost felt like I was only half myself.

After a short break for a meal at noon, we changed horses and continued on. Lulled to sleep by the food and the sunshine outside, Mrs. Rawlings's head tipped against the door. She did not snore, quite fittingly. That would be unacceptable.

I glanced across the carriage at Alexander. He was watching me. It was the first moment we'd had to talk since we'd left Briarstone. The silence built between us, a knowing thing.

"You are eager to return to London," Alexander said quietly, so as not to wake his mother.

"This will come as a shock to you," I said, "but I did not want to leave in the first place."

I thought he might smile at my jest, but there was something very serious in his eyes.

"You'll be glad to see Mrs. Travers," he said.

"Yes, very glad." I eyed him. He was acting strangely.

"And Jack and Verity." He cleared his throat. "And the others."

What was he—

Oh.

He was speaking about Mr. Drake.

For some reason, the idea that he was even thinking of my previous attachment to his friend produced within me a disbelieving laugh. I clamped a hand over my mouth, not wishing to disturb Mrs. Rawlings.

He frowned, a crease in his brow. "What?"

"You cannot truly be jealous again," I said. "Heavens, what a vice, Alexander. You really must aim to improve."

He sat back. "I'm not jealous."

"Oh?"

"No, I'm . . ." He paused. "Well, perhaps I am."

His admission sent a jolt of awareness and a rush of pleasure through me. It was not like him to admit to so much. To admit to *anything*, really. It was a risk he was taking, and I could see it.

"You preferred him before." He inspected me as if my expression might give away my thoughts. But I had nothing to hide.

"*Before* being the key word," I pointed out with a smile. "Besides, you did not like me either, you'll recall."

"I was deluding myself," he said. "I don't wish to do so again now."

I leaned forward. "I am eager to return to London to see Ginny," I said sincerely, "and to put this entire business behind us. That is all."

The carriage bumped, and our knees jostled together. That simple touch sent warmth spiraling through my chest, and when I met his eyes, he watched me with that new intensity—the same one I'd seen before he'd kissed me in his study. But Mrs. Rawlings shifted beside me, and we both sat back quickly, realizing how close we'd been leaning toward each other. We sat in still silence until Mrs. Rawlings settled again, hands crossed primly across her stomach.

"I do hope Ginny hasn't had the baby while I've been away," I said a few moments later, trying to guide our conversation into safer, less tempting territory. "I would be terribly put out with her."

"She has a few weeks yet, does she not?"

"Yes, but it would be just my luck to miss the birth." I sighed. "I do love babies, and I am quite excited to dote upon hers. I plan to claim aunthood unequivocally."

Alexander's face softened. "A lucky child indeed."

I smiled wistfully. "I never had brothers or sisters, which made for a quiet childhood. I always imagined that when I married, I would have a great brood of children to scurry underfoot, to make me laugh and fill my days. Assuming my husband wanted that also, of course." I stopped suddenly, realizing how my words might have sounded to him. My cheeks filled with heat.

He said nothing for a long moment, his gaze moving to stare out the window.

"He would be a fool not to want that with you," he said finally, softer than I'd ever heard him before. "A life of laughter sounds like a dream."

My lips curved into a smile.

The coach hit another deep rut and bounced, waking Mrs. Rawlings with a start. She began complaining about the state of the roads, which was a very good thing, considering how seriously I'd been contemplating kissing Alexander right there in the carriage.

The day wore on, and as night fell, we drew closer to London. Finally, at nearly ten o'clock, our coach pulled even with the front steps of the Travers home. My anticipation rose like an ocean swell inside of me. Finally.

Alexander handed me down, then turned to offer his hand to Mrs. Rawlings. I could not wait. I darted up the stairs and rapped sharply on the front door. Would Ginny and Jack be asleep? It was late, but not terribly.

Footsteps sounded, heavy and quick, and then the door opened. Jack stood there, brow furrowed, but when he spotted me, his expression lifted in surprise. "Beatrice?"

I beamed at him. "Good evening, Jack. Is your wife in?"

A clatter of footsteps came from the parlor to the left, and then Ginny appeared, gaping at me. "Beatrice!"

I laughed and ran to her, throwing my arms around her.

"Oh, my dear!" she exclaimed. "I've been so worried."

I pulled back, holding her shoulders. "No need for that anymore."

"What do you mean?" Jack asked, thoroughly confused. "Did you not receive our message? We haven't caught your attacker yet. You're still in danger."

Alexander followed me inside. "We received the message," he said. "But we had a few developments of our own that demanded a return to Town immediately."

Mrs. Rawlings came up behind him, shrewdly taking in the details of the house and her son's friends.

Alexander gestured to her. "First, might I present my mother, Mrs. Ruth Rawlings. Mother, this is Jack and Genevieve Travers."

She curtsied. "A pleasure."

Ginny curtsied as well, though she shot me a curious glance, no doubt wondering how we'd come to be traveling with Alexander's mother.

"Won't you come in?" Ginny offered. "I'll send for some tea."

"No, thank you," Mrs. Rawlings said. "It is late. I will go on with the coach to Alexander's rooms."

She patted Alexander on the arm, then glanced at me. "Miss Lacey," she said, then left. I hid a smile. I knew behind the aloofness existed a woman who cared very deeply, even if she disliked showing it.

"First, you must tell us about the man you arrested for the viscount's murder," Alexander said as he and Jack headed into the parlor, Ginny and I following. "Who was it?"

Jack looked grim as we seated ourselves in front of the fire. "It was the viscount's coachman. Apparently, Lord Somerton had dallied with the man's sister years ago, and the coachman's been seeking revenge all this time. A rather tawdry affair, truth be told. The papers have gone wild with news of it."

Alexander sat back, shaking his head. "His coachman," he mused. "How was he found out?"

"Another servant, the viscount's valet, found the coachman sodden with drink on the street," Jack said. "As the valet helped him home, the coachman was muttering, ranting about the whole affair. Apparently, guilt was tearing him apart. The valet came to us, and when we confronted the coachman, he confessed immediately."

"The coachman looked very much like Verity's sketch," Ginny said. "We assumed he was one and the same, so we summoned you home."

"Until you learned he had an alibi," Alexander said.

Jack nodded, brow furrowed. "Why *did* you return if you knew your attacker had not been apprehended?"

"Because he apprehended us," I said darkly.

Ginny paled. "He found you?"

Alexander and I spoke in turns, telling them everything that had happened since we'd left London a fortnight ago. Well, not *everything*. Neither of us mentioned sharing a room at the inn, the conversations we'd shared, our dance—or our kiss. That would certainly have made both of their jaws drop. But we told them all we'd learned about the robberies, my realizations about my past with Clarissa, and the events of that rainy night.

"So you see," I said to finish, "the attack at Vauxhall was never about the viscount's murder. This man and Clarissa Haythorne were in league together, and I was the target all along."

Jack and Ginny sat in stunned silence.

"I expected a story," Jack managed. "I did not expect that one."

I offered a weary smile. "Neither did we, I assure you."

"You are quite certain?" he pressed. "That this Rowde fellow was the same man you saw the night of the robbery at the ball?"

I nodded. "I am positive. And he confirmed it as well, that night when he—" My mouth went dry. I did not want to talk about Rowde, how close he'd come to killing me.

Ginny reached for my hand, gripping it intensely. "He is dead now?" she asked, voice tight. "He can't hurt you again?"

"He's dead." My throat ached. "Alexander made certain of that."

Ginny's brow furrowed slightly, and she glanced at Alexander.

"How are we to connect Miss Haythorne to Rowde?" Jack asked. "If he is dead, we can hardly garner a confession."

"Miss Haythorne is the key to everything," Alexander said. "But time is not on our side. If Miss Haythorne somehow learns what happened to Rowde, she will flee, I have no doubt. We must act quickly before she can slip through our fingers."

Jack nodded. "I agree. We need solid evidence against her."

"Irrefutable evidence," Alexander said forcefully. "I won't have her escaping a guilty verdict because we did not do our jobs. Beatrice has been haunted by this woman long enough."

His eyes were filled with a brutal determination as they met mine, and I almost felt sorry for Clarissa. *Almost*, because she truly was the wickedest woman I knew. Having Alexander come so strongly to my defense caused a surge of contentment inside me. How different this was from two years ago, the last time I'd tangled with her. Now I had friends on my side. I had Alexander.

"Beatrice, my dear," Ginny said suddenly. "Do come with me for a few minutes. You can refresh yourself after the journey and the men can speak."

I raised one eyebrow. "Very well."

She was obviously up to something, but I said nothing more as I stood and followed her from the room. We went upstairs to the guest room I'd occupied before we'd left. All my things were still here, the ones I hadn't packed in my great hurry to leave for Briarstone, and I felt an unexpected relief at seeing them. The world had gone on in my absence, but these small tokens of my life remained.

Ginny closed the door behind her, then turned in a whirl, her large belly almost throwing her off-balance. "What on earth," she said, "happened between you and Mr. Rawlings?"

"Me and Mr. Rawlings?" I repeated as if I hadn't heard her correctly.

"Yes," she said. "The last time I saw you both, you were at each other's throats. Now you are using your Christian names like you've known each other all your lives, and there is such a strange energy between the two of you, almost like . . ." Her voice faded, and her gaze narrowed.

"Like what?" I asked innocently, sitting on the edge of the bed.

She took one step forward. "When you left London," she said, a suspicious gleam in her eye, "you had never been kissed."

"That is true." I nodded quite seriously.

"Has that *changed*?" She drew out the word.

"Are you asking if Mr. Rawlings kissed me?" I paused, tilting my head as if considering the question. "Well, yes. Yes, he did. And he is shockingly good at it, though I've little to compare it to."

"Bea." Ginny stared at me. "Are you quite serious?"

"Indeed," I said. "The man kisses like his life depends upon it. It's rather thrilling."

"No," she said with a sudden laugh. "Not that. Only, he *did* kiss you? And you were . . . receptive?"

I grinned. “One could say that, considering I’ve been trying to convince him to kiss me again ever since.”

She crossed the room in two great steps and sat on the bed beside me, taking my hands. “Tell me everything.”

I did. I filled in all the details Alexander and I had left out of our report downstairs—the type suited only for sharing with one’s closest friend. She listened in astounded wonder, mouth wide as I spoke.

“Heavens, Bea,” she said quietly once I’d finished. “That is much more than a kiss.”

My smile faded, and my hands squeezed hers. “Yes,” I said simply. “It is far more than that. I’m afraid I’m rather in love with him.”

I thought she might squeal, throw her arms around me, laugh in delight. Instead, her eyes filled with tears.

“Oh, darling,” she whispered. “That is wonderful.”

My own eyes grew blurry. “It is, isn’t it?”

“I do not even need to ask if he feels the same.” She swiped at a tear on her cheek. “I sensed it the moment he stepped in the door. The way he looks at you, the way he treats you—it is everything I’ve dreamed of for you.”

“Just perhaps with a different man than you’d originally intended?” I gave a small laugh.

She smiled. “But the right one, I think.”

“The only one.”

She leaned forward and pressed her forehead to mine. “I do not believe I have ever been happier.”

“I’m sure Jack would take issue with that,” I said in amusement.

She only shook her head. “He would understand. Your joy only adds to mine. There is no limit, I’m quite certain.”

“That is good,” I said, resting a hand on her belly, “or this little one would surely push you past it.”

Ginny patted my hand. “How glad I am that you are back. You are safe, and everything is as it should be.”

“Not quite yet.” I sighed. “There is still the matter of Clarissa.”

For the first time since our conversation began, Ginny's eyes darkened. "Yes, there is. But I have little doubt she will get her just reward."

"Come," I said, standing. "Let us go back down. Alexander grows anxious when I'm out of sight."

We returned to the parlor, and as I'd guessed, Alexander was standing at the mantel, fingers drumming on the polished wood. He turned when we entered, and his shoulders lowered slightly as soon as he saw me.

"There you are," he said shortly.

"Missed me, did you?" I swept into the room and seated myself again before the fire. Ginny followed, going to sit beside Jack.

"You are *not* out of danger," he pointed out. "Rowde clearly had accomplices. We haven't any idea who might still be after you."

"They would be determined assassins, indeed, to sneak past the pair of you," I said dryly.

"I'll not grow complacent." Alexander crossed his arms. "And neither do you wish me to, I would wager."

"No," I said with a saucy smile. "Not in the least."

Ginny pressed her lips together, hiding a grin.

Jack looked between the two of us, a sharp crease between his brows. "I am not entirely sure what is going on," he said, "but while you were upstairs, we did have an idea."

"An idea?" I repeated.

"On how to entrap Miss Haythorne," Jack said.

Alexander nodded. "We need a confession from her, or as close to one as we can get. The only way we can think to achieve that is with you."

"Me?" I glanced between the two of them. "How?"

"We want you to meet with her," Jack said grimly. "Convince her to speak of what she's done, who she's colluded with, so we can overhear. If you can do that and we can testify to what we've heard, we have a solid chance at a prosecution against her."

I met Alexander's eyes. He watched me, expression steely. "If I could have you avoid this, I would," he said. "But Jack is right. It is the best way, the surest way, to end this once and for all."

I swallowed, my euphoria from my conversation with Ginny fading. I'd known I would have to testify against Clarissa once she was arrested. I'd been ready to face her, preparing myself. But I never imagined I would be involved in setting a trap for her. I wasn't a Bow Street officer. I wasn't Verity. How could I be clever enough—brave enough—to catch Clarissa in her lies?

But I looked among the three of them, all with determination etched into their faces, and my own resolve steadied and grew. I would not be alone. I could do this. I took a deep breath. "Tell me what I must do."

CHAPTER 25

Normally, the streets of London were my favorite place in the world. They invigorated me with their energy and vitality, and I never grew tired of watching people cross to and fro.

Today, however, not even the fascinating melee of London's busy Mayfair could distract me from the nerves that buzzed inside me, like a swarm of bees in a summer meadow.

"Are you ready?" Alexander spoke in my ear, his voice a deep rumble in his chest.

He stood right beside me, and though we did not touch, I could feel the warmth of his body, the air around us cold and blustery.

"I'm ready." My voice creaked, giving me away.

"I'll be there," he promised gruffly. "Just out of sight but close enough to hear everything. You needn't be afraid."

I looked up at him. "I'm not afraid for my safety," I said. "I'm only afraid I won't be able to do what I need to, that this will continue to hang over my life like an axe. I want to—" I had to stop, swallow hard. "I want to be free from this. From *her*."

He gazed down at me, his eyes holding a familiar understanding. "You *can* do this, Beatrice," he said quietly. "Only you can end this the way you deserve."

His voice was a balm to my nerves, his words a reminder of all I had overcome. He was right. This was my battle, and I intended to win it decisively.

He glanced up. "Here is Drake."

Mr. Drake was crossing the street, his sandy hair tucked under a hat and his hands in his pockets. He spotted us on the corner and made his way over. He smiled at me. "Miss Lacey."

"Mr. Drake," I greeted him. I'd seen him this morning when we had all met together at Bow Street—Mr. Drake, Jack, Verity, Mr. Denning, Alexander, and I—to go over the specifics of our plan. I had thought that perhaps there would be some awkwardness between us, perhaps a flash of embarrassment on either of our sides. But he had been all that was professional and good-natured, and I'd been immediately at ease.

"Drake will wait here with you until it is time," Alexander said, though we'd gone over the plan a dozen times at least. "He will observe from here once you've gone in."

I nodded.

Alexander shot a glance at Mr. Drake, who apparently received some sort of signal from his friend because he coughed and turned away.

Alexander stepped closer to me. "Be careful," he said in a low, rough voice that sent a shiver across my skin. This man really should not be allowed to whisper anything in a lady's ear. It made me feel rather scandalous, though we stood on a public street.

"I doubt Clarissa will pull a weapon on me," I managed lightly.

"One never knows what a cornered rat will do." His expression hardened. "Stay alert. If anything feels wrong, just leave."

"You know I won't do that."

He exhaled. "I know." His fingertips trailed from the inside of my wrist up my forearm, leaving a streak of fire behind.

"I have to finish this," I whispered. I knew what I had to say and what I had to make Clarissa say.

"I know," he said again. His hand settled behind my elbow. One small tug would bring me close enough to kiss him. But he only swallowed hard, the muscles in his throat tight, and gave the smallest press of his fingers against my arm. Then he turned and strode away, setting his hat on his head with both hands as he made his way through the crowd.

My pulse escalated as soon as he left my side. It only reaffirmed to me how settled he made me feel, how safe. It was a feeling I would never take for granted.

Alexander crossed the street and opened the door to Hatchards bookshop. That was where we'd planned to make our stand against Clarissa, if she deigned to show. I could just make out the red flash of Verity's pelisse through the bow window. She and Jack were already inside, pretending to shop, while Mr. Denning kept watch up the street.

"Everything will be fine, Miss Lacey," Mr. Drake said from behind me, his confidence a palpable thing.

I glanced at him. He really was a handsome gentleman, with a contagious smile and shoulders any girl would swoon over. But there was no flutter in my stomach when he spoke nor any heat in my cheeks when he looked my way.

My heart was spoken for.

"I hope so," I replied.

We stood in silence, both of us watching around the corner for Clarissa. It was nearly three o'clock. Would she come?

Then I caught sight of a dark-blue cloak weaving through the crowd toward the bookshop. It was a woman, from the build of the figure and the make of the cloak. She wore her hood, though it wasn't raining, and when she glanced to the side, I caught her face in profile: slightly squashed nose, freckles, and clever eyes.

"That's her," I said, my mouth dry.

Mr. Drake moved up beside me, and we watched as she reached the doors of the bookshop, looked up and down the street, then entered.

"That is your cue, Miss Lacey," Mr. Drake said quietly. "Good luck."

I nodded disjointedly. My lungs were too tight, and I felt like I might be ill. I inhaled deeply, set my shoulders, and strode across the street.

Entering the bookshop, I glanced around as nonchalantly as I could manage. To my right were Verity and Jack, inspecting a shelf of books behind the counter. Neither looked at me—professionals, the both of them. I did not see Alexander. He must have made himself scarce in one of the other rooms nearby. He would come closer once I engaged Clarissa and distracted her.

I swept my gaze to the left, and there she was, just entering another room full of bookshelves. She moved slowly, cautiously. She wouldn't know who to expect. I'd had an anonymous note delivered to her home early that morning, a note that demanded a meeting at this time at Hatchards. Alexander hadn't been at all certain she would come, but I'd had a sense that she would not be able to resist. I'd been right.

Her back was to me, so I had the advantage as I approached. I stopped in the doorway, noting the other door beyond Clarissa, the room being almost more of a passageway, albeit lined with books.

"Miss Haythorne." My voice was low but steady.

She turned sharply, and I was rather gratified to see the shock cross her face, her mouth parting. She stared at me a moment, then straightened, seeming to connect her thoughts. "*You* sent me that note?"

I stepped farther into the room so it was just the two of us having a private conversation. Or so she would think. But I knew Alexander, Verity, and Jack would all be shifting closer now outside the doors on either side of us.

"I did," I said evenly.

Her eyes razed over me, intelligent and hard. She did not like this. She was a woman who always knew everything.

"I'm leaving," she said shortly and started forward.

My stomach turned. I had not anticipated this. I'd thought her curiosity would keep her here, but she was too careful.

I stepped to block her. "I think you might reconsider once you hear what I have to say."

"I doubt it." She then turned on her heel and went toward the other door.

"I know what you and that man were doing the night of the Granville ball."

My words had their intended effect. Clarissa stopped abruptly, paused, then whirled on me. I was in the thick of it now.

"What did you say?" she asked dangerously.

I narrowed my eyes. She'd intimidated me long enough. She had no power anymore. "That night when I interrupted your assignation," I said, stepping closer. "But it was much more than that, wasn't it?"

"You don't know the first thing about what you saw." Her lip curled.

"Oh?" I tilted my head. "So you and Jasper Rowde weren't working together to steal from Lord Granville?"

Her sneer fled in an instant, replaced by a stunned incredulity.

"Oh yes," I said. "I know his name. And I know that you two have been partners for years. You infiltrated parties and balls, then found a way to sneak him inside to rob people blind. Am I right?"

She said nothing, her expression twisting into something cold and angry.

"I know that I am," I said, "though I cannot figure why you would do it. You have everything, Clarissa: wealth, status, influence. Why would you risk it all for a common thief? For money you don't need?"

"He isn't common," she bit back, then looked like she regretted it immediately.

Her answer told me a great deal, and I was taken aback. Whatever her relationship was with Rowde, she cared for the man. Or at least, however much a creature like her could care for another person. I felt a small pang of sadness for her—warring with my anger—at the loss she did not even know was coming.

"Is *he* the reason you never married?" I gripped my skirts with both hands. "I did wonder. You must have had prospects."

"Of course I had prospects," she snapped, then quickly glanced behind her as if realizing how her words might carry. "Stifling, boring, enormously irritating prospects."

"So Mr. Rowde is . . . exciting?"

She sniffed, nose in the air. "You wouldn't understand, dull girl that you are."

"Yes, so dull I cannot keep two thoughts in my head at the same time," I said dryly.

She eyed me, then moved closer. "You know as well as I how empty our lives are." Her voice was low and sharp. "Preening and primping for Society, a society that only cares if we are married or not. I needed more, you see. And Jasper showed me that. He was a footman in my own house, and I caught him stealing from us. But instead of turning him in, we fell in together."

I stared at her, trying to hide my surprise at every word that fell from her lips. "The risk though," I managed. "How could it be worth it to you?"

"What is life without risk?" she said. "Besides, it isn't as if the people we steal from do not deserve it. They are hypocritical monsters, the lot of them. Jasper helped me see that."

"Did he?" I asked. "Or does he simply see you as a means to a greater quarry?"

She gave a curt laugh. "Oh, Beatrice, you are naive. I am well aware he sees me that way, just as I see him as a way to inject a bit of excitement into my life."

"Excitement?" I echoed. "Does that include trying to kill me at Vauxhall?"

Her expression froze. "I . . . I did not approve of that action on his part."

"So you weren't responsible for informing him that I'd returned to London?"

She gulped. "I was. But I told him I would ensure you stayed silent about what you saw at the Granville ball. We were never sure if you believed our ruse of a romantic tryst in the library."

"I did," I said. "Until recently."

She shook her head. "That was why I started those rumors, to drive you away from London—and Jasper. I only just stopped him from going after you that very night."

"So I should be thanking you?" I said, a harsh edge to my voice. "For ruining my life two years ago so your paramour did not kill me?"

Clarissa's face was tight, intent. "Perhaps you *should* thank me. Jasper does not like leaving things to chance. That was why he followed you when he learned about your return to London. He watched you go into Bow Street, saw you in the company of two Runners at Vauxhall. He imagined that you might finally be reporting the robbery. His blood runs hot when he feels threatened, and he does not think properly." She leaned forward and spoke in a rough whisper. "I do not know what you are about, Beatrice, but I will warn you: Jasper is not a man to be trifled with. If you swear to keep quiet and return to your tiresome little country house, I can convince him to leave you be."

"Can you?" I asked. "He seems to be a rabid dog with a very long lead."

"He can see reason," she snapped. "I will ensure it. Just swear you will not tell, and I will keep my end of the bargain."

I looked at her, my stomach rioting in absolute disbelief at the woman in front of me. Because she'd been *bored*, she'd allowed herself to get swept away with a man like Jasper Rowde. She'd just implicated herself in attempted murder, for heaven's sake.

I shook my head slowly. "I am sorry, Clarissa, but I cannot keep silent any longer."

Her eyes turned to ice. "That is a dangerous path to take. I know Jasper far too well."

"Knew," I said.

Clarissa blinked. "What?"

"You *knew* Jasper."

She said nothing. She stood stock-still.

"Do you know where he is?" I asked. "Where he went?"

"He told me—" She was gripping her reticule hard. "He told me he was leaving Town for business. To sell some of our goods."

"He lied," I said. "He came after me."

"I told him not to," she hissed. "I swear it! I told him he'd frightened you off, that we should leave it be."

"He did not listen." I swallowed before going on, the words sticking to my tongue like dried honey. "He's dead, Clarissa."

There was no pleasure in delivering such news. Even if Rowde was a monster and deserved his fate, even if she was a conniving, stealing wretch, I thought she might actually have loved the man. And death was not something that ever knocked lightly on anyone's door.

Her face went utterly pale, leaving her freckles in stark contrast. "You're lying," she whispered.

I shook my head, chest aching. I hated her, but she deserved the truth. "He followed a servant from London to the house where I was hiding. He waited until the middle of the night, then broke inside."

She gave a wordless shake of her head.

"He chased me from the house with a knife." I tried to hold my voice steady. "He would have killed me. But I was not without protection." The memory of Alexander appearing through the rain and dark shot a burst of light through me. It gave me determination, courage. "Jasper was shot and killed," I managed.

Her body was rigid, as if her bones were made of sharp pins. "I don't believe you."

I opened my reticule and pulled out the note we'd found on Rowde, the one signed with *C. H.* I hadn't been sure I would need it, but she was clinging so desperately to her denial. "Then how did we come into possession of this letter?" I asked quietly, holding it out for her to see.

Clarissa did not move, her eyes fixed on the letter. Then they turned to me, burning and boiling. "You little cow," she said in a gasp. "You killed him. You killed him!"

She charged at me. Her hands lashed at my face, fingers bent into claws. I threw up my arms, blocking her. My heart choked in my throat. She railed against me, her rage unbridled.

"You killed him," she shrieked, not caring one whit that we stood within a public shop.

I shoved her away, and she stumbled back a step. She found her balance, then flew forward again.

Something primitive and raw rose up inside me. Acting on instinct only, I formed a fist with my right hand and drove it at her face with all my might.

It connected with her jaw, and she dropped, falling to her knees and yowling like a cat. I gasped, clutching my hand against my chest. Blast, but it hurt!

Then Alexander was there, grasping Clarissa's arms and yanking her to her feet. She fought him, though she looked dazed and confused. Jack darted through the opposite door and took over, pulling her arms behind her back. Verity appeared with iron fetters and worked with Jack to contain her.

I stood there, shaking, as Alexander turned to me.

He grasped my elbows. "Are you well?" His hold on me was almost too tight, as if he were reassuring himself.

I nodded, then shook my head. "I've hurt my hand," I said, holding it against my chest.

He released a breath through his nose, then took my hand in his, gently cradling it as he removed my glove. He examined the skin of my knuckles, already turning red and purple. I hissed in pain as he bent one of my fingers.

"I really must teach you to plant a facer," he said. "You've likely fractured it."

"I have no regrets."

His eyes flicked up to mine. "No. I do not imagine you do."

Clarissa was cursing, language I was quite certain her mother would have fainted to hear her use.

Verity and Jack each took one of her arms and led her from the shop while the other patrons gawped and whispered.

I took several deep breaths and focused on Alexander's face. "Did you hear enough?"

"We heard everything," he said, his fingers pressing into my palm. "You did perfectly. She will not escape this time."

I closed my eyes, relief sweeping over me. It was done. *I'd* done it. The truth would come out, and I would be vindicated after the last two years of torture. No one could argue against this—an arrest and prosecution by Bow Street.

I felt his fingers brush back a curl from my face, and I looked up at him. He watched me, so intent I felt like I ought to be a great painting in a museum.

"You're a marvel," he murmured.

How three simple words could make me want to melt into a puddle, I wasn't entirely sure. But said by this man . . .

"I am, aren't I?" I managed.

He exhaled a laugh, dropping a kiss to the tips of my fingers. "Confidence becomes you."

"Beatrice." Verity had come back into the shop, concern across her face as she approached us. "Are you—" Then she saw my hand in his, our closeness, and understanding dawned.

"She's hurt her hand," Alexander said, turning and setting his palm against the small of my back. "I'm taking her back to the Traverses' and sending for a doctor."

Verity nodded, a sly grin on her face. "We'll need you at Bow Street after. Both of you."

"In time," he said. "Do what you can without us."

Alexander guided me through the shop with that masculine surety I'd once thought off-putting but now found maddeningly alluring.

"Delaying your work?" I asked. "That doesn't sound like you."

"I *am* working," he said. "Minding you is a full-time occupation."

"You do not seem terribly bothered by it."

His fingertips pressed more firmly into my back. "No."

We stepped out onto the street, and it was utterly baffling how so many dozens of people could be passing by in total ignorance of what had just happened inside Hatchards. My life had been drastically altered, while theirs continued on in day-to-day normality.

A coach waited down the street. Mr. Drake was helping—forcing?—Clarissa inside, her face a mask of pure hatred. He followed, then Jack as well. Mr. Denning closed the door behind them, and the coach started off. Several passersby had stopped to watch, whispering behind their hands. I had little doubt that news of Clarissa's arrest would spread like wildfire through the *ton*.

Verity had followed us from the shop and, seeing her husband just ahead, hurried to his side. He took her hand and held it with such sweet familiarity as he looked down at her. She touched his waistcoat and leaned up to press a kiss to his cheek.

It seemed like something of an intimate moment, so I turned to Alexander. Strangely enough, he was also watching Verity and Mr. Denning, brow furrowed as if he were considering some great moral dilemma.

He caught me watching him. "Yes?"

I smiled. "Nothing." I bent my fingers again and found the pain had lessened. "Only, I think I really am well enough. I'd rather go to Bow Street and have this over and done with."

He frowned, then nodded. "Very well. We'll go to Bow Street. But we are still sending for a doctor."

Verity and Mr. Denning walked back to join us, his hand at her elbow, his eyes skimming across the street in constant awareness.

I thought of Jack and how ferociously defensive he was of Ginny. These Bow Street men. There was something innately chivalrous and protective in all of them. Perhaps that was what had drawn them to their profession, a desire to guard and preserve.

I felt Alexander's hand slide from my back to wrap around my waist. A flurry of heat burst through my stomach. I was a capable, intelligent, forward-thinking woman, but I had no defense to his staking so public a claim on my person. He was telling the world I was his. And I quite liked it.

"It seemed everything went according to plan?" Mr. Denning said when they reached us. He did not glance at Alexander's arm around me, though perhaps that careful avoidance only made it more obvious.

Verity had no such qualms. She looked at me, eyes bright, mouth quirked.

"Yes," Alexander said. "Quite thankfully, as our plans go awry more often than we care to admit."

"I see you only mention that after the fact," I said with a raised eyebrow.

Alexander shrugged, uncaring. "In this case, it worked. I have no complaints."

Mr. Denning hailed a hack. As it came to a stop beside us, I glanced back at Hatchards. I released one long, heavy breath, consumed once again by the fullest relief I'd ever felt in my life. I did not know what my life would hold after today, but I knew I was finally free from the shadow that had been my constant companion for so long. And while I hoped the rumors surrounding me would subside eventually, I found I did not care so much as I had in the past. My life was my own again, and I would make anything I wished of it.

Mr. Denning helped Verity inside the hack, then followed her. Alexander held out a hand to me. I took it but paused.

"Thank you," I said softly.

He nodded, eyes fixed on mine, a world opening inside those dark-brown irises. "You're welcome," he said.

Chapter 26

I winced as Dr. Moulton adjusted my hand, inspecting it carefully.

"Fractured, I'm quite sure," he said. "I will wrap it, and you'll need to take care for a few weeks."

We had taken up residence in an empty interview room at Bow Street. Dr. Moulton and I sat at the table, his bag open, while Ginny and Jack observed. Though Ginny had wished to come to Hatchards, Jack had responded so strongly in the negative—"Do see reason, Ginny. None of us is carrying a child"—that she'd relented and compromised by waiting at Bow Street until we'd returned.

"Really, Bea," Ginny said, standing just behind my shoulder. "You ought to have let Mr. Rawlings do the fighting."

"I hardly had the time," I protested.

"Still," she said. "There was a reason we did not send you alone. He knows better how to handle such things."

"Rather rich," Jack said, "coming from a woman who nearly brought me to my knees with her own fist."

I tipped my head to stare at Ginny. "Really? This is a story I haven't heard."

Ginny's face flushed. "And you won't." She turned resolutely back to the doctor. "Any other instructions, Dr. Moulton?"

As Dr. Moulton showed Ginny how to wrap my hand, I glanced out the open door to where Alexander paced in the main office. What he was anxious about, I wasn't entirely certain. I wasn't so grievously injured as to inspire *pacing*.

Mr. Moulton finished the wrapping. "Limited use for four weeks," he advised.

"I suppose my harp practice will have to wait," I quipped.

Ginny shook her head with a smile. "It's waited for twenty-four years. I think it can wait a while longer."

After the doctor left, we went out into the main office, desks and chairs and tables spread throughout. Thankfully, Clarissa had been taken to an upstairs room, so I did not have to see her. I had no qualms about anything that had happened today—she deserved every bit of justice she got—but I'd finally begun to reclaim a sense of calm. Seeing her again would only disrupt that.

Alexander came to meet me halfway across the room. "What did the doctor say?"

I sighed dramatically, holding up my bandaged hand. "He says I will likely never use my hand again. A tragedy, to be sure, but—"

"She will be well enough," Ginny said as she passed. "A few weeks to heal is all."

I glared after her. "A fine friend you are. I only wanted a bit of attention; is that too much to ask?"

She just laughed, going to sit beside Verity. I turned back to Alexander, his lips twitching.

"You have my full attention," he said. "I assure you."

"Good," I said. "A girl can only injure herself so many times."

He shook his head, his dark eyes somehow both serious and amused. "Let us hope this is the last time."

The next few hours passed in a haze of interviews, questions, and far too many cups of tea. I knew it was vital to record all the details of a case as soon as possible, but heavens, it was exhausting being at the center of it all.

It was growing late, the purple sky outside claimed by the coming night, when I noticed how very tired Ginny looked sitting beside me for all those hours. I might have been bearing the brunt of the questions, but she was nearing her ninth month. No doubt worrying for me the last fortnight had not helped anything.

"Ginny, you ought to go home," I said. "You look weary to the bone."

"When you're finished," she said. "I'm well enough."

"Jack?" I needed reinforcement.

He'd been working at a nearby desk but, overhearing our conversation, had already stood. "She's right, Ginny. Let me take you back."

"I don't want to leave Beatrice alone," Ginny said.

Alexander, who sat by Mr. Drake as he recorded my answers to all their questions, leaned forward. "I'll bring her when we've finished," he said. "Likely only another half hour or so."

Ginny finally acquiesced, which spoke to how truly exhausted she was. She and Jack left, then Verity and Mr. Denning soon after. The office quieted, with only a few clerks and other officers finishing a few tasks.

When at last Mr. Drake seemed satisfied, he closed his notes and offered a smile. "I am sorry for what you have been through, Miss Lacey, but I hope we can carry this forward with as little effect on your life as possible."

"Thank you," I said sincerely. "Truly, I am so grateful for your help. For everyone's help."

"I daresay none of us minded in the least," he said. "Rather, we were eager to help, considering—" He stopped midsentence, glancing at Alexander. "That is, of course. You are welcome."

What had that glance meant? *Considering* what?

Mr. Drake stood, and Alexander and I followed suit. "We will contact you if anything else is needed," he said. "I imagine Rawlings will be our go-between."

"Quite," Alexander said.

Mr. Drake smiled and gave a short bow. "Good night, Miss Lacey."

He left, and then it was just Alexander and me.

"I'll see you home," he said. "Mrs. Travers said she would send the coach back for you."

"It's hardly a few minutes to walk," I protested.

"Let us humor her, shall we?"

I gathered my things—gloves, reticule, and bonnet—then followed Alexander toward the front door. Ginny's coach was indeed waiting for us outside, the driver standing beside the horses and looking very familiar.

"Mr. Barton!" I exclaimed. "How do you do?"

"Well enough," he said, smiling broadly. "Pleased to see you. It feels as though I just left the pair of you at that inn."

It did not seem that way to me. Rather, it felt like a lifetime had passed since then, an age that had changed me in so many ways. But I did not need to delve into those feelings with Mr. Barton. "It does indeed," I said, returning his smile.

Alexander helped me into the coach, then followed me inside and sat beside me. He closed the door, and we started off.

I could not help a glance back at Bow Street, to the lighted window, where I imagined Clarissa was being kept. I swallowed hard. "What will become of her?"

Alexander did not ask who I meant. "England's laws do not look kindly on thieves. If she is convicted, I've little doubt the sentencing will be harsh."

I shook my head. "That her life should come to this while mine is . . ." I sighed. "I only mean to say, she and I are more alike than you might think."

"You and Miss Haythorne?" Disbelief was stark in his voice. "As alike as a butterfly and a cockroach."

"Let us hope I am the butterfly in this comparison."

"You're nothing like her," he said flatly.

"And you're wrong," I said. "You do not know what it is to be a woman, to be raised with certain expectations and rules. Clarissa and

I both longed for a life outside what was demanded of us. We both wished for adventure, excitement, romance. In truth, our desires were uncannily similar."

"You, however, did not stoop to grand larceny in your pursuit of such desires."

"Yet," I said, a mischievous tilt to my head.

He exhaled a short noise of amusement. "You should feel not one ounce of sympathy for that woman."

"I cannot help it," I replied. "She lost the man she loved. I can only imagine how that feels." I paused. "It makes one think how one decision can affect a lifetime . . ." My voice faded off, then I shook my head. He was right. I was being too sentimental. Clarissa did not deserve any more of my thoughts. Not now. Not ever.

"What is it you want now?" His voiced had changed, more guarded, careful.

I regarded him. "What do you mean?"

"You said that you wanted adventure, excitement, and romance," he said. "I only wondered if after the last fortnight, that might have changed."

I smiled. "I've had adventure and excitement aplenty. Perhaps enough for a lifetime, but one never knows." I tipped my head. "Romance, however, I could do with a great deal more of."

We passed a streetlamp, and it cast half his face in steep angles, the other half softened by shadow. He looked at me. Oh, how he looked at me. And I realized that this was the first time we'd ever sat beside each other in a coach. Before, he'd always sat across from me, keeping a certain amount of distance. Now, however, the side of his leg brushed my skirts, his boots only inches from mine. I felt a stirring in my stomach. A delicious foretelling.

"Do you know," I said, "that we haven't been alone since we left Briarstone?"

"Trust me," he said, his words thick with meaning, "I am fully aware."

His gaze pierced through me, so intense that I found I could not breathe. I'd faced down both a murderous thief and a vengeful lover in the last three days, but this new awareness between us brought more trepidation than the two of them combined. I knew what I wanted. I knew what I longed for. But what if our hopes were not the same? He'd been a bachelor officer of Bow Street for so long. What if I was not enough to—

"When we were at Briarstone," he said, the rumble of his deep voice interrupting my thoughts, "there were certain subjects I could not breach."

"Because I was under your protection."

"Yes."

I had to look away, my breaths coming too quickly. "I am not under your protection anymore," I said quietly. My hands were clasped neatly in my lap, proper as I never was. I hardly knew what to do with myself. This conversation could go a million different ways.

Or it could go the one way I hoped for the most.

"That is where you are wrong."

His words forced me to look at him again, the wishing inside me so strong my chest seemed to swell with it. Sometime during the ride, we'd both turned toward each other, as if drawn by a force neither of us fully understood.

"You will always be under my protection, Beatrice Lacey," he murmured. He lifted one hand, trapping my chin between his thumb and forefinger, ensuring I did not look away. "I will always be your defender."

I dared not move. "That sounds terribly expensive," I managed, my voice unapologetically breathless. "Having a Bow Street officer on retainer."

He exhaled a shadow of a laugh. "I have a drastically different arrangement in mind."

"Oh?" I gave a sly smile. "Will you be paying *me*, then? Perhaps a consulting fee? I did solve this case practically alone."

His eyes narrowed, and his thumb brushed over my bottom lip. "Do not play coy, Beatrice," he said in that low, delicious brogue that drove me to distraction.

"I'll play whatever I like," I said, tipping my face up to him, daring him. "I daresay you're going to kiss me either way."

"Considering I've thought of little else in the last three days?" His eyes slid languidly down to my lips. "The chances are very, very good."

"Well then," I whispered, "I shall take that gamble."

He made me wait for it, the horrid man. He leaned forward, taking his time, his movements smooth and unhurried. The air between us felt like the night sky on the edge of a lightning strike. I closed my eyes, felt the brush of his breath against my skin.

His lips touched mine, and that beautiful anticipation burst into pure pleasure. He kissed me slowly, a rich longing unfurling in my chest. I was grateful for the seat beneath me, my knees weak. Alexander Rawlings might be an aloof, serious, sharp sort of man—but he knew how to kiss a woman.

My hands slid up his chest, roving over buttons and wool and the skin above his collar. I took his strong jaw between my hands, and I kissed him back, telling him everything I felt, showing him everything I wanted. His hands dropped to my waist, cinching tight, fingers pressing into my lower ribs.

Our coach rolled to a stop.

We pulled apart just an inch, staring at one another. His eyes were dark, shadowed, beautifully unfocused.

"The Traverses really ought to live farther away," I whispered.

He brushed his lips across mine once more. "I will ensure they hear my full complaint."

Reluctantly, we untangled ourselves from one another, straightening clothing and hair. Upon my nod, Alexander opened the door and stepped down, helping me out after him.

Mr. Barton waited until we climbed the steps, then gave a knowing little wave as he started off. I sighed, moving to open the front door.

Alexander intercepted my hand. "I'm not quite ready to give you up yet," he said, and his words filled every remaining space in my heart.

He pulled me into the deepest-angled shadows beside the door. He kissed me again and again, our hearts melding, our lips dancing. We might've kissed all night. I imagine we both would have preferred that.

But one also needed to breathe, and so we finally parted, chests rising and falling in sync. He leaned his forehead on mine, and I kept my eyes closed, relishing every intoxicating moment.

"What have you done to me, Beatrice Lacey?" he murmured.

I could relate. He'd stolen into my heart, right into the very center of me. The most unexpected, glorious thing. We'd been perfect strangers thrown together by circumstance. Now though . . . Now I *knew* him. I knew what sort of man he was, the values he held dear, the people he loved, and the trials that had formed him. And I loved him so deeply it hurt, like my heart wished to leap from my chest. It was his, fully and completely.

He shook his head, forehead still touched to mine. "I managed to dodge marriage left and right for years," he said, "and yet here I am."

I finally opened my eyes and stared up at him. His expression was set and serious, even as one hand traced up the path of my spine.

"A statement like that, Mr. Rawlings," I breathed, "is sure to keep me from any thought of sleep, so I will beg you to continue."

"It seems fair retribution," he replied, "for all the sleep you have stolen from me."

I frowned. "You'll recall I did not *ask* you to sleep outside my—"

He laughed. "Not that. I'm speaking of every night from the one we met. How often I lie awake thinking of you."

"Oh." I dragged my hands down his lapels and waistcoat, my insides feeling rather like warm porridge. "Well, that is a bit more romantic, I'll give you."

"I'm not romantic," he said, hands coming to rest against my back, a delicious, solid weight. "You know I'm not."

"You sell yourself short." I fiddled with one of his buttons. "But I find I am quite—*quite*—taken with you, romantic or not."

"A mystery in and of itself." His voice grew quieter. "One I cannot solve."

It did not seem possible he should feel that way. Of course I would love him. He was the best of men. He wore honor and strength like a shield. His intelligence dazzled me. He was kind and compassionate beneath his gruff exterior. Heavens, he even had wealth and position—and was as near to the perfect physical specimen of a man as I'd ever seen.

That he should want *me* was the real mystery.

"I should warn you," I said lightly, though my words were serious enough, "that I am *precisely* what I appear. I do not improve upon further acquaintance. I am bold and brash, impulsive and vexatious. Not precisely the makings of a good wife."

Alexander's cheek twitched. "Are you attempting to frighten me off?"

"I only want you to be sure," I said. "It would be better to know it all now, before—

"I know everything I need to know." He bent to catch my eyes, sobering. "You are brave and beautiful, Beatrice. Generous, sincere but with a backbone made of iron. You are too clever by half, as you are well aware, and a force of nature who often drives me half mad. But I would not have it any other way." He paused. "In fact, it feels inevitable."

"What does?" Was I holding my breath?

His gaze lingered, seeing me—all of me—as he held me close. "Loving you."

My smile spread slowly, like sunshine slipping over a misty morning. "You love me."

"Have I not been kissing you right?" he said. "I do not think I can make myself clearer."

"Oh, you've been kissing me splendidly." I tapped his delightfully firm chest. "Only, a girl likes to be told outright every once in a while just what a man intends."

He exhaled a sigh of long-suffering, though I knew there was more than a touch of amusement behind it.

"What I intend," he said, leaning forward, placing one hand on the door over my shoulder, "is to marry you at the first opportunity. I intend to kiss you every chance I get. I intend to fight with you, laugh with you, live with you. I *intend*"—the word tightened like a promise between us—"to make you mine. Forever."

I stared up at him, my heart so full, so brightly buoyant that I felt I might slip off into the sky.

"You, Alexander Rawlings, have no business calling yourself unromantic," I whispered.

His gaze drifted over my face, a caress, an embrace. "And you have yet to give me an answer."

I thought of making another joke, teasing him and testing him, as I was wont to do. But I allowed my face to settle into earnestness, my eyes keeping hold of his, my hands at his lapels. "I want everything you said." My voice was the barest drape of a whisper. "I want it so badly." I pressed one hand to his chest, directly over his heart. "I want *you*."

He swallowed, his throat bobbing, and looked at me one long moment, as if memorizing a poem. Then he gathered me into his arms, pressed his face into the bend of my shoulder, and held me.

My arms slipped around his waist, inside the warmth of his jacket, and pulled him even closer. "I love you, Alexander," I whispered. "I'm yours. Forever."

He did not answer, though I felt the lightest brush of his lips against the slope of my shoulder.

He held me there on the front steps, the night cool and dark around us, and I'd never been so perfectly, wonderfully, beautifully happy.

Epilogue

"Oh, Ginny," I murmured. "She is so lovely."

I gazed down at the sleeping babe in my arms, bundled up against the January cold in a thick, white blanket. The skirts of her billowing christening gown escaped past the blanket and fluttered against my dress. A lace cap covered her head, lips perfectly pink, red-tinged lashes splayed against her cheeks.

"She is, isn't she?" Ginny said, beaming. "A just reward, I think, considering the work it took to bring her into the world."

"Troublesome little creature," I cooed at the baby. "Your mama was not very pleased with you that day. Why, I thought I would finally hear her swear. Perhaps next time."

"Just wait until it is *your* turn," Ginny said, entirely unfazed. "You shall be a terror at childbirth. I do not think Alexander has any idea what he's gotten himself into."

"Oh, undoubtedly," I said cheerfully. "Why do you think we married so quickly? I couldn't very well give him time to reconsider."

The church bells rang behind us, the sound loud and clear on this winter day. The churchyard was frozen over, an inch of snow crunching beneath my feet, but there was warmth in the hum of conversation and laughter around us. Ginny and Jack had invited a great many friends and family to the christening, and the service had been all that was beautiful and touching. Mr. Denning had announced the child's name—Lillian—as was custom from the godfather, while Verity and I, godmothers both, stood beside him at the front of the church. I'd held Lillian as the vicar had poured the water over her head and used oil to mark a cross on her forehead. I hadn't stopped smiling the entire time.

Now I tilted my head and pressed a kiss to the soft skin of Lillian's temple. "You are loved," I whispered. "More than you know."

Her lips curved in sleep, as if she had heard and understood my words.

"Are you going to share her at all?"

That familiar, delectable heat flooded me at Alexander's amused tone, and I faced him as he came to stand beside me.

"Why, do you wish for a turn?" I'd been attempting to convince him to hold Lillian since yesterday, but to no avail.

"I shall let others more inclined take my time." He crossed his arms in that devilishly attractive way of his, though he had no idea. "I'd hardly know what to do with a babe."

"Well, there is no time like the present to learn," I said brightly. Without warning, I settled the bundled mass of blankets and muslin in his arms.

He was so very surprised he did not even think to stop me. He froze as I stepped away, grinning at him.

"Beatrice," he warned. "Come take her. I am not at all qualified."

"No, thank you," I said. "I like the sight far too much."

I certainly meant it. Seeing my new husband holding a baby prompted a delightful blend of maternal instincts and marital desire within me. Alexander stood so stiff and awkward, his arms perhaps a bit too tight around the baby, and it was impossibly endearing.

"Try to relax," I encouraged him.

"She is so tiny," he muttered, looking down at Lillian. "I shall drop her, and Jack will have my head."

Ginny laughed. "She is bundled so well that I doubt it would even hurt her."

Alexander gazed at the baby, tracing over her perfect nose and rounded cheeks. He said nothing, but when he looked up at me, there was perhaps a slight glaze to his eyes. He cleared his throat and held her out. "There, I've had my turn."

"I shall take her," Verity said, approaching from my right. "I have not had nearly enough time."

She eased Lillian from Alexander's arms as Mr. Denning came to join her. The two leaned over the baby with clear delight. I wondered if they had hopes to start a family soon; they would be wonderful parents, both of them.

Alexander fell into conversation with Mr. Denning about a case they'd been recently assigned involving counterfeit banknotes. My mind wandered as I glanced around the churchyard. Many parishioners from Little Sowerby lingered after the service, people I'd known for years. Neighbors, acquaintances, one-time friends. I'd felt many of their gazes on me in the church, curious and judgmental and everything between. But things were changing. I could feel it.

Catherine Davenport, or Catty, as I'd often called her, stood across the churchyard. She was Ginny's half sister, and they'd had something of a difficult relationship over the years, though they seemed to have turned a new leaf since Ginny's marriage to Jack. Indeed, Catherine had been much more civil to me today, nearly verging on friendly. I could only hope the rest of Little Sowerby would follow suit. Not that I hadn't grown adept at ignoring other's opinions of me, but it would be terribly nice not to have to.

I spotted Mother approaching. Father had already disappeared inside the carriage.

"Beatrice, darling," she said. "Your father wants to leave for Wimborne. You know how he dislikes the cold."

He disliked nearly everything except a warm fire, *The Times*, and his dogs, but I did not mention that.

"You go on ahead," I said, reluctant to leave such a merry scene. "Alexander and I can walk. It's not far."

Mother patted my arm. "Very well." She glanced over at Alexander, so darkly handsome and intimidating, and seemed about to say something. But she only nodded and took her leave. She still did not feel terribly comfortable around my husband, but we'd been married barely a month now. She'd only just begun to recover from the shock of our unexpected courtship and engagement. It would take time, but I was certain Alexander would win her over, as he had me.

Father, on the other hand, had received the news of our match with such indifference one would think him a distant, uninterested cousin rather than a father. Upon meeting Alexander, he'd asked a few questions regarding his financial situation and family name, then had given his blessing. I could be thankful for that, at least.

Mr. Drake and Mrs. Travers joined our group, and we chatted a few minutes about her upcoming performance of *The London Merchant*. In a break in our conversation, I noticed Ginny had slipped away. Furrowing my brow, I inspected the churchyard again and found her with Jack, speaking to a man I did not recognize. He was dressed in an outlandish striped jacket and bright-green waistcoat, a hat tipped low over ruddy cheeks. He shifted his wiry frame as if nervous, eyes darting around the churchyard.

After a few moments, Ginny and Jack bade farewell to the man and started back toward us, arm in arm.

"Who is that?" I asked Ginny curiously.

She grinned. "That, my dear, is Wily Greaves."

I brightened. "Really?" I'd heard a great deal about Wily, from his shadowy connections with the London underworld to his unlikely friendships with Jack, Ginny, and Verity. He was a fence and, as such, often skirted both sides of the law. I found him absolutely fascinating, though I'd never met him.

Ginny seemed to read my thoughts. "I doubt he is looking to garner new acquaintances at the moment," she said with a small laugh. "Not with so many of Bow Street's finest officers out in force. If you approached, I daresay he'd vanish with the wind."

Disappointing indeed.

But when I looked over again, Wily was looking straight at me. He offered a jaunty tip of his hat and a mischievous grin, then disappeared around the corner of the stone church. I liked him already.

"He had a gift for little Lillian." Jack held up a small golden spoon, elaborately detailed and clearly expensive. "He swore it was bought and paid for honestly."

"But by whom?" Ginny quipped.

Jack smirked. "That is indeed the question."

The party began to separate and depart for Wimborne, where Ginny and Jack had prepared a festive meal. They reclaimed Lillian from Verity's arms and departed in their carriage. The rest of us followed after, some in carriages and some walking.

Alexander sought me through the happy crowd of family and friends, and I did not think I would ever grow used to it—the sight of him intent on me, eyes focused as if he had no greater aim than to be at my side.

"Mrs. Rawlings," he said, offering me his arm.

I scrunched up my nose. "I still have yet to banish the image of your mother that appears in my mind each time you say that."

His lips twitched. "Don't think on it overmuch, then."

"It is as if you do not know me at all. Overthinking is one of my special skills." I slipped my hand around the firmness of his upper arm and drew myself against his side. I craved being close to him, and a month of marriage had only heightened that desire.

He did not seem to mind, his free hand coming to draw tantalizing circles over the back of my kidskin gloves. "Then perhaps distraction is the order of the day."

"Oh?" Silly how my heartbeat still quickened, even after all we'd been through. "Do tell."

"I do not think the vicar would approve of me kissing you senseless in the churchyard."

I laughed and shoved him with my shoulder. "Alexander Rawlings, you shall make me blush."

He only gave a knowing, crooked smile and pulled me back against him. "I doubt that very much."

He smiled a great deal these days, certainly far more than in those first few weeks of our acquaintance. I liked to think it had something to do with me, wonderful wife that I was.

We fell into step behind Verity and Mr. Denning, who walked with Mr. Drake. The couple spoke animatedly, but Mr. Drake walked with his hands in his pockets, head bowed slightly. He was quiet, a strange occurrence for the man. Did he feel out of sorts, being the only bachelor guest in attendance? He shouldn't, considering he was Jack's closest and oldest friend, but his curious change in mood did make one wonder.

"I think," I said to Alexander in a low voice, "it is high time we found someone for Mr. Drake."

Alexander narrowed his eyes. "Is matchmaking also one of your special skills?"

"There is much you've yet to learn about me, husband." I tapped him smartly on the arm. "Mr. Drake is in need of the stability and contentment that comes from having a woman in his life."

"Stability?" He exhaled an amused chuckle. "You do know you threw every stable and orderly facet of my life into chaos the moment you entered it?"

"Yes, yes, you are welcome."

He shook his head. "Drake can manage himself. The last thing he needs is us meddling in his affairs."

I only hummed a noncommittal sound. I would take every opportunity I could once we returned to London to find Mr. Drake a proper match. It was the least I could do for all the aid he had rendered me. Besides, it wouldn't be terribly difficult to convince any decent, halfway intelligent woman that a handsome Bow Street officer would make an excellent husband.

I knew that very well for myself.

"Are you certain you wish to return to London with me tomorrow morning?" Alexander asked. "You could always stay another few days with Ginny."

I was still growing accustomed to living farther than four miles from my closest friend. Though London was but an afternoon's journey from Little Sowerby, it was an adjustment. One that was very much worth it. "I've far too much to do at home," I replied, which was true enough.

We were nearing the end of some fairly substantial renovations in our new townhome, conveniently located near Bow Street. It was not so large or grand as to provoke too many questions, but it was perhaps a bit more than could strictly be afforded on Bow Street wages. Not that it mattered terribly much—Alexander had finally told his friends about his history, about Briarstone and his wealth. Beyond their teasing insistence that he now pay for drinks every time they stopped at The Brown Bear at the end of the day, they treated him precisely the same as before.

"And," I went on, "we both know you'll pine for me endlessly, and it will distract you from your work."

He exhaled. "There is more truth to that than you know."

I tightened my hand around his arm. During our time at Briarstone, he hadn't dared voice any of his feelings. He'd held so much of himself back then. But since our engagement and wedding, a new openness had bloomed between us—a sweet closeness, a vulnerable honesty. I loved it. I loved seeing behind each and every one of Alexander's layers.

"Besides," I said lightly, "your mother and Helen arrive in a week. I want to ensure the house is ready for them."

"A good point," he replied. "Mother is a most particular houseguest."

"Shocking, to be sure." I grinned up at him. "At least we shall have Elijah there to soften her."

"Quite thankfully," he said with a low chuckle.

"He is most keen to see Vauxhall," I reminded him, our steps crunching through the snow. We'd fallen behind the others, their conversation and laughter echoing through the trees, our steps lazy and slow. "And I've also yet to fully appreciate its delights."

"Yes, so you've said," Alexander said, amused long-suffering clear in his voice. "I shall do my best to ensure we are not interrupted by a thief bent on revenge."

"I'm not so concerned about that." I brandished a saucy smile. "Only I am very curious as to whether you shall dance with me this time."

"Marriage has not altered my views on dancing." Alexander narrowed his eyes slightly.

I released his arm, spinning to walk backward a few steps as he followed just a pace behind. "So you would not dance even to please your wife?"

"Why would I do that when there are other, more enjoyable ways to gain her favor?" He caught my hand and pulled me against him.

A sudden bolt of fire blazed over my skin, and my heart tumbled inside my chest. I looked up at him, my hands grasping his arms. His eyes . . . He gazed down at me with such desire, such devotion that my throat went dry.

"Such as?" I did not bother to hide the raspy anticipation in my voice.

He lifted my chin with one finger and gently brushed a kiss to my lips. "You seem quite partial to kissing," he murmured.

"I suppose," I attempted nonchalantly, our lips a breath apart.

He glanced up and down the path, flashed me a wicked grin, then pulled me behind the trunk of a great oak tree with low, thick branches spreading out above us. Then he kissed me, a dizzying press of his lips that sent a cascade of delightful tingles up and down my spine. I slipped my arms around his neck even as his hands fell to the dip of my waist, his thumbs brushing against my stomach. Our lips matched in pace and fervor, this connection now familiar but no less thrilling. He knew I had no resistance to a kiss like this—no reserves of strength to deny myself this heady awareness, this delightful, tangible intoxication.

Alexander finally pulled away, though he also seemed less than inclined, his chest rising and falling. We stood there in the still shadow of the oak, surrounded by a frozen countryside, cold creeping through our clothes. I barely felt it, enclosed in the warmth of Alexander's arms.

"Very well," I breathed. "I suppose I can forgive you for not dancing. But that is because I am a generous and thoughtful wife, not because of your thoroughly masculine wiles."

He made a sound of pure disbelief. "Masculine wiles?"

"What else would you call kissing me until I'm dizzy to get what you want?"

"A highly enjoyable pastime?" he replied indignantly.

I laughed. "Wiles, Alexander. Nothing more than *wiles*."

"I do not need wiles," he said in that gruff, knee-weakening tone. "You know I will dance with you if you wish it."

Oh. My breath was snatched away, stolen by the underlying care in his words. It was more than simply agreeing to a dance. It was the fact that he thought of me before anything, that he put my desires and wishes before and beyond his own. I saw it in his every action and word, and my chest felt as if I might fly into a million glittering pieces. This. This was the sort of man a girl dreamed of. And he was mine.

I rose up onto my toes and kissed him again, this time a soft caress of my lips that somehow felt more intimate than the deep kiss we'd just shared.

"What was that for?" He sounded caught off guard.

"Nothing." My throat suddenly ached, tears pricking. "Only I am reminded every day how very fortunate I am. That you should love me. That you should want me."

His hands tightened at my waist. He swallowed, gazing down at me, his expression shifting into something deeper. Something more real and more vibrant. "I know a man is not supposed to disagree with his new bride," he said roughly, "but in this case, you are most certainly wrong. *I* am the fortunate one. There was no love before you, Beatrice. My life was half lived, my soul barely formed. You have made—" His voice broke off, and he had to clear his throat. "You have made me whole. And I shall never stop wanting you."

I pressed my forehead against his chest, closing my eyes against my suddenly blurry vision. "How I love you," I murmured.

His arms came around me. I relished his nearness, his steadying, deliberate warmth. It was a reminder that he would be with me through every part of our life together, whatever we faced.

We held each other close—a promise, a vow.

That *this* would be our forever.

Acknowledgments

The experience of writing this book was both exhilarating and exhausting. I hadn't felt this same thrill—or obsession with a story—since the beginning of my career. Something about Beatrice and Alexander just spoke to me, and their romance flew onto the pages. That being said, once I finished the rough draft, I looked at it and immediately knew it needed the TLC of those I trust the most with my stories. Thankfully, I have the best team behind me!

First of all, my books are never possible without my husband's support. With four kids and counting, it's not easy to fit in writing, book tours, marketing, and all the rest that comes with this career. But I'm eternally grateful for a partner who makes my dreams his as well. And one day, we'll go on that Alaskan cruise—my treat.

Thank you to my sister Jessica, for your encouragement as you read bits and pieces of this story (and for sending me funny reels on Instagram when I needed it most). I hope you enjoy this book as a beautiful, polished whole! Love you!

Thank you to my wonderful beta readers, who have been with me for years and whom I beg to stay with me, for their fantastic feedback and kind words: Esther Hatch, Jillian Christensen, Deborah Hathaway, Cassy Watson, and Jan Lance. You are all rock stars, and I am so grateful for your expertise!

To my square—Heidi Kimball, Megan Walker, and Arlem Hawks. I would not be where I am today without you! In fact, I think I would be a much less funny and far more stressed version of myself.

So thank you for the daily texts, the laughter, the tears, and everything that has kept our friendships going for eight years now! Hugs!

Thank you to my incredible editor, Samantha Millburn, for not only making my words the best they can be but for also helping behind the scenes with many different struggles. I'm so grateful for your kindness and your compassion.

Thank you to Heather Ward for the most *beautiful* cover and to my Shadow Mountain team for all the work and time you put behind this book.

Lastly, thank you once again to my readers. Whether you've been with me every step of my journey or you're picking up one of my books for the first time, I'm forever grateful to have you with me. And if you feel the beginnings of your own story inside you, I hope you find the courage to put pen to paper.

Discussion Questions

1. Beatrice arrives in London determined to reclaim her life after years of scandal and exile. What did you think of her approach to facing her past? Would you have handled it differently?
2. Alexander begins the story closed off and guarded. How did your perception of him change as the story unfolded?
3. Mrs. Rawlings made assumptions about Beatrice and treated her unkindly. Do you believe her actions were justified once you learned her reasoning? What would you have done in her place?
4. The murder investigation and robberies added a layer of danger to the romance. How did this heighten the stakes of the love story?
5. Both Beatrice and Alexander carry deep wounds from their pasts. How did these experiences influence the way they viewed each other—and themselves?
6. Which supporting character was most memorable to you, and why? What role did they play in shaping the main characters' growth?
7. The Regency setting is full of societal rules and limitations, especially for women. How does the setting shape Beatrice's choices and her willingness to take risks?
8. The mystery contains twists and reveals different clues about the antagonist. Were you able to guess the culprit, or did the ending catch you off guard?
9. If *A Love Most Daring* were adapted into a film or series, which scenes would you be most excited to see on screen?

10. If Joanna Barker were to write a spin-off following a side character from this book, who would you want it to be, and what would you hope for in their story?

Enjoy More Tales from Bow Street

Photo by Brynn Eyre

JOANNA BARKER firmly believes that romance makes everything better, which is why she has fallen in love with writing Regency romances. When she's not typing away on her next book, she's listening to podcasts, eating her secret stash of chocolate, or adding things to her Amazon cart. She thinks being an author is the second-best job in the world—right after being a mom. She is just a little crazy about her husband and four wild but lovable kids.